MAVERICK

MAYHEM MAKERS

USA Today Bestselling Author

Morgan Jane Mitchell

Copyright Maverick, Road Monsters MC © 2024 Morgan Jane Mitchell

All rights reserved under the International and Pan-American Copyright Conventions. No part of this book may be reproduced or transmitted in any form or by any means, electronic or mechanical, including photocopying, recording, or by any information storage and retrieval system, without permission in writing from the publisher.

This is a work of fiction. Names, places, characters and incidents are either the product of the author's imagination or are used fictitiously, and any resemblance to any actual persons, living or dead, organizations, events or locales is entirely coincidental.

Warning: the unauthorized reproduction or distribution of this copyrighted work is illegal. Criminal copyright infringement, including infringement without monetary gain, is investigated by the FBI and is punishable by up to 5 years in prison and a fine of $250,000.

www.morganjanemitchell.com

Models: Tony Brettman
Photographer: CJC Photography/ Christopher John
Cover Designer: Clarise Tan/ CT Cover Creations

ISBN: 9798309721221

Imprint: Independently published

Motorcycles, Mobsters, and Mayhem Author Event proudly presents *The Mayhem Makers Series*, novels brought to you by several bestselling authors specializing in writing twisted chaos. You'll get all the bikers, mobsters, and dark romance your heart can handle.

Disclaimer: ***The Mayhem Makers Series*** *is a collection of works of fiction that mention the author signing* **Motorcycles, Mobsters, and Mayhem Author Event** *in each novel. No authors, assistants, models, or readers attending the event were harmed in the writing of these fictional works. Events mentioned are fictional additions to each author's novel and do not reflect what actually goes on at the aforementioned signing.*

From USA Today Bestselling Author,

Morgan Jane Mitchell comes

ACKNOWLEDGEMENT

A big thank you to model Tony Brettman, along with photographer Christopher John and cover designer Clarise Tan for this beautiful cover.

Thank you, Sapphire Knight, for inviting me to Motorcycles, Mobsters, and Mayhem Author Event years ago and for hosting such an amazing event. This will be my fourth year, and they just keep getting better.

DEDICATION

To my readers who love a Happy Ending, and not just the one I gave him in a previous book, after a massage, that caused all of his heartache.

I hope you enjoy the rest of Hallow/ Maverick's story.

I loved writing it.

I wish you many Happy Endings of your own, both kinds.

MJM

From USA Today Bestselling Author, Morgan Jane Mitchell comes Maverick, Road Monsters MC

(a Royal Bastards MC: Nashville, TN Crossover that can be read as a Standalone)

Welcome to the Road Monsters MC

When my brothers betrayed me and my world fell apart, I ditched the Royal Bastards MC in Nashville and found a new home with the Road Monsters MC. Hallow became Maverick. Love? It died with the loss of Eve and then Sky. The open highway was all I had. Until Lexi crashed into my life.

She's a lawyer on the run from the mob, and now protecting her is my mission. She's fiery, irresistible, and makes me feel things I swore I'd never feel again.

Lexi's past is a ticking time bomb. With secrets that could bring down a dangerous man, she's got a target on her back. My past as a detective before my MC days taught me to fight for justice, and protecting Lexi feels like my last chance to do the right thing. But every mile with Lexi blurs the lines between duty and desire. And the fight to keep her safe can only be won by a ruthless outlaw.

Lexi's world and mine couldn't be more different. Can she love an outlaw like me? Can I keep Lexi safe without completely losing myself, or will our pasts tear us apart?

Mayhem Makers Series - https://amzn.to/3xTszFQ

Find all my books - www.morganjanemitchell.com

CHAPTER 1

Lexi

A cheesy grin spread across my face as I hugged my newest signed paperback. The author's name was scrawled in a bold, looping signature across the title page, and I had to keep myself from squealing with delight.

Nova shot me a teasing look, which I promptly ignored. I was in heaven at the Motorcycles, Mobsters and Mayhem author event. Rows and rows of tables filled the massive conference hall in Frisco, Texas, each one manned by a romance author or cover model who I'd only ever seen online or plastered across my Kindle screen.

Lots of noise, bright banners, lines of excited readers chatting and fanning themselves with bookmarks, I was breathless and a little sweaty from the sheer press of bodies, but none of that mattered. It wasn't every day that I got to meet a hundred authors I practically worshipped.

Cover models strutted around in leather, showing off tattoos that made me flush from head to toe. Nova kept raising an eyebrow at me every time my eyes lingered on a particularly muscular torso.

"Smutty," she murmured as we shuffled forward in another line. Nova had a special bookish nickname for me. "You look like you're about to combust. Do you need a minute?"

A laugh escaped me as I adjusted my glasses and tucked a dark lock of hair behind my ear. "What can I say? I'm a book nerd, and these guys look like they just walked off the page. It's...too much."

She rolled her eyes in amusement, but I caught a hint of shared enthusiasm in her smirk. I knew Nova loved being here almost as much as I did, especially since we'd both devoured these Motorcycle Club Romance novels in college as our guilty pleasure.

Something about the outlaws, the freedom, the headstrong, take-no-prisoners kind of alpha guys. I'd always found it thrilling in fiction.

Fiction, I repeated to myself.

Real-life bikers probably weren't anywhere near as romantic. More likely, they were dangerous assholes. And I'd had enough cautionary tales from my mom, Diana, growing up to know that the biker world could be downright terrifying.

Still, seeing these gorgeous cover models dressed in leather cuts and tight jeans, hair slicked back or braided, a shit ton of tattoos rippling across arms and chests. I couldn't help but swoon a little.

Hell, I was swooning a lot.

Especially now that I'd finished law school and passed the bar, I was determined to soak in a little fun whenever I could. I might've been a newly minted lawyer, but I was still a sucker for a bad boy with a deep voice and a nice ass. Even if it was just for my imagination.

I'd been waiting for this weekend for months. Studying, I'd barely had time to breathe, much less indulge in my biggest passion, reading smut. If someone asked me where I was going after my big win, this was it. Stepping into that conference center was as if I was stepping into my own personal Disney World, except instead of fairy Godmothers and princes, there were authors and cover models, the place full of the kind of worlds I loved to lose myself in.

"God, Lex, check out that walking snack over there." My best friend, Nova, nudged me. She kinda secretly pointed out the hot, ripped model in the black shirt. Tattoos of dragons, skulls, and flames covered his arms, from wrists to shoulders. He was chatting with a bunch of giggling women in "Reading is my Favorite Position" T-shirts. "They should rename this place *Men, Muscles & Mayhem*. I'm in trouble already."

My eyes wide, I radiated. Because I was experiencing a little flutter of my own at the sight of so much male eye candy. It was impossible not to. "Down, Slutty," I teased. I had a nickname for her, too. "We just got here. You can't jump the first hot guy you see."

Nova rolled her big blue eyes. "I can't? Challenge accepted." Her long dark-blonde hair poured over her shoulders, and her bright red lipstick gave her that extra bit of sass she carried so well. "I am *definitely* looking for trouble, Smutty." She was tall, model-thin, and drop-dead gorgeous. She'd been engaged once, but that relationship imploded, leaving her with a vow to never settle for anything mediocre again, especially not in the bedroom.

Nova and I were halfway through the line to meet another author when my phone rang. The caller ID showed a California area code, which was strange enough to get my immediate attention. I stepped out of line, placing my large tote of books on a nearby chair.

"Hello?" I said, pressing the phone to my ear.

"Lexi?" a raspy voice croaked. My mother. "It's mom."

"Mom?" My eyebrows shot up. Diana, *AKA Dirty Diana*, as she called herself, was the last person I expected to hear from right now. "Where are you calling from? You never call me out of the blue."

She coughed, like she was trying to clear a scratchy throat, and paused and I could imagine her looking over her shoulder. Woman was paranoid even when she wasn't on drugs. "I'm in California, baby. You know, at a…well, I guess you'd call it a biker rally."

I sucked in a breath. Of course, she was at a biker rally. That was her scene, always had been, no matter how many times she promised to stay away from that life. "What's going on?" I asked. "You usually text."

"Yeah, well," she said, her voice dropping to a whisper, "text messages leave a trail. I need…shit, I need some legal advice, Lexi. You're the only lawyer I know."

My stomach twisted into a giant knot. I'd been official for all of five minutes, and the thought of my own mother needing legal help, no doubt for something shady, instantly made me anxious. "What's going on, Mom? Are you in trouble?"

"Maybe. I don't know. There's a man." She hesitated. "Threatening me. He says he's going to sue me, among other things. I just…I need your advice."

I exhaled, pressing my forehead with two fingers. This was so typical. "Okay, can you give me more details? Who is he? What's the nature of the lawsuit?"

"I can't talk about it here. Too many ears. I just... I'm in Anarchy, California, at this big Kings of Anarchy rally. Please, can you come out here? I know it's a lot to ask."

I glanced around at the chaos of the book conference and my friend Nova's curious expression. "Mom, I'm at an event, and I'm supposed to be at work next week."

"You said you had some time off, right?" she pressed. Of course, she'd been fishing for that info the last time we exchanged texts. "Please, Lexi. I wouldn't ask if I wasn't desperate."

My thoughts raced. I did have the next week off. Eight whole days after today. I'd asked for it after a long string of grueling nights at the office. The plan was to relax, catch up on reading, and enjoy this conference. But perhaps I could see my mother, figure out what was going on, and then come right back. "I guess...maybe I can. Let me talk to my friend. We could drive out there."

She let out a shaky sigh of relief. "Thank you, baby. I'm sorry to do this to you."

I ended the call, and Nova hustled over. "Who was that? You look pale."

I stuffed my phone in my bag, ignoring the trembling in my stomach. "That was my mom. She's in California at a biker rally. Says she needs legal advice. Something about a man threatening her with a lawsuit. She wants me to come out there."

Nova's eyes widened. "A biker rally in California? And your mom wants *you*, a brand-new lawyer, to help her?"

"Yeah, can you believe it?" I forced a cutting smile. "But she sounded really worried, Nova. I can't just blow her off."

She raised her perfect brows. "Your mom's that wandering free spirit, right? A real wild child? I remember you telling me she used to run with bikers."

I bit my lip. "Yes. She's always drifting around, partying, hooking up with random guys, living off who-knows-what. She's gone by *Dirty Diana* since I was little. She's...well, let's just say it's complicated."

Nova took my arm, pulling me away from the crowd to a quieter corner. "What are you going to do? She said she's in trouble?"

I fiddled with my glasses, pushing them up my nose. "She wants me there, but I have no idea what kind of trouble this is. She's been threatened before. She's gotten mixed up with guys who want money, who do drugs, you name it."

Nova nodded, crossing her arms. She had that thoughtful expression on her face, the one she got when she was weighing all the pros and cons. "Then I say we go," she said finally, a grin tugging at her lips. "I mean, we planned on spending a few more days here, but we can bail. We've met most of our favorite authors anyway. It's your mom. Let's just do it."

Her quick agreement surprised me. I hesitated, piddling with the straps of my tote. "Are you sure? It's a biker rally, Nova. There will be, like, real bikers. Not these romance cover models who smell like fancy cologne and do push-ups for photo ops."

She wiggled her eyebrows. "All the more reason. A real adventure."

A trickle of excitement ran through me, despite my groan. I'd never stepped foot into my mother's biker world. I knew only glimpses of it, the secondhand smoke, the leather, the sketchy bars she dragged me to when I was a kid before I went to live with my aunt. Still, something about stepping out of my comfort zone made my heart race. I was a grown woman, a brand-new lawyer, single, though I'd been practically married to my books for years. It was time for a break from the monotony.

"All right," I conceded. "We'll drive out after the event tonight." I wasn't going to miss this occasion for anything.

Nova clapped her hands. "Yes! Road trip!"

I mustered a laugh, but the flutter of nerves in my stomach wouldn't settle. My mother had always been a drifter, hooking up with random bikers and coasting in and out of my life at her convenience. I'd spent considerable time resenting her, but my sense of loyalty remained strong enough to bring me when she required my presence. Maybe that was a weakness in me. But I had another weakness, the yearning to experience what I'd only read about.

CHAPTER 2

We left Frisco in the late afternoon, the trunk of my car stuffed with signed books and suitcases of clothes we'd barely touched. My silver sedan wasn't exactly a road warrior, but it would get us to California.

The miles melted away under the scorching Texas sun as we sped west, talking about anything and everything. Nova and I had been friends since college, and we had a comfortable rhythm.

She'd been engaged once, briefly, to a guy who turned out to be controlling and unfaithful. James was a sex addict who liked her being submissive. He also liked to video tape her. She figured she was all over the internet by now. Needless to say, they broke it off. She moved on, but ever since, she'd been reluctant to settle down again. James was always a topic of conversation.

For me, relationships never even began. My big secret, I was twenty-five and still a virgin. Not because I was prudish or anything, or because I wasn't as thin as Nova, but because, well... I never met the right guy, never felt like risking my heart and body with some random fling. Books were safe. Studying was safe. And men rarely found me approachable. Tall, curvy, and wearing glasses, I was not your typical girl. I'd get flustered. I tended to babble, which apparently wasn't sexy. Not sexy enough to get swept off my feet.

At least Nova always hyped me up.

"Smutty," she teased as we merged onto a highway through New Mexico. "When we get to California, if you see a man who makes you moist, promise me you'll let him buy you a drink?"

I sighed dramatically. "You know I hate that word... Slutty, you know how I feel about random men, especially bikers. The only bikers I like are the ones in my books."

"Then it could be time to see if reality measures up," she said with a wink.

I couldn't help but snicker. "Trust me, the real ones are not as dreamy as in the stories. My dad was probably some random biker my mom hooked up with once. I never even knew him."

Nova grew thoughtful. "Still, you can't work 24/7. You're a lawyer now, Lex. You're allowed to get 'moist'."

My nose wrinkled. "Will you stop that?"

"You deserve some throbbing manhood. A glistening manroot invading your meatcurtains and inching up your musty cavern."

"Stop!" I sputtered a laugh. As much as we loved smut, we also loved to laugh about the worst of it.

"Or you could masturbate each other," she went on, cackling.

"That was the worst," I agreed.

But she wasn't wrong. The thought of stepping into a biker rally made me nervous, strangely intrigued, and I hated to say it, 'moist'.

"I really don't understand your dislike of the word," Nova started. "Moist is cake. Dessert. Wet is much worse. Makes me think of a basement or a smelly dog."

Shaking my head, I didn't want to get into what would be the best way to describe what the thought of hot bikers did to my privates. "If I'm going to help my mom, I have no choice but to go to this rally."

"See, it's already a romance novel. The heroine has no choice." The back of her hand to her forehead, she fake fainted.

"Real funny."

We pushed through two days on the road, stopping only for gas, cheap motels, and drive-thru food. Each time my phone rang, I hoped it would be my mother with more details, but she only sent a few cryptic texts. *Hurry up* or *please get here soon*. She gave me the address of a big open field near Anarchy, California, where the Kings of Anarchy MC was hosting their rally.

After hours of bleary-eyed driving, we finally arrived in Anarchy. It wasn't a big city by any means, more like a large town that had grown around a chaotic intersection of highways. Relentless desert sun beat down, its glare shimmering on the asphalt.

We found a cheap motel on the edge of town that had a half-broken sign reading *Anarchy Inn—Vacancy*. The place looked... well, not exactly five-star, or even three, but at least it was somewhat clean and had a working lock on the door. That was about as much as we could hope for. We checked in, rolling our suitcases into a surprisingly clean room with two queen beds and a rattling air conditioner.

"So," Nova announced, flipping through her phone as she perched on her bed, "I say we freshen up, grab some outfits that won't scream *lawyer ladies from Dallas*, and then head over to see your mom."

She didn't have to twist my arm too much. If I was going to step into this place, I wanted to at least attempt blending in. I had no illusions that I'd pass as a regular, but I hoped I wouldn't look like a total fish out of water.

We found a nearby strip mall with a boutique that apparently specialized in biker attire, or so said the neon sign in the window. *Anarchy Outfitters*. It seemed like this town had a theme.

Tight leather pants hung from racks, along with cropped tops, studded belts, and riding gear. We both nearly died laughing as we tried on increasingly scandalous outfits.

"Smutty!" Nova gasped, wiping a tear from her eye as she held up a tiny black leather vest that could barely qualify as a garment. "You *have* to try this on."

I rolled my eyes but took it from her. "Fine. But if my boobs pop out, I'm blaming you."

Sure enough, the black leather vest was snug and sexy, showing off more boob than I usually cared to. Paired with a very short matching mini-skirt and tall boots, I looked like I was dressed for a costume party. But Nova insisted it was perfect. She ended up with a short denim cut-off skirt, fishnet tights, a black Harley tank top that showed off her cleavage, and a studded leather belt and short boots to match.

By the time we got back to the motel, we were giggling like teenagers, half-horrified, half-excited. We changed into our new outfits, curled our hair, put on makeup that was far bolder than my usual neutral look.

I stared at myself in the mirror. My long dark hair hung in beach waves over my bare shoulders, my green eyes popping behind my thick rimmed red glasses. The vest was unzipped just enough to show all my cleavage down to the nips. My thick hips and thighs were poured into the mini-skirt, and my boots gave my legs a decent shape, but also made me look a bit taller than I already was. All in all, I felt hot, like a different woman, someone braver.

"All right," Nova said, giving herself one final once-over. She was tall and slim, her dark-blonde hair tumbling artfully down her back, so she looked like some runway model with a dangerous streak. "Shall we, Smutty?"

I nodded, swallowing the knots in my stomach. "Slutty. Let's do this."

CHAPTER 5

The rally was like landing on a different planet. The venue was a massive stretch of desert land filled with motorcycles, rows upon rows of gleaming chrome under the blistering sun. Music boomed from makeshift stages, competing with the roar of engines. Tents lined the dirt pathways, selling everything from beer to bongs to leather gear. There were stands advertising tattoos, piercings, even mud wrestling. The smell of dust, exhaust, and weed hung in the stifling air.

We parked the car on the edge of the madness and stepped out, both of us instantly hit by a wave of intense heat. It felt like we were walking into a real-life version of those MC romance books, but infinitely rougher, grittier.

"This is like Burning Man for bikers," Nova shouted over the noise, eyes wide. "Look at those bikes!"

"Yeah, don't point," I agreed, experiencing a slight dizziness. "Or maybe Burning Man for criminals." I'd studied enough cases to know the lawlessness that went down at these events. But that was all the more reason to find my mother. "I'm not even sure where to start looking for my mom."

We began weaving through the crowds. I gawked at the carnival-like atmosphere, complete with freaks and even some bikers with their faces painted like evil clowns. People were wearing bandanas and leather vests with patches from clubs I didn't recognize because they were real. But to my delight, several guys were shirtless, showing off heavily inked muscular torsos that were as yummy as the models in Texas.

As for the women, we discovered we were overdressed as they paraded around in thong bikinis or nothing at all, holding beer cans or hooking their arms around the men. Not to mention, riding their shoulders, in nothing at all. I felt like I was trespassing on some hedonistic playground.

Nova nudged me. "Smutty, don't freak out, but that group of bikers is staring at us." She gestured subtly with her chin to a knot of rough-looking men near a tent that boasted *Ice-Cold Tequila Shots*.

Sure enough, they were eyeing us like fresh meat. One of them, a lanky guy with a shaved head, flicked his gaze up and down my body. I fought the urge to shrink back.

"Hey there, jailbait," the shaved-headed guy said, stepping forward with a grin that showed off tobacco-stained teeth. "Want to ride this hog?" The biker grabbed his crotch.

My mouth went dry.

Nova, apparently bolder, spoke up. "We're over eighteen, shithead."

"Just looking for someone," I said, as if it would erase her insult.

"We can help you find what you need," another man leered, his eyes roaming over Nova's legs.

"Thanks, but we're good." I tried to keep my voice steady and firm.

The skinhead barked a laugh. "No need to be shy. Stick around. We'll show you a good time."

Nova grabbed my hand, and we attempted to move along. But the men closed in, weaving around us, offering drinks and asking all kinds of intrusive questions.

"Are you a real blonde?" they asked Nova. "Does the carpet match the drapes?"

My discomfort skyrocketed. I tried to be polite, but they weren't taking the hint.

One of them with a thick braided beard nudged the other before he got too close to me.

I stiffened. "Don't touch me."

Somehow, we kept walking. "Let's grab some water. I'm about to pass out."

We found a vendor selling bottled water and took a moment to chug it. Another biker gang rolled by, checking us out like we were a side of beef.

One of them, a tall mountain of a man with a scraggly mustache and stained shirt, smirked at me. "Look at the fresh faces. You looking for a man, sweetheart?"

Nova stepped forward, ever the bold one. "We're not taking applications."

"Feisty. I like it. The feisty ones are fun to break."

Then his gaze latched onto me. His eyes raked over my curves, lingering on the exposed skin at my waist. I tried to keep my cool, but something about his stare made my skin crawl. "We're busy," I said curtly, turning away.

"Bet she's real smooth under that leather. Nowadays, these young thangs always shave their snatch bald."

Turning, I crossed my arms. Fuming, I was feeling brave, brave enough to fuck with him. "Really? I guess you don't know the new trends. Full bush is back."

Nova joined in the fun. "Yeah, full bush with accessories, just like how we do our Crocs."

"You ladies think that'll make my dick limp? Now, *sugar puss*, I've got to see that full bush." The big guy reached out and gripped my vest, yanking me to him. In a motion so swift that my brain could barely register it, he yanked it down, causing my bra and breast to slip and pop out completely before the whole crowd.

I gasped, terror flashing through me. "Hey!"

Before I knew it, a blur of motion cut between us, and a large fist collided with mustache-guy's jaw. He reeled back, stumbling into the dirt. I clutched my vest closed, eyes flying to our savior.

If mustache had been a mountain, this biker was Mount Everest. He was tall, broad shouldered, with dark hair that curled at the nape of his neck. A neatly trimmed beard framed a handsome and strong jaw, but his face looked like he'd recently been in a fight. His arms were roped with muscle, tattoos covering his forearms, one of a sad woman's face, the other depicting a set of black wings. His leather vest read *Road Monsters MC*, and the nametag over his chest said *Maverick*.

"Back the fuck off," Maverick growled at the men, his deep voice rumbling through me like thunder. "You don't put your hands on a woman who doesn't want it."

The mustache guy spat dirt out of his mouth, then glared at Maverick. "Who the hell are you to..."

He didn't finish because Maverick just lunged forward, hooking him in the gut with a punch that made the man collapse to his knees. The others muttered curses but backed away, not willing to tangle with this biker.

"Take your shit elsewhere or I'll break your goddamn jaw," he barked.

I fiddled with my vest, trying to get it straight as my heart pounded out of my chest. Nova stepped beside me, eyes wide, breathing hard. Maverick glanced at us. When his gaze locked on mine, a flicker of concern, it seemed, crossed his gorgeous eyes.

"You all right?" he asked, his tone a touch gentler, but still carrying an edge.

I nodded, my cheeks burning so hot I thought I might catch fire. "Yeah. Thanks. I was handling it."

He raised a sexy eyebrow, unconvinced. "Sure you were, princess," he said dryly, but he offered a nod of respect all the same. Then he stepped closer, as if to shield me from prying eyes, as I was still trying to fix myself. He said nothing for a moment, just studied me, my hands digging in the vest to pull up the cup of my bra. His eyes flicked over my curves, but not in a leering way. More like he was assessing whether I was genuinely okay.

Finally, he extended a hand. "Name's Maverick."

Done righting myself, I took it, noticing how large and warm his hand was. I opened my mouth, but Lexi spoke. "She's Smutty, and I'm Slutty."

I gave her a look of death.

"What? Maverick's not his real name," she argued.

"Smutty?" he asked, a smirk on his handsome face. "With a full bush?"

Fuck, he heard that. Cringing inside, I died from embarrassment. That was so not true. I was as bald below as any twenty-five year old. Nevertheless, I was too mortified to even address it.

"Lexi," I murmured, pushing my glasses up. "This is my friend, Nova. Or at least she was."

He bowed at Nova, then turned back to me. "What're you doing here? You're obviously not from this crowd."

Before I could answer, a familiar voice slurred out behind him. "There you are, big boy!"

I craned my neck to look around the big hunk of a biker, only to see my mother. *Dirty Diana*, in the flesh, stumbling toward us with a half-empty bottle of liquor in one hand. My stomach sank at the sight of her. She looked way older than her fifty-five years, her skin weathered from too much sun and too many late nights, dark hair sticking up in all directions. She wore a denim vest that showed off her skinny arms and a skirt that left little to the imagination, as in her belly. I'd never seen another woman with a beer gut.

But the biggest blow was seeing her wrap a wrinkly arm around Maverick's bicep like she owned him. "Hey, baby," she purred, pressing herself to his side. "I've been looking all over for you."

Maverick didn't reject her. He simply gave her a small, tight smile. And I stood there, with a twisting stomach.

Was this the man my mom was...with?

He seemed about my age, possibly thirty, undoubtedly younger than mid-thirties. The difference in their ages and the sight of her pawing at him made my cheeks flame in frustration.

Nova, clueless to my inner turmoil, leaned over and whispered, "Is *that* your mom?"

I swallowed. "Yes."

Mom's eyes swung to me. She blinked as if trying to focus. "Lexi, baby, you made it!" She broke into a grin, releasing Maverick to sway in my direction. She flung her arms around my neck, nearly toppling me with her liquor-laced breath. "Oh, I'm so glad you're here.

I was telling Maverick all about you. My sweet, smart daughter, who's a lawyer now!"

I forced a smile, embarrassed and worried all at once. "Yeah, Mom, I'm here. You said you needed my help."

She bowed, then tossed back another swig from the bottle in her hand, ignoring the crowd around us. "Yes, yes," she muttered. "Some asshole's threatening me, claiming I...well...that's not important right now."

"Uh, it *is* important," I insisted, but she waved me off. "Mom, are you drunk right now?" I asked, my tone sharper than I intended as my childhood came rushing back to me.

She shrugged, blinking rapidly. "It's a party, ain't it?" Then she cackled, planting a sloppy kiss on Maverick's cheek. "Look at this hunk-a-dunk," she slurred. "He's been real sweet, taking care of me."

I wanted to melt into the ground. Nova sent me a wide-eyed glance that said, *Holy shit, your mom is hooking up with that.*

Meanwhile, Maverick's expression was unreadable. He wasn't trying to get away.

"I see you've found a...friend," I said slowly, unable to hide my disapproval.

Mom rolled her eyes. "Oh, don't start. I'm a grown woman, Lexi. I can sleep with whoever I want. You kids today are missing out. We burned our bras, so you didn't have to keep your legs glued shut. You're the one who's here to help me. Not to judge me." She wobbled on her feet again.

Maverick stabilized her, looking stoic as ever.

Was he sleeping with my mom?

Maverick stepped in, hooking a thumb in his belt. "Diana's told me a little about it, but not enough to figure out who's behind the threats. She's...not real specific."

I frowned at him, unsure how to handle the protective note in his voice. Was he genuinely looking out for my mom, or was he using her for something else? My gaze caught on the patch on his vest that read *Maverick* again, remembering the raw moment he'd saved me a second ago. A swirl of confused gratitude and distaste for his closeness to my mother curled inside me.

Nova cleared her throat. "Perhaps we can all find somewhere quieter to talk?"

"Yeah," my mom piped up with a giggle. "Let's get more drinks first."

She was sloshed. It was mortifying. People nearby were starting to stare. Maverick raked a hand through his hair, looking vaguely uncomfortable. "We can move over to the bar tent," he suggested. "Less dust, at least."

We ended up at a makeshift bar under a large canopy tent. Dozens of folks milled around, music burning my ears, bartenders pouring shots. Fans whirred overhead but did little against the California desert heat. With our drinks in hand, we all found a rickety wooden table near the corner, and Mom slid into a seat between Nova and Maverick, effectively leaving me to perch on the edge of the bench opposite them.

"So," I tried again, leaning in to speak over the noise, "who's threatening you, Mom? And what exactly are they threatening you with?"

She glanced away, eyes darting around. "Just...someone who doesn't like that I know certain...information."

I let out an exasperated breath. "Can you be more vague?"

Maverick gave a half-smile, closing in to whisper something to me. "Your mom's known around here as Dirty Diana. She's, uh...gathered a lot of intel on different clubs, different men, all that. Some of them might not want their secrets out in the open."

"Secrets," I repeated, eyeing my mother warily. I'd always known she had a reputation, but hearing it laid out was something else.

She lifted both shoulders, not meeting my eyes. "I've had to...survive, Lexi. You do what you gotta do. But anyway, this man who's threatening me says he'll sue me for defamation if I ever breathe a word about him or his...connections."

Nova exchanged a confused look with me. I cleared my throat, summoning my newly minted legal knowledge. "If it's defamation, that means you'd have to be making false statements. Are you? Or do you have evidence to back up these alleged secrets?"

Mom pursed her lips. "I... Well, let's just say I've got some stuff locked away. And he might not want it out in the open."

I groaned. Typical. She was being so cryptic I couldn't do my job. "Mom, I can't help if you won't give me details."

"Later," she insisted, patting my arm. "Tonight's for fun. This rally only happens once a year, baby. Relax. You look so tense. You need to get drunk and get laid."

Her idea of fun apparently included another round of tequila shots that Maverick ordered. I noticed he paid for all of them out of a fat wallet full of cash, then casually pulled a flask out of his pocket to top off his own glass. Nova seemed more than happy to join in.

"Cheers to new friends," she announced, clinking her shot glass against Chigger's, some cornfed biker who materialized from nowhere.

He matched Maverick's height but carried his burly build on a thinner frame. With his sandy blond hair in a ponytail complete with blond patchy beard, he was Nova's type. At least his eyes sparkled with easy humor. Maverick introduced him as another Road Monster. Chigger wore a cocky grin and had a playful gleam in his eye as he scooted closer to Nova. They were already hitting it off.

I sighed, forced into another shot by my mother's insistent beam. The liquor burned going down, but the warm rush in my veins dulled the edges of my anxiety.

For a while, the conversation shifted to random small talk as Chigger and Nova got to know one another. The rest of us were merely audience members to this *meet cute*. My mother got more and more wasted, clinging to Maverick, giggling, and then she was telling embarrassing stories about me as a kid.

"I once caught Lexi kissing the pages of a book. She was eleven. No... no... I mean she was really kissing it. So much so she broke her glasses. Can you believe it?"

I wanted to sink through the floor. But I adjusted my glasses feeling the same way I did back then. Utterly invisible. Maverick seemed distant, though he occasionally offered polite nods or half-smiles when Nova or I tried to include him. Something about him felt...wounded, under all that tough exterior, but I couldn't be sure.

Eventually, Mom decided she needed to dance. She dragged Nova and Chigger along, leaving me and Maverick to wander to the bar. An awkward silence stretched between us as he ordered us another shot.

I sipped my tequila because my throat was burning. "Thanks again for stepping in earlier," I said quietly, recalling how he'd punched that creep who exposed me. My cheeks warmed at the memory of my vest being yanked down.

Had he seen my nip slip?

He shrugged, like it was nothing, rolling his broad shoulders. "No big deal. I don't tolerate that shit. But I do expect a peek at that full bush you're sporting."

I opened my mouth to deny the bush, but he quickly backtracked.

"I'm joking."

As I tried to figure out what he was joking about, believing I had a full bush or wanting to see it, my eyes wandered to the tattoos on his forearms. I noticed a stylized letter "E" near the black wings, partially obscured by new ink. He purposely shifted, and I quickly looked away, not wanting to stare or to pry.

"You're new here," he said. "Never seen you around."

I let out a short laugh. "I'm not a biker groupie, if that's what you're asking."

He gave a faint, almost amused snort. "Figured that much. Since your mom said you're a lawyer. You carry yourself like it. This isn't your scene."

I raised a brow at his perceptiveness. "I am a lawyer," I answered, ignoring the impulse to brag about recently passing the bar and landing my dream job. Something told me that in this crowd, brand-new or not, it wouldn't make much difference. "Mom called me for help, or I would never be here. What about you? You didn't get that black eye from rescuing me, earlier."

"I'm a fighter, in the ring and out." He gingerly touched his scarred lip. "Recently went a couple rounds with a grizzly."

"A bear?" I asked.

"No. An asshole." He leaned closer, a scent of leather, sweat, and something musky tickling my nose. "Your mom's a handful," he murmured, voice low enough to be drowned out by the nearby chatter. "She's been stirring up a hornet's nest for a while."

"Why are you with her, then?" I asked, unable to keep the edge out of my voice. "She's... She's quite a bit older than you."

A flicker of something passed through his eyes, but he simply gave a careless nod. "She's a grown woman. We have...business."

Heat rose to my cheeks again. Some jealousy, which made no sense, and protective anger for my mom. "Right. Well, do me a favor and don't hurt her. She's all I've got."

He inclined his head, his expression unreadable. "I won't."

Mom called to us, and soon, the group of us swayed in the crowd near a small makeshift stage, the music throbbing. My mother was drunkenly dancing, her arms around Maverick's neck, pressing her body to his. I couldn't tear my eyes away from the sight. Jealousy and revulsion warred in my stomach. He was far too young for her, and from the quick, dismissive glances he kept sending me, I wondered if he was just humoring her.

Nova and Chigger were laughing in a corner, leaning in close. I felt like the odd one out, clutching my empty shot glass, watching my mother flirt outrageously with a man who, less than an hour ago, knocked out someone for pulling down my top. It was all too bizarre. But maybe he would've done that for anyone. I wasn't special.

After a while, my mother staggered, nearly falling, and I rushed to catch her. "Mom, you need to slow down," I scolded, though I couldn't hide the worry in my tone. "You've had too many shots."

She just giggled, an obnoxious, drunken sound. "You're such a good girl, Lexi. Too good for this world." She patted my cheek.

Nova stumbled over, hooking a finger at me. "We should probably get your mom to her tent, yeah?" She looked tipsy too, her lipstick slightly smeared from sucking face with Chigger.

Maverick agreed, sliding an arm under mom's shoulders. "Come on, Dirty D. Let's get you lying down."

We half-carried, half-dragged my mother through the crowd toward the labyrinth of tents pitched in the far corner of the rally grounds. It was a messy sprawl, some tents were big and fancy, others were battered and old. Then there were the RVs and campers farther out. The smell of weed thickened as we passed groups of partiers around fire pits. And I was getting a contact buzz.

We finally found my mom's tent, which was a small, battered thing with pink ribbons on the entrance flap. She stumbled inside, nearly face-planting on the sleeping bag. She was out cold within seconds, barely responding when I tried to ask if she'd be okay.

"Are you staying with her?" I asked Maverick, noticing that he was lingering by the tent flap.

He raked a hand through his dark hair. "She's hammered. But I got somewhere to be, so I can't babysit right now. You two should stay with her."

I scowled. "What's that supposed to mean? You're with her, right? Or...something?"

His eyebrows rose. "Diana does her own thing. Don't worry about it."

That stung a little, though I wasn't sure why. Part of me wished for his denial of a romantic relationship with my mother. I hoped he wasn't that sort of man. The sort of man to use her. But he didn't say otherwise, and I didn't want to pry any more.

"So, you're just gonna leave her here?" I demanded.

He stared at me, unflinching. "She's got you, doesn't she? And your friend?" He jerked his chin toward Nova, who was leaning against Chigger, completely distracted.

I crossed my arms, torn between relief and annoyance. If he had crawled into the tent with her, I would've lost it. "Fine," I said. But

I wasn't staying here all night. I had a room in town. "But I prefer an actual bed."

Maverick's lips twitched in a ghost of a smile. "You might find out you like it out here, princess. A real bed can get overrated."

I bristled at the teasing note in his voice. "I'm not a princess."

"Whatever you say. You do you, lawyer girl." Then, without another glance, he turned and walked off into the darkness, broad shoulders disappearing among the other tents and drunk bikers.

I let out my breath, flustered. Part of me wanted to chase after him, demand to know more about him, about my mom, about this weird arrangement. Another part of me was grateful to see him go, because he unsettled me in a way I didn't want to examine too closely.

My mother moaned for water, so Nova grabbed a bottle from the cooler, and we helped her drink a bit before she passed out entirely. Apparently, wherever Maverick went, Chigger followed because he was gone as well.

We exchanged a glance.

"What a shitshow," Nova whispered, brushing hair back from Mom's face.

I sighed, mind swirling. "I can't believe she's messing around with that guy. He can't be much older than us. And he's... God, I don't even know. I'm not sure I trust him."

Nova carelessly lifted her shoulder, her expression half-dazed from all the tequila. "He did save you from that creep. He might not be so bad."

"He's banging my mom," I said, clearly agitated.

"Possibly he is, but not tonight. Let's get your mom settled and then we can head back to our room. I can't sleep on the ground tonight. I'll break my neck."

Nodding, I tucked a blanket around my unconscious mother. She snored softly, reeking of tequila. "All right. I'll see her tomorrow. She can fill me in on who's threatening her, and maybe we can figure out how to handle it."

Morgan Jane Mitchell

We left the rally, weaving past bikers who whistled at us or offered more drinks. My nerves were on edge, but Nova was valiantly ignoring them, hustling me toward the safety of the car.

CHAPTER 4

The next morning, I woke early, head throbbing from too many shots. And forced down a few cups of motel coffee. Nova was sprawled across her bed, moaning about the sunlight creeping through the thin curtains.

"You alive, Slutty?" I asked with a yawn.

"Barely," she groaned. "I'm never drinking tequila again."

I took a swig of coffee, steeling myself. "I should go check on my mom. Make sure she's okay...maybe get more info on this threat."

"Fine," Nova said, yawning. "I'll shower and meet you there, okay? You go ahead."

That worked for me. I wanted to talk to Mom alone, anyway. So I dressed in simpler clothes, a pair of jeans and a book T-shirt, since that was what I packed for Frisco. It read, 'Men are Better in Books'. But I was still wearing my knee-high boots. I drove back to the rally grounds.

I parked closer this time. The atmosphere was quieter in the morning, many people probably sleeping off hangovers as I approached the tents, scanning for my mother's pink ribbons.

I found it soon enough, noticing the flap was hanging open. "Mom? Mom, are you awake, yet?"

The words died in my throat as I saw her lying on her back inside the tent, eyes like mine staring blankly at the canvas ceiling. Her chest didn't rise or fall. A dark bruise marred her neck, and her lips were blue-tinged.

"Oh, my God." My voice wavered. I crawled inside, shaking her shoulder. The stiffness of her body made me recoil.

She was...dead.

No, no, no.

Tears burned my eyes. "Mom," I whispered brokenly, checking her pulse even though I knew it was pointless. Her skin was cold. Bile rose in my throat. This couldn't be happening.

I stumbled out of the tent, shaky and gasping. I had to get help. Grabbing my phone from my pocket, I dialed 911, rattling off the location as best I could. My thoughts were a jumbled mess. My mother, drunken, irresponsible, vexing, was...gone.

My heart ached, but my head kicked into high gear. Had someone hurt her? That bruise on her neck looked suspicious as hell. Why would anyone kill my mom? *Because she knew secrets.* The threat. My pulse hammered.

I staggered away from the tent, scanning the area. Where was Maverick?

He was with her last night.

I spotted a few men with Road Monsters patches milling about, but not him.

Finally, a woman giggled from behind another tent, the flap partially open. I heard a man's low voice, too familiar. Fury ignited in my chest. I marched over, fueled by shock and grief, and yanked the tent flap aside.

Inside, Maverick was indeed in the midst of hooking up with some scantily clad woman. His bare ass was out, and her top was off, and I couldn't see the rest of her. They both jerked in surprise at my intrusion.

"What the hell?" Maverick growled, eyes narrowing.

"You!" My voice broke. I pointed a shaking finger at him. "My mother is dead, and you're in here screwing some random chick?"

The woman gasped, covering herself, glaring at me like I was the intruder. Maverick's face darkened, and he shoved off her, standing up. "Wait, *dead*? Dirty D?"

"Yes, *Diana*," I spat, tears threatening to choke me. But as much as I cried, I noticed Maverick didn't cover up. His erect dick, complete with slimy condom, was on full display. I tried not to let it distract me. "She's in her tent, cold as ice, and there's a bruise on her neck. You were the last person seen with her."

His expression flickered with something, shock, or even grief. But then it morphed into anger. "Calm down, princess. I had nothing to do with that."

"You expect me to believe that?" I shouted, ignoring the woman who was scrambling for her clothes. "You left her. She was threatened. She's dead. And you're here, going to town on another woman."

He stepped forward, pulling up his pants. "I didn't kill her, all right? Don't come in here accusing me."

My eyes burned with tears, heartbreak twisting inside me. "She's dead," I choked, my voice cracking. "My mother is *dead*. Someone strangled her."

Maverick froze, fists clenching. His jaw tightened. "Who else knows?"

"You should worry less about that," I snapped. "And more about explaining where you were last night. Because I called the cops."

He grabbed my arm. "No cops!"

I wrenched free. "Stay away from me."

Everything was chaos then, the sound of sirens in the distance, the woman pulling on her shirt and cursing at Maverick, me stumbling back, half-blinded by tears and rage. If he didn't kill my mother, he sure as hell didn't seem innocent. And the fact that he was having sex with someone while my mother's body lay in a tent just yards away made me sick.

Police cars began to pull up at the edge of the rally, creating a buzz of alarm among the bikers. Everyone scurried to hide their drugs or vanish before the cops could question them. I spun on my heel, dashing back to my mother's tent, wanting to be near her, wanting to protect her even though it was too late.

One of the officers, a gray-haired man with a somber look, took in the scene, noticing the tears on my face and the lifeless form of my mother. He immediately radioed for more assistance. The crowd pressed in, curious onlookers, but parted for the cops.

I felt someone's hand on my shoulder. Nova, newly arrived, face pale as a sheet. "Lexi, oh my God, I got your text. I came as fast as I could. Is she...?"

I nodded, tears slipping free. "Yeah. She's gone."

"Jesus," Nova whispered, eyes brimming with sympathy. She hauled me into a hug, and I buried my face in her shoulder, trembling.

Over her shoulder, I saw Maverick standing a few yards away, arms folded, watching me with a troubled look. Our eyes met, and I glared at him, rage pulsing under my skin. My mind screamed that he was involved, that he was no good, that he was trying to protect whoever really did it, or it was him.

But for now, I had no answers. Just a dead mother, a bruised heart, and a sickening, ugly suspicion that Maverick knew far more than he was saying.

And as the cops swarmed around to secure the scene, I realized my life had just taken a sharp turn into the darkest parts of the biker world, a place I had never wanted to go. The ache in my chest told me there was no going back to normal.

CHAPTER 5

Maverick

A Week Ago

The smell of spilled beer and stale smoke hit my nose the moment I shoved open the door of the Velvet Rooster. The place always reminded me of a cheap, run-down whorehouse, only with more broken glass on the floor and fewer illusions about class.

A neon-red glow bathed the walls, flickering off the battered jukebox in the corner that blasted some ear-splitting heavy metal track. Looked like the same scrawny waitress was slinging drinks behind the bar, but she didn't give me a second glance. Nobody here gave a damn about any new face unless you gave them a reason. I liked that about this dive.

But I wasn't in the mood for nostalgia. I was here because Kingpin had called me out, the son of a bitch. The bastard who'd stolen my first love, then married her. The same man I'd stolen another woman from, his wife, if we're being real technical. Shit was complicated as hell, dirty, but in my line of work, dirty deeds were the only real currency we traded in.

My road name nowadays was Maverick, which felt ironic as hell, considering I was once a law-abiding detective named August Adam Hart. But "Maverick" fit better than "Hallow," which was the name I had carried back in Nashville during my stint with the Royal Bastards MC, when I met Kingpin. And it sure as shit felt better than "detective." That label left a sour taste in my mouth now, like I'd swallowed a mouthful of burnt coffee grounds. I'd left that world of law and order far behind.

"Hey, kid," growled Merc, the old-timer behind the bar. His potbelly hung over a thick leather belt with a tarnished buckle. He was wearing a sleeveless T-shirt that read: *Velvet Rooster - Love It or Leave It*. That was his favorite line. The man was consistent. I'd give him that. "You look like you're fixin' to start trouble. You want a beer first?"

I slid onto a battered stool by the bar. "Merc, I'm not a *kid* anymore. It's 'Maverick' now," I said, tapping the splintered wood with my knuckles. "And yeah, I'll take a beer." I could pretend to be calm. Hell, maybe I was for about two seconds.

"Sure thing, Maverick," he muttered, emphasizing my name in a way that said he'd always see me as Hallow or that pig from Columbus, didn't matter. He slid a bottle down the counter. A swirl of foam sloshed at the top. I took a swig, ignoring the bitterness. Beer wasn't my top choice anymore, but I needed the cold bite of it. Needed the distraction.

Over Merc's shoulder, I spotted Kingpin sitting in a dark corner booth, leaning back like he owned the entire joint, which wasn't far from the truth. He had a presence that spoke of years in the MC world, of deals cut in back alleys and bodies left behind in shallow graves.

He had slicked back his long black hair, a thick beard covered half his face, and his silver ear piercings caught the red lights. He folded his arms across his broad, black leather-clad chest. The silver rings on his knuckles glinted ominously, and I remembered too well the damage they could do.

I took another lengthy sip from the long neck, bracing myself for what was coming. Even after all this time, Kingpin looking at me with those cold, half-lidded eyes ignited something twisted inside. Loathing. Shame. Regret. Most of all, I felt the old fury, that unstoppable wave of anger that'd led me to steal his wife, Sky, once upon a fucked-up time.

Yeah, we had some baggage. My ex-fiancée, Eve, had cheated on me with him. But he'd also been married to Sky at that same time. And Sky... She's the one I kidnapped after I found out. Well, not really. She wanted to leave Kingpin, or so she said. I gave her the chance, so we took off. Then he had the nerve to marry Eve. The bastard turned around, gave Sky and me new identities, and left us the fuck alone until recently. Until Sky left me.

I slid off the barstool, my boots scraping over the sticky floor. In the bar's mirrorlike reflection, I glimpsed the man I'd become, hair longer than it used to be, scars visible on my neck and arms, remnants of close calls on the road, fights I'd barely won. My Road Monsters MC cut felt light on my shoulders. Though it reminded me I wasn't just drifting without purpose. No, I had a purpose, even if it was just to survive.

Merc ambled around to the far side of the bar. "You two try not to kill each other in my place, all right?" he grumbled, jerking his chin in Kingpin's direction.

Before I could respond, Kingpin raised his hand and snapped his fingers. Immediately, the straggling customers finished their drinks or poured them out and left. It was like a silent alarm had gone off. Hell, maybe it had. People in the Velvet Rooster knew better than to stick around when men like us had business. Merc locked the front door behind the last body and flipped the "Closed" sign.

All at once, the music felt louder in the emptier room, but Kingpin got up and snapped off the jukebox. That bar was dead quiet, apart from the neon lights and noisy vents. I walked forward, ignoring the flutter in my gut. My heart beat fast, but I wasn't scared. It hammered from hating. Out of anger. From a past that just wouldn't let me fucking go.

Kingpin waited until I was close. I could see the black swirling tattoos creeping up his neck. He smirked, flashing that evil grin of his. "Hallow," he said. He knew damn well that wasn't my name anymore.

"It's Maverick," I corrected, tossing my half-empty beer bottle on a nearby table. "You called me out here, so let's hear it."

He just shook his head and let out a low, mocking laugh. "Maverick, Hallow, Pig, whatever you call yourself these days. Why the hell do you always come back for more?" He stepped forward. I noticed he had an old scar across his forehead. I'd put that there once. He'd never let me forget it.

I curled my fists, that old detective instinct telling me to stay measured, watch his hands, his eyes. "I'm here because you told me you had intel about Sky. You had said she was kidnapped. We found out that was bullshit, remember? She went back to that asshole Ralph Getty on her own."

"Don't you mean you ran?"

"I've checked into it. She's with him, alright."

"Aw, the big bad ex-cop has done his investigating," he taunted. "Turns out you can't let that uniform go, can you? Always snooping. It's the only good skill you ever had. That, and running away."

He wasn't just talking about me looking into Sky. I knew his secret. Once I let that cat out of the bag, I was sure he'd want to have a talk.

He took a step toward me. "You ran from Columbus when your partner shot that kid. You ran from Charleston when the MC had you pinned for trouble. And you ran from me in Nashville." He jabbed a finger in my face. "You always fucking run, Pig."

I wanted to punch him right then, but I held back, barely. My entire life had been a chain of escapes and hearing him rub it in my face made my blood boil. But it was also painfully true. "Fuck you," I muttered. "I don't owe you any explanation."

"Nah, you owe me a hell of a lot, boy," he said, eyes narrowing. "You stole my wife, remember? Kidnapped her, took the child that wasn't even mine, then ran off to Alaska and lived under the radar. I gave you those new IDs."

I had to grit my teeth, because it was all true. "Sky wanted to leave you. I did what she asked. I took her away from your bullshit. She was under my protection. And yeah, you helped with new names, but I didn't realize I was walking right back under your thumb. Road Monsters MC, you running the top, playing the fucking puppet master. I guess you always find a way to screw me over."

His lip curled. "If I wanted to screw you over, you'd be six feet under by now. Let's not forget that. You're still breathing because I have bigger fish to fry."

"Fish," I repeated with a sneer. "That's your name too, right? Ace of Spades. The big Fish. The grand puppet master pulling all the strings in the Road Monsters MC. Kingpin, I know who you are. I know the shit you're into. I could out you in a second."

He let out a short, barking laugh, stepping closer until we were practically chest to chest. I could smell the bourbon on his breath. "You think I don't know that, Pig? Go ahead. See how far you get before someone puts a bullet in your skull. There are four Aces in the Road Monsters MC. You really think you can tangle with us all, all alone?"

I'd be lying if I said the threat didn't rattle me. Once upon a time, I'd been some hotshot detective who believed in justice and righting wrongs. That was a lifetime ago. Now, I was just a man stuck between outlaws, criminals, and regrets. "I'll take my chances," I growled.

He stared hard, measuring me. The tension was thick enough to choke on. My muscles coiled, every inch ready for the fight I knew was coming. Because Kingpin and I were never going to have a peaceful conversation. We were two dogs in a cage, neither willing to back down. It was a good thing we left our weapons at the door.

He smirked. "Yeah, you always do." A quick flash of movement was my only warning before his fist slammed into my jaw.

CHAPTER 6

The impact of Kingpin's fist exploded across my face. I stumbled back, cursing. I tasted blood on my tongue, metallic and hot. Adrenaline pumped through my veins, and I launched myself forward. My knuckles connected with his gut, driving the air from his lungs. He grunted but didn't back down. Instead, he grabbed my shoulders and yanked me into a brutal knee that connected with my ribs.

"Fuck," I gasped, but I drove my elbow down onto his thigh, enough to make him buckle. We crashed onto a nearby table, the old wood splintering under our combined weight. Beer bottles shattered around us, glass fragments cutting into my arms. The smell of sour ale and blood hit my nose.

Kingpin was heavier, older, and cunning. He fought dirty, always had. He raked his black nails across my face, aiming for my eyes, and I barely jerked back in time. I wrapped my arm around his neck, trying to twist his head into a choke hold. Twist the damn thing clear off, if I could. He slammed an elbow into my side with enough force to make my vision blur.

My boots scraped for purchase on the wet, sticky floor. We both tumbled sideways, crashing into a row of freestanding stools. They scattered like bowling pins. He pinned me for half a second, hooking his arm around my throat. I snarled, bringing my fist up into his ribs, hooking him under the beard. Anything to break free.

"Just like old times, Pig!" he spat.

Memories of our first real fight, years ago, flashed in my head. He'd always had the advantage in weight and experience, but I'd had a detective's training in self-defense. I gritted my teeth, ignoring the pain, and planted my foot in his gut, shoving with everything I had. He flew back, arms flailing, slamming against a sticky table.

Gasping for breath, I forced myself up, fists raised. A cut above my right eyebrow dripped blood into my eye. I wiped it away with the back of my hand. Glass crunched under my boots. We circled each other, chests heaving.

"You could've killed me," I ground out, trying to steady my breathing. "But you didn't. Why are we doing this all over again?"

He spat on the floor, a fleck of red in it. "Because you need reminding who the fuck is in charge, Maverick."

Something about hearing him say my name instead of "Pig" or "Hallow" made me pause. My rage was still there, but I felt a flicker of confusion. That was all Kingpin needed. He lunged, slamming a fist across my cheek. My head snapped to the side, and I staggered, nearly blacking out. I tasted blood and sweat, felt my veins pounding in my skull.

"No more running," he hissed. He grabbed my cut, yanking me upright, his breath hot on my face. I stared into those cold eyes, wishing I could just tear them out.

"Fuck you," I rasped, ignoring the splitting pain in my ribs. "I ain't runnin' from you."

He hauled back for another strike, but I managed to block it, hooking my arm around his. With a twist, I got leverage, ramming him into the bar with a sickening crunch. He let out a grating moan, sliding down to one knee.

Merc's voice cut through the haze, distant and frantic. "Shit. Hey. Don't break my damn bar, you bastards!"

I ground Kingpin's face into the edge, my weight pressing him down. "Call me Pig one more fucking time," I snarled.

He chuckled, even as his lip smashed against wood. "Pig."

My fury surged. I let him go just enough to land a savage punch across his jaw. Something cracked. We both lost our balance, and I ended up sprawled on the floor. Before I could get up, he scrambled to his feet, snatching up a broken bottle. The jagged edge glinted in the neon light.

I cursed and backed up a step. My left hand fumbled blindly for a weapon of my own. My fingertips closed around another shard of glass, and I lifted it between us. We stood there, gasping, bleeding, just staring, broken glass as dueling swords. Neither of us gave a shit about how ridiculous we looked.

Merc's voice echoed again, louder, more desperate. "Christ, you two are fuckin' insane. If someone's dyin', do it out back. Not in my bar."

Neither of us moved. Kingpin's eyes narrowed, blood streaking down his chin, into that black beard. "I could kill you right now, and no one would say a damn thing. You realize that?"

My grip on the shard tightened. "Do it, then. I got nothin' left to lose. Sky's gone. Eve's gone. My illusions about the Road Monsters are long gone. I'm just your fucking pawn again."

He gave an ugly laugh. "You never had illusions about this life, Pig. You always knew what we were, criminals, outlaws, scumbags. You joined up because you had nowhere else to go. After losing your detective job and your precious love, you're adrift. You need us just to survive."

My breathing slowed, the fight-or-flight tension still vibrating in my muscles. But part of me realized he was telling the absolute truth. I swallowed thickly, ignoring the fresh blood on my tongue. "You took Eve from me," I said, voice trembling with rage. "Then I took Sky from you, because you turned your back and cheated on her. Let's not pretend we're saints."

"Sky was never truly mine," he shot back, spitting on the floor. "I just claimed her. Then you claimed her. Now she's with Getty. So, seems she'd been using us all along." A twisted grin. "But that's not my business anymore. Eve's all I need."

I felt a pang of old pain at her name. Eve, my first real love, the woman I was gonna marry. She'd lost my baby once, we never recovered, and next thing I knew, she was with Kingpin. "Good for you," I sneered. "Congratulations on your little vow renewal or whatever you called that bullshit ceremony. Heard you got two babies now, too."

He wiped his mouth with the back of his hand. "Yeah. Two little ones. A real family. More than you've got, Pig. You lose them all in the end, don't you?"

Rage flared again, and I had to force myself not to strike. At the corner of my vision, I saw Merc inching closer, as if to intervene. "Knock it off," he hissed, brandishing a shotgun from behind the bar.

"I don't need a murder scene in my place. Not this week. *Take it outside or I'm gonna kill you both.*"

Kingpin and I traded one last stare. Then Kingpin dropped the broken bottle with a clatter. I followed suit. I was shaking, desperate for more violence, but it seemed the worst of it was over. For now.

He looked at me, breathing hard. "Still a tough bastard, Hallow. Or Maverick, whatever. I gotta say, if you'd been any weaker, I'd have left you in a pool of blood. But you can handle yourself."

I wiped blood from my face and spat it on the floor. "Yeah, I can. So, what the fuck do you want from me, Kingpin? Spit it out, or I'm done."

He flicked a glance around the wrecked bar, broken tables, shattered glass, splintered stools. We'd done a number on the place. Merc was muttering curses, but no way in hell was he going to try to throw us out until he and Kingpin settled up. At least I wouldn't be paying for this shit.

Kingpin lifted a sore shoulder. "I needed to remind you who's in charge. But more than that, I got a job for you."

"A job?" I let out a harsh laugh. "Since when am I your goddamn errand boy?" Why wasn't he ordering me through the Road Monsters' chain of command?

He cracked his neck, wincing. "Since you realized I could've had you taken out for kidnapping my wife and child. But I didn't. Not only that, I gave you new names and let you live in peace in Alaska for a while. I don't owe you a damn thing, but it sure seems like you owe me. So even if I wasn't technically the boss of you, which I am, consider this mission a chance to make good and stay alive a little longer."

I sneered, my fists still trembling from the fight. But he was right. I owed him in a twisted, fucked-up way. And if I didn't do what he asked, I'd have a target on my back. "What's the job?"

Kingpin lowered his voice, glancing at Merc like he didn't want the old guy to overhear this. "We're heading out to a rally in Anarchy, California. The Royal Bastards in Charleston and Nashville are both wanting to see this club in action. The Kings of Anarchy MC. Rumor has it they're hosting an event that could open some doors or close 'em. The Road Monsters are interested in alliances. Some of the top clubs are always looking for ways to expand or shift power. It's all talk right now, but talk can turn real fast."

CHAPTER 7

I frowned, trying to keep up. My head still throbbed from the beating. "So you want me to come along on a field trip? That's it?"

He gave a dark chuckle. "Not exactly. There's a woman out there, goes by Dirty Diana. She's a whore with a knack for collecting secrets. She's blackmailing some of the top folks in the biker world, or at least threatening to. I'm not about to let her hold shit over my head. I need someone to get close to her, find out if she's talked to anyone. If she's messing with my name or my club, I want to know. I want you to handle it."

Despite myself, I gave a short laugh. "You want me to babysit a whore who might spill secrets about you? Sounds like your problem, not mine."

"It becomes your problem if you want to keep your Road Monsters' patch and your head attached to your shoulders. I can make sure good things come your way. Or I can make sure you're cast out as a traitor and a pig to the entire MC world. Take your pick."

My jaw clenched. I glanced at Merc, who was still standing near the bar, shotgun lowered but ready. This was too big to blow off. I'd pissed off a lot of folks over the years, cops, criminals, people in between. Having Kingpin's protection, twisted as it was, had probably saved my ass more times than I cared to admit. "Fine," I said finally. "I'll shake down this Dirty Diana. But I'm not killing someone."

"Hold on, I didn't tell you to kill her."

"What's her story?"

"She's a tricky one," he announced, his fingers brushing his beard. "Money talks. She pays for her men, young men, buys them new gear, the works. Half of them, she manipulates and steals their secrets. Then sells them to whoever's got the biggest checkbook. She's not as physically dangerous as she is cunning. But word is someone wants her real quiet. Someone's aiming to kill her, and it isn't me. But there's talk. Diana saying something to do with me could be her ace in the hole. Could be the same people who want her dead, want to blackmail me, and she's willing to sell me out. I need you to keep her alive long enough to find out."

I studied him, anger still smoldering in my gut. But I had nothing else going for me right now. Sky was gone, voluntarily or not, she'd walked away. I'd lost everything, even my illusions that the Road Monsters were truly independent. They answered to hidden puppet masters like Kingpin, one of the Four Aces. Bastard. "So be it," I bit out. "I'll go to California and deal with your problem."

Kingpin nodded slowly, as if sealing a truce. "Good. The rally's happening soon. You'll ride alone. And watch yourself. This business has a lot of shit swirling. The Royal Bastards are restless. The Road Monsters want to expand. It's a big fucking pot, and we're all throwing in chips. Don't get caught in the crossfire."

My anger flared again. "And if I decide to blow your cover? Tell everyone you're the Ace of Spades running the show behind the scenes?"

He bared his teeth in a feral grin. "Then I'll kill you where you stand. Simple as that." His gaze flicked to the shards of glass around us. "I'm giving you another chance, Pig. Take it or leave it. But you know which choice ends with you breathing tomorrow."

I forced myself to swallow the words I wanted to hurl at him. Instead, I gave a short, tense nod. "You have my number. Let me know when and where to meet in Anarchy. I'll do the damn job. After that, I'm out."

He smirked. "Sure, Maverick. After that, you're out. If that's what you want to believe. You can't run from the biker world. Ask Monster about that."

My mind spun with hatred and self-loathing all at once. Monster had tried to run, and they skinned him alive. He was a Road Monster like me now. The fact gave me some hope. Kingpin didn't want us all dead.

I'd always prided myself on being one step ahead, first as a detective, then as a runaway, then as an outlaw. But Kingpin always seemed ten steps ahead. Why he let me live, I never fully understood. Surely, it was because I'd done the dirty work for him. Perhaps he saw some twisted reflection of himself in me. Or more likely he just enjoyed holding something over my head, so he could get whatever he wanted.

I turned to leave, ignoring the protest in my ribs. Every part of me hurt like a motherfucker. My face was swelling, my lip split, and blood trickled down my arms from random glass cuts. I felt half-dead.

Before I reached the door, Kingpin spoke up one last time. "You better be ready to ride soon. The Nashville chapter is rolling out next week. We're meeting with the Charleston group, and potentially some from other chapters. Could be that we all end up wearing fresh cuts soon."

I glanced over my shoulder. "You do what you gotta do. I can't say I give a damn about your business."

He raised a brow, dabbing at the blood on his split lip. "Don't kid yourself. If we patch over, that changes the entire dynamic for the Road Monsters. The four Aces might shift alliances, might even rearrange leadership. Hell, you might find yourself taking orders from a whole new set of scumbags. Keep your ears open."

I remained silent. I'd had enough of his voice for the night. I jerked the door open, ignoring Merc's curses about the damage. Didn't even bother tossing him a tip for the trouble. Kingpin was undoubtedly going to handle that. One glance back at the bar, I saw Kingpin leaning on the counter, exchanging some low words with Merc. He had that gleam in his eye that said I was just another piece in his chess game.

But I was too tired to fight it anymore.

Outside, the cool night air soothed my battered face. My motorcycle, a new matte black Harley, waited in the narrow lot behind the bar, reminding me I didn't completely hate being a Road Monster. I fished out a rag from my saddlebag and wiped the blood off my arms as best I could. The distant hum of city traffic reminded me I was still in the underbelly of some nameless backstreet. Places like the Velvet Rooster drew outlaws like me. We drifted in, we drifted out, leaving disasters in our wake.

I took a moment to breathe, resting against the seat. Memories coursed through my skull, each one like a fresh bruise. The first time I met Kingpin in Nashville, the way he set his sights on Eve right away. Then me finding out she cheated while I was still reeling from the miscarriage she and I had suffered. But the truth was, I hadn't been faithful to her either. I hadn't even been kind. I drove her to it.

I thought of the rage that consumed me as I pushed her away, pushed her toward Kingpin. My petty revenge, stealing away *his* woman, Sky, who turned out not to be carrying his baby at all. The baby was some other bastard's, and eventually I learned that bastard wasn't a Royal Bastard, not a biker at all, but a mobster named Ralph Getty.

Sky and I had ended up in Alaska, living under the names Owen and Savannah Black, with her kid Caden. We even got married. Then we came back when I joined the Road Monsters, ran a safe house. For a while, it felt normal, stable. But fate always had a twisted sense of humor.

Our baby died in a miscarriage, just like the one I'd lost with Eve. And that's when the wedge drove between Sky and me. Next thing I knew, she was gone, not even giving me a chance to fix things. Or maybe I was too broken to fix shit. She'd run off, or so I thought, got kidnapped but no, after that dust settled, she went to Getty, her son's real father all on her own, helped him double cross his uncle and cousin, kill them to take over the Music City Syndicate.

Learning that Kingpin was behind the Road Monsters MC I'd joined just added another layer to the betrayal. I'd come full circle, right back to this asshole's sphere of influence. And now I was in his pocket again, heading off on some mission to guard some bitch called, Dirty Diana.

"Fuck me," I muttered under my breath. The emptiness in my chest felt colder than the night air. I had no one left, no reason to fight except for my own pride and survival. The open road was all that made sense anymore. And, ironically, the MC was the only place that let me be the brand of savage I'd become.

I swung a leg over my Harley, aware of every ache and pain from the fight. My ribs objected when I breathed too deep. My lip stung. But I'd had it worse. I'd keep riding. It's what I did best, ride away from problems, or ride straight into them, whichever kept me moving.

The engine roared as I kicked it to life. The vibrations coursed through my arms, and for a split second, I felt the freedom I loved more than any woman. I tore out of that parking lot, my headlight splitting the darkness. My head pounded, blood drying on my face, but I didn't stop. Couldn't stop.

I needed the highway beneath my tires, the rhythmic hum that drowned out the pounding in my skull like I needed air to breathe. Because if I stopped, I'd have to face the truth. I'd lost Eve. Sky was long gone, too. I had no family that would claim me. I had nothing except a battered MC cut and a new name that felt as empty as the rest.

Hallow... August Adam Hart... each name was drenched in shame and regret. The quiet detective who once believed in justice was a distant memory. The outlaw I'd become as a Nomad as Maverick was all I had left.

As I sped down the deserted back roads, red taillights reflecting off wet asphalt, my mind inevitably drifted to the next step. I'd have to pack up what little I had and prepare for the ride to Anarchy, California. I'd meet up with the Nashville chapter, or possibly the Road Monsters from wherever. Then I'd locate this Dirty Diana, see what the fuss was about, figure out if she was leaking intel on Kingpin and the rest of the MC. Then what? Did I turn her over? The details were never clear with Kingpin. He just wanted me to be his eyes and ears, and also his fists. But if there was blackmail involved... let's just say I'd seen how far he'd go to silence a threat.

My bike thundered over the interstate, weaving around slow-moving cars. At nighttime, anonymity was my shield. Headlights flashed by, an endless stream of strangers with their own problems. No one gave a shit about me, about the blood staining my clothes. The open road was the only judge now. I'd gone from detective to outlaw, and sometimes I struggled to see the line where my old moral code ended. Maybe it ended the day Eve left. Or it could have ended when I first crossed the line to protect my partner in Columbus.

The panic of the night my partner shot that suspect lingered in my mind. *A young father who ran a red light. The guy wasn't armed. He wasn't our suspect from the bank robbery, either. That fact didn't save the guy's life. My partner claimed he was. Internal Affairs grilled us. I tried to do the right thing, but the brass wanted me to cover it up. The scandal tore me apart, even though I never pulled the trigger. I hopped on my bike and rode, leaving behind a career in tatters and a city that now hated me.*

Another memory, another regret. No matter how fast I rode, I couldn't escape them. But I sure as hell tried.

CHAPTER 8

I was almost out of the city when dawn started to break. My body screamed for rest, but I resisted. However, I noticed a cheap motel off the highway. It was the kind of dump that wouldn't blink at a bruised, bloody biker paying cash for a room. I parked the Harley in front of my door and limped inside.

Tossing my cut on the bed, I locked the door. I checked my reflection in the mirror above the cracked sink. I looked like I'd lost a street fight with a fucking grizzly. My right eye was bruised, lip busted, eyebrow sporting a fresh gash. My ribs felt like they'd been pounded by a sledgehammer. "Fuck Kingpin," I muttered, wincing as I gingerly pressed my side. Probably nothing broken, but I'd feel it for weeks.

I couldn't stop thinking about everything. I was tempted to get wasted, pass out, and forget the world. But I had to keep my head clear. If Kingpin was serious about some rally in Anarchy, I needed to be on my game.

Instead of sleeping, I slumped onto the edge of the bed and pulled out my phone. A battered, older model, less traceable. Not that it mattered if the Aces were tracking me. They already had me by the balls. I stared at the blank screen for a moment, considering who I could call. No one. There were whores in every town, willing to video call for some phone sex, but there was no one left to call.

I thought about Sky. A surge of bitterness twisted my gut. I'd truly loved her or tried to. We'd built something of a life together, me going by Owen Black, her going by Savannah, raising little Caden. Then she had a miscarriage. And everything crumbled. Sometimes I wondered if she blamed me for that. Or if it was just her old life calling her back.

She said she was done with Kingpin's shit. But apparently, she wasn't done with Getty. She ended up in the arms of the mobster father of her kid. She'd said she loved me. People can't be trusted to tell the truth, not even to themselves.

I squeezed the phone until my knuckles burned. Then I put it aside. If she wanted me, she'd know how to reach me. If she was in trouble, she'd either dig herself out or not. I couldn't be her savior again. That nearly broke me the first time.

I flicked on the TV, letting the fuzzy images distract me. Some old Western was playing. A ragtag gunslinger was staring down a line of lawmen, one revolver on his hip. I almost laughed at the irony. I used to be one of those lawmen. Now I was a gunslinger on the wrong side of everything.

Reaching behind me, I pulled out a half-crumpled pack of cigarettes and lit one. The motel's no-smoking sign might as well have been written in a foreign language. I inhaled deeply, letting the nicotine mingle with the residual taste of blood in my mouth. I didn't even like cigarettes much, preferred the occasional cigar. But it gave me something to do with my hands, kept me from punching another hole in the goddamn wall.

Kingpin had said to ride out next week. That gave me seven days to figure my shit out. Time for my face to heal. Get some new clothes, make sure the Harley was in top shape for a cross-country trip. The Road Monsters from my current charter might ride with me, or maybe I'd go alone. I was a nomad, anyway, free to drift. Then we'd all converge in California for this rally. The idea of crossing paths with more outlaws, more drama, hardly thrilled me. But it was my ticket to keep living.

I stared at the ceiling, the battered fan spinning overhead. My head still pounded, but now the adrenaline had drained away, leaving a deep ache that went past bruises and cuts. It was an ache in my soul, if I even had one left. Eve was gone, living the life she wanted with Kingpin, two little babies. No doubt she was the queen of the Royal Bastards. Hell, perhaps she was happy. Remembering how she looked at me the last time I faced her, it's as if she forgot I ever existed.

A flicker of a memory rolled in. Eve's tear-streaked face when she first told me she was pregnant with my kid all those years ago. The glow in her eyes, the hope in her voice. Then when I found out that she'd lost the baby. My guilt at not being there, the wedge that formed... And soon after, she'd found comfort in Kingpin's bed. That was it. The end.

I might have been cursed. My child with Eve had died, then my child with Sky. Love was a crock of shit. Some men aren't meant for it. I was one of those men, obviously.

If I was wise, I'd let the entire scenario go. I'd cut ties, burn my patch, run again. But Kingpin was right. Where the fuck would I run? The entire MC world was connected, especially at the top level. The Road Monsters spanned the country, led by four Aces, Kingpin among them. They had tendrils in each region, alliances with cartels, local mobs, you name it. He'd find me. Or if not him, then someone else he hired.

Still, the thought of sneaking away in the dead of night toyed with my mind. I envisioned the open road, a new identity, some small town where I could vanish. But if I'd learned one thing from my time as a detective and later as an outlaw, it was that your sins always catch up to you.

I took another long drag of the cigarette, coughed out a cloud of smoke. "Dirty Diana," I muttered aloud. The name sounded like trouble waiting to happen. Some cunning woman who fucked for money and secrets. If she was blackmailing Kingpin, I almost wanted to shake her hand for having the stones. But I also knew the bastard well enough to realize he would not stop until he either owned her or destroyed her. Possibly both. And I was stuck in the middle. Perfect.

My phone buzzed on the nightstand. I glanced at it, expecting some message from Kingpin detailing our next move. But the number was unknown. I almost ignored it. My instincts, though, told me to check.

I picked it up, slid my thumb across the screen. A single line of text greeted me:

Heard you're going to California. Some piece of advice, watch your back.

No name. No signature. Could be from a variety of people, an old contact, a half-friend, or some leech that wanted to stir the pot. The phone beeped again.

Sky didn't betray you. Not in the way you think.

My eyes glued to the text, a hot wave of anger and confusion rolling over me. I knew better than to respond.

I muttered a curse, tossing the phone aside. Great. Another puzzle I didn't need. She *did* betray me. She went back to Getty. But the text said not in the way I thought. Was she a prisoner again? Was it all an elaborate ruse? We had rescued her, but she left again on her own. I was there. Still, my detective brain latched onto the questions, but I forced them down. I'd been six months and not a word. I couldn't afford to chase ghosts. My next priority was surviving Kingpin's mission. I'd worry about Sky if she ever gave me a reason to hope again.

When the cigarette burned down to my fingertips, I snuffed it out in the ashtray. My entire body ached, telling me to lie down. So I did, collapsing onto the lumpy mattress. I watched the flickering motel sign through the window blinds. Scenes from the fight played in my head. Scenes from my entire cursed life.

I closed my eyes. The inside of my eyelids was a red swirl of bitterness and pain. I'd get a couple hours of rest before the nightmares kicked in. But even if I didn't, I was used to it. This was the life I'd chosen. Or possibly it had picked me.

Either way, come next week, I'd be on the road to Anarchy, California, searching for a woman named Dirty Diana. Guarding her, fucking her over, or saving her, whatever Kingpin decided "handling" meant. The only certain thing was that trouble would follow me like a shadow. And I'd do what I always did, face it with clenched fists, a bitter heart, and an empty soul.

I woke up sometime later to a throb in my skull and the stench of stale cigarette smoke. The TV was still droning on about some paid programming for kitchen knives. My side ached like I'd been trampled by a stampede of bulls. But for once, my mind felt sharp, free of illusions.

I hauled myself off the bed, ignoring the dryness in my throat. In the dingy bathroom, I turned on the faucet and splashed cold water over my face. It stung the cuts and bruises, but at least it cleared my head a bit. I rummaged in my bag for a first-aid kit. Dabbing disinfectant on the cuts made me hiss, but it was better than letting them fester. My phone was silent. No messages from Kingpin or the unknown number. Just me in this shithole of a motel room.

Kingpin thought he could control me. Perhaps he was correct. But I'd play his game just long enough to slip the noose around someone else's neck. If Dirty Diana was the key, I'd find out. When I rolled into Anarchy, California, I'd do what I had to.

I didn't give a shit about love or loyalty or any of that garbage anymore. I had an MC cut on my back and a bitter heart in my chest. And if the devil wanted me to ride with him, I'd ride. Just so I could burn him when the time was right.

CHAPTER 9

I cruised into Anarchy, California, just as the sun dipped low, the sky ablaze with amazing colors. Didn't mean shit to me except that it was getting late. The day had been hot as hell, and the wind biting at my face as I roared down the highway didn't cool me off nearly enough. My Harley rumbled beneath me, a familiar promise of speed and power.

I'd been on the road for days. Not that I really *wanted* to. Kingpin had made it clear I was on babysitting duty, and I was never good at playing babysitter. Sure as shit never wanted to play it to some older broad who'd messed with the wrong criminals. But I was in deep with Kingpin. He had me by the balls, and if he said "fetch," I had to fetch. Being stuck as a puppet for that bastard wasn't exactly how I'd pictured my life, but I'd had plenty of illusions beaten out of me already.

As I neared the edge of the rally, I could hear the thunder of bikes and the blare of rock music. The place was a goddamn zoo. Tents and tarps lined up on a dusty field, bonfires going, random crowds shouting and laughing. Engines revved, women giggled, men hollered. It was everything you'd expect from a massive biker event, drugs, booze, fights waiting to happen. It might've been my scene once, back when I still got some kick out of chaos. Now, it felt like just another job.

I found a spot to park among a sea of motorcycles. Some engines still humming around me gave the impression I was stepping into a hornet's nest. Perfect for a guy like me, someone who'd be gone before dawn, if I had any goddamn luck.

I took a quick walk around, letting my gaze slide over the scene. Men in leather, sporting cuts from different MCs, the Kings of Anarchy, a few from Royal Bastards, random independents. Women tottered around in heels, some in fishnets, some wearing practically nothing at all, tits out for the world to see. Usually, that'd make my day, but I tried to stay focused. Vendors hawked cheap beer, questionable meat off a grill, and T-shirts with slogans like *Live Fast, Die Last*.

Kingpin's intel told me Dirty Diana was already set up here. She was supposedly the queen of gossip, a woman who sold secrets or traded them like currency. On the trip here, if I wasn't riding, I was digging, questioning my contacts.

Half the men in the biker underground had warmed her bed, or so the rumors went. Except, from what I'd heard, she was pushing mid-fifties and no spring chicken. Not exactly top of my personal to-do list. But Kingpin wanted me up close, and said she had blackmail potential. Or she was being blackmailed, one of the two. He needed to know if she'd talk to the wrong ears. So, yeah. Lucky me.

I spotted her near a bonfire, nursing a beer and laughing raucously with a cluster of old dudes that looked like they'd stepped right out of 1978. She stood out because she had dark dyed hair, too much makeup, and clothes meant for a woman half her age and size. She wasn't as big as some had hinted, but she had a roundness to her. Looked older than her years, too. Life had not been kind to her. Neither had her own choices, if I had to guess.

Time to play nice. I plastered on my best charming grin. The one I used to bust out when I was an undercover cop, back in a life that felt like it belonged to someone else and strolled up to the fire. "Hey, sweetheart," I said, letting my gaze flick over her in a way that usually works wonders on lonely women. "You look like you could use some company."

She blinked at me, eyes bloodshot, lips cracked from the heat of the flames and probably too many cigs. "Company?" She dragged out the word, a little uncertain.

I gave a slow shrug, letting the patches on my vest catch her attention. *Road Monsters MC.* She'd know that name carried some weight, even if it wasn't as flashy as the local clubs. "Yeah, or maybe you want me to fuck off?" I teased, playing the line between confidence and arrogance.

She stared a moment longer, then a big grin split her face. "Shit, honey. Don't you know old Dirty Diana never says no to a handsome face?"

I tried not to cringe. Jesus. *This is your life now, Maverick,* I told myself. *Deal with it.*

I sat down on a log next to her, ignoring the smirks of the old guys she'd been chatting with. They lost interest fast once I joined in, drifting off to find more drinks or easier women. She turned to face me, leaning in close.

Her breath reeked of stale beer and cigarettes. I forced myself not to recoil. "You're new," she purred, letting a hand settle on my upper thigh. "What's your name, sugar?"

Thankfully, my cock didn't even twitch. I gave her a lazy grin. "Maverick."

She made a show of batting her lashes, though they were caked with cheap mascara that'd started to flake. "Maverick. Mmm, I like that."

She leaned closer, but I twisted slightly so her hand slid off my leg. The last damn thing I wanted was to have her pawing all over me. Still, I needed to keep the conversation flowing. "I hear you've got a story or two to tell, Dirty Diana. Word says you collect secrets like some folks collect baseball cards."

A flash of something. Fear? Excitement? Crossed her eyes. "Who told you that?" she asked, voice sharper.

I shrugged. "People talk. Or it could be that I simply have good ears."

She snorted. "Yeah, well, maybe they should keep their mouths shut." She took a long swig from her beer can. Then, abruptly, she turned to me, eyes wide. "You know what? You might not be safe talkin' to me. There's a man named Grinder, some big mob boss. He's put a hit out on me."

Fuck, that was easy. The woman really did have loose lips. I kept my face neutral. "A hit, huh?" I asked. "Why'd he do that?"

She glanced around, lowering her voice. "'Cause he thinks I'm talkin' about stuff, I shouldn't. I know a lot of shit, Maverick. Dangerous shit. And he wants me dead. Hell, he wants my daughter dead, too. He threatened her name specifically."

My detective instincts, long buried, stirred. She was either telling the truth or spinning a story. She had that sweaty, jittery look of someone in real fear, but it could be an act. I'd known plenty of hustlers. "Your daughter?" I asked. "Does she know she's in danger?"

Diana's eyes darted. "I... mighta hinted. But she's busy, you know, has her own life. She's in Texas. No sense dragging her into my mess, right?"

What a load of bullshit. If she really thought her kid was in danger, she'd call her. Well, maybe a normal mother would. Then again, Dirty Diana sure as hell wasn't normal. "If Grinder is for real, you should warn her," I said flatly. "More than a hint. Unless you want to see her in a casket."

She pursed her lips, her face twisted with concern or guilt. "Yeah, yeah," she mumbled. "Maybe I will. Could use a lawyer's mind on this anyway, and she just passed the bar." She rummaged for another cigarette, lighting it with shaky fingers. "But what about me, Maverick? You gonna keep me safe?"

I avoided making any promises. "We'll see. Let's talk more after I catch my breath."

She gave me a considering look, then nodded. Seemed I'd earned a tiny shred of trust.

I left her by the fire, telling her I needed to take a leak. In reality, I had to find Kingpin. He'd texted me earlier that he was in a big black RV near the south side of the field. I was supposed to give him updates, like some fucking errand boy. My lip curled with anger, but I forced it down.

CHAPTER 10

Spotting the RV, I knocked once and stepped in. The inside was surprisingly spacious, with a little living area. Kingpin sat at a small table, a cigar clamped between his teeth, while a man I recognized as Murder, the president in Charleston, sat across from him, swirling moonshine in a plastic cup. Both turned at my entrance.

"About goddamn time," Kingpin growled, exhaling a cloud of smoke.

Murder lifted his chin in greeting, though he gave me a once-over. "So, you're the one Kingpin set to sniffin' around for that mouthy broad?" He had a gravelly voice that reminded me of a man who'd smoked a hundred cigarettes for breakfast.

"Lucky me." I crossed my arms over my chest. I hated being in the same room with Kingpin. He'd stolen everything from me, my first love, my illusions, my sense of belonging. Now I was his lacky, forced to do his bidding so he wouldn't have me fucking killed. Living the dream.

Murder poured me some moonshine. "Good to see you, again. Picked some up from the Black Rebel Riders on our way," he explained. "Local shit's the best."

"Mind the smoke," Kingpin said with a sneer, blowing another puff in my direction. "Eve hates it, so I gotta catch my puffs when I can."

I nearly flinched at the mention of Eve's name, but I covered it by taking a long drink of moonshine. Shit was good. But I didn't want to think about Eve, or how she'd been mine once upon a time, how we'd lost a baby, how she'd run to Kingpin after. *Fuck*, I hated even hearing her name.

"She's not here, so you can calm your tits, son," Kingpin said dismissively.

Murder gave a wheezing laugh. "Poor old Kingpin, pussy-whipped by his hot, young, new wife."

Kingpin shot him a glare but didn't disagree. "So, Maverick," he said, turning his gaze on me. "You find ol' Dirty D yet?"

I nodded, knowing he was inviting me to speak in front of Murder. Made sense. The two presidents were as thick as thieves, and twice as cunning. I wondered momentarily if he was one of the Road Monsters' aces himself before I answered Kingpin, "She's here, all right. Says some mob boss named Grinder put a hit on her. She's spooked. Told me the asshole's after her daughter, too."

Kingpin cocked his head, "Diana has a daughter? That's news."

Murder snorted. "A hit. Probably a crock of shit. That woman would say anything for attention."

Kingpin took a long drag of his cigar. "Perhaps. But I ain't takin' chances. I need to know if she's got anything on me or my club. Something she might trade to the highest bidder. You keep her close."

I resisted, rolling my eyes. "Yeah, I'll keep her close. But I'm not screwing her, if that's what you're aiming for," I added, letting a note of sarcasm slip. "She's older than my damn mother."

Murder burst out laughing, nearly spilling his whiskey. "Fuck, son, no one's asking you to pork her."

My jaw set, ignoring that little dig. Murder wasn't my enemy.

Kingpin smirked, half-lidded eyes glinting at Murders quip. "You do whatever you gotta do, Maverick. If you can keep your dick in your pants, more power to you."

Murder pointed a finger at me, still grinning. "Ah, you poor bastard. Diana used to be a wildcat in the sack, when she was young and hot. We all get old, eventually."

Kingpin spoke up. "We all had a turn with Dirty D over the years."

Murder continued, "Yeah, before we knew, she would suck us dry in a whole other way. Then we used to have new prospects handle her so that no one else had to. They'd get a new Harley out of being on her arm for a while, in her bed, and when they tried to leave her, they'd get blackmailed. They'd learn their lesson to steer clear of a sugar mama."

Kingpin chimed in, "We had to stop doing that when it backfired. She had too much to hold over the clubs. She drifted west."

"I'll do what I need to. Just make sure I'm compensated for this bullshit."

Kingpin didn't even blink. "You keep me informed, and I'll keep you alive. That's enough compensation for a Pig like you."

I stiffened. He never missed a chance to remind me I was an ex-cop. "Fuck you, Kingpin," I muttered, but we both knew there wasn't much bite to my words. He had all the leverage.

Murder cleared his throat. "So, about that other shit... I hear he wants more money outta you guys."

Kingpin nodded, stubbing out the cigar in a little ashtray. "He's pushin' for bigger dues, more loyalty. Says if we don't show we're 'all in,' he'll strip us of our territory. But we built these chapters ourselves. No thanks to that asshole. We pay enough. Hell, we do all the heavy lifting. He just sits on his ass, counting money."

Murder took a swig of his moonshine. "And rumor has it he might be behind our Cloud Nine drug fiasco in Charleston. Pushing that shit to line his own pockets."

Kingpin's features darkened. "Wouldn't surprise me. Also, we got word from the guys in Nashville that some info got leaked to the mob. Stuff only he would know. Might be him fucking us over, dealing with them behind our backs. I ain't got proof yet, but it smells rotten."

Murder let out a dangerous chuckle. "Are we thinking of ditching them?"

Kingpin shrugged. "Might or might start something new. We got options. If we can get enough allies, who knows? Either way, he's welcome to gargle my balls."

I listened, stone-faced, but my mind buzzed. So, Kingpin was planning to jump ship, maybe align with another club or form his own coalition. That spelled big changes. And if I was being honest, I didn't give a damn, so long as it didn't screw *me* over.

A scuff of boots sounded behind me, and I turned to see a large, red-haired biker stepping inside, a smattering of freckles on his brawny arms. He bowed to Kingpin, ignoring me at first. Then his gaze slid over, and his expression shifted. "Ah, well, if it ain't Hallow," he said in a thick Irish brogue I struggled to decipher.

I swallowed a curse. "Name's Maverick," I corrected him, trying to keep my tone neutral.

He flashed me a friendly smirk. "Aye, you can change your name, but I remember my brother."

I gave a curt nod, forcing a tight smile. "Good to see you too, Irish." The last thing I needed was reminding of my past, but Irish was a genuine soul.

He looked me up and down. "You were trouble then. Guess you're trouble now. Glad to see you survived. Surprised you're not signed up to fight."

"Not this time. My new boss, whoever's over the Road Monsters is a real piece of shit. Has no interest in having me do what I'm good at," I said to Irish, getting a dig at Kingpin, since I wasn't supposed to know who called the shots.

Irish's curiosity was piqued. He asked, "Is that so. What's wrong with the bastard. You're one of the best fighters, you are."

"Yeah, guys got small dick syndrome or something. So, I'm too busy."

Kingpin tapped a finger on the table, clearly done with the pleasantries. "All right, enough. Irish, go find some whores to amuse yourself with until we reconvene."

Irish laughed, heading back out. He threw me one last knowing look over his shoulder as he left.

Murder and Kingpin turned back to me, but I raised a hand. "If we're done, I gotta get back to Diana. Don't want her running off or opening that big mouth."

Murder shrugged, lifting his whiskey. Kingpin waved me off, bored, his eyes already drifting to the phone on the table.

I stepped out of the RV, relief washing through me as I breathed the night air. Something about being so close to Kingpin for more than a few minutes made my skin crawl. I liked to pretend I was free, even though I wasn't, not really.

I started cutting back through the tents, heading in Diana's direction, when I heard the pulsing beat of music from a corner. A ring of people had gathered, watching something. Curious, I coasted over.

In the center, a short, lithe red head wearing shimmering booty shorts and a cropped top was dancing with several large, color-changing hula hoops. Her skill was mesmerizing, spinning them around her waist, arms, and neck in a rapid, hypnotic swirl. The flickering lights made patterns in the dark. With a whoop and a holler, the men cheered. The women clapped.

When the music ended, the woman, took a playful bow. She had a wild grin, blue eyes dazzling with mischief. I found myself oddly captivated. She looked up, and our gazes locked. Without warning, she beckoned me closer with a flick of her finger.

Like pulled by a string, I moved forward. She looped her arms around my waist, pressing her body close. "You look like trouble," she said, her tiny voice high and sickeningly sweet. "I'm a big fan of trouble."

I smirked. "Then you're in luck. I'm Trouble."

"Hoops," she purred, lifting a slender hand in a wave. Then she traced a fingertip along my shirt collar, noting the patches and that my name wasn't Trouble. In this crowd it could've been.

"Trouble is my middle name," I quipped.

"You also look like big dick. I'm a big big fan."

I cleared my throat. "Last name, Big Dick."

She licked her lips. "Maverick Trouble Big Dick of the Road Monsters MC, huh? New in town?"

"Just passing through," I replied watching her tongue.

She leaned in, her lips brushing my ear, making my dick spring to life. "Come find me at my tent tonight, Mr. Big Dick. I'm over there by the red banner." She pointed to a distant bright flag swaying on a pole. "I got a bottle of tequila with your full name on it."

My grin widened. "I'll see what I can do."

And just like that, Hoops disappeared into the crowd, her hips swaying, leaving me with a renewed appreciation for the night's possibilities. *Maybe this trip isn't all shit,* I thought, continuing my trek to check on Diana.

I was trudging around the rally grounds to find Diana when I saw a familiar face leaning against a battered truck. I'd glimpsed him the other night, but we weren't able to catch up.

"Smoke," I called.

He turned, and a huge grin split his face. "Well, I'll be damned. Hallow, or should I say Maverick?" He grabbed me in a rough, friendly embrace. Smoke was from Charleston, a Royal Bastards brother from my first club. He'd always been laid back, the type to share a joint and a laugh more than start a fight.

I clapped him on the shoulder. "Good to see you, brother. Didn't know you'd be here."

He punched at my arm. "The Charleston guys wanted to scope out the rally, see what the Kings of Anarchy had to offer. A big patch-over might be in the works."

I inclined my head, not surprised since hearing it from Kingpin. "How's life in the hills?"

Smoke grinned big. "Got engaged, actually. We got a baby on the way." He rubbed the back of his neck, looking sheepish. "Never thought I'd settle down, but here I am."

I gave a genuine smile, ignoring the pang of envy in my gut. "Good for you, brother. Proud of you."

He nodded, glancing around. "So, I hear you're stuck with Dirty Diana. She cornered me earlier this morning, asked if I had any weed. Then told me some crazy story about a mob boss wanting her dead." He snorted. "That woman lives in her own reality, I swear."

I rubbed my beard. "She told me the same. Says it's some guy named Grinder. Put a hit out on her and her daughter."

Smoke folded his arms. "Half the time, she makes shit up. Think the old girl's senile. But who knows, she's been tangled up with shady crowds before."

"Yeah," I muttered, the old detective itch present at the back of my mind. I needed to figure out if she was lying or not. "Well, watch your back. If there's truth to it, we might have trouble."

Smoke nodded. "Sure thing. But we're heading home soon. Good luck to you."

We said our goodbyes. I continued onward, eventually spotting Diana near a mud-wrestling pit, spectating with a giggly group of women. She seemed in high spirits, her paranoia from last night either faded or drowned in liquor. I cursed under my breath. Babysitting a half-sober old woman was one thing. Babysitting a wasted liability was another.

CHAPTER 11

It was hotter than the devil's asshole out there, so I ducked into the shade of a makeshift bar area, just some big tent with crates of beer. That's when I heard a commotion. I was half listening, as a man with a scraggly mustache accosted some girls.

I spit out my beer. Did she just say she had a full bush? *What the hell?* That had my attention. The biker suddenly had a grip on some girl's vest, yanking it down. I heard her startled yelp over the noise.

I stepped forward instinctively, eyes zeroing in on the woman. She was tall, with dark, wavy hair, green eyes wide in shock. She had glasses perched on her nose, fogged slightly with the heat. Her body was insane. Curvy in all the right places, hips that filled her tight black skirt, and to top it off, a perfectly plump and perky breast that had just spilled out of the half-torn vest. The combo of that sexy body and the nerdy glasses made my brain short-circuit for a hot second.

When I saw the asshole pull her top so low that a succulent breast popped free, before I even thought it through, I was shoving him back, my fist connecting with his jaw. He staggered, cursing. The girl scrambled to cover herself, cheeks flaming.

"Back the fuck off," I snarled, grabbing him by the collar. "You don't put your hands on a woman who doesn't want it."

He spat blood. "Mind your own business, Road Monster."

I tightened my grip. "Take your shit elsewhere or I'll break your goddamn jaw."

He blanched, dropping his gaze. "Fuck you," he mumbled, but he stumbled away, nursing his busted lip.

I turned to the girl, her chest still heaving with anger. She was adjusting her clothes, face flushed. A blonde friend stood beside her, looking ready to throw punches herself.

"You all right?" I asked gruffly, forcing myself not to stare at the generous cleavage she was covering, but my eyes went elsewhere to her exposed belly. Damn, her flawless skin. She was downright gorgeous.

She nodded, swallowing hard. "Yeah. Thanks. I was handling it." Her voice trembled a bit, but her eyes were fierce, even behind those foggy lenses.

"Sure you were, princess," I jibed.

Goddamn, she was pretty. Like real pretty, akin to a pinup girl of days gone by. That dark hair fell around her face in intoxicating curls. When she looked up at me with larger-than-life green eyes, I felt a jolt, like she was electrocuting me.

No. She was a fucking defibrillator, bringing my dead heart back to fucking life.

Her hand was in her vest, adjusting the breast I just saw. My dick noticed, instantly becoming an unmovable rock. How I wished her hand was mine. I reached out. "Name's Maverick."

Her tiny hand slipped into mine, warm and soft, and I imagined it was that titty. Her pretty lips parted, but her friend spoke. "She's Smutty, and I'm Slutty."

This princess's face scrunched up as she glared at her friend. Damn, she was adorable when she was angry.

"What? Maverick's not his real name," her friend said, and I couldn't argue with that.

"Smutty?" I asked, thinking my dream had come true. My tent plans for the evening just changed. "With a full bush?" On her, it didn't matter. I'd bring my machete to get inside her.

Her cheeks turned bright red. "Lexi," she breathed, pushing her fogged glasses up.

Fuck, I wanted to rip them off her face and kiss her.

"This is my friend, Nova. Or at least she was."

I acknowledged her friend, but I couldn't keep my eyes off her as she bit her bottom lip nervously. "What're you doing here? You're obviously not from this crowd."

Before I could say more, a familiar, boozy voice chimed in from behind me, "There you are, big boy!"

I turned to see Diana stumbling over, arms outstretched like she wanted to hug me. I stepped aside to avoid her wet-lipped kiss. She pouted, then noticed the dark-haired girl. A flicker of recognition passed over her drunken features as she caught herself on my arm.

"Hey, baby." Was she talking to Lexi? "I've been looking all over for you."

My gut tightened as I saw the likeness, but Lexi was so beautiful. Diana was probably beautiful too before life chewed her up and spit her out.

So that's Diana's daughter.

The brunette's eyes flew to Diana, then to me, confusion etched on her face. Her friend looked equally dumbfounded.

"Mom?" the girl said, voice tight. "What are you... Who is...?"

Dirty Diana giggled drunkenly, leaning on me. "This is Maverick. He's been takin' real good care of your mama." She patted my chest like she owned me. "Isn't he fine?"

My face flamed for reasons I couldn't quite name. That was the last introduction I wanted right then. "Hey, so you're her daughter," I said, trying not to sound like a complete dumbass.

She crossed her arms over her chest, eyes narrowing under her glasses. "Yeah. I just got here. She called me for help. Didn't realize she was...preoccupied." She shot me a look that screamed, she did not approve of whatever she thought was going on.

I bit back a sigh. Although I wished to clarify the misunderstanding, I was on a mission. I couldn't blow my cover.

Diana cackled, apparently missing the tension. "He's shy," she teased, throwing me a saucy wink. "But oh, you should see him in action." She gave me a not-so-subtle up-and-down.

Lexi looked appalled. Her friend, that tall blonde, rolled her eyes. The moment was awkward as fuck. I cleared my throat.

"Lexi, baby, you made it!" Diana wrapped her arms around her daughter. "Oh, I'm so glad you're here. I was telling Maverick all about you. My sweet, smart daughter, who's a lawyer now!"

My mind was everywhere at once learning the fact that Diana did in fact have a daughter, and she must've taken my advice and told her of the danger. Her daughter was panicked, asking her a million questions, and Diana wasn't being too forthcoming. Since she was shitfaced.

I leaned into Lexi to let her know what I knew. "Diana's told me a little about it, but not enough to figure out who's behind the threats. She's...not real specific."

Lexi frowned. So, Diana told her someone was threatening to kill them.

Her friend cleared her throat. "Perhaps we can all find somewhere quieter to talk?"

Diana wanted more drinks and after everything, I figured getting her sloshed was our best bet when it came to milking the truth out of her.

"We can move over to the bar tent," I suggested. "Less dust, at least."

Lexi continued to pepper her mom with questions, but Diana didn't want to talk here. I had another excuse to get close as I whispered in her ear, "Your mom's known around here as Dirty Diana. She's, uh...gathered a lot of intel on different clubs, different men, all that. Some of them might not want their secrets out in the open."

"Secrets," Lexi practically shouted.

Diana creaked out, "I've had to...survive, Lexi. You do what you gotta do. But anyway, this man who's threatening me says he'll sue me for defamation if I ever breathe a word about him or his...connections."

As Lexi and her mother argued, I spotted Chigger and flagged him down. I introduced him around, pretending he was just another Road Monster, not a man who could've been my brother-in-law. I never knew him before the Road Monsters, so I tried not to think of him that way. He was my brother, and that was it. Him and Nova made eyes at each other almost immediately. Knowing Lexi and I were a dead end, I ignored her. I needed info from her mother. I couldn't make any moves on the daughter.

So, we drank, and I listened. Diana wasn't giving up anything. I danced with her, did all I could to loosen her up. But soon, the old woman was too plastered and hadn't even told her daughter anything useful. I let her wander off to the dance floor with Chigger and Nova as Lexi and I stayed behind at the bar.

"Thanks again for stepping in earlier," Lexi said, surprising me. She'd had quite a lot to drink.

I recalled that perfect titty. "No big deal. I don't tolerate that shit. But I do expect a peek at that full bush you're sporting."

The girl looked like I about killed her, turning beet red.

"I'm joking."

Her eyes drifted over my arms, over my tattoos. The ones I'd gotten in haste for lovers long gone. I moved my arm out of her view.

"You're new here," I said, trying to take her mind off my ink. "Never seen you around."

Her laugh was music to my ears. "I'm not a biker groupie, if that's what you're asking."

No shit. "Figured that much. Since your mom said you're a lawyer. You carry yourself like it. This isn't your scene."

"I am a lawyer. Mom called me for help, or I would never be here. What about you? You didn't get that black eye from rescuing me earlier."

"I'm a fighter, in the ring and out." I probably looked like ground beef. "Recently went a couple rounds with a grizzly."

"A bear?" she asked as if she took me literally.

"No. An asshole." I bent to her ear. "Your mom's a handful," I said, wanting to tell her of all the danger. Not just the death threats, but that I was trying to figure out what she knows, but I couldn't. "She's been stirring up a hornet's nest for a while."

"Why are you with her, then?" she asked, like she gave a damn. Damn, she was disappointed, thinking I was taken. Or maybe just thinking I was with her mother. "She's... She's quite a bit older than you."

I couldn't give up my cover. "She's a grown woman. We have...business."

"Right. Well, do me a favor and don't hurt her. She's all I've got."

"I won't," I started before her mom was calling us to the dancefloor.

I had to hold the old woman up, but I couldn't keep my eyes off Lexi as she swayed, dancing alone. I longed to scoop her up in my arms. Soon, Diana was too wasted to walk, so we took her back to her tent.

"Are you staying with her?" Lexi asked me, like she was asking if I was sleeping with her. I had to make a choice.

"She's hammered. But I got somewhere to be, so I can't babysit right now. You two should stay with her." I wanted her to know I wasn't sleeping with her mom. Plus, I had to do some digging. Diana, her and her friend should be safe from the mob here, surrounded by hundreds of bikers.

"What's that supposed to mean? You're with her, right? Or...something?"

"Diana does her own thing. Don't worry about it."

"So, you're just gonna leave her here?"

"She's got you, doesn't she? And your friend?"

"Fine. But I prefer an actual bed."

I had the tent beside Diana. Maybe when I got back, I could ask Lexi to join me in mine. "You might find out you like it out here, princess. A real bed can get overrated."

"I'm not a princess," she tried, but damn, she was my princess.

I made the rounds, rubbing elbows and getting the lowdown from any and every biker who ever had dealings with Diana, but came up short. When I got back to my tent, my mind was on Lexi. Pulling back the flaps of Diana's tent first, I only found the old woman snoozing, her chest rising and falling. Damn.

Needing rest, I went to my tent. Inside, a red headed pixie waited for me. I remembered Hoops and her invitation. The memory of those lithe hips spinning, those neon rings stuck in my mind.

Her eyes lit up. "You came." She yanked me in by the front of my vest. We wasted no time with small talk. She pressed her lips to my cock, and I let the tension of the day slip away in the heat of that moment. She wasn't shy, and I sure as hell appreciated it. There was a bottle of tequila, as promised, but we barely touched it. I was too busy burying my frustration and my cock into some easy pussy, while I thought about another. About that curvy lawyer, princess with glasses and possibly a jungle in her panties.

At some point, we collapsed on her sleeping bag, dozing in the humid night air. And the next morning, sunlight filtered through the tent's thin fabric, jolting me awake. Hoops stirred, half-naked beside me. I kissed her shoulder, muttering something about needing a drink. She giggled, pulling me back down. I wasn't a man to refuse.

We were mid-round two when I heard a frantic voice outside. A woman's voice, angry, shouting. A whoosh of air. Then my name. "Maverick!"

I froze. *What the fuck now?* I looked over my shoulder. My stomach dropped when I saw Lexi, tears in her red-rimmed eyes, hair disheveled, her glasses askew. "Diana's dead," she gasped, choking on the words.

I disentangled from Hoops, yanked on my jeans.

"She's... in her tent."

It felt like someone punched me in the chest. Dirty Diana? Dead? My mind spun, half from shock, half from the remnants of last night's lust-filled haze. "When? How?" I managed, my voice hoarse.

Her face twisted in grief and fury. "I don't know! I found her this morning. She wasn't breathing." Her tone became accusatory. "Where the hell were you? You said you were taking care of her!"

I bit down on my jaw. "I told *you* to watch her, remember?" The words came out sharper than I intended. A flash of guilt cut through me, though. *Dammit.*

Lexi's eyes flashed with anger. "So it's our fault?" She wiped at her cheeks, trembling. "Just... The cops are coming. They'll want to talk to you."

Fuck. My ex-cop senses lit up like a siren. If the cops poked around too much, they'd find all kinds of skeletons, not just with me, but the rally in general. And Kingpin would have my hide for bringing the law down on this place.

Hoops peeked out, eyebrows lifting at the drama as she sounded like a siren herself. I ignored her as I zipped up my jeans fully and shoved my arms through my cut. "All right, calm down," I told Lexi, though I knew calm was the last thing she'd feel.

But as we hurried toward Diana's tent, I saw the flashing lights of a police cruiser on the horizon. Sure enough, the rally was already abuzz with folks either scattering or stepping forward to gawk. My insides churned. Kingpin had told me to keep her safe, and now she was fucking dead. *Shit.*

We arrived at the tent. Lexi's blonde friend, Nova, I recalled, was near tears, trying to give a statement to a pair of uniformed cops who looked overwhelmed by the chaotic scene. A paramedic was crouched inside, presumably confirming that Diana was gone. With each step, my heart hammered harder. I peered inside, glimpsing Diana's lifeless form. The sharp smell of vomit and stale booze stung my nostrils.

"She's..." I started, but the words died.

Lexi turned on me, her voice quivering. "I blame you," she hissed, eyes brimming with tears. "She trusted you, and you vanished."

I bit back my retort. Now wasn't the time to argue. People were gawking, the cops were watching. I saw Kingpin in the distance, a dark scowl on his face, and I figured he was about to blow a gasket. This was all going sideways.

CHAPTER 12

Lexi

Nothing felt real anymore. Not the gray morning sky, not the cracked sand of the rally grounds, not the police lights flashing behind me as they asked endless questions about my mother. I was stuck in a nightmare loop. Mom was *dead*, and no one could tell me how or why. All I got were suspicious looks from the officers, halfhearted condolences, and a million questions I couldn't answer.

"Miss, can you spell your mother's full name one more time?" asked the taller cop for what felt like the tenth time. He was young, fresh-faced, and trying way too hard to sound authoritative.

I swallowed the lump in my throat and repeated, "D-i-a-n-a... last name's basically a guess. Could be Bryan, like mine." My eyes flicked to his partner, a woman with thinning hair who was scribbling notes on a pad. "She changed her last name a dozen times. She never told me who my father was. She just, she *drifted*. She went by *Dirty Diana*. I don't even know if she has an ID."

The female cop frowned. "So, you're not even certain of her legal last name?"

I shook my head, with tears imminent. "She'd call herself Dirty Diana. I don't think she used her real name in years."

It was humiliating, standing there in the middle of the dusty rally site, the ground littered with beer cans and cigarette butts. Everyone around me, bikers, groupies, vendors, had paused their partying to stare. Mom's body had just been carted off, and the cops kept repeating the same questions, over and over.

"Miss," the female cop pressed gently, "do you have any idea if your mother was taking drugs? Or did she have health issues?"

I struggled to keep my composure. "She drank a lot. Could've been pills sometimes, but I don't know. She's... She was always..." My voice cracked, so I cleared my throat. "Look, do you think this was an OD, or...?"

She hesitated, glancing at her partner. "We're not ruling anything out right now. The coroner will have to determine cause of death. We'll be in touch."

They took down my phone number and my Dallas address. I gave them Nova's too. The moment they finally let me go, I felt as though I'd collapsed inside. *Mom, what happened to you?*

Stepping away from the crime scene, I nearly bumped into a hulking man in a black vest embroidered with *Kings of Anarchy MC*. He had arms the size of tree trunks and a dark beard with some flecks of grey. He looked intimidating, but his gaze was surprisingly kind.

He held up his hands. "You must be Diana's kid," he said softly, his deep voice rumbling. "I'm Big Daddy, President of the Kings of Anarchy. I'm real sorry for your loss."

I nodded, forcing the tears back. "Thanks. I just...don't know what happened."

He lowered his gaze, sympathy shining there. "We'll get to the bottom of it, if we can. This is our rally, and if someone did your mother dirty, we'll see justice done. You got my word." He fished in his vest pocket and pulled out a crinkled business card. "Call me if you remember anything. Or if you need help."

I managed a nod. "Thank you." I gave him my number too, a sense of relief flickering for a moment. At least *someone* around here offered help.

After that, I wanted nothing more than to vanish back to the motel and cry in peace. Nova was already waiting by our car, arms folded protectively over her chest. We didn't speak as we got in. She just rested her hand on my shoulder in silent comfort. We drove off, leaving behind that hellish rally, the cops, and my mother's final moment of shame.

When we returned to the motel, I felt a crushing weight of exhaustion. My head pounded, and my eyes burned from crying. We trudged up to our room in silence. I had no idea what to do next. Mom was gone, and the police had no answers. I was stuck hundreds of miles from home in a seedy little motel, reeling with grief.

Inside, the stale air did nothing to soothe me. I flopped onto the edge of the bed, staring at the wall.

Nova perched beside me, rubbing my back. "I'm so sorry, Lex. I wish I knew what to say."

My throat constricted. "I just... I can't believe she's gone." A tear slipped out, and I wiped it hastily. "She called me for help, Nova. She said she was in trouble. And I..." My voice cracked again. "I couldn't protect her."

Nova's face was grim. "That's not on you. She made her choices. You came as soon as she asked."

I nodded, though it didn't stop the guilt. She was my mom, irresponsible as hell, but my mom. I never got the chance to say a real goodbye. To find out what kind of trouble she'd stirred up this time.

Before I could sink deeper into my despair, there was a knock at the door. Nova and I exchanged glances, both of us were on edge, especially after the cops had asked if we'd heard any threats. "Who is it?" I called from the bed as Nova went to open the door.

A low voice answered, "Maverick."

My heart stumbled in my chest. That damn biker. Part of me wanted to slam the door in his face. Another part felt a surge of relief. He'd helped me before, maybe he knew something I didn't.

"Hey," he said quietly. "Can I come in?"

Nova peeked over my shoulder, her protective posture obvious. But she stepped aside. "Sure."

Inside, he closed the door and raked a hand through his hair. Maverick stood there, looking grim and tense. His dark hair fell around his forehead, and the vest with *Road Monsters MC* was dusty from the rally. There was something about his brown eyes that tugged at me, like a magnetic pull I couldn't explain. *Stop it*, I told myself. *He's trouble.*

"Look, I, uh... I'm sorry about your mom. And I hate to pile on more shit, but you need to know that you're in danger."

A jolt of fear sparked in my stomach. "Danger?" I repeated.

CHAPTER 13

Maverick

I backed off, letting the cops do their job. They didn't zero in on me immediately. Hopefully, they had no clue who the fuck I was yet, which was good. I kept my head down, drifting around the periphery. The paramedics eventually brought Diana's body out on a stretcher, covering her with a sheet. Lexi and Nova watched, tears streaking their faces. My gut twisted at the sight.

I was about to slip away to check in with Kingpin when I caught a snippet of conversation behind a row of bikes. Two men, wearing brain buckets and dark shades, were speaking in hushed voices.

"That's the old bat's gone," one said. "But the daughter's still a problem."

The other spat on the ground. "Yeah, well, we wait until the cops clear out. We know where she's staying, some flea-bitten motel near the main road. We'll finish the job tomorrow."

Adrenaline spiked in my veins. *They're planning to kill Lexi.* Must be connected to this Grinder shit, or maybe some other angle. Either way, they were talking murder, plain and simple. I tensed, stepping forward, but one of them must've sensed my presence. They both jumped on their bikes, engines roaring to life. I barely got a glimpse of a patch, couldn't tell which MC or group. Then they sped off in a cloud of dust.

Fuck, I swore under my breath. Chasing them now would be useless. They had too big a head start, and I had no idea which direction they'd go once they hit the highway. *Fuck.* But I had to warn Lexi. If these assholes came after her, she was screwed, especially if she was naïve enough to trust random guys. Random bikers like me.

By then, they'd had loaded Diana into an ambulance, presumably to take her to the morgue. I hovered at a distance, noticing that more cops were swarming. Some of the bikers had already started scattering, not wanting to risk a random search or warrant. It wouldn't be long before tensions rose even more.

I saw Kingpin lurking near a lineup of black Harleys, scowling at the scene. Our eyes met, and he jerked his head. A silent command to vanish. He didn't want me around when the cops were asking questions, no sense exposing ourselves further. That was fine by me. I slipped through the crowd, found my bike, and kicked the engine into gear.

I had one destination in mind, Lexi's motel. If those assholes really planned to come for her, I had to warn her first, maybe get her out of town. I told myself it was just because Kingpin would want the daughter alive, that she might have secrets or could unravel something bigger if she died. But deep down, I knew there was something else. I couldn't let some scumbags off her just when she'd lost her mother. A mother I'd failed to protect, even if I hadn't truly wanted to.

It took me about half an hour to locate the motel I'd heard them mention, hell, it wasn't like Anarchy was brimming with five-star resorts. The sign blinked in neon: *Anarchy Inn*. Perfect. The lot was half-empty, a row of shitty vehicles and a couple bikes on the far side.

I parked, scanning the area. No sign of the men I'd overheard. I went into the lobby where the aroma was stale coffee and mildew. An elderly clerk raised an eyebrow at me.

"I'm looking for Lexi," I said curtly, giving her last name if I remembered it from that quick mention... Shit, I realized I didn't actually know her last name. "She's with a friend named Nova," I tried. "They got here recently."

He shrugged, flipping through a binder. "We got a couple women who checked in from out of state. Brown-haired and blonde, right?"

"That's them."

He gave me a suspicious once-over. "Room 214. But don't cause trouble here."

I ignored that last part and headed upstairs, the hallway reeking of old carpet and cigarettes. Door 214 was at the end. I knocked, then realized how this might look, me showing up out of nowhere after her mother died. But there wasn't time for niceties if these scumbags were coming.

The door cracked open a sliver. Nova's face appeared, eyes rimmed with red from crying. She saw me and gasped, "Maverick?"

Flattening my lips, I gave her a solemn look. "Let me in. It's important."

She hesitated, glancing over her shoulder. Then she unlatched the chain. I stepped inside to find Lexi perched on the edge of one of the beds, hugging her arms around her middle, eyes bloodshot behind her glasses. She looked up, and her expression hardened.

"What the hell are you doing here?" she demanded, voice raw. "You have the nerve..."

I raised both hands in a placating gesture. "Look, I know you're pissed at me, but you and your friend are in danger. I overheard some guys talking after your mom's body was taken away. They want to come after you next. They know you're here."

Her face went blank. "W-what?"

Nova's eyes widened. "Are you fucking serious?"

I nodded grimly. "They said they'd wait until the cops cleared out, then come here tomorrow. I don't know who they are, maybe tied to that mob boss Diana was yammering about wanting to kill you all. But it sounded legit."

Lexi swallowed hard, her knuckles white where they gripped the bedspread. "What the hell are you talking about, wanting to kill us?"

"Did she not tell you? She told me someone named Grinder was threatening to kill her and her daughter."

"No. She didn't tell me anything of the sort. Said she needed legal advice. The defamation. Remember? You heard her being all cryptic and shit," Lexi said.

"Listen. Diana has a reputation for not exactly telling the truth. So, I didn't believe her at first."

Lexi nodded, like she related to that fact.

"So, once I found out there was actually a daughter, I thought she told you about the hit, when she called you."

"A hit?" Lexi repeated my words like they were foreign.

"I told Diana to let you know you were in danger. I just figured she did, and supposed that's why you were desperately wanting answers last night." I spoke mostly to myself. "So, you didn't understand that you two should have stayed with her. Because you didn't know she was in real danger."

"Well, you left her in her tent," Lexi cried out, blaming me, rightfully.

"I came back in the middle of the night, and Diana was fine, breathing. I went to bed, thinking I was right beside her, and the sea of bikers would protect her from the mob. But I should've known, the mob would have bikers do their bidding."

"You mean, you were distracted by some loose woman. What do you call them? Club whores? Sweetbutts? Club Bunnies? Roadhouse Rabbits?" Her voice raised and got high at the same time.

"I'm sorry, Lexi. I put your mom's life in danger and yours."

"My life? Are you sure? I—I can't even process this. Why would they want me dead?"

I gave a rough shrug. "Because your mom might've said something. Or they think you know something. Shit, I don't know. But if they're serious, you need to get out of here. Tonight."

Nova made a strangled sound. "We can't just, leave. The police might have more questions, and Lexi... You can't trust some random biker."

"I promise, I'm just trying to help," I tried, meeting Lexi's wet eyes.

"She needs to plan her mom's funeral. Or something," Nova huffed out.

Lexi let out a shuddering breath, tears brimming again. "She can't just...be gone."

Guilt twisted in my gut. I knelt near the bed, forcing Lexi to meet my gaze. Up close, I noticed the faint freckles across her nose, the redness in her eyes, the tremble of her bottom lip. She was so damn beautiful it almost hurt to look at her. "I'm sorry," I said quietly, meaning it more than I wanted to admit. "But if these assholes come for you, you might end up just like her. You got any family, friends who can help? Anyone you trust?"

She shook her head, blinking back tears. "My dad's never been in the picture. I have some extended family in Dallas, but... I don't know. There's Mark, my boss from the office, but I'm not sure I want to get work involved."

"Then I'll help," I said, surprising myself with how quickly the words came out. But it was the proper course of action, and I could find a way to placate Kingpin during this. "I can move you two to a safer place, somewhere these guys won't find you. Then we'll determine the next steps."

"Tell me why I should trust you," Lexi said, putting me on the spot.

"Well, once upon a time I was a good guy..." I started, but that explanation died in my throat. Hell, I didn't want anything to happen to her for selfish reasons, but I'd gotten her mom killed. I tried a more reasoned approach. "If anything, your mom knew secrets, secrets about a man I work for and he asked me to keep her alive. If you don't trust me, trust that my boss would want to know why someone wanted Diana dead, and you might be our only lead."

Lexi puckered sideways, trying to decide.

I looked at her shirt that read, 'Men are Better in Books'. Tears streaked her pretty face, and it was right, no romance hero would have left her mom unguarded to pork some whore.

"Listen, Princess, I'll be real honest with you. Come clean, lay it all out. I won't let anyone hurt you because from the moment I met you, I wanted to haul those glasses off your pretty face and give you a kiss to make you notice me, really notice me. Make your knees weak and land you under me, in my tent, my bed. So, I came looking for you in Diana's tent. When you weren't there, I found someone in mine, so I buried my bone in her, wishing she was you. So, don't go thinking I'm going to let you get killed when I want to fuck you."

Lexi swallowed hard. She parted her lips but nothing came out.

"Besides, I got to see that full bush," I added, smiling.

Nova and Lexi exchanged looks. Finally, Lexi exhaled, shoulders sagging. "Okay," she whispered. "I don't know what else to do. And I don't have a full bush. I don't want to disappoint you." She almost laughed.

Nova glanced at me, her expression still wary. "Just promise you're not going to kidnap us or something."

I snorted. "Kidnapping ain't my style." I lied. "I'm trying to stop them from killing you."

Lexi nodded, wiping her eyes under her glasses. "Fine. We'll go. Let me just... God, I don't even have time to process my mother's death." Her voice cracked, and she took a moment to breathe. "But if we stay here, I might end up dead too, right?"

I stood up, shoving my hands into my pockets, wishing I could take away her pain. But I couldn't. I could only keep her alive. "We'll handle everything, step by step. Right now, pack up your shit. We'll find a different spot."

Nova got up, rummaging for her keys. Lexi remained on the bed for a beat longer, looking lost. Then she rose, moving stiffly, like a woman in a dream or a nightmare, more like. I took one more glance at her trembling figure, that wave of protectiveness flaring in my chest again.

What the hell am I doing? I was an outlaw biker. I owed her nothing. But something about Lexi made me want to keep her safe. It could have been the guilt from failing her mother, or perhaps the sight of her tears, or I simply needed to do one decent thing in my messed-up life.

"All right," I said, clearing my throat. "Let's move fast. Those bastards won't wait long."

She looked at me with a mixture of resentment, uncertainty, and, beneath it all, hope that maybe I could fix this. I doubted that, but I'd sure as shit try. Because I was Maverick, and if there was one thing I hated more than Kingpin's manipulations, it was seeing an innocent woman get dragged into the underground's crosshairs.

And so, battered by guilt and responsibility, I prepared to lead Lexi and her friend into the unknown, all while some faceless hitmen lurked somewhere out there, starting their engines, planning to strike. One thing was certain, Kingpin's assignment had just turned from babysitting an old hag into protecting her daughter. And I had a sinking feeling that *this* job would be a hell of a lot more complicated.

CHAPTER 14

Lexi

Maverick pulled out his phone and stepped into the hallway. I heard him speaking in low tones, calling someone. Minutes later, a knock sounded again. I opened the door to find another biker leaning casually against the frame, Chigger.

"Maverick told me we're escorting you ladies outta here."

Nova's cheeks pinked slightly, and I remembered her cozying up to him at the rally.

Chigger threw a look over his shoulder at Maverick, who was gathering some of our bags. "We all set?"

Maverick nodded. "We ride. The ladies will follow in their car. We'll keep an eye on 'em."

Fifteen minutes later, we were on the road again. Maverick and Chigger rode their bikes in tandem, one in front, one behind, while Nova and I drove in the middle. The night was dark, the headlights illuminating a winding country highway that twisted through endless trees and brush. I clenched the steering wheel, nerves on edge, scanning the mirrors for any suspicious vehicles.

Nova glanced at me. "You okay, Lex? You look pale."

"I feel like I'm in a goddamn spy movie," I muttered. "But yeah, I'm managing."

She gave a shaky laugh. "Right? Just a day ago, we were at a book convention, swooning over cover models. Now we're running from hitmen with two bikers we barely know."

I cleared my throat. "I just... Mom is gone. And I can't even process it because I'm too busy worrying about the next threat."

Nova reached over to squeeze my hand. "You'll get through this. We both will."

I nodded, though tears pricked my eyes again. Eventually, the road turned to a narrow, gravel path that led deep into a wooded area. Maverick signaled for us to follow, and after what felt like an eternity of bumping over rocks and potholes, we emerged into a small clearing. A weather-worn cabin stood at the end of a short driveway, surrounded by dense trees. No other houses in sight.

Maverick killed his engine, Chigger following suit. We parked next to them. The night was eerily silent, broken only by the chirping of insects. I stepped out, eyes adjusting to the darkness. The cabin looked old but surprisingly sturdy, with a wraparound porch and a single lamp glowing by the door.

"Welcome to your new hideaway," Chigger said, gesturing grandly.

Nova laughed nervously. "Yay. Rustic."

Maverick pulled a set of keys from his pocket. "We maintain a few of these in different states," he said, leading us inside. "No one knows about them except the Road Monsters and maybe a couple of our allies. You'll be safe here."

Inside, it was tiny but relatively clean. A small living room opened to a cramped kitchen. There were two bedrooms on either side, and a bathroom with minimal amenities. A faint scent of dust was present, but I preferred that to the musty motel we'd left behind.

"See?" Chigger said. "Cozy enough, right? I'll open some windows, let fresh air in. Nova, we can go grab some provisions in the morning, unless you two are starvin' now?"

She moved her head from side to side. "I'm not super hungry. But I could eat." She threw me a guilty look, as if uncertain if it was okay to be hungry when I was grieving. I forced a small smile.

Maverick nodded toward the bedrooms at the hall's end. "You two can bunk in there." He pointed to the first door. "Me and Chigger will take the other one." Then he turned to me, his voice low. "Look, I promise I'll figure out what's going on. If your mom was targeted, there's a reason behind it."

My chest tightened again at the mention of Mom. "Thank you," I whispered.

Nova and Chigger set off to open windows in the living room, rummage for blankets, and look for anything edible in the cabinets. Not finding a thing, they decided they would run to the small grocer we saw on the way.

I lingered near the bedroom door, and Maverick hovered close. The weight of the day hit me like a tidal wave, and I started to shake, tears welling up again.

"Hey," he murmured, stepping closer.

I tried to hold it in, but the sobs broke free. All the fear, confusion, and grief flooded out of me. "I can't... I can't believe she's gone," I gasped, pressing my hands over my face. "We might not have been close, but she was still my mom. I—oh, God..."

He hesitated only a moment before gently pulling me into his arms. His body was solid, warm, the leather of his vest creaking softly as he wrapped me in a secure hold. I clung to him, burying my face against his chest. A spark of comfort seeped through me. It felt oddly safe, even though I hardly knew him.

"It's okay," he murmured, one large hand stroking my hair. "Let it out."

For a second, I closed my eyes, letting the tears flow. A faint aroma of engine oil, sweat, and an unnamed manly fragrance emanated from the biker. Despite everything, my heart fluttered, a traitorous little flip. My mother was dead, and I was standing here craving the scent of a biker who'd been vaguely involved with her. *What is wrong with me?*

I sniffled, pulling back slightly. My cheeks burned with embarrassment. "Sorry."

He shook his head. "Don't apologize."

I swallowed hard, about to retreat into the bedroom, when he reached up to brush a strand of hair from my face. His callused thumb stroked away a tear on my cheek. The simple gesture made my pulse thrum. I looked up into his eyes, and for half a second, everything around us disappeared.

Then, shockingly, he *kissed* me.

His lips were warm and firm, pressing against mine in a heartbeat that seemed to stretch forever. My mind went blank. I instinctively leaned in, kissing him back. A spark ignited in my chest, something raw and desperate.

But the moment I realized what was happening, I jerked away, heart pounding. "What the hell?" I managed, voice trembling.

He pulled back, expression unreadable. "I'm... sorry," he said roughly. "I didn't mean..."

I shook my head, anger warring with the leftover warmth of that kiss. "You were hooking up with my *mother*." My voice cracked on the word. "She was all over you. And now..." I wiped my mouth, tears pricking my eyes again. "This is messed up."

Maverick's jaw tightened. "Look, it wasn't like that. Someone sent me to watch over her, keep her out of trouble. I never... I *didn't* touch her, if that's what you think."

I stared at him, trying to sort lies from truth. "You could've said something last night. You let me believe, everyone believe, that you were with her."

A grimace flashed over his face. "I wasn't sure if her danger story was real, and I had a job to do. I was trying not to blow my cover." He exhaled sharply. "Diana was a wild one, yeah, but I never laid a hand on her."

A wave of relief and guilt washed through me. "Mom always lied, so I... You're saying you *didn't* sleep with her? Not ever?"

He shook his head. "Not even close. Trust me, I'm not into older women. I was just doing a favor for my... boss." There was bitterness in his tone at that word.

I sighed, covering my face with my hands for a second. "I guess it's no telling what my mom told people. She might've put me in all this danger with her big mouth."

He stepped closer again, gaze determined. "Then I'll find out who did this, why, and I'll stop them from hurting you."

"Why do you even care?" I asked, voice raw. "You're some outlaw biker, probably just like her. Why not walk away and save yourself the headache?"

He stared at me for a moment, expression pained. "Because my previous profession was a detective. Before all this. I can't shake that part of me that needs to see justice done. Even if I'm not the same guy I used to be."

My eyes widened. "A detective? But you're..."

"Yeah," he said, voice dropping. "I was a cop in Columbus, Ohio. Long story. Let's just say it ended badly, and I ended up here, in the biker world."

I was momentarily speechless. An ex-cop turned outlaw? My mind reeled. But it explained the way he carried himself, the sharp, assessing glances, the sense of moral obligation, buried beneath the leather and tattoos.

He sighed. "Look, get some rest. I need to see if I can shake some leads out of folks who might know more about your mom's situation. Stay here with Chigger. He's good people. He'll keep you safe while I'm gone."

I wanted to ask more, but Nova and Chigger returned with a thud of bags being set down.

Maverick stepped back, picking up his keys. "I'll be back tonight, or tomorrow morning at the latest," he said. "Don't leave this cabin. Got it?"

I nodded, oddly bereft at the thought of him riding off. "Okay."

With that, he strode out the door. Moments later, his Harley's engine roared, fading into the distance.

CHAPTER 15

I didn't realize how numb I felt until he was gone. Nova and Chigger bustled around the small kitchen, finding a pack of tortillas and some random supplies from the cupboards to go with what they bought. They put together a passable meal of chicken fajitas, the savory aroma filling the cabin.

I sat at the worn wooden table, picking at my food without much appetite. Nova and Chigger were chatting like old friends. Actually, more like flirtatious new friends. It was sweet, but I couldn't shake the pang of resentment twisting in my stomach. My mother had just died, and here was my best friend giggling over chopped onions and sizzling chicken.

Eventually, Chigger looked over at me. "You doin' okay, Lexi?"

I forced a thin smile. "As okay as I can be, given…everything."

He nodded sympathetically. "Maverick will find answers, trust me. He's relentless when he sets his mind on something."

Nova propped her chin in her hand. "How do you know Maverick so well?"

Chigger grinned, leaning back in his chair. "We met a while back, after he left his first MC. He's been drifting for a bit. Joined the Road Monsters. He's a hell of a fighter, used to be a detective, you know."

"Yeah," I interjected softly. "He told me."

Chigger nodded. "Then you know the gist. He's got a complicated past. Something about his ex, Eve, screwing him over, losing their baby, and hooking up with Kingpin, his old MC president."

Nova and I exchanged looks, from our books we knew all about the motorcycle club hierarchy.

Chigger grimaced. "My sister, Eve Angel… She messed him up."

"Your sister?" I asked, my face probably giving away my surprise.

"Yeah. It's a small world when you're from Arkansas."

"Maverick's from Arkansas?"

"No, Eve and me. Maverick's from Ohio, though I'm rubbing off on him. Man used to have a bright future, you know? Now he's... I don't want to say broken, but he's definitely a different breed. Me, myself, I never had prospects like him, so I'm good with who I am."

Nova smiled and touched his hand lovingly.

But I focused on getting info on Maverick. "What do you mean different breed?"

"Man's been dead inside. I think the fact his wife left him, really put the final nail in the coffin."

"Eve? He married her?" I asked, getting whiplash.

"No, another woman. His president's wife. He ran off with her."

"Oh, what happened to him then?" Nova asked, as we tried to keep up.

Chigger motioned to the cabin. "You're looking at it. He got exiled to another club."

"So, is the guy single?" Nova asked what I was thinking.

"Oh, yeah," Chigger replied, like the answer was obvious.

My heart twisted. Maverick had loved a woman named Eve, they'd lost a child, and then she'd betrayed him? Then he was married and that's over now too. No wonder he seemed so dark and guarded.

"Chigger, if Maverick's so broken, do you trust him?" I asked the burning question.

Chigger met my gaze. "With my life. And just between you and me, Eve's my real blood and flesh sister. Don't get me wrong. I love her. But man's been real good to me even though I stir up shit memories for him. He's got a dark cloud following him, sure. But under all that tough shit, he cares. He's got a code, his own code, even if he tries to hide it."

Nova smiled. "That's good to know." She glanced at me. "Hear that, Lex?"

I nodded, chewing my lip. Part of me felt a warmth spread through my chest. A code. That explained the unwavering sense of responsibility he'd shown in trying to protect me. But it also made me wary, I'd seen my mother latch onto men who had "codes," only to be disappointed when they turned out to be scumbags.

We ate in relative silence after that. I concentrated on the fajitas' flavor profile, spicy, tangy, actually quite palatable for a rushed meal. Chigger and Nova chatted softly about random topics. The best bars in Dallas, funny stories from the road. I felt like an outsider, my grief too raw, my thoughts too consumed by everything that had happened.

Maverick never returned that evening. Eventually, the only light came from a single lamp in the living room. I sat on the small couch, phone in hand, repeatedly checking for any messages or calls. Nothing.

"Any word?" Nova asked around ten o'clock, yawning.

I gave my head a little shake, worry gnawing at me. "No."

Chigger checked his phone, then dialed a number. He spoke in hushed tones, then hung up. "He's fine," he assured me. "Just said he's tied up with something, and not to wait up. He'll see us in the morning."

Relief loosened my tight muscles, though a thread of anxiety remained. What was he doing out there? And would he really find answers? I sighed, exhaustion weighing me down. "I guess I'll go to bed."

Nova stood too. "Me too." She shot Chigger a little smile. "Thanks for dinner."

He winked. "My pleasure. You ladies sleep well. I'll keep watch."

Despite my best attempts, I couldn't sleep. My mind replayed the day's horror like a broken record. Mom's lifeless face, the bruise on her neck, the cops' questions, Maverick's intense gaze, his little speech about keeping me alive because he wanted to fuck me. At some point, I must have drifted off, because I woke with a start sometime after midnight, a chill creeping over me.

I blinked in the darkness, realizing I was alone in the bedroom. Where's Nova? Her bed was empty. Confusion pulsed through me. It wasn't like her to wander off in the middle of the night, especially not in a strange place.

Fear prickled along my spine. My first thought was Are we being attacked? I shoved the blankets aside, heart racing. Quietly, I grabbed my glasses from the nightstand and slipped out of bed, tiptoeing across the cabin. I flipped on a small lamp in the living room, noticing it was empty.

Then, from down the hall, I heard noises. Distinct moans, followed by muffled laughter. Oh, God. My cheeks heated. It was coming from the second bedroom. Chigger's room.

I realized what was happening at once. Nova was hooking up with Chigger. My stomach churned with a weird mix of relief at the fact at least she wasn't kidnapped and embarrassment. Still, the moans sounded urgent and echoey, and part of me panicked. Perhaps she required assistance?

I crept closer, picking up a cast-iron pan from the stove, my brain in a half-asleep panic mode. God, Lexi, calm down. But adrenaline spiked. If there was danger, I wasn't going to be caught unarmed.

The sounds got louder as I reached the doorway, moans, creaking of the bed, breathless gasps. My face flushed bright red. They're definitely not in trouble. I decided to slink away before I humiliated myself further.

But as I turned to retreat, I smacked right into a solid wall of bare chest. A startled yelp escaped me, and I almost dropped the pan.

A low chuckle rumbled above me. "Easy, princess," Maverick whispered. "You planning on bashing someone's skull in?"

I looked up, heart hammering. It was dark, but enough moonlight filtered through the cabin window to reveal Maverick's silhouette, tall and broad as ever, and very deliciously shirtless. My gaze roamed over the cords of muscle in his thick arms, the dark outlines of tattoos on his chest. His nipples, were larger than I imagined, but made sense his chest was so vast. God, he looked too good. My mouth went dry, and I licked my lips.

Though I had no saliva, I swallowed hard, flustered. "I heard noises," I explained lamely. "I thought maybe we were being attacked."

He smirked, leaning in closer. "Just your friend and Chigger having themselves a little midnight fun. The walls here aren't exactly thick."

Heat rushed to my face. "Right. Um... You're back."

"Got back a few minutes ago," he murmured, glancing over his shoulder at the sounds still echoing from the other bedroom. "Didn't feel like stepping into that, so I was gonna crash on the futon in the living room. But now...." He gestured at the noise with a crooked grin. "I doubt I'll get any peace with that going on."

I realized how close we were, close enough that my arm brushed his bare torso. My stomach flipped. "You can, uh, take Nova's bed in my room, if you want," I found myself offering. The words came out before I could think them through. "I mean, she's obviously not using it."

His eyebrow arched, a flicker of surprise in his eyes. "You sure?" he asked softly.

I nodded, my pulse racing. "Yeah. It's fine. Let's just...sleep."

He studied me for a moment. "All right," he said finally. "Lead the way."

We crept back into my bedroom, the pan still in my hand for some stupid reason. I set it down on a small table, feeling like an idiot. Darkness cloaked the room except for a faint glow from the moon outside. Maverick hovered near the twin bed meant for Nova, while I slipped under the covers of mine.

For a few heartbeats, I just watched him. He toed off his boots, wearing only jeans now, the faint line of his abs visible in the low light. My mouth went even drier. Damn, I was thirsty and finally got the slang. The earlier spark of that kiss flickered in my memory, sending a rush of heat through my veins, through all my bodily fluids. But I had no right to want this. My mother had just died, and I was in mortal danger.

He lay down on Nova's bed, exhaling a quiet sigh. "Night, princess."

I swallowed thickly. "Good night."

I rolled onto my side, trying to ignore the awareness of him just a few feet away. My heart pounded so loudly I wondered if he could hear it. He didn't say anything else, though. Maybe he was as confused as I was.

Eventually, exhaustion claimed me. As I drifted off, the faint murmurs of Nova and Chigger's passion died away, replaced by the gentle rhythm of Maverick's breathing. Safe, my tired mind whispered. I felt... safe.

Despite the grief threatening to swallow me, despite the swirling questions about who killed my mom, I found a pocket of comfort in the dark, knowing that a man who once was a detective, now a hardened biker, was just a few feet away, vowing to protect me until this nightmare ended.

CHAPTER 16

Maverick

I'd always hated the tail end of a rally. When the booze ran low, the dust and sweat caked every inch of your skin, and the noise was too damn loud to think. But I had business to handle before I could ditch Anarchy, California. Specifically, one more face-to-face with Kingpin, the asshole who owned me, or so it felt. I needed to look him in the eye and be damn sure he wasn't behind Dirty Diana's death.

I found him exactly where I expected, outside of his RV bordering the rally field, smoking a cigarette like it was the last one on earth. His once-smug expression was set in a dark scowl, and I knew he was pissed about the cops sniffing around.

He spotted me and lifted his chin. "Well, look who decided to drop by."

I parked my Harley and swung a leg off. "We gotta talk." My voice came out rough, layered with the leftover adrenaline from the shitstorm that'd gone down with Diana.

He blew a plume of smoke, eyes narrowed. "Yeah, we do. Figure you want to know if I had anything to do with the old broad's death."

I didn't say anything, just stared him down. We'd both seen more violence than we'd ever admit, so it was best to be direct.

Kingpin snorted. "If I wanted her dead, I wouldn't have sent you to get close to her. I'd have done it a long time ago, no middleman required." He spat on the ground. "But she's gone now, so what I wanna know is, does the daughter know anything? Did Dirty Diana pass on all those secrets to Lexi? Or does she have zero intel?"

I fought the urge to punch him in that smug mouth. Instead, I kept my voice even. "Lexi doesn't know jack shit. She's mourning her mom. She's not exactly rummaging through some secret file."

He pursed his lips. "Lexi, huh? Women like Diana don't go quietly. She might have given her kid something, a clue, a ledger, a flash drive, who the fuck knows. Don't be stupid, Maverick. The mob doesn't just go after someone for no reason. So fucking figure it out. We can't have them sniffing around our operations because of some dead whore's secrets."

My jaw clenched at the callous way he talked about Diana. Sure, I hadn't liked the old lady. She was a drunk, had borderline zero morals, but still, she was Lexi's mom, and she'd died under suspicious circumstances. "I'm not doing this for you," I ground out. "I'm protecting Lexi because she's in danger, not because you say so."

Kingpin shook his head, a half-smile twisting his lips. "Don't start getting noble on me, Pig." He flicked his cigarette butt away, grinding it under his boot. "We've got bigger fish to fry. That mob boss, Grinder, runs parts of Texas. Word is Diana used to hang with some biker out in Dallas who was originally from the SOS MC in San Diego. Might be Lexi's daddy, might be just another fling, but either way, the rumor is he pissed off the wrong people. If the girl's connected to that old bastard, that could be why these assholes want her gone. Or perhaps Diana was holding onto something that ties Lexi to a bigger scheme. Documents, blackmail, who knows?"

I exhaled slowly. "If you hear anything else about Grinder's real motive, you let me know. I'm not letting Lexi end up like her mother."

He raised a brow, chuckling darkly. "Getting attached, are we? You always did have a soft spot for these helpless women."

A stab of anger shot through me. "Fuck off, Kingpin. I didn't come here for a therapy session."

He shrugged. "Fine. Just remember your place. If that girl has anything that might compromise me or the Road Monsters, you get the intel. Then we decide what to do with her."

I grimaced, biting back the urge to deck him. "She doesn't have shit that'll compromise you. But if I find out differently, I'll let you know."

Kingpin rubbed his beard. "Last thing. You said you got some cryptic texts about Sky? That's old business. She left. Hell, if I wanted to haul her back, I would have done it by now. Figured you would, too, if you had any questions. But... it's possible another person is stirring the pot."

My gut twisted at her name. "You don't think it's from her?"

He shrugged. "No clue. She's still in the wind, presumably with Getty, as you know. I'll dig around, see if something pops up. Nashville's my territory, my business. If someone's messing around with Sky's name, I wanna know who it is."

I caught the flicker in his eyes. Deep down, he'd always had a thing for Sky. Didn't matter that he'd married Eve, or that he'd had a twisted relationship with both women. The man was a fucking black hole of desire, never satisfied. But in that moment, I realized I didn't care anymore about Eve or Kingpin's personal shit. Sky and her betrayal were the last thing on my mind. My mind was consumed by Lexi, her emerald eyes, her fear, her grief.

I turned to leave, flicking a glance over my shoulder. "We're done here."

Kingpin barked a laugh. "For now, Maverick. But if you screw me over..."

"I won't," I snapped, then stomped back to my Harley. My blood pounded with anger, and something else. The need to keep Lexi safe, no matter who was behind this.

On my way out, I weaved between the thinning crowds. The rally was winding down, but there were still pockets of chaos, men swigging from beer bottles, women dancing, random bikes roaring. I was just about to pass a row of tents when a familiar high voice called, "Maverick..."

I turned to see Hoops stepping out of her rainbow-colored tent, wearing the same skimpy top I'd peeled off her a couple of nights ago. She gave me a flirty grin, her hula hoop on one arm.

"Hey, big dick," she crooned, stepping in close and sliding a hand over my crotch. "You going somewhere? Thought we could have another good time."

She grabbed me by the balls, literally, and I let out a hiss. "Jesus, woman, I'm kinda busy."

She pouted. "Aw, come on. Don't tell me you're still playing white knight for that old lady's daughter."

I shoved her hand away, gently but firmly. "That's exactly what I'm doing. Sorry, Hoops. Not interested."

Her eyes narrowed. "You used me for a little fun, and now you're blowing me off?"

I forced a tight smile. "It was mutual fun. Don't pretend otherwise. Look, I got shit going on. That's it." And with that, I turned and headed for my Harley. I heard her curse under her breath, but I didn't care. All I could think about was Lexi, her wide, tear-filled eyes and the way her voice quivered when she put all her faith in me.

Hoops was old news, just another distraction in a world full of them. Right now, I needed a clear head, and Lexi.

CHAPTER 17

When I finally returned to the safe-house cabin, it was late. My headlights shone on the tiny porch in the darkness, and my eyes scanned for trouble. So far, Lexi's car and Chigger's Harley was just where they'd left them. I killed the engine and stepped inside, finding the place mostly silent.

The bedroom I was supposed to share with Chigger's door was shut and locked. I didn't have to press my ear to the door to hear what was going on inside. Typical. Those two had become practically inseparable, which annoyed me a little, but I wasn't their keeper.

In the bathroom, I scrubbed the dirt from the rally off my face. Tearing off my shirt, I planned to take a scalding shower. But I heard a noise. Stepping out into the hall, I ran into Lexi, still dressed in the clothes from earlier, holding a damn frying pan in the air. She froze when she saw me, relief flashing across her face.

"Easy, princess," I whispered. "You planning on bashing someone's skull in?"

"I heard noises," she blurted. "I thought maybe we were being attacked."

Drawn in by her, I couldn't resist getting closer. "Just your friend and Chigger having themselves a little midnight fun. The walls here aren't exactly thick."

Her face turned bright red. "Right. Um... You're back."

"Got back a few minutes ago," I explained, shooting a glance to the cries of passion coming from the bedroom. "Didn't feel like stepping into that, so I was gonna crash on the futon in the living room. But now...." I thought about the lumpy cushions. "I doubt I'll get any peace with that going on."

"You can, uh, take Nova's bed in my room, if you want. I mean, she's obviously not using it."

My heart did a funny twist. "You sure?"

Lexi nodded eagerly. "Yeah. It's fine. Let's just...sleep."

Damn, she was sexy. The way her lips trembled as her breathing quickened. This girl wanted me. It was written all over her face, but for some reason she was holding back. "All right. Lead the way."

We headed down the hallway to her room. Sure enough, it had two small twin beds. Nova's bed was empty. Since she'd obviously moved on to warmer company. Lexi cleared her throat and sat down the pan she'd still been clutching. She turned out the light, plunging the room into darkness. The faint moonlight through the curtains showed her silhouette as she crawled under the blanket of the other bed.

Getting rid of my boots, I sank onto the bed's edge nearest the door. Determined to give Lexi some space, my eyes fixed on the ceiling, letting my mind drift. The day had been pure chaos, from Kingpin's bullshit to Hoops grabbing me to the never-ending swirl of confusion around Diana's murder. But at least here, with Lexi a few feet away, I felt... calmer. She was within arm's reach, so that meant I could get some rest.

I woke before dawn, a little light creeping in. Lexi was still out cold, facing the window. She looked oddly peaceful, no tension across her brow like I'd seen before. A protective urge swelled in my chest as I watched her. There's nothing I wanted more than to slip behind her, spoon her, comfort her. And then maybe have my way with her. But the girl was grieving the loss of her mother.

Quietly, I left the bedroom and went to the cramped bathroom. I showered quickly, cursing under my breath at the lukewarm water that sputtered from the old showerhead. When I emerged, dressed in fresh clothes, I noticed Chigger and Nova were still knocked out in the other room. No surprise there.

I rummaged in the kitchen and found instant coffee packets, water, and an old drip coffee machine. Soon, the rich aroma of coffee filled the cabin. I was pouring myself a cup when Lexi shuffled out, hair tussled, eyes squinting.

"Smells good," she murmured. "Gimme."

I handed her a mug. "Morning, princess."

She sipped, sighing in delight as the caffeine hit her system. Then her expression sobered. "Why do you call me that?"

"You're not like anyone in the circles I run in now, lawyer girl."

"I'm just a girl who finished school and passed the bar. I'm no one special."

"In my eyes you are," I said, thinking about all the women in my world I could have with a snap of my fingers. Lexi looked like she at least had some standards. "And I bet a girl like you wouldn't give a biker like me the time of day."

Lexi made a face. "Men don't give me the time of day, usually."

"They're intimidated. You're confident, smart, sexy. Probably have a good job. Men want someone to rescue."

"Like you're rescuing me?" Her eyes darted to the floor as she shook her head. She was changing the subject. "Did you find out anything from last night?"

Leaning against the counter, I came out with it. "There's a mob boss named Grinder, runs shit around Texas. That's where you live, right?"

Leix nodded.

"Possibly your mom messed with him somehow. Also heard rumors of a biker from the SOS MC in San Diego, some old guy your mom might've been with, who could be your father. Maybe that guy had a beef with Grinder. We don't know yet."

She blinked. "That's... a lot to process. A father I never knew, and a mob boss who might want me dead."

I took a long drink of coffee. "Anything your mom left behind that you can think of? Documents, a box of stuff, maybe a computer file? Sometimes blackmail or secrets get stashed."

She frowned. "She never let me near her personal things. But a few times she dumped some crap at my apartment in Dallas, then left without explanation. I didn't dig through it. It's mostly old clothes, random junk. But maybe there's something hidden in there."

I set my mug down. "Then that's our next stop. We need to see what the hell your mom left. If she has anything incriminating, that'd explain why people want you gone."

"You're right." Then she paused. "So… about this possible father? If that's even true, I don't know if I want to meet him."

Lifting my shoulder, I understood. "Maybe you never have to. Kingpin's info is sketchy. Could just be gossip. But if it's real, it might tie into the bigger picture."

Her features hardened. "Kingpin? Your old president?"

"How do you know that?" I asked in a rush, my mind whirling.

"Chigger said the name. He told us about your past."

"Fuck," I said automatically. Chigger and I would be having a talk. I was fuming.

"He said the man used to be your president. That's all. Nova and I grilled him last night. Don't be upset."

Fighting to temper my anger, I focused on our next moves. "To Dallas then?"

"Fine. Let's go. I just want answers."

By the time Chigger and Nova woke up, we'd finished half the pot of coffee. We filled them in on our plan to drive to Dallas. They agreed without question. Therefore, we packed up the minimal gear we had to shove into Lexi's trunk, and stepped outside…

…only to find her car's front tires slashed.

Lexi stood there, jaw slack. "Are you fucking kidding me?" She nudged one of the tires with her foot, rubber torn to shreds. "Why the hell would they slash my tires and not just kill us in our sleep?"

Nova crossed her arms, looking around nervously. "Perhaps they only wished to frighten us? Slow us down? Who knows?"

I kicked the other tire, cursing myself. "And they didn't touch the bikes?"

At my words, Chigger shot me a guilty look, one that said he was the one who did the deed. He slashed her tires. It all made sense. But did Chigger do it to get closer to Nova or because taking the car was a liability? After all, it was in Lexi's name. It could be tracked. It was something I'd have to put on my list to talk to him about later.

I covered for him. "Could be a message. Could be they got spooked so didn't have time to finish or to take us all out. Either way, you can't drive this piece of junk now."

Chigger grunted, scanning the tree line. "Well, guess the ladies ride with us."

Lexi looked between our two Harleys, her expression uneasy. "I've never ridden on a motorcycle."

Chigger had Nova right beside him. She was practically buzzing with excitement. "I have! Well... once. When I was, like, nineteen." She didn't look too worried.

I gave Lexi a reassuring nod and my helmet. "It's not that bad."

She chewed her lip, glancing at the slashed tires again. "I guess we don't have a choice, huh?"

"Nope." I hoisted my bag over my shoulder. "We'll need to travel light. I'll have someone from the club come pick up your stuff later. Right now, we need to get on the road."

Bending over the trunk, Nova and Lexi speedily went through their luggage, tossing some of our stuff, and filled the two saddlebags. Chigger and I stood back and watched. Enjoyed the view.

He leaned sideways and whispered. "You can thank me later."

I whispered back, "For what? Causing a problem?"

"That car is a liability. Get your head on straight, brother."

"You're the one distracted," I challenged him.

"No, I'm getting mine. I'm keeping Nova out of your hair. You need to get some pussy, stat, so you don't make such obvious mistakes."

When Lexi hopped on my bike and hugged me from behind, I said, "Hold on and lean with me."

The beginning of the trip was smooth sailing. Riding for miles with a scared but determined woman holding onto me should be no big deal. Lexi's grip on my waist got tighter every time we turned. Oddly enough, I was totally worried sick about her. But she chilled out pretty quick, letting me handle the bike. Weirdly, having her close, her warmth on my cut, felt pretty good. But Chigger was right, I was distracted by her. It was something I'd have to take care of soon, just so I could keep her safe.

Nova rode on the back of Chigger's hog, and we'd occasionally stop for gas or a quick bite. The sun was brutal, sweat pouring down my face, but the faster we got to Dallas the faster we got answers. We zipped across the border, arriving in Texas by late afternoon.

The sky turned dark, and we all decided to call it a night. We stopped at a crappy motel off the highway. A burned-out neon sign, flickering, barely showed "VACANCY". The four of us stood at the reception counter, haggling with the bored clerk.

"Two rooms, one night," Chigger said, flashing the man a casual smile.

"Two beds in each room," Lexi added.

The clerk gave us a suspicious glance. Bikers often got that reaction. He shrugged, taking our cash, then handed over two keys. Rooms 204 and 205, upstairs. Perfect.

Nova clung to Chigger's arm, so it was obvious they weren't separating. Me and Lexi ended up in the other room again.

"Probably for the best," I mumbled, leading her to our door. "No sense leaving you girls alone in a room."

She blushed. "Right."

We realized we forgot our bag, and I stretched out my sore shoulders, preparing to head back out. My stomach rumbled. "Damn, I could eat."

Lexi smiled faintly. "I think there's a diner next door. Want to check it out?"

"Absolutely. Let's see if they at least have real food."

CHAPTER 18

We walked across the dusty lot to a diner that looked straight out of the seventies. Inside, a waitress in a pink uniform led us to a booth, handed us sticky menus, and poured stale coffee into chipped mugs.

I glanced at Lexi from across the table, noticing how tired she looked. Still, there was a quiet determination behind the lenses of her glasses. Maybe it was the heat of the coffee after a long ride, but I felt all warm and fuzzy inside when she looked at me. She was so damn beautiful, even with dark circles under her eyes.

"How you holding up?" I asked softly.

She shrugged. "Tired. Confused. Grieving. Terrified. The usual." Then she gave a wry smile, as if laughing at her own misery.

I reached across the table, brushed a strand of hair behind her ear. "We'll figure it out."

She studied me, something flickering in her eyes. "You keep saying that," she said, voice trembling. "And I keep wanting to believe you."

I pulled my hand back, forcing a casual grin. "I'm a man of my word."

The waitress interrupted them, setting down plates of greasy burgers and fries. We ate quickly, exchanging quiet words about tomorrow's plan, arrive at her apartment, dig through Diana's junk, see if we hit some kind of jackpot that explained everything.

At one point, I caught myself staring at Lexi's lips, coated with grease from the burger. I remembering the taste of them from that impulsive kiss. She noticed, her cheeks instantly coloring, and I had to look away, overcome by a rush of heat of my own. She dabbed her lips with a napkin, reminding me she was off-limits. Damn it. She'd just lost her mother. And she didn't need me complicating her life. But damn if my body disagreed as I adjusted myself under the table.

"You okay?" she asked, brow furrowed.

I cleared my throat. "Yeah. I was just... thinking we should get some rest. Big day tomorrow." Liar, I thought. But at least it was half true. I was imagining getting her back to the room and tearing off her glasses and her latest ridiculous book t-shirt, with a racoon, saying she reads trashy books. See that titty again, and the other one. I'd show her that not all men are better in books.

We rolled out of that diner, full of burgers and coffee, and the night air felt great. Without thinking, I reached for her hand, lacing our fingers together. She blinked, but didn't pull away. For a few seconds, we walked in silence, that small connection feeling more intimate than it had any right to be.

Then gunshots shattered the quiet, echoing from the motel parking lot.

Lexi gasped, and I whipped my head around to see Chigger and Nova sprinting toward us. Chigger's face was grim, Nova's eyes wide with terror.

"Run!" Chigger yelled. "They've found us. We gotta get the fuck out of here!"

My stomach lurched. I grabbed Lexi's hand tighter. "Let's go."

The four of us bolted for the motorcycles, bullets whizzing by. Shouts erupted from behind some parked cars. Whoever it was, they weren't shy about making noise. I yanked Lexi onto the back of my Harley and fired up the engine.

"Hang on!" I roared.

Nova and Chigger did the same on his bike. Tires squealed as we tore out of the parking lot. Headlights pierced the darkness, as the boom of our engines mingling with the gunshots. I ducked and weaved, evading possible shots from the rear. Lexi clung to me with a death grip, her face buried against my back.

Glancing in the mirror, I saw a pair of bikes chasing us, muzzle flashes lighting up the night. Shit. I gunned the throttle. We bobbed and weaved, taking random turns to lose them. One bullet pinged off the pavement too close to my front tire.

At last, after cutting through a maze of side streets and back roads, we lost the bastards. I slowed, scanning for any sign of them. Nothing. Just a long, empty highway with a few sad streetlights.

But Chigger and Nova were nowhere to be seen.

"Where the hell did they go?" Lexi asked, her voice shaky.

Pulling off onto a side road, I shook my head. "No clue. We got separated." My blood still pounded in my ears. "We have to assume they're okay. Chigger can handle himself."

She gasped shallowly. "So now what?"

I surveyed the area. We were in the middle of nowhere, a highway lined with a few rundown buildings. A cheap motel sign flickered in the distance. Every muscle ached, and Lexi was trembling.

"We lie low," I said. "At least until morning."

I pulled into the grim parking lot of a rundown single-level motel. Inside the office, a bored-looking woman took my cash without much comment, though she eyed our rumpled, panicked appearances.

A minute later, we stood outside room 10, a key in my hand. I opened the door to a dull, stale space with one bed, a tiny TV, and the faint smell of cigarette smoke. Good enough for the night.

"Safe and sound," I muttered, flipping the deadbolt once we were in. My shoulders finally relaxed. "No gunshots. That's an improvement."

Lexi hugged herself, eyes haunted. "I can't believe this is happening. People shooting at us in the middle of nowhere..."

I set her helmet on the dresser, turning to her. "We'll figure out who they are. Tomorrow, we can try to reach Chigger, see if they're safe."

She nodded, rubbing her arms. "I, uh, think I'll shower. I feel gross from the road."

"Sure," I said softly. "Bathroom's all yours."

She grabbed a change of clothes from my saddlebag, stuff we'd hastily shoved in there earlier, and disappeared into the tiny bathroom. I heard the water squeak on. My mind buzzed with the day's events. Bullets, Kingpin's demands, this potential father in Texas, and now we were holed up in yet another shitty motel.

After a few minutes of pacing, my nerves got the better of me. An urgency from the escape was still spiking, and the image of Lexi's terrified face kept flashing in my head. I couldn't just stand here. I found myself drawn to the bathroom door.

The rush of the water was loud behind the thin wood. *Calm down, Maverick.* But a wave of protectiveness surged, maybe even something more. I couldn't wait any longer. I pushed the door open, half hoping she'd already be done.

Steam billowed out, the shower curtain drawn. I could just make out her silhouette. Her voice startled me. "Who's there?"

I swallowed. "It's me," I said softly, stepping closer. "Princess, I..."

She squeaked, probably noticing a figure looming behind the curtain. "Maverick?!"

I reached out without thinking, tugging the flimsy plastic aside a few inches. She was turned away, water streaming down her shoulders, beads tracing over soft curves. She yelped and spun, covering herself with an arm.

My cock hammered at the sight of her wet skin. "Shit," I muttered, instantly regretting my intrusion. "I'm sorry... I just..."

High on adrenaline, confusion, and the overwhelming urge to make sure she was okay, I hadn't thought this through. Now I was face-to-face with her naked form, half concealed by the curtain.

Her eyes were wild, cheeks flushing. "You couldn't wait until I was out?!"

I kept my gaze on her face, trying not to stare at what little I could see. "I just... I'm sorry," I repeated, breath catching.

My pulse pounded, half from embarrassment, half from the undeniable attraction that slammed into me. But I managed to yank the curtain closed, stepping back. "I'll, uh, let you finish."

She didn't say anything, probably too shocked. I retreated, heart thudding like a jackhammer, every sense on high alert. The door clicked shut behind me. For a second, I stood there, hands fisted at my side.

Smooth move, asshole. I'd never felt more like a dumb teenage boy in my life. The thrill, the guilt, the embarrassment all warred in my chest. I cursed under my breath and backed away from the bathroom, sinking onto the edge of the bed.

Outside, the hum of traffic was quiet, and inside, all I could hear was the rush of water and my own hammering heartbeat. I realized that despite all the chaos, the danger, the grief... she was the only thing I was thinking about right now. And that scared me more than any bullet ever could.

CHAPTER 19

Lexi

My entire body trembled with shock as I watched the bathroom door slam shut behind Maverick. I stood under the stream of hot water, mind spinning like a rollercoaster stuck on fast-forward. Had he really just marched in and yanked the shower curtain back?

For a brief moment, I'd been convinced we were under some new attack. The adrenaline spike made me drop the bar of soap and shriek. Then my brain registered that the intruder was none other than Maverick. I'd caught the outline of his broad shoulders through the curtain. My heart practically burst through my chest.

Why did he do that? A dozen irrational reasons leapt to mind. He may have thought I was in danger. Possibly he desired to see me. All of me. It's likely he was powerless. Unable to control himself.

The water pounded against my skin, but I couldn't feel it. All my senses hummed with the aftershock of Maverick's sudden intrusion. I squeezed my eyes shut, remembering the urgent way he'd called my name, and the raw expression on his face. A tiny part of me had *wanted* to fling open that curtain, let him really see me, let him crash into me. But there was a stronger voice in my head screaming, *No, your mother just died, and you barely know this man. This biker.*

But it did no good. My hand trailed down my body until my fingers found my sensitive nub. I rubbed her until she was satisfied, all the while imagining what the biker could do to me. Then I swallowed hard, trying to ground myself. I was calming down, but I couldn't stop picturing Maverick, his scruffy face, his tattoos covering hard muscles, and that deep voice of his.

Besides, it was the worst possible time to be fantasizing. My friend Nova and her new biker beau were missing in action for all I knew. People wanted me dead. My mom was gone, murdered, leaving behind a swirl of secrets and chaos. And yet... *here I was, masturbating to the outlaw who just almost saw me naked.* My face burned.

I forced myself to rinse off and twist the shower knob off. Steam billowed around me. I reached for a towel, mind spinning.

What the hell is wrong with me?

He barged in for a reason. The cynical side of me insisted it was just leftover excitement from earlier. The romantic side fed by too many MC romance novels whispered that he wanted me more than he could stand. That side also whispered, *He's your knight in battered leather armor, princess.*

But that was nonsense, right?

I dried off and wrapped a second towel around me, padding out to the sink. The mirror was fogged up, so I wiped it clean to find my reflection, wide green eyes, damp hair plastered to my cheeks, mouth drawn in a tense line.

What does he even see in me?

I wasn't some sexy bombshell with perfect curves. Though I had enough hips to fill out my jeans and then some, they weren't perfect by any means. They were lumpy and dimpled. I wasn't a patched-in biker babe with tattoos or killer confidence. I was just... *Lexi.* The nerdy, grieving lawyer whose mother had just died.

And yet, he was helping me. He'd stuck around even after the bullets, the drama, the tears.

My phone, which I'd left on the edge of the counter, gave a faint ding. I snatched it up, heart lurching. A text from Nova:

Nova: *We're okay, at a hotel a bit farther into Texas. Phones died, just charged up. Sorry for the scare. We'll meet in the morning. I'm so sorry, Lex. Stay safe.*

A rush of relief flooded my chest. *Thank God.* She was safe. *They were safe.* No more anxious thoughts about her lying in a ditch somewhere.

I quickly typed back:

Me: *It's okay, just glad you're safe. See you tomorrow.*

Setting the phone down, I stared at my reflection again. "Okay, Lexi. You're all alone with a biker who apparently can't keep his eyes to himself." I tried to sound stern, but my voice shook. "He's trouble. Focus on staying alive, not hooking up."

But that little voice that read romance novels day and night whispered, *You like trouble. If this were a book, you'd have jumped him by now.*

I growled at my own reflection. This was insanity. My mother had just been murdered. My best friend was missing until five seconds ago. Why the *hell* was I even entertaining thoughts of jumping Maverick's bones?

Steeling myself, I dressed in an old T-shirt and shorts, the only clean clothes I had left. My shirt read, "Morally Gray Men Give Me All the Feels" and my shorts might as well have been underwear, tight and thin. Taking a breath, I squared my shoulders and opened the bathroom door.

Only a weak lamp lit the dark motel room. Maverick stood near the window, shirtless, rummaging through a saddlebag on the small table. My gaze roamed over the large tattoo on his back, a biker patch, not the Road Monsters MC but possibly from the club he was in before. I couldn't make out the words, so I focused on the muscles underneath his inked skin. I was swooning.

He turned at the sound of the door, catching me staring. A faint smirk tugged at his lips. "Sorry about earlier. I, uh, guess I panicked."

I swallowed hard, trying not to eye his bare chest again. "No worries," I mumbled, noticing my cheeks grow warm. "It's your turn now, if you want to shower."

He scratched the back of his head, looking oddly nervous. "Yeah. Definitely. I should probably... y'know, rinse off too."

I stepped aside, giving him room to pass. As he brushed by, a wave of heat rolled off his skin. Suddenly, my throat was parched. He slipped into the bathroom, closing the door softly behind him. For a few seconds, I just stood there frozen by lust.

When I finally remembered how to move, I took stock of the room. *One queen-sized bed.* The corners were suspiciously saggy, but at least the sheets looked clean-ish. The same old romance-novel trope popped into my head. *Only one bed. Oh no, how ever will we manage?*

I almost laughed at how ridiculous it was. "Come on, Lexi, you've been studying this trope for years," I muttered under my breath.

I thought, *He'll offer to sleep on the floor, you'll protest, but he will anyway. In the middle of the night, something will happen, maybe danger, and you'll both end up tangled in the sheets.* I frowned at my own reflection in the dark TV screen. *Well, not likely. Dead mother. Potential assassins. Real life is not a romance novel.*

Still, a flutter stirred in my stomach. Would we share the bed tonight? Did I *want* to? A big part of me was absolutely terrified, physically and emotionally. I was a virgin, for one. And I was still reeling from losing Mom. But the memory of him barging into my shower made something ache low in my belly. I couldn't deny it. I was fucking moist. I made a face at the word in my mind. No, I was dripping wet and not just from the shower.

Suddenly, Maverick's muffled voice came from the bathroom. "Hey, Lexi?"

I jumped, crossing to the door. "Yeah?"

"I need some clean clothes," he said. "Could you grab something from my bag?"

I froze, eyeing the saddlebag he'd been rummaging through. That was *his* bag. I'd stuffed it with my clothes in a hurry. Our packing situation was a disaster. "Uh, are you sure you have any in there? I think that's all my stuff."

"Just look, princess," he called, voice echoing slightly in the tiled space.

I couldn't stop a little flutter at the nickname. Biting my lip, I dug through the saddlebag. Sure enough, I only found my clothes, plus a random spare bullet or two, a first-aid kit, and some bandanas. And the kicker, a condom... Nothing that resembled boxers or jeans.

"Um... Maverick?" I pressed a hand to the bathroom door. "There's, uh, nothing in here for you."

"What?" His voice was muffled, but I heard frustration. "Shit. Maybe I left it all in your trunk before we hopped on the bikes."

I winced. "Which we left in California."

"Fantastic," he grumbled, voice dripping with sarcasm. A moment later, the door opened a crack. He stuck his head out, dark hair damp. "So, I guess I have to wear the same clothes tomorrow?"

"Looks that way," I said.

He sighed, pulling the door wider. For a second, my eyes went straight to his muscled chest. He clutched a small towel at his waist, but it wasn't quite long enough. I kept my eyes on his tanned abs. My face flamed.

"Well, that's just perfect," he muttered. Then he looked at the single bed, brow creasing. "I'll take the floor. Least I can do."

"In just a towel?" I blurted, my mouth running ahead of my brain.

He arched an eyebrow. "I can't exactly sleep in my wet jeans," he pointed out where he haphazardly left them in the floor as he was stepping out of the shower. "They're all I've got."

I wanted to shrivel up. "Oh. Right."

He grabbed his old clothes, giving them a sniff. Apparently not satisfied, he tossed them aside. Then, without warning, he let the towel drop.

"*Oh my God,*" I squeaked, instinctively covering my eyes with my forearm. I thought I'd pass out. "Warn a girl, would you?"

There was a quiet chuckle. "Look at me, princess," he said, voice low and serious.

"I can't," I whispered, mortified. But a dangerous curiosity simmered in my veins.

"I want you," he said in a husky tone that made my stomach flip. "I'm not gonna pretend I don't. Hell, seeing you under that water earlier... it messed me up."

I swallowed, eyes still squeezed shut. "I've never done anything like this before." The words spilled out in a panicked rush. "I'm not that kind of girl. And my mom just died, and..."

I heard him exhale sharply. Then some rustling, and the soft whisper of cloth. A moment later, he murmured, "Shit, Lex, I'm sorry."

I lowered my arm a fraction, peeking. He'd grabbed the towel from the floor and was covering himself again. His gaze held genuine remorse.

"This is too much," I managed. "I can't. My brain can't process it. My mother's death, the threats, you... I just can't."

He bowed his head, stepping back. "I get it." He turned and strode back into the bathroom, rummaging. After a minute, he pulled on his damp jeans, wincing as he buttoned them. Then he came out, toweling off his hair. "Lexi, I'm sorry. Sometimes I don't think, especially when I'm... worked up."

I stood there, arms wrapped around my torso, trying to stop the shakes. "It's fine," I croaked. "This is all just. Yeah, it's a lot."

He set the towel aside and looked at me with an intensity that made my breath catch. "I know we barely know each other. But I can't ignore this pull I feel. It could be the rush, the danger, it could be something different. But I want you to know, you aren't alone. You hear me?"

A tremor coursed through me. "Why?" I whispered. "Why do you want to help me, or be with me, or anything? All we have in common is a bunch of bullets whizzing by."

His eyes flickered. "Because you fill a hole in me, I didn't know was still raw. I've lost people, too, Lexi. People I cared about. And you... you make me want to do better. Don't ask me to explain it, I can't. Attraction, chemistry, destiny, whatever. It doesn't matter."

Heat flooded my cheeks. "So, it's just lust, basically?"

A half-grin pulled at his lips. "Not just lust. But damn, you are *fine,* princess. You got these curves, that mouth, those eyes... I've been trying not to stare at your ass since day one."

My jaw dropped. "That's... crude."

He shrugged. "I'm a crude guy. But it's the truth."

A strange flutter warmed my chest. Despite everything, I felt a surge of gratitude that he found me attractive. But the grief and confusion overshadowed it. "I'm sorry," I said, my voice giving away my inner turmoil. "I just can't jump into bed with you right now. It's all too fresh, my mom..."

He stepped closer, placing a comforting hand on my shoulder. "I know," he said softly. "I'm sorry about the timing. I'm just being honest about what I feel. We don't have to act on it."

I nodded, tears prickling my eyes. "Thank you."

He exhaled, a long sigh that seemed to carry the weight of the world. "I'll sleep on the floor, all right? No arguments. You need space."

I wiped at my eyes. "I appreciate that."

With that, he grabbed a thin blanket from the closet, tossed a pillow onto the carpet, and made himself a makeshift bed. He stripped off his jeans again, this time more discreetly, leaving on a pair of boxer briefs that clung to his hips. He avoided my gaze, clearly trying not to stir up more tension.

I climbed into the queen-sized bed, heart aching and mind exhausted. The sheets felt scratchy, and I could hear Maverick shifting on the floor, trying to get comfortable. Trying to rest I was haunted by Maverick's words, saying I filled some hole in him. Little did he know, I longed for him to fill a hole in me. I was just too chicken.

CHAPTER 20

My body ached from too little sleep. Sunlight leaked around the edges of the cheap shade. For a second, I forgot where I was, then it all came crashing back. My mother's death, bullets, Maverick.

I rolled over, expecting to see him on the floor, but the blanket was empty. My heart seized. "Maverick?"

The door opened, and he appeared, carrying two takeout cups of coffee from somewhere. "Morning, princess," he murmured, handing one to me.

I sat up, blinking in surprise. "Where'd you get these?"

He offered a slight smile and a shrug. "Found a gas station across the street. Figured we could both use some fuel."

I sipped, nearly moaning at the heat and bitter flavor. "Mmm, thank you."

He positioned himself on the edge of the bed, sipping his own. The morning light highlighted the stubble on his jaw and the scar near his temple. "We should go find Chigger and Nova. They texted me they're at a diner off the interstate."

A relief washed over me. "Thank God they're okay. Let's go."

I lost my shorts for my jeans. Maverick's clothes had at least dried. Soon, we pulled into the diner's parking lot and spotted Chigger's bike right away. I hopped off Maverick's Harley, rolling my shoulders to ease the stiffness. Inside, the smell of bacon and coffee welcomed us.

We found Nova and Chigger in a booth, heads bowed together. Nova perked up the moment she saw me. "Lex!" she squealed, practically climbing over the table to hug me.

I laughed, a swell of relief filling my chest. "You're alive," I murmured into her hair. "I was so worried."

She pulled back, wide grin on her face. "We're fine, just had to dodge some bullets. No big deal." Her eyes sparkled with that too-familiar mischief. "And then we... well, we found a place to crash, obviously."

Chigger cleared his throat, hand resting possessively on Nova's hip. "Sorry about ditchin' you last night. Shit got crazy."

Maverick slid into the booth, making room for me. "We're all in one piece, that's what matters."

Nova snuggled closer to Chigger, ignoring the mild eyeroll I shot her way. "We ended up at a little motel an hour down the road. We, uh, kinda crashed hard."

I couldn't help but notice the way they kept kissing, soft, quick kisses between sentences. *They were definitely not shy.*

"I'm just glad you're safe," I said sincerely, though their open affection was a tiny stab of envy. They were obviously hitting it off. Meanwhile, my own relationship with Maverick was complicated beyond belief.

Nova must've noticed my tight expression, because she tugged me away to the bathroom after we placed our orders.

She locked the door, turned to me, and practically squealed, "Smutty. I have so much to tell you!"

I braced myself, leaning against the sink. "Spare no detail, obviously."

She giggled, cheeks flushing. "We've been going at it like rabbits. Chigger's so... *mmm.*" She fanned herself. "I'm sorry if that's TMI, but I have zero filter right now."

I raised an eyebrow, trying to hide a wry smile. "Nova, my mother was just *murdered*, remember? And we were shot at."

Her face fell. "Oh my God, I know. I'm a horrible friend." She grabbed my hands, eyes wide. "I'm so sorry, Lexi. It's just that... we're traveling with these hot bikers, I'm stressed, and sex is my coping mechanism, I guess."

I squeezed her hands. "It's okay. You're not horrible. It's just... *a lot.* I'm still trying to sort through losing Mom, plus all these near-death experiences."

She nodded fervently. "I understand. And I feel shitty for hooking up while you're suffering. I promise I'm here for you, no matter what."

I gave her a shaky smile. "I know. You don't need to feel guilty. We all handle things differently, Slutty."

She laughed at me calling her by her nickname and wiped an imaginary tear from her eye. "Glad we cleared that up. So how about you and Maverick? Anything... happen?"

My cheeks heated as I thought of his naked figure, the sexual tension crackling between us, that moment he saw me in the shower. "No. Not really."

Nova's brow arched. "He's totally into you, though. You can't deny it."

I flushed harder. "I don't know. Maybe. But I'm grieving, and... and I'm still a virgin, Nova. I can't just fling myself into bed with a guy I barely know, even if he's saved my life."

She nodded, expression gentler. "I get it. It's your choice. Whenever you're ready. If you're ready."

A rueful smile touched my lips. "Yeah. And let's face it, if it were up to me, I'd never have the courage. That's why all those romance novels have the man practically dragging the heroine to bed."

She laughed, patting my shoulder. "I guess we'll see what happens. No pressure. Just... if you want it, don't let your fears hold you back, Lex. Life's too short."

Her words echoed in my head. *Life's too short*. Mom was proof of that. And it gave me pause. We'd barely escaped death last night. Did I want to die a virgin?

We finished up, washed our hands, and returned to the table where the guys waited. Chigger had his arm slung around Nova like they were an old married couple, and Maverick gave me a small, private smile as I slid in next to him. The warmth in his eyes did something funny to my stomach.

After breakfast, we stepped outside, the morning sun bright. The plan was simple, drive the rest of the way through Texas, to Dallas, so I could check my apartment for anything Mom might have hidden.

But Nova cleared her throat. "Hey, so... we're thinking we'll go to *my* place." She glanced at Chigger. "We might still be in danger, but I need to get some clothes, catch my breath."

Chigger nodded. "I'll stay with her, keep her safe until this is over. Could be I'm also looking forward to, uh, some extended alone time." He waggled his eyebrows.

Maverick sighed, crossing his arms. "Fine. But you two watch your backs, understand? If we were targeted once, it can happen again."

Nova gave him a big smile. "Duh, of course." Then she pulled me aside. "We'll still be close by, but maybe not right next to you. We can handle ourselves."

I nodded, understanding that my drama might not need to drag Nova down further. "Thank you for everything. But be safe, please."

Chigger clapped Maverick on the shoulder. "We'll check in. If we see any suspicious shit, I'll call. Don't worry."

Nova gave me a tight hug, whispering in my ear, "Go easy on yourself. And if that sexy biker decides to make a move, maybe let him." She pulled back and winked, making me blush. "Just a suggestion."

I rolled my eyes but couldn't hide a small smile. "I'll keep that in mind."

Then Maverick and I got on his motorcycle, while Nova climbed behind Chigger on his. We parted ways in the parking lot with waves and screaming engines, the sound of potential danger still echoing in my head.

I wrapped my arms around Maverick's waist as we roared back onto the highway. My heart hammered from the powerful vibration of the bike, or maybe it was from the warmth of Maverick's back under my fingers. This was our reality now. Hunted by who-knows-who, chasing secrets I didn't ask for, leaning on each other because we had no other choice.

The wind whipped my hair into a frenzy. My body pressed tight against his, and despite everything, I felt the faucet of desire dripping on my thighs. Something about hugging a strong biker on a growling motorcycle was undeniably thrilling.

He turned his head slightly, voice carrying over the engine's roar. "You good back there, princess?"

I nodded, cheeks flushing at the endearment. "I'm good."

I wondered if he felt my heart drumming. The open road stretched ahead, and we had hours before we'd reach Dallas and my apartment, the place that might hold the key to my mother's secrets. I didn't know what we'd find, but I knew one thing. I wasn't facing it alone.

Yes, I was scared out of my mind. But the biker in front of me, guiding the motorcycle with confident hands, was letting me cling to him for my safety. I was starting to believe, the real thing was better than any of the heroes from my books.

CHAPTER 21

Maverick

I'd never expected to roll into Dallas with a woman clinging to me so tightly that I could practically feel her heart pounding against my back. Or was that my own? But there we were, weaving through traffic on my Harley. The city sprawled around us, tall skyscrapers glinting in the late afternoon sun, highways tangled like spaghetti, and an endless barrage of cars honking in frustration.

Lexi's arms were wrapped around my waist, her cheek pressed between my shoulder blades. I could definitely feel her relief when we veered off the main drag and turned onto quieter streets. Or was that my own as well? The further we got into her neighborhood, the more we both relaxed. It was as if the comfort of familiar territory lessened her fear of being shot at yet again. As soon as she settled, I settled.

We'd first parted from Nova and Chigger last night, but it felt like a lifetime ago. Since then, Lexi and I had been chased out of our motel, nearly gunned down, and forced to keep moving like fugitives with targets on our backs. She'd lost her mother. Granted, Diana wasn't exactly a model parent, but still her mother. Everything in her world had crumbled in less than a week. And me? I was playing bodyguard, detective, and borderline loverboy all at once, trying not to lose my head.

Lexi's apartment complex rose before us, a squat, three-story building that looked older than either of us. A row of tall oak trees lined the sidewalk, and a small metal gate stood partially open, giving a glimpse of a shaded courtyard. As I pulled into a visitor's spot, I felt Lexi's grip tighten.

She didn't let go until the bike's engine died. Then she slid off, pulling off her helmet, her hair tumbling in wild waves around her face.

She exhaled, staring at the building. It wasn't the nicest place, faded paint, a cracked walkway. But it was hers.

"Home sweet home," she murmured, her voice laced with exhaustion. "I can't believe we're finally here."

I climbed off the bike and ran my fingers through my hair, scanning the area like a hawk. No immediate signs of danger, no tinted SUVs lurking, no suspicious characters on the sidewalk. But that didn't mean we were safe. "You feel okay?" I asked quietly, stepping closer so only she could hear. "We can get in and get out. We don't have to linger."

Her lips pressed into a thin line. "Yeah... I just... we need to see if there's any sign of whatever my mom stashed here. This is the only place I can think of." She squared her shoulders with a determined look that made my chest tighten. "But let's be careful."

I gave a curt nod. "Always."

We made our way through the courtyard, stepping over uneven paving stones. The space had a shabby charm, a few potted plants, a small fountain that wasn't running. Lexi led us up a narrow stairwell to the second floor, then down an open-air walkway. Her apartment door was near the end. It took her a moment to fish out her keys. Her fingers trembled, betraying her nervousness.

"You okay?" I asked again, softly, hovering just behind her.

She shot me a quick look over her shoulder, mouth curving in a half-smile. "Yes. Just... wondering if someone's inside, waiting to blow our heads off."

The tension in her voice made me want to pull her close, but I just rested my hand lightly on her shoulder. "If so, I'll handle it." I forced a little bravado to my tone.

She exhaled, slid the key into the lock, and twisted. The door opened onto a small living room with a worn beige couch, a low coffee table stacked with law books, and an assortment of mismatched rugs covering the scuffed wood floor.

Lexi stepped inside cautiously, half expecting an armed thug to leap out. I followed close behind, scanning corners, my senses on high alert. But nothing looked disturbed. No overturned furniture, no footprints in the dust. The place smelled slightly stale from being closed up for days, but otherwise normal.

"Clear," I muttered, though I never truly let my guard down.

She let out a shaky breath, locking the door behind us. "Thank God." Then she flicked on a lamp near the couch, bathing the space in a soft glow. "I guess no one decided to sabotage my apartment."

"Seems that way. But stay sharp," I reminded her.

She gave a small nod, dropping our bag on the couch. "I will. Let me show you around. Though there's not much to see."

I took in the room like a detective scanning a crime scene, neat rows of law journals on a bookshelf, a second-hand TV stand holding a modest flat-screen, a stuffed armchair in the corner. On the walls, she'd hung a few framed prints of famous court decisions, alongside a poster of some half-naked male cover model for a romance novel. My lips twitched at that. She definitely had a thing for smut.

She noticed my gaze and blushed. "Hey, a girl's allowed to have fantasies," she mumbled, crossing her arms.

"I'm not judging, princess," I said with a half-smile. "I'd just pegged you more for the serious attorney type. Not the cover-model-lusting type."

Her cheeks reddened. "I can be both, you know."

"Mm. I do know." My tone rumbled with innuendo as I took in her shirt. "What's a morally gray man?"

"A bad boy, basically."

"Like a biker?"

She cleared her throat, turning to lead me down a short hallway.

We stopped at a closed door at the end. She hesitated, hand hovering over the knob. "This is it," she murmured. "I keep all of my mom's old stuff in here, at least, the stuff that belonged to her that I couldn't throw away. Some of it used to be at my aunt's place. She raised me, but after my aunt died, I had nowhere else to store it. So, I... stuck it in here."

I studied her profile, noticing the flicker of sadness in her eyes. She'd lost her aunt, the woman who truly reared her, then her mother, no matter how flawed. It was no wonder she was guarded. "You sure you're ready?"

She pressed her pretty lips together. "I have to be." Then she twisted the knob and pushed the door open.

Lexi clicked on the overhead light, and a single naked bulb flickered. The room was small, filled with boxes. Some were stacked neatly along the walls, others haphazardly piled in the corner. A battered trunk sat against the far side, and a few plastic bins were labeled with marker. I smelled a faint mustiness, like old clothes and yellowing paper.

She took a step inside and gestured helplessly. "Here we are. A lifetime of Dirty Diana's junk."

I whistled low. "We got our work cut out for us." Part of me was impatient to rummage through everything, but I also sensed Lexi's emotional turmoil. "We'll find whatever we can, if it's here."

She nodded, swallowing. "Yeah."

"Let's do this systematically," I said, letting my old detective instincts surface. "We'll open each box one by one, see if there's anything relevant, documents, receipts, letters, anything that could link your mom to that Grinder guy or the mob or the SOS MC folks."

"Right." She took an unstable breath. "Let's start with those bins." She pointed to a trio of plastic containers near the trunk.

We settled on the floor, side by side, and pried the lids off. The first bin was stuffed with old clothes, feather boas, sparkly tops, fishnet stockings, like some leftover relics of Diana's freewheeling days. Lexi rolled her eyes and tossed them aside, clearly unimpressed.

The second bin was full of random knick-knacks, cheap jewelry, half-burned candles, a handful of photos from who-knows-when. I paused over a polaroid of a younger Diana, wearing a leather jacket and pouting at the camera. She was in a parking lot filled with motorcycles, a man's arm around her waist. Only half the man's face was visible. A tall guy, moustache, beard, big grin. No patch or sign of affiliation that I could see. Possibly the father Lexi never met, but there was no obvious clue.

"You recognize him?" I asked, showing Lexi.

She squinted, a faint line forming between her brows. "I don't think so. My mom had a different boyfriend every year, so it's hard to keep track. She never told me his name if he was around, anyway. Just called him 'baby' or 'darling.'"

I slipped the photo into my jacket pocket. "Might be worth checking out further."

She nodded, a flash of sadness crossing her face. I suspected the idea that she might see a photo of her dad stirred complicated feelings. But she pressed on, rummaging through the rest of the bin. Some diaries with missing pages, a deck of tarot cards, a half-empty perfume bottle. Nothing that screamed incriminating. We set the bin aside.

The third bin held more of the same: random clothes, old lipsticks, a stack of cheap romance paperbacks. I couldn't help but smirk at that. The apple didn't fall far from the tree. We found a battered notebook with half the pages torn out and a typed letter from a small claims court referencing overdue rent in some place in Nevada. No mention of the mob or blackmail or anything relevant to a target on Lexi's head.

"Damn," I muttered, running a hand through my hair. "So far, this is a bust."

Lexi sat back on her heels, blowing out a breath that fluttered a strand of hair from her eyes. "We still have boxes. And that trunk." She eyed the trunk warily.

"Let's tackle it."

We moved a few smaller boxes to get to the trunk. The boxes contained old Christmas decorations, some random children's toys, which Lexi explained were hers from when she was a kid, though how her mom ended up with them was a mystery. I flipped through the final small box. More photos, mostly blurry, a few letters from men who wrote "I love you, Dirty Diana," with no last name or real address.

Finally, we pried open the trunk. It creaked ominously, revealing piles of crocheted blankets and doilies. Lexi gave me a quizzical look, rummaging through them. Underneath, there were old receipts from a roadside diner in Colorado, a few postcards, some from Alaska, ironically enough. My heart twinged at the mention of Alaska, remembering my time there, but I pushed that aside.

"This is insane," she murmured, frustration sharpening her tone. "I don't see a single document that screams blackmail or mafia dealings. It's just junk. My mom's entire life was junk."

I touched her shoulder gently. "Could be we haven't found it yet. Could also be that your mom kept her secrets somewhere else. Or maybe she really didn't have any. Could be the threat was about something else entirely."

She sighed, slumping. "Or maybe she just lied to everyone, including me."

We searched for another twenty minutes with no real luck. I snapped pictures of some older letters, just in case a random signature might mean something. But I doubted it. As we closed the trunk, Lexi flopped onto her butt, a wave of exhaustion washing over her features.

"Ugh, I'm so tired of sifting through my mother's half-life," she said softly. "I didn't want to do this when she was alive. Now I have no choice."

My heart constricted. "I'm sorry," I muttered, wishing I had better news or a comforting truth. But I was never good at sugarcoating. "It might mean the mob's after you for some other reason. Or someone else orchestrated it all to look like a mob hit."

She nodded, eyes downcast. "So, we found nothing." She let out a long breath, then mustered a weak smile. "Thanks for helping me dig. At least I know now."

Lexi burst into tears, and I wrapped my arms around her, just holding her against my chest as she cried. After a few minutes, she settled down. Releasing her, I stood up and reached out. I tugged her gently by the arm, helping her stand.

"Let's bag a few of the photos, the diaries, anything that might have even a scrap of info. I'll keep them safe. We can comb through more thoroughly when we have time."

She agreed, so we did that quickly, stuffing them into a bag. When we were done, we both stared at the messy room, boxes and bins scattered in disarray.

"So that's it?" she asked quietly.

"For now," I said. "We should probably get out of here soon. No telling if someone's tailing us. We've already been here a few hours."

She glanced at her phone. It was late. "You're right. But... can I at least cook dinner first? I'm starving."

I was about to protest, but something in the way she said it stopped me. She looked so worn, so desperate for a shred of normalcy. And honestly, so was I. We'd been eating diner food, gas station junk, and fast bites for days. The idea of a home-cooked meal made my stomach rumble.

"All right, princess," I relented, a half-smile tugging at my lips. "Cook me something. But we gotta keep an eye out."

She beamed, relief flooding her face. "Deal."

CHAPTER 22

Lexi's kitchen was small, Formica countertops, old linoleum floor that peeled at the edges, and cupboards that creaked whenever we opened them. But she had an impressive collection of spices and cooking tools for such a tiny space. I perched on a stool near the counter, watching as she bustled around with an excitement I hadn't seen since we got shot at in the last motel.

"What are you in the mood for?" she asked, rummaging through the fridge. "I've got some frozen chicken, veggies. I can do a stir-fry?"

"Sounds good," I said, leaning an elbow on the counter. "I'll eat whatever you whip up. Just don't poison me."

She shot me a playful glare. "I'm a better cook than you might think."

I smirked. "I don't doubt it. I'm just used to bar food and takeout, so anything homemade is a treat."

She laughed, pulling out a bag of chicken, a variety of vegetables, and some sauce bottles. Soon, she was chopping onions, peppers, carrots, the rhythmic thunk of the knife oddly soothing. I watched the way her hair fell across her cheek, the curve of her jaw, the grace in her movements. Beneath the exhaustion and tension, there was a woman who knew how to take care of herself, and who found comfort in cooking. A caretaker, even if she pretended she wasn't.

"You said you love to read," I said, my gaze flicking to a shelf of romance novels in the corner of the open space. "Gotta say you have quite the collection. Must be hundreds, maybe thousands, of pages about big, tough guys and the women they fall for, huh?"

Her cheeks turned pink as she stirred the chicken in a pan. "Um, yeah, well, it's my escape. Some people watch reality TV or go clubbing. I read. And I guess... I always liked the idea that the men in those books wouldn't let anything happen to the heroine, you know? No matter how dangerous the world got, they'd protect her. It was comforting, in a weird way. Not having parents, maybe I wanted to be protected like that."

I nodded, a pang of guilt hitting me. She'd lost her mother, was nearly killed multiple times, and here I was, a real-life biker with a complicated past, trying to protect her. Did I measure up to those fantasy heroes? Probably not. But I sure as hell was trying.

Telling her I also lost my parents as a child, and I turned to books too, studying to become a cop felt too cheesy. We had so much in common, but I was reluctant to open up. "You never had a boyfriend or anything?" I asked quietly, watching her body language.

She paused, the spatula in hand. "Not really. I mean, I dated guys in college, but it never worked out. They found me too nerdy, too bookish. Or they were intimidated by me wanting to be a lawyer. I don't know. It's not like I aim to be some power-hungry lawyer. I just want to help people. And after law school started, I just... didn't have time. So, no. After that, I somehow landed my dream job, and now that I've passed the bar, that job is only going to consume more of my life. The men in my books have been my only consistent relationship."

I felt a strange protective surge, annoyance at those men who'd brushed her off. "Their loss," I said, voice firm.

Her eyes flicked up, a soft smile curving her lips. Then she turned back to the stove. "How about you?" she asked. "You said you had an ex... two, actually. Eve and Sky?"

My stomach twisted at their names. Fuck Chigger for telling my business. But if she was opening up, perhaps I could do the same. "Yeah. Eve was my fiancée back in Nashville, before I joined the Road Monsters. We... lost a baby. Things fell apart. She ended up with my president, of all people."

Lexi frowned, her gaze sympathetic. "I'm sorry. That sounds awful."

I shrugged, forcing the old pain away. "It is what it is. Then there was Sky. Another complicated story. She was Kingpin's wife, but she wanted out. We ran to Alaska together, had our own heartbreak. She left me for someone else. A mobster. Seems I have a knack for choosing women who prefer men in powerful positions." The bitterness in my voice surprised me.

She set the spatula down and turned off the burner, stepping closer. "Then... why are you here helping me?"

I met her gaze, unable to look away from those green eyes. "Because you needed it," I said simply. "Because I can't let you get killed. And maybe because... I'm not quite as jaded as I pretend to be. Something about you, it's different."

Her face colored. "Oh."

"Yeah. 'Oh.'" I swallowed. "I told you I was passionate for you. Maybe I'm just a fool, but I can't ignore that pull."

She breathed out shakily, then turned back to the stove, fiddling with the pan. "I, um, the stir-fry's basically done. Let me just get it on plates."

I smiled softly, letting her have that moment of composure. The fact that she was flustered around me gave me a thrill I hadn't felt in a long time.

We ended up at her small dining table, a rickety wooden thing that wobbled unless we set a folded napkin under one leg. She'd plated the stir-fry and served it with rice.

"Damn, this smells incredible," I said, taking a bite of chicken. "You weren't kidding about being a wonderful cook, princess."

"Thanks," she murmured. "I didn't get to do it much with law school... but it's nice to share it with someone."

I caught the slight tremor in her hand as she lifted her fork. Fear still clung to her, no matter how relaxed we tried to be. My protective instincts flared again.

Over dinner, we talked more about everything and nothing, her law school memories, the time she spent preparing for the bar, how she'd always dreamed of working in criminal defense to help the underprivileged. And how she was stuck at some high-powered firm for now.

I told her about my own dreams once upon a time, about how I'd joined the police force in Columbus as a fresh-faced recruit who believed in justice. "My illusions were shattered when my partner shot an unarmed guy. I attempted to do what was right, but the system ate me alive. That was how I ended up on the road, drifting, eventually crossing paths with the Royal Bastards MC and then the Road Monsters."

Then I told her about the endless string of meaningless women. "None of them hold a candle to you."

"How many women?" she asked, crinkling her nose.

"Honestly, countless. And you, how many men have you been with, Princess?"

She gave me a confused look. Then she reached across the table, curling her fingers around mine. My heart thumped as I looked into her eyes, soft, vulnerable, but shining with curiosity. She licked her lips, voice barely above a whisper. "I have to admit something."

"Shoot." My own voice was hoarse.

"I've never... done this. Or anything, really. You know, physically. Sexually." Her gaze darted to the plate, cheeks reddening. "I'm a virgin."

Oh, I recalled her words from the other night at the hotel. When she said she'd never done anything like this before, she meant literally, not just that things were moving too fast or that she didn't know me well enough.

I stayed quiet for a long moment, letting it sink in. A swirl of emotions ran through me, surprise, protectiveness, and a flicker of something raw and primal. She was twenty-five, a lawyer, gorgeous, and somehow untouched. I forced myself to speak calmly. "I should've figured, from what you said before. And it doesn't bother me, if that's what you're worried about."

Her lips parted. "You're not put off?"

I squeezed her hand gently. "Hell no. If anything... it makes me want to be careful with you. Make sure your first time, whenever it happens, is right. Not overshadowed by fear or bullets."

She exhaled shakily, relief washing over her face. "Thank you. I just... Everyone in those romance novels, they jump into bed so fast. I guess I'm... behind."

My chest tightened with affection. "You're not behind, princess. You're just living your own story, not a cliché. And trust me, with how we've been shot at, chased, and threatened, you're more than heroic enough."

She let out a breathy laugh. "Good to know." Her hand tightened on mine. "I... I'm glad you're here with me, Maverick."

My heart thudded. "Me too."

We both leaned in, our faces inches apart. I could feel the warmth of her breath, smell the faint fragrance of the soy sauce on her lips. Slowly, we tilted our heads, and my lips brushed hers, a gentle, tentative kiss. She sighed softly against my mouth, her hand sliding up to grip my shirt.

My entire body lit up at the soft pressure of her lips. I deepened the kiss slightly, letting her feel my hunger, but also holding back so I wouldn't scare her. She trembled, kissing me back, a sweet uncertainty in her response. I was already hard as a rock, just from her saying she was a virgin. Our brief connection was driving me insane. Fuck, I needed more. But I kept it gentle.

Then, suddenly, there was a crash. The kitchen window shattered, shards of glass spraying inward. I instinctively threw myself forward, knocking Lexi off her chair and onto the floor. A bullet whizzed through the space we'd occupied a split second earlier, embedding in the opposite wall with a thud. Another shot rang out, blowing chunks of drywall near the doorframe.

"Shit!" I roared, scrambling to shield Lexi with my body. She let out a sharp gasp, eyes wide with terror.

A third shot splintered the door. My heart pounded like a war drum. "We gotta move!" I hissed, flattening us both against the floor.

She nodded, face pale. "Yes."

I risked a glance around the table. The window was gone, glass all over the floor. I couldn't see the shooter, but I knew the vantage, probably from a building or alley across the way. Another bullet pinged, hitting the stove. We were sitting ducks.

I dragged Lexi to her feet, half-crouched, and bobbed into the hallway. "We're going out the front. Stay behind me." She clung to my jacket, trembling. We inched toward the door, praying the shooter didn't have an angle. No more shots rang out for the moment.

I yanked open the door, scanning left and right. The courtyard was empty, however that didn't ensure our safety. "Go, now!" I hissed, pushing her forward. We sprinted down the walkway, footsteps echoing in the still air. Another shot ricocheted off the railing behind us. Apparently the bastard had repositioned. My chest hammered with fear and rage, but I forced us onward.

We flew down the stairs and around to the parking lot to find my Harley. A bullet whizzed overhead, and my shoulders stiffened. We had to get out.

"Helmet!" I barked, tossing Lexi hers. She jammed it on, hands shaking. I swung my leg over the bike, turned the key, and fired it up with a roar. She scrambled onto the seat behind me, arms locked around my waist.

Tires squealing, I tore out of the lot, ignoring the startled shouts of a couple of neighbors who'd come outside. Another shot pinged off the pavement behind us. But then we were on the main road, weaving into traffic. Lexi clung to me desperately, and I tried to calm my breathing, scanning the rearview mirror for any sign of pursuit.

Whoever it was, they didn't follow. Or if they did, they were too far behind for me to see. After a few hectic turns, I relaxed fractionally, though my pulse still raced like I'd downed a pot of black coffee.

Lexi's voice trembled behind me as we idled. "That's it," she said. "I'm never going back there. That was my home, Maverick. And they shot it up like it was nothing."

A swell of anger burned in my gut. These bastards had taken everything from her. Her mother, her security, even her personal space. Enough was enough. "I'm not letting them keep you on the run forever," I growled. "But for now, we need to be smart."

She nodded, pressing her helmet against my shoulder. "Yes," she whispered. "I'm so tired of running. But I don't see another option."

"I have a plan, or something close to it. We're going to Kansas."

She stiffened slightly. "Kansas?"

"Yeah. The Road Monsters MC has a clubhouse there, somewhere safe, with men I can trust to keep watch on you while I do what needs to be done. I can't guard you twenty-four-seven and also track down whoever's gunning for you. So, we'll hole up at the clubhouse. Then I start pulling strings, calling in favors, sniffing out leads."

She was quiet for a moment, then she nodded. "All right. I'll trust you."

My chest squeezed. "Thank you." I merged onto a busier street.

CHAPTER 23

We didn't make it out of Texas that night. I wasn't about to ride hundreds of miles in the dark with the possibility of more ambushes. We found ourselves in yet another no-name motel off the interstate. If I had a dollar for every seedy place I'd bunked in the last few years, I could've bought one by now.

The desk clerk barely glanced at us, accepting cash without question. We got a room with two double beds. Neither of us said much as we entered, flicking on a single lamp. The day's chaos weighed heavily.

Lexi sagged onto the first bed, burying her face in her hands. "This is insane," she muttered, voice muffled. "I thought maybe going to my apartment would help us find answers. Instead, we nearly got killed again."

I let out a humorless laugh, tossing my jacket onto a chipped dresser. "Welcome to my world, princess."

She lifted her head, eyes glistening with unshed tears. "A world where everyone's out to kill you?"

I gave a half-shrug. "Sometimes. Listen... we'll figure this out. Maybe in Kansas I'll get leads on who's behind these attacks. Might not even be that Grinder guy, just some other jerk with a grudge. One way or another, I'll find them." My voice went harder than I intended. I realized how furious I was that they'd targeted her again.

Her expression softened. "Thank you. For everything."

I exhaled. "Don't thank me yet." Then I nodded at the beds, changing the subject. "We should get some sleep. Tomorrow's a long ride."

She glanced at the two beds, then back at me. "Yeah. I guess so."

I hesitated, part of me wanting to comfort her physically, hold her, maybe stroke her hair until she drifted off. But I sensed she needed space after the assault. "If you need anything during the night... just wake me," I said quietly.

She nodded, mustering a small smile. "Same goes for you."

With that, she slipped off her shoes and climbed under the covers, still wearing her jeans and T-shirt. I flicked off the overhead light and sank onto the other bed, boots still on, my mind too wired to sleep easily. But eventually, exhaustion claimed me, and the room faded into darkness.

I woke before dawn, my internal clock permanently tuned to an early schedule. Stretching my sore muscles, I decided to do a quick workout, push-ups, crunches, anything to clear my head. The day ahead promised a long ride and God knows what danger.

I started with push-ups, arms pumping as I tried to regulate my breathing and keep my mind from swirling with anxiety about last night's bullets. Halfway through my second set, a soft gasp made me pause. I glanced up to see Lexi sitting on the edge of her bed, hair tousled, eyes still heavy with sleep.

"Good morning, princess," I murmured, continuing my push-ups.

She blinked, a shy smile curving her lips. "Good morning. That's... quite a view."

I smirked, finishing the set and rolling onto my back for a moment. "Didn't realize I had an audience."

She laughed softly. "Sorry, I guess I'm not used to seeing a half-naked man doing push-ups in my motel room." Her gaze traveled over my chest and abs. I felt my skin warm under her scrutiny.

"Better than a bullet in your window, right?" I quipped.

She grimaced. "Definitely. I can handle a man in boxers over gunmen any day."

I stood, running a hand through my sweaty hair. "You want the shower first, or should I go?"

She yawned. "Go ahead. I'll freshen up after."

I grabbed my old shirt that I'd washed in the sink and hung to dry on the air conditioner, heading for the bathroom. Then I paused, turning back to her. "Princess?"

"Yeah?" She looked up, half-lidded eyes still hazy from sleep.

I crossed the distance in two strides and took her hand, pulling her to her feet. My voice dropped low. "It's killing me, you know. Being near you, wanting to hold you, comfort you. But I'm trying to be respectful, when all I really want to do is throw you on that bed and see your titties again."

Her breath caught. "I... I don't know how," she admitted, voice trembling with vulnerability as she pushed up her glasses.

Don't know how? I leaned in, eyes flicking to her mouth. "You read all those romances, right? Smut?"

"The men just... take charge."

"They do?"

A faint blush tinged her cheeks. "Yes, that's generally how it goes. They just do it."

I exhaled, my hands sliding to her waist. I tugged her body against my erection. "If that's all you need, me to just do it, all you gotta do is say the word."

She gazed at me for a heartbeat, then parted her lips. My chest tightened. Unable to resist, I lowered my head, capturing her mouth in a deep kiss. She gasped against my lips, her fingers clutching my shoulders. Heat surged through my veins, a hunger I'd been tamping down for days.

She melted into me, her soft curves pressing against my bare torso. My heart thundered like I was fighting for my life. Hell, maybe I was, fighting for a new life. Our tongues brushed, tasting one another. That soft moan of hers really got to me.

I wanted to scoop her up, throw her onto the bed, devour every inch of her. But she was still so new to this, and we had a mission. With a low growl, I pulled away, resting my forehead against hers.

She breathed heavily, eyes dazed. "That was..."

"Yeah," I agreed, chest heaving. "And it's just a preview, princess. If we had more time..." My gaze drifted to the rumpled bed.

Her face lit with a shy smile. "Then you'd throw me down and have your way with me?"

I chuckled, brushing a stray lock of hair from her forehead. "I have half a mind to do it now, but I don't want to scare you. Especially after what you told me."

She leaned up, pressing a feather-light kiss to my jaw. "I might need some scaring, if that's the only way it'll happen," she teased, though her voice was tentative.

Heat flared. "Fuck, you're killing me." I kissed her again, briefly, savoring the softness of her lips. Then I forced myself to step back. "We gotta hit the road. If we keep this up, we won't leave until lunchtime."

She laughed nervously, her cheeks flaming. "Right. Reality."

"Yeah. Reality sucks." I winked and headed to the bathroom, glancing back once to see her touching her lips, as if marveling at what had just happened.

Part of me hated leaving her there. Another part was grateful for the break, so I could get my raging libido under control. Since she was a virgin, I needed to be sure her first time wasn't overshadowed by fear or regret. The last thing I wanted was to traumatize her while bullets whizzed past our heads.

In the shower, the water pounded my sore shoulders, and I let out a low groan. My thoughts kept drifting to her, how she felt in my arms, how her lips tasted. How her tongue felt, and how it would feel on my dick. Pulling on my cock, I imagined popping her sweet cherry in one hard go. I pictured her breasts in my mind, her wet skin from the other night. Her nervous stammer. Her innocence. She doesn't know what to do. I longed to teach her. Damn, sliding into her was going to feel so damn good. She was all mine. My fist pumped as a red-hot release spurted over my hand.

After that, I forced myself to focus on the day's plan instead of my raging hormones. We'd head north, keep to back roads, and eventually reach the Road Monsters MC in Kansas by nightfall or tomorrow morning. Once there, I'd have reinforcements, access to intel, and a safe place for Lexi to hide.

When I emerged, towel slung around my waist, she was folding up the blankets on her bed, phone in hand. She gave me a once-over that made my blood stir again, but I quickly changed into my clothes. Couldn't risk another meltdown of self-control.

We checked out, hopped on the Harley, and roared onto the highway. The sky spread vast and blue above us. I kept my eyes peeled for any sign of a tail, but the roads were relatively calm. Lexi clung to me, arms around my waist.

Halfway through the trip, we stopped for gas at a dusty station in Oklahoma. She stretched her legs, yawning, while I filled up. The attendant eyed us warily but said nothing. We grabbed a few snacks, protein bars, bottled water. No time for a leisurely lunch. We had them there. The sooner we got to the clubhouse, the better. Capturing her lips, I didn't want her to forget about what was in store for her. In Kansas, I'd find some peace, find time to treat her right and take what's mine. Her virginity. After I ended our kiss, we hopped back on the bike.

As miles bled into more miles, Lexi shifted behind me whenever we idled, occasionally pointing out random sights. A dilapidated barn, a roadside antique shop. I found myself smiling at her attempts to lighten the mood. Even in the midst of chaos, she had a spark of curiosity, a desire to see something good in the world.

We spoke little, thanks to the wind whipping past us. But the silences felt comfortable, at least in my mind. She seemed at ease too, or as much as one could be while fleeing gunmen. By late afternoon, we crossed into Kansas, fields stretching on either side of the road. The horizon felt infinite.

"I guess I never pictured you as a farm kinda guy," Lexi joked at one point, bending closer to speak over the wind.

Laughter escaped my lips. "I'm not. But trust me, the Road Monsters clubhouse is nowhere near an actual farm. They just picked a remote location, so no one bothers them."

Sure enough, by dusk, we turned down a gravel road lined with trees. My stomach tightened with anticipation. Would they welcome me with a stranger in tow? It'd been a while since I'd shown my face. But we had no other choice. Lexi's life was on the line, and I couldn't handle it alone.

As the clubhouse came into view, a sprawling low building with a fenced perimeter, I felt Lexi's grip tighten. I reached down to pat her hand, a silent reassurance. Anything necessary, I would do. I'd keep her safe.

CHAPTER 24

Lexi

Dust swirled around us as Maverick and I rumbled off the main highway onto a gravel road. The bike's tires kicked up loose stones, and I clung to him, my heart fluttering more from anticipation than fear. We were riding through the flat, endless plains of Kansas, the geographic center of the lower forty-eight states, or so he told me. There wasn't a building for miles, except for a battered sign announcing *Welcome to Lebanon* in faded paint.

Finally, we spotted what looked like a low-slung compound behind a tall chain-link fence. A large patch of land surrounded it, dotted with a few scraggly trees. The building itself was long and rectangular, topped with a rusted metal roof. Several motorcycles were parked out front, a handful of men milling about, wearing cuts with the same *Road Monsters'* insignia Maverick wore.

We pulled into the makeshift parking lot. A dirt patch, really. The men turned to stare, eyes narrowing at our arrival. Maverick cut the engine, and the sudden silence felt deafening.

He gave my thigh a reassuring squeeze before I swung off the bike. My legs were sore from the long ride, my mind still reeling from the past events. Gunshots in Dallas, fleeing to a shitty motel, then this trek north across two states. But somehow, just knowing I was with Maverick made me feel marginally safer.

A gigantic man with a long, bushy beard, nearly down to his belt, stepped forward. His cut read Sarge in white lettering. He had arms as thick as logs and tattoos everywhere I could see, coiling snakes, flaming skulls, a giant cross, a heart, like he was checking off boxes. He eyed me suspiciously.

"Maverick," he greeted, voice as gravelly as the road leading here. "Didn't figure I'd see your face 'round here again so soon."

Maverick lifted his chin in a silent nod. "It's been a while, I know."

"Got to check in. Them's the rules."

"Had business. Brought my..." he hesitated a fraction of a second, then forged on, "...my woman."

The words clanged in my head. *My woman.* I swallowed hard, self-conscious before all those biker men with Maverick's patch. *Woman, property, old lady,* the terms I'd read in countless MC romance books. Now, it seemed I was living it for real.

Sarge's gaze flicked to me, taking in my worn jeans and dusty T-shirt. "Your property, huh?" he asked, tone testing.

Maverick didn't hesitate this time. "Yeah, she's mine."

The big man grunted. "All right, brother. Let's see if the others are on board with you bringing an outsider."

I stiffened at the word outsider, but did my best to keep my face neutral. I'd known we'd face some hostility or suspicion. After all, these men wouldn't just let anyone waltz into their secret clubhouse. Some part of me was flattered that Maverick was introducing me as his so firmly, but another part bristled at being labeled that way. Yet I had to remind myself, we're in danger, and I'm not about to question what keeps me alive.

Another man appeared, this one with a long, red beard parted in the middle and braided at the end, like a Viking. He was short but stocky, and a patch on his cut read Stumpy. I tried not to stare, but the beard was mesmerizing.

"Who's she?" Stumpy asked, hooking a thumb in my direction.

"Lexi," Maverick answered quickly, slinging an arm around my shoulders. "She's with me."

Stumpy scratched at his braided beard, shooting me an assessing look. "All right. Long ride?"

I nodded, forcing a polite smile. "Very long."

He let out a grunt that might've been acknowledgment or amusement, then jerked his head toward the building. "C'mon in, then. We got cold beer."

I couldn't miss the hush that fell among the other men, tall, short, heavy, lean, each with his own scowl or suspicious glance. *Jesus,* I thought, *this is intense.* But I stuck close to Maverick, letting him navigate me through the cluster of bikers who parted like wary animals. Every so often, he'd murmur, "She's with me," in a tone that brooked no argument. And every so often, I'd catch a flicker of interest in one of their eyes that made my blood run cold. *God, this is so much like the books I read... but real.*

A small voice in my head whispered, *You're safer as his.* Something about that knowledge both comforted me and made me uneasy. Because was I really just "his" so men wouldn't make a move on me or see me as a free-for-all?

Sarge led us inside. The clubhouse's interior was surprisingly large, a wide-open common area with a bar along one wall, several worn leather couches, a pool table, and a couple of doors that presumably led to more private rooms. Emblems and trophies, likely from charitable events or rides, decorated the walls. However, I also noticed a large symbol on the back wall. A flaming motorcycle and skull with four playing cards fanned out. *Four Aces.* It matched the patch on Maverick's cut, Road Monsters MC logo.

"Yo, Maverick!" called a voice from across the room. A man with a buzz cut and a spider tattoo creeping up his neck stood there, raising a beer. "Didn't expect to see your sorry ass again."

Maverick gave him a mock salute. "Taz. Been a while."

Taz sauntered over, giving me a once-over before focusing on Maverick. "Who's the sweet piece?"

I bristled. Maverick's arm tightened around my shoulders. "Her name's Lexi," he said, voice edging with warning. "Watch your mouth, Taz."

Taz raised his hands in surrender. "Hey, I'm just sayin' she's pretty. Calm down." Then he stuck his hand out to me. "I'm Taz. I do ink for the club."

Some tension left me. "Nice to meet you." I managed a tiny smile, shaking his hand.

A tall, barrel-chested man approached next, wearing a cut that read Tank. He gave me a curt nod, as if barely tolerating my presence. A guy behind him, ironically named Tiny, was anything but easily six-five with hands like shovels. Another man, dark as night, Hammer, lingered near a dartboard, casting suspicious looks.

A woman with bright red short hair approached, who looked a bit older, wearing a low-cut black tank top that showed off ample cleavage and a patch reading Ruby. She flashed a perfect grin at me.

"Don't mind the grunts," Ruby said, jerking her thumb at the men. "Half of 'em can't string two words together around a pretty face." She winked, and I felt a little wave of relief.

I returned a shy grin. "Thanks. I'm Lexi. Sorry to crash your clubhouse."

She waved me off. "We get new faces all the time, just usually it's not so tense. We got word about the danger following you." She turned to Maverick. "You keepin' her safe, honey?"

"As safe as I can," he replied.

A couple of other women hung around. A petite, dark-haired girl named Charlie nodded hello, while a blonde in ripped jeans, BonBon, sized me up with what could have been nothing more than a mild curiosity. But I couldn't be sure she wasn't jealous that Maverick brought a woman around.

Over by the bar, another redhead with long hair, Pep, was playing darts, sending them flying with practiced precision. The place felt like an odd combination of party central and war zone, with danger thrumming under the surface.

Sarge led us to a table near the bar. "Sit," he commanded. Maverick and I did, while half a dozen bikers circled us. My gut tightened with nerves. I had no idea what would happen next, some kind of interrogation, presumably.

"We gotta talk," Sarge said, lighting a cigarette. "About you bringing in an outsider. You know the rules, Maverick."

Maverick gave a brusque nod. "I do. She's with me." Then his arm tightened around my shoulders again. "She's mine, my property."

I swallowed, trying not to show how strange that word felt on my tongue. *Property.* But I stayed silent, trusting Maverick's knowledge of MC protocol. I knew from my books it's not that I wasn't allowed to be here, it's that if the Road Monsters didn't see me as claimed, they might treat me like free game. The idea rattled my spine.

Sarge stared at me through the haze of smoke, then nodded slowly. "The last time you brought a woman around saying the same, a fight broke out."

"Won't happen again," Maverick said through his teeth.

"Fine. She's your woman. We respect that. But she ain't to roam around, cause trouble. You keep her close. Understood?" Sarge stamped out the cigarette.

Maverick glanced at me, then back at Sarge. "Understood."

Stumpy, Taz, Tank, Tiny, and Hammer lingered, offering wary nods or shrugs of agreement. Ruby caught my eye, gave me a quick wink that seemed encouraging. *At least one woman here is on my side,* I thought, exhaling.

"You two want a beer?" Sarge asked.

Maverick nodded. "Yeah, we could use a drink."

Sarge waved Tiny over, who handed us a couple of cold bottles. The glass felt reassuringly solid in my hand, though I wasn't sure how relaxed I should be.

"How 'bout the rest of y'all get lost," Maverick growled under his breath to the nearby men. "We need a minute."

They didn't like being dismissed, Hammer sneered, Taz muttered something under his breath but eventually drifted away. I suspected they'd keep a close watch, though, because I was an unknown element, an outsider and apparently the property of Maverick. Though maybe not the only one he's brought here under that guise.

CHAPTER 25

We sipped our beers as slowly the group around us dissipated, returning to their previous activities of shooting pool, playing darts, or slumping on couches. Maverick gestured for me to stand, and we moved across the room so we wouldn't be in the center of the clubhouse.

He leaned down to murmur in my ear. "You okay?"

I nodded, still scanning the crowd. "I think so. This is intense. I'm not used to being called property, though," I admitted with a tight smile.

He brushed his knuckles gently along my jaw. "I know it's weird. But it's how it works here. It's the best way to keep you safe. No one messes with another man's old lady. Understood?"

I let out a shaky laugh. "Yeah, I get it. Like in my books. Except it's, you know... real. And maybe less romantic than I imagined. And aren't old ladies your wives?"

A flicker of a smirk played on his lips. "Don't worry, princess. We'll get to the romantic part, eventually. And yes, once you claim a woman as yours might as well be married to her."

My chest fluttered at the way he said *married*. I had no business feeling giddy, but damn if his voice didn't make me weak in the knees.

He cleared his throat, standing straighter. "Lemme show you around a bit. Then we'll head to my room. I gotta talk to some of the guys, see if anyone's got leads on who might be after you."

I nodded, letting him guide me through the clubhouse. We passed a hallway lined with doors, bedrooms or offices. A loud snore drifted from one, while music thumped from another. The entire place reeked of beer, leather, and cigarette smoke, weed, too, with a faint undercurrent of motor oil.

In a glass display case near the end of the hall, I saw old patches from members who'd presumably died or retired. My gaze lingered on a battered black-and-white photo, a group of bikers from decades ago, staring defiantly at the camera.

Maverick pointed to a heavy steel door. "That's the back entrance. Locked up tight at night." Then he led me farther, stopping in front of a door with a menacing skull decal. "This is mine."

I raised my brows. "You have a room? You live here?"

He produced a key. "I move around a lot. Being a nomad has perks. But yeah, there's a space here for me for whenever I pass through." He grasped the knob and swung the door open.

Inside, the room was surprisingly spacious. A double bed sat against one wall, covered in a plain black comforter. A small dresser, a desk, and a closet took up the rest of the space. A single lamp provided a dim glow, revealing that it was actually neater than I expected. No clothes strewn about, no beer cans. Just a slight stuffy scent, like it hadn't been used in a while.

"Sit," he said, gesturing to the bed. "Make yourself comfortable. I'll be back."

I sank onto the mattress, which creaked under me. "Where are you going?"

He exhaled, rubbing the back of his neck. "Club business. Gotta talk to Sarge and the others about who might've followed us or who could be behind your mom's murder. Maybe get them to help dig into Grinder or any other asshole who'd want you dead. These guys have been in the life forever. They'll know something."

A lump rose in my throat at the reminder of everything that'd happened. "Right. Of course."

His expression softened. "I won't be long. Promise. Try to relax. You're safe here." He rested a hand on my shoulder. "Lock the door behind me, okay?"

I nodded silently. As he turned to go, I caught his wrist. "Maverick?"

He looked back. "Yeah?"

"Thank you. For bringing me here. For keeping me alive."

He gave a half-smile, leaning down to press a soft kiss to my forehead. "Don't thank me yet, princess. I plan on a bigger reward someday." Then he slipped out, closing the door gently behind him.

I stared after him, heart fluttering. Then I stood, turning the lock as he'd asked. I tested it. It was solid. Good. Letting out a long breath, I surveyed the room again. It felt surreal that I was in a biker clubhouse in the middle of nowhere, surrounded by men who might do who knows what to me if I wasn't under Maverick's protection. But for some reason, I felt safer than I had in days.

Exhaustion weighed me down, so I kicked off my shoes and curled up on the bed. My body ached from all the traveling, my mind from the stress. Maybe just a quick nap... *Just a little rest.*

Time blurred. At some point, I drifted off, lulled by the faint thump of music through the walls and the distant laughter of bikers.

I dreamed of bullets shattering windows and the roar of an engine, of Maverick's arms around me. Then a gentle touch on my shoulder drew me out of the dream.

I opened my eyes to see Maverick leaning over me, his features shadowed in the near dark. "Hey," he murmured. "Didn't mean to wake you."

I blinked, disoriented. "What time is it?"

"After midnight," he said softly, brushing hair from my forehead. "I'm sorry. Didn't realize you'd zonk out so hard."

I sat up, rubbing my eyes. "You're done with club business?"

He nodded. "For now. Sarge and some others are following leads, but it'll take time." His gaze flicked over my face. "You hungry? I can get you something."

I moved my head from side to side, then paused, remembering the words he'd used in front of the others. "Maverick, thank you for... for introducing me as your woman, I guess. For letting me stay. I know it's not easy."

His jaw tightened. "It's the only way, Lexi. This club doesn't do half measures. A woman here is either claimed or fought over. The winner gets the spoils, if you catch my drift. That's the ugly truth." He exhaled. "I told you, I won't let them lay a finger on you. But that means playing by their rules."

I shivered, meeting his eyes. "I understand. And what did they mean, you've done this before? There was a fight?" I was really curious about that.

"Princess, I told you there's been countless women," he said, like that explained everything.

"There's been another woman you claimed was yours that wasn't?"

Maverick lifted a shoulder. "Last time I was here, I had a date. No, I didn't follow the rules. I only said it with no proof. Found out they were more serious about this shit than my last club. Yeah, I was challenged."

"What happened to the woman you claimed?"

Maverick looked down, smiling shyly. "Well, you met her. Bonbon. She wasn't really mine. I wouldn't do what it took to keep her, anyway. She hangs at the club now."

"Yikes," I said. But I hadn't meant to say it out loud. "It's just... I've read about all this in my MC romances, but experiencing it is something else."

A flicker of interest lit his gaze. "Yeah... So, tell me. What do they say about claiming a woman, about being someone's property?"

I swallowed, trying to recall all the tropes. "They say, usually, the biker claims her in front of the whole club, might give her a cut with a property patch, or a tattoo marking her as his. Some stories mention branding or forcibly tattooing. In others, it's more consensual but still intense. Sometimes the women are thrilled, sometimes they're reluctant." I gave a half-laugh. "I'm sure it's a lot more romantic on paper or scary, depending."

Maverick met my eyes. "Well, it's not all romance out here. But yeah, that's basically how it goes. I could prove it in front of my brothers. Fuck you out in the club. Give them a show. Or you get a property patch, some ink, you become off-limits to other bikers. The club protects you as one of their own. So, if you fuck with her, you fuck with the entire MC."

I bit my lip, anxiety creeping in. "So... is that what you're suggesting I do?"

He shifted on the bed, leaning closer, the mattress dipping. "I can't watch over you around the clock, Lexi. I have to leave, gather intel, maybe chase down leads. If you're gonna stay here, I need to ensure you're safe." He brushed his knuckles over my cheek, voice softening. "That means an official mark of belonging, so no one questions your status. *Any* question about you being fair game could get you hurt. Or worse."

I tensed. "You mean, if I don't do it, they might... they might?"

He exhaled, frustration evident. "I won't let it happen. But I can't be here every second."

"You're suggesting I should get a tattoo? Marking me as your property?"

"That's how it works. Doesn't have to be big or showy. Just enough that the club sees you as one of ours."

This was happening too fast. *I barely know him.* We'd kissed a few times, sure, but a permanent ink brand. That was insane. "I'm freaking out," I admitted, hearing my voice tremble.

"Hey, Princess," He took my hand, lacing our fingers together. "They can remove tattoos now if you really want it gone later. Just... for now, it's the best way."

My eyes fluttered closed, tears threatening. "It's too much. We've barely kissed, we're not even... we're not lovers. And now I'm supposed to brand my body with your name? Or the club's name?"

He studied me, his brow creasing. "Lexi, I need this. I can't concentrate on hunting down these bastards if I'm scared shitless that you're one step away from being assaulted, or worse. Please."

A heavy silence followed. I could almost hear my anxiety. He lifted my wrist, bringing it to his mouth, kissing the pulse point there, a soft, persuasive kiss.

"Please," he repeated. And he licked my wrist.

I looked into his eyes, seeing genuine concern and something else. Regret, maybe, at having to ask this. My throat tightened. "Fine," I croaked. "I'll do it."

His gaze flickered with relief. "Thank you."

I tried to breathe through the panic. "But I want it small. Somewhere I can cover it up easily. I get to decide, all right?"

"Deal." A smile curved his lips. "I'll arrange it."

CHAPTER 26

Not ten minutes later, we were in another room deeper in the clubhouse, a small, windowless space that smelled of disinfectant and cigarette smoke. Taz was there, setting up a tattoo station that consisted of a swivel chair, a tray of ink bottles, and a buzzing machine. I was going to be sick. I'd never had a tattoo, never even considered it.

Maverick's hand was on my back. "Think about where you want it," he murmured in my ear. "Something that says 'Property of Maverick' and just the Road Monsters' patch."

Taz looked up, raising an eyebrow. "Hey, man. Let's do a small property patch. She's new to this." He shot me a reassuring grin that did little to calm my racing heart. "Where's it going?"

I hesitated, glancing down at my arms, my legs. Maverick made a low sound, stepping up behind me, fingers slipping beneath the hem of my shirt. "Here," he said, lifting the fabric just a bit, exposing my navel.

Heat flooded my face. "Maverick..." I started to protest, but the look in his eyes silenced me.

"It'll be hidden under your clothes most of the time," he murmured, leaning close so only I could hear. "I want it here, near your stomach. Symbolic, I guess." His hand pressed gently on my waist, stirring a flutter in my belly that was half fear, half holy shit hot.

"That okay with you?" Taz asked, glancing between us.

I swallowed. "Yes. Fine."

Taz nodded, grabbing a small stencil. "Then have a seat, sugar."

Instead of leading me to the tattoo chair, Maverick sank down first. He spread his legs, pulling me onto his lap. I let out a little gasp at the feel of his strong thighs beneath me and something else pressing, growing harder against my backside. My cheeks burned.

"This all right?" Taz asked, snapping on latex gloves. "Sometimes the old ladies get nervous. Having the man there can help."

I couldn't find my voice, so I just nodded, heart rattling in my chest. Taz produced a shot of liquor. "You look real nervous, sugar."

Maverick's arm encircled my waist, steadying me as I took the shot. Knocking it back, I noticed how strong it was. I about gagged. "What the hell is that?"

"Tequilla and Molly," Taz remarked.

"Molly?... Drugs?" I asked, horrified.

Maverick grumbled, maybe at Taz. "Don't worry. I'll be here."

Taz carefully pulled my shirt up, exposing the lower half of my stomach. The chill of the air made my skin prickle. "Small patch, right?" he confirmed.

"Yeah," Maverick said. "Make it say 'Property of Maverick of the Road Monsters MC with the small flaming skull, the standard design for ol' ladies."

He glanced down at me, his lips brushing my ear. "You good?"

I gave another nod, my heart banging. My head swam with the significance. I was getting a permanent mark that said I belonged to this club... and by extension, to Maverick. And I felt all fuzzy.

Taz cleaned the skin with alcohol and placed a stencil. I felt Maverick's breath warm on my neck, his hand gripping my hip. "You're doing great," he murmured.

Then Taz switched on the tattoo machine, and the buzzing filled the room. The first prick of the needle stung more than I expected. I winced, inhaling sharply through my teeth. But I laughed out loud. My head was floating around the room like a helium balloon.

Maverick pressed his mouth to my ear, whispering, "Easy, princess. Breathe."

I did, focusing on the steady drum of my heart, on Maverick's arm holding me close. But I was also liquid, flowing. Part of me knew it was the laced shot. Part of me didn't know a damn thing. My nails dug into Maverick's thigh as Taz worked. But after a minute, the pain dulled to a constant burn, bearable, if uncomfortable.

Maverick's hot lips brushed my earlobe, sending shivers that competed with the sting of the tattoo. "I'm proud of you," he whispered. "When I get back, I'm gonna make this real. Claim you for good."

My cheeks burned. "This wasn't real enough?"

He chuckled, his breath ghosting over my neck. "The tattoo makes you off-limits to the club, but I'm talking about *us*." His free hand slid under my shirt a fraction, resting on my rib cage. "I want to claim you, Lexi. For real. You, me, no fear, no interruptions. Show you what it's like to be mine in every sense. Claim your soul, mind, your pussy."

"My pussy," I repeated his words. Or rather, the drugs did. I would never say such a word aloud.

My pussy pulsated, half terror, all desire.

"Yeah, that full bush."

"You know that's not true. I don't have any hair down there. I've waxed so long, it barely grows back."

The needle buzzed, Taz oblivious to our conversation. Maverick's hand had slipped lower, and he was petting me, petting my pussy. Well, my jeans over my pussy. I was sure Taz could see that, but nothing was said. And somehow, I didn't give a damn. Oh God, this is intense, I thought, biting back a moan that was definitely not from pain alone.

"I can't wait till I come back and get inside you. Make you mine," Maverick rumbled in my ear.

"You... you talk like it's guaranteed," I mumbled, breath catching.

He tightened his hold, his cock beneath me pressing into my ass as he rubbed me. "Because it is, princess. Very soon, I'm coming back for you. And I'll make sure you're never afraid again."

I swallowed, heart thudding so loudly I swore Taz could hear it. Or maybe my pussy was pounding. "Maverick..."

He kissed the side of my neck, and I almost got off. "Just breathe. Focus on me." He whispered other things, half-promises, half-sins. "I plan to kiss every inch of you. And when I'm finished, I'm going to tie you to the bed and fuck you so hard, you'll think this tattoo was a breeze."

His words sent me over the edge, as I got off just with him rubbing my jeans. I was trembling by the time Taz announced he was nearly done.

When Taz finally killed the machine and wiped away the excess ink, I let out a ragged breath. The area stung fiercely, but the realization that I now had a permanent *Property of Maverick of the Road Monsters* MC mark on my skin was the bigger shock. Taz grinned as he applied a bandage, telling me the usual aftercare instructions: keep it clean, apply ointment, that sort of thing.

I nodded, barely processing his words. Maverick's hand stroked my back now, yet my entire mind buzzed with the knowledge that I'd just taken a step deeper into this world. *A world that once existed only in my books.* Now it was etched on my skin.

"You okay, sugar?" Taz asked as I carefully stood, pulling my shirt down.

I giggled. "Yeah, thanks."

He eyed Maverick. "She's a trooper. Most first-timers squirm a lot more."

Maverick smirked proudly. "Don't let her looks fool you. She can handle this life."

My face heated, but I tried to play it cool. "I'll be fine. Just... need to lie down." The drugs were starting to wear off.

Taz nodded. "Sure thing." He started cleaning his station. "Take care of that tat, y'hear?"

Maverick guided me out of the room, his hand sliding around my waist protectively. We made our way back through the narrow hallways until we reached his room again. My brain felt foggy from the adrenaline and the lingering sting in my abdomen, not to mention the Molly.

As soon as the door clicked shut behind us, Maverick turned me around, cupping my face in his hands. He kissed me with a desperation that nearly stole my breath, mouth slanting over mine, tongue urging me open. I grabbed ahold of his cut, pulling him close, gasping against his lips, still reeling from the sensation of the tattoo and the promises he'd whispered in my ear.

The memory of his words, the promise to come back and claim me, pulsed between my thighs. I wanted to lose myself in him, to forget the terror and the pain of the last few days. But we had no time, no privacy, not really. And I still wasn't sure I was ready to cross that final line.

He tore away, breathing ragged. "Lexi," he muttered, looking sorry. "I gotta go. Sarge found me a lead, someone who might be familiar with your mom, and I need to chase it."

My heart sank. "Right now?"

He nodded, regret shadowing his eyes. "Yeah. I'm sorry. I don't want to leave you here alone, but it's the best shot at tracking down who wants you dead. And now you've got the tat, so the men know you're under my protection."

"But what if something happens?"

"Then Sarge is your go-to. He'll keep you safe. Just show them the tattoo if anyone gives you trouble. They see that brand. They know you're not to be messed with." He brushed his thumb over my lip.

"What will happen if they do mess with me?" I asked, crossing my arms.

"I'll kill them," he said, dead serious.

"You're serious?"

He cocked an eyebrow that said I was silly for asking. "You'll be safe. I promise. Don't go anywhere."

Safe in an outlaw biker clubhouse. *The irony wasn't lost on me.* But given the alternative, being hunted on the open road, maybe this was safer indeed.

I exhaled shakily. "Where would I even go if I tried to run? So, yeah, I'll stay."

He hauled me into another fierce kiss, his hand fisting in my hair. His essence, the feeling of pure pent-up longing, nearly buckled my knees. His hands slid down to my crotch again, as he spoke into my gaping mouth. "Wait for me. I don't want you to even touch yourself. I want you to be horny from the time I leave until I get back to claim your pussy." Then, with a groan, he tore himself away, grabbed his jacket, and headed for the door.

"One more thing," he said, turning back. "If you need anything, food, clothes, first aid for your tattoo, tell Sarge. Or Ruby, if you prefer a woman's help."

My fingers pressed over the bandage on my stomach, reality crashing in. "Maverick... come back."

His eyes flickered with emotion. "I will." A final glance at me. Then he was gone, the door clicking shut behind him.

I stood there, alone in that unfamiliar room, trying to steady my heart. *Now what?* His scent lingered, stirring a longing I wasn't ready to face.

Stifling a sigh, I reached down to lift the hem of my shirt, peering at the fresh bandage. Underneath it was a brand-new symbol, the tiny, flaming skull with *Property of Maverick of the Road Monsters MC* inked in swirling script. *Property.* My mind tottered at what that implied. I had no clue how I got here so fast. But part of me couldn't ignore the twisted thrill that came with belonging to a biker like Maverick, if only to survive.

I slipped onto the bed, hugging my knees to my chest. *I can do this,* I told myself, ignoring the ache in my abdomen. Because I had no other choice, right? *He'll come back.* And maybe then, once this nightmare was over, I'd find out if those heated promises of his were anything like the fantasies I'd clung to for so long.

For now, I was alone, a *Road Monster ol' lady* in name, if nothing else. And all I could do was wait for my hero in leather to come back and claim me.

CHAPTER 27

Maverick

I blasted out of the Kansas clubhouse before the sun rose, dust clouds trailing behind my Harley. The open road was familiar, a friend, a confidant, the only fucking piece of stability in my life these days. Until Lexi. The engine's rumble rattled my bones, but it also calmed me. Took me back to a time when I thought I was in control, back when I only had my own problems to worry about. That was before Lexi, before I realized I could actually care about someone other than myself again.

Damn it, it was all so fucked. Just moments ago, I'd locked eyes with her, pressed my mouth to hers, breathed her in like she was the last bit of oxygen left on earth, and now I was riding away. Leaving her behind in that clubhouse. I hated myself for it, but there was no choice. If I wanted to keep her alive, I had to go figure out who exactly wanted her dead. And the best lead I had right now pointed me south, to the last place on earth I wanted to be. Nashville, Tennessee.

More specifically, I was about to stick my head in the lion's den of the Music City Syndicate, run by Ralph Getty. But if the intel from Sarge was right, and Sarge is an old bastard who usually nails this kind of shit, it wasn't just Ralph Getty. It was *Sky* who had some stake in it, too. The same Sky who used to warm my bed in Alaska, the same Sky who'd run from Kingpin with me, the very Sky who left me for that piece-of-shit mobster. The same fucking Sky who apparently was helping Ralph run the Syndicate now that Ralph had popped his Uncle and claimed the throne. Didn't that beat all?

I felt sick just thinking about it, but I couldn't ignore the chatter from the Road Monsters. My brothers traveled all over the country and knew all the secrets. Lexi's father wasn't some unknown biker. And Grinder, who was behind the threat was working for another mob boss, a cousin in the East. So, my brothers seem to think Lexi's father might've been the late, notorious criminal mastermind named

Alexzander Getty. They explained that Getty was at least where Diana was said to have been getting all the money she threw around for the last twenty-five years.

Diana being with Getty twenty six years ago, getting pregnant and holding it over the mobster was feasible, to say the least. That would make Lexi actually a Getty by blood. And if that was the case, maybe Ralph had reasons, the typical mob politics to want her snuffed out. Hell, he might see her as competition, or as some loose end that could unravel the entire family if she decided to stake a claim. After all, he just recently killed his Uncle Alex to become the head of the Music City Syndicate. Who the fuck knows how these insane families think?

Kingpin had worried Dirty Diana was offering to funnel secrets about him to whoever wanted her dead, but it turns out it was simpler, and more complicated, than that. So, if she'd been in Nashville at some point long enough to know anything about Kingpin, she may have also been in the right place and time to have gotten pregnant by Alex Getty. The big problem was, if Lexi was truly the daughter of Alexzander Getty, that was enough to put a big red target on her back. And now that Diana was dead, Lexi would be next. Because families like the Gettys tie up loose ends with bullets, not with court orders.

But none of that explained how Kingpin fit in. Or how the hell my ex, Sky, had a role in Diana's murder, if she had one at all. Or if Kingpin was working behind the scenes, pulling strings, maybe trying to pit me against Ralph for his own ends. Trusting that bastard was like hugging a rattlesnake. He was an Ace of the Road Monsters MC, but that doesn't mean he was loyal to me. Hell, we had a history that's so twisted it tied my brain into knots.

Despite it all, I had one advantage. *Eve*. She was Kingpin's wife, mother of his kids, the woman who'd once been my fiancée. That old heartbreak still left a bitter taste in my mouth. But if there was one thing I knew about Eve, it was that she wasn't a liar. Secretive, yes. She'd hide shit like a professional gambler, but she didn't lie straight to your face. Not without reason, anyway. So maybe I could corner her, get the truth about Kingpin's involvement, about Sky, about the entire fucked-up mess. She might not be thrilled to help me, but she'd do it if it meant keeping her own life stable.

Hence my plan to ride to Nashville, call Eve, and arrange a meeting somewhere neutral. *Yeah, real fucking brilliant.* I was basically inviting Kingpin's wrath if he found out. But I never claimed to be a genius, just a desperate bastard.

The first day on the road was hell. I blasted through Missouri's rural highways, fueling up at grimy gas stations, choking down stale coffee, constantly checking my mirrors to see if I had a tail. If Grinder's men who were working for Ralph Getty were onto me, I'd spot them, but so far, I was alone. The bike's engine sang a monotonous lullaby, and I let my mind drift to Lexi.

Fuck, I missed her. I'd only known her a short time, but she'd carved a place in my chest that felt deeper than anything I'd felt since... well, since I lost my first unborn child with Eve. And then when I gave love a chance again, with Sky, my heart shattered again. That old sorrow nearly shattered me for good. I'd never let myself get close to that kind of pain again until Lexi happened. And now here I was, in deeper than ever. Couldn't even think of losing her. Not after everything.

She was so different from Sky. Sky thrived on chaos, on drama, on men with power. Lexi? She valued justice, something I once believed in. She wanted to help people, actually do good in the world. That shit's rare, especially in my circle. And I found I wanted to protect her hope, her goodness, no matter what. *Christ, look at me, turning into a sappy motherfucker.* But that's what caring does to a man, makes him reckless, makes him do stupid things like leaving her behind in an outlaw clubhouse while I chase answers in a city that wants me dead. Great plan.

I reached the outskirts of Nashville late the next day, having crashed at a cheap motel in Kentucky the night before. My nerves were shot, my body aching, but I pressed on. The city skyline, all bright lights and glitz, stirred up old memories. The last time I'd been here, I'd been forced to kneel before Kingpin, literally and figuratively. That bastard had me by the balls. Now? I wasn't sure if I was coming back to wage war or to beg for help. *Possibly both.*

I pulled into a Dolly Parton themed diner on the outskirts, a tacky little spot with neon pink lettering, pictures of Dolly plastered on every surface. I could hear country music twanging out from the speakers above the door. Perfect for a clandestine meeting with your ex, who used to sing on Broadway, right?

CHAPTER 28

I stepped inside, the smell of fried food and sugary pies hitting me. A waitress in a Dolly Parton T-shirt greeted me with a forced smile. The place was mostly empty. Good. My eyes scanned the booths until I spotted her. *Eve.* Blonde hair sprayed stiff and way past her shoulders, manicured nails tapping anxiously on the tabletop. She still had that angelic face I once fell for, but now she looked... a bit older, more tired. Parenting two kids with Kingpin would do that, I guess.

She locked eyes with me and tensed. For a split second, her eyes flicked to my cut. Then she forced a smile, trying to appear casual. I stalked over, slid into the booth across from her. Fuck this was awkward as hell.

"Eve," I greeted, keeping my voice low.

She folded her arms. "I told you I'd come, but this better not take long. Kingpin would tan my hide if he knew I was meeting you, *Hallow.*"

I flinched at the old name but forced a smirk. "It's Maverick now."

She snorted delicately. "I know what it is. I just don't care to use it. I know that's what you used to call your you know what."

A deep bellied laugh escaped me. Shit, she was right. I didn't think I told anyone that but must've let it slip to Eve at some point.

"So, forgive me, Hallow. It's not who you were when I knew you." Her southern drawl thickened, a sign she was stressed. "Now hurry up. I ain't got all day."

I sat back, taking her in. She was still beautiful in that sweet, southern-belle way, big brown eyes, soft features, the kind of woman men line up to protect. But where once she'd made my heart twist into knots, now I felt a distant affection, maybe a spark of bitterness. She's nothing like Lexi, I realized again. Lexi was strong in a different way.

"Glad you could make it, Eve," I said finally. "I need to know if Kingpin's fucking me over. That's the short version."

She raised a perfectly shaped eyebrow. "Fucking you over how?" She sipped from a frosty glass of sweet tea, refusing to meet my gaze for a second. Then she set the glass down, tinkling ice. "He wouldn't tell me even if he was. Why do you think I can help?"

"Because you've got eyes and ears," I replied, cutting to the chase. "He can't hide everything from you. Hell, I used to hide shit from you, but you always found out." I softened my tone.

She took a sharp breath, color rising to her cheeks. "Are you trying to butter me up, *Hallow*? 'Cause that dog won't hunt. I ain't the same naive girl you once knew."

I shrugged. "Maybe not. But I trust you more than I trust Kingpin."

Her eyes narrowed. "Trust me? That's rich coming from you."

I kept my temper in check. *Focus.* "Look, a lot's changed. I'm not the same either. But I need to know if Kingpin's spoken to Sky behind my back, or if he's dealing with Ralph Getty, or if he's feeding intel to the fucking mob. Because I have a woman, someone I'm trying to protect, and Kingpin's tied up in the strings somehow. Or he might be."

Eve's lips parted in surprise. "Another woman, Hallow?" She shook her head. "You've got a type, I guess, picking up strays in trouble. That's how you ended up with me once upon a time." She tapped her nails on the tabletop. "So, who is she? What does my ol' man have to do with her?"

I leaned forward. "Her name's Lexi. She's... I'm guarding her, or was. Dirty Diana's daughter."

"Lord almighty," Eve gasped, her accent thickening. "Dirty Diana? She's the one who up and died at that rally Kingpin was at, right? I heard rumors she was found in a tent. So that's real?"

"Yeah, why wouldn't it be real?"

She studied her nails. "I wasn't there. My husband can be a bit dramatic. He likes to exaggerate sometimes."

"Yeah, it's real. She's dead. I was there. And her daughter's in danger now, someone's trying to kill her. Word is it's connected to the Getty family. Possibly because Lexi's father might've been Alexzander

Getty, Ralph's Uncle." I exhaled heavily, trying to keep the frustration out of my voice. "And apparently, Sky is involved with Ralph."

Eve's expression flickered with something like pity. "You always did have a knack for love triangles and messed-up relationships, Hallow. But... yeah, I know about Sky and that mob boss. Kingpin's got no shortage of talk about it after what happened before. He's real sore about that betrayal." She paused. "So, you're worried Kingpin's playing you, or maybe working with them to get rid of the daughter?"

"Or using me as a pawn for some bigger plan." I spat the words.

"But why?"

"Wouldn't be the first time. I also wonder if Sky's pulling strings behind the scenes. Maybe she's got Kingpin's ear. Maybe she's whispering in it. I don't know. Everything's so tangled."

Eve sighed, looking away. "Why aren't you meeting with him directly? Why me?"

I snorted. "Because I don't know if I can trust him. Plus, if he's in bed with the mob, the second I show my face, they'll know. I can't risk that. And I sure as shit can't risk bringing Lexi near them."

"Well, I can tell you he's not in bed with the mob, Hallow. That's ridiculous. As for Sky reaching out to him, using him to get to you..." Her shoulders slumped. She fiddled with the sweet tea again, the ice clinking. "You do realize if Kingpin finds out I met with you, he'd be fit to be tied. He hates any mention of you. Our entire marriage is built on not talking about the past."

I forced a chuckle. "You sure about that? Because you used to talk about me all the time, from what I heard." I let the insinuation hang, but she just glared.

"Shut it," she hissed, scanning the diner to make sure no one overheard. "I only slip up occasionally. And I'm paying for it every time. So keep your voice down, or I'll walk out."

I lifted my hands in surrender. "Fine, sorry."

She sipped her tea, regaining composure. "All right, so what exactly do you want from me, Hallow?"

"*Maverick*," I corrected. But she just rolled her eyes. "I need you to do some digging. See if Kingpin has any arrangement with Ralph Getty. Or if Sky's been talking to him about me or about Lexi. I also want to know if anyone in Texas might be connected to this. Any mention of Grinder working for the Getty's or being related to them. I need the truth before Lexi ends up dead."

Eve studied me for a long moment. The overhead lights glinted off her blonde hair. She's changed, I realized. Gone was the starry-eyed girl who once talked about our future kids and a house in the suburbs. But she didn't looked hardened, worn down by life with Kingpin like I'd hoped. I knew Eve had what she wanted in Nashville, a budding singing career. Hell, even on the road, I didn't miss the news of her going on tour with Kingpin's famous brother. Eve had the life I never wanted to give her. And she looked satisfied. "Are you asking me to commit espionage on my own husband?" she said finally, voice wavering with sarcasm.

"Yes," I said bluntly. "Or something close to it."

She released a humorless laugh. "Well, butter my butt and call me a biscuit. You sure know how to put a woman in a tight spot." She shook her head, exhaling. "But I guess I owe you something, after everything."

My chest tightened. "Eve, you don't owe me a damn thing. You left me for Kingpin, remember? We both fucked up. I'm not here to relive that. I just know you're the only person who might tell me the truth."

Her gaze flicked up, surprise etched in her expression. "You're real serious about this girl, aren't you?"

"Lexi," I said her name, tasting it like a prayer. "I might be. If she survives." The words felt like gravel in my throat. "I think... I think I can love her."

Eve's lips parted slightly. Possibly due to shock, possibly due to pity. Her chest rose and fell. "Well, at least you found someone you love. That's more than I can say for your sorry ass in the past."

I gave a grim smile. "Don't get too sentimental."

She leaned back, crossing her arms. "All right, let's do it your way. I'll see what I can find out about Kingpin's connections, about whether he's been in contact with Sky or the Gettys. But you gotta give me some time. He doesn't exactly leave his phone unlocked on the kitchen counter."

I nodded. "Time, I can do. In the meantime, I'll be back in Kansas, watching over Lexi."

She arched a brow. "Kansas? Is that where you stashed her?"

"Yeah. Safer than taking her anywhere near Ralph Getty. Or near Kingpin," I added pointedly.

Eve snorted. "So, you're trusting a bunch of savage bikers to guard her?"

I thought of Sarge, Taz, the others. They had their flaws, but I believed they'd keep her from harm if she wore my mark. "They're less savage than the Syndicate. Less ruthless than your husband. At least we have a code they actually follow."

"Now, that's a sad statement. If Kingpin followed his own rules, you'd be dead." She drummed her nails. "All right, I'll poke around. But you keep your ass out of Nashville unless I call you, got it? If Kingpin even suspects I'm talking to you, he'll lose his mind. And if he finds out I'm feeding you information, he'll... I don't even want to think about it. Not to mention what the Road Monsters might do if they think you're double-crossing one of the Aces."

I clenched my jaw. "I get it. Don't worry. I won't blow your cover."

She studied me with an odd mixture of nostalgia and scorn. "You always were a fucking magnet for trouble, Hallow. I guess some things never change."

I bit back a retort. She's not wrong. Instead, I tossed a few bills on the table for her tea. "Thanks for meeting me. You can text me on my burner if you want. I'll keep it quiet."

She nodded, fishing out her phone, tapping quickly. "Gimme that number."

I rattled it off. She typed it in, glancing at me. "If this messes up my marriage, I swear to God, I'll drag you to the barn and skin you alive myself."

A wry grin tugged at my lips. "Look at you, all badass."

She rolled her eyes. "Don't test me. Now get out of here. Go to your girl. Let me do my part."

I hesitated a moment, remembering the old us, the broken dreams, the baby we lost. But that was a lifetime ago. "Take care, Eve," I said softly.

She offered a half-smile. "Yeah, you too, Hallow. Good luck."

Without another word, I slid out of the booth, ducked my head, and strode out into the sweltering Tennessee heat. Climbing onto my Harley, I exhaled with a tremor. That could've gone worse. Or better. But at least I'd planted a seed. If Eve sniffed out anything about Kingpin's involvement with the Gettys or how Sky was tied in, I'd have a better shot at protecting Lexi.

CHAPTER 29

I had zero reason to linger in Nashville. The second I fired up the engine, my mind was already on the road back to Kansas. Something about the idea of Lexi alone among my brothers, some of whom were cutthroats, made me uneasy, no matter how safe I believed she'd be. And maybe, deep down, I just wanted to be there in case she needed me, in case she got scared or lonely or fucking bored. I wanted to see her face again, hear that voice that trembled every time I stepped too close.

I pushed the bike to its limits, ignoring the soreness in my back. The wind whipped across my face, stinging my eyes. I only stopped for gas and bathroom breaks, munching on stale jerky for sustenance. The miles blurred, but every time I thought about turning off to rest, I remembered Lexi's smile, the small laugh she gave when she thought something I said was funny. The faint moan that slipped out when I kissed her in that motel. *Shit,* I had it bad.

My phone stayed quiet the entire ride. No texts from Eve, no warnings from Sarge, no calls from Kingpin. That could be good or bad. Maybe it meant no one had discovered my meeting. Or maybe they had, and the hammer just hadn't dropped yet.

Despite my best efforts, my mind kept drifting to *Sky.* The mention of her name always twisted my gut. Did she really orchestrate this attempt to kill Lexi? Or was she just playing the game with Ralph Getty, not knowing or caring who got caught in the crossfire? She always was cunning. Maybe she'd recognized that Lexi was a potential threat or a piece on the chessboard, and she needed to be removed. Or maybe it had nothing to do with her, and I was imagining connections where none existed.

But the puzzle was too big to ignore: Kingpin, Sky, Ralph Getty, the late Alexzander Getty, Dirty Diana, Lexi... They were all pieces of a puzzle I didn't quite see yet. *Fuck, I used to be a detective. Why is this so damn hard?* Because emotions were tangled in it, that's why. My mind got cloudy when my heart was involved.

It was late afternoon, the following day by the time I found myself once again on the dusty road leading to the Road Monsters' clubhouse in Lebanon, Kansas. The heat was oppressive, shimmering waves rising from the asphalt. My engine growled in protest as I pulled into the compound, the gates manned by a couple prospects who gave me curt nods.

I parked, swung off the bike, and blew out a breath. The place looked the same, quiet, remote, half-deserted except for a handful of bikes outside. My heart pounded as I scanned for any sign of Lexi. *God, please let her be all right.* I'd only been gone a couple of days, but it seemed like a fucking eternity.

The door creaked as I stepped in. A few heads turned, Taz, leaning against the bar, arms folded. Hammer, messing with a pool cue. I recognized that suspicion in their eyes. They're curious why I left and came back so fast. I ignored them, heading down the hallway toward my room. Each step quickened with anticipation.

I reached my door, turned the knob, and realized it was locked from the inside. Good. I knocked softly. "Princess, you in there?"

A second later, the lock clicked, and the door opened. She peered out, eyes wide with relief. "Maverick?"

I exhaled, tension draining. "Yeah, it's me, princess."

She threw the door wide, stepping aside so I could enter. I stepped in, shutting it behind me, and found myself staring at her. She wore a simple tank top and jeans. Looked like Ruby gave her some clothes. Her hair was a bit messy, and her face was flushed. Damn, she looked so good. I longed to yank her into my arms, but I held back a second, scanning for any sign of injury. She looked tired, but intact.

"You came back," she whispered.

"Of course I did." I emitted a trembling chuckle. "I said I would. I'm not a total piece of shit, you know."

She swallowed, eyes glistening like she was about to cry. Then, all at once, she launched herself at me, arms around my neck. I caught her, pressing her tight against me, inhaling the faint scent of shampoo. She was so small, so vulnerable, yet so fucking strong in her own way.

"What happened?" she asked, muffled against my chest. "Did you find out who wants me dead?"

I clenched my jaw, burying my nose in her hair. "I got leads. It's complicated. But I'm working on it. You're safe here for now, right?"

She nodded, pulling back to look at me. "Yes. No one bothered me. Though Taz asked if I wanted to hang out in the rec room, and Ruby tried to talk to me. Everyone's curious. But I stayed in your room, mostly. I was... I was scared."

Guilt stabbed me. "Shit, I'm sorry. I didn't mean to lock you in a cage."

She swayed her head. "No, I just... I feel safer here than wandering around with them. Some of them have that hungry look in their eyes." She gave a nervous laugh. "But your brand is working. None of them will touch me."

My gaze dropped to her stomach, remembering the fresh tattoo. "How's it healing?"

She lifted the edge of her tank top, showing me the small bandage. "It's sore, but it's okay. Taz said I was doing fine with the aftercare."

A surge of pride and possessiveness flared in my chest. She fucking marked herself for me. I reached out, skimming my knuckles over the bandage. "Thank you," I murmured.

Her cheeks colored. "You already thanked me, in a way, with that last kiss before you left."

I let out a dark chuckle. "Princess, that was just a preview." I slid my hand around her waist, pulling her curvy body flush against me. Her eyes fluttered shut, lips parting as I leaned in. I kissed her deeply, letting days of pent-up tension and longing flood through me. She responded with a soft moan, her hands gripping my shoulders.

For a minute, we just stood there, losing ourselves in the taste of each other. My dick ached for her as it solidified. My hands went to rest on her shapely ass. I looked down at her cleavage. Shit, I could stay like this forever. But eventually, I forced myself to ease back, resting my forehead against hers.

"How about we talk first, yeah?" I said softly, though I wanted to rip her clothes off right then.

She blushed, nodding. "Yeah, sorry."

I pressed a finger to her lips. "No apologies, princess. I've been craving that since I left."

She bit her lip, eyes shining. "Then let's talk quickly so we can do more."

A grin tugged at my mouth. "Damn, you're dangerous." I steered her over to the bed, where we sat, side by side. I still didn't let go of her hand. "So, I went to Nashville. Met up with someone. See, before I left, I found out. Well, it's not confirmed, but it looks like Grinder's working for someone. And your father might've been Alexzander Getty. That means you might be."

"A Getty," she finished, voice hollow.

"Yeah, word is that's how your mom survived, off Alex's dirty money."

"Well, she did call herself Dirty Diana. And it was more than the fact she loved Michael Jackson. She always had a way. She made sure things got paid for."

"Alex was a mob boss in Nashville. His nephew Ralph offed him and his son to take power. So, we figure he could want you dead, too."

"So, does that mean he wants me dead because... I'm some sort of threat to his empire?"

"Could be." I rubbed my face, frustration boiling. "Ralph's an egomaniac. If you're a rightful heir or something, he might see you as a problem. Or maybe he's just cleaning up the family's dirty secrets. We don't know yet."

She swallowed hard. "And my mother never told me any of this. She just let me live, thinking my dad was some random biker. She even said it a few times, that he was a biker. But it's a mobster. Great." Her voice cracked with anger and sadness.

I squeezed her hand. "I'm sorry, Lexi. I wish I had better news. The good part is, now I know who to go after. Ralph Getty, possibly in cahoots with Sky."

"Your ex? She's with the guy who wants me dead, right? That's a big coincidence."

"Yeah, I don't believe in coincidences."

Lexi shrugged. "Well, I do. Circumstantial evidence means little."

"But I was asked by Kingpin to talk to Diana and find out what she knows about him. I'm not sure how Kingpin ties into this. He might be dealing with them, or maybe he's trying to sabotage them and using me. Hard to say. It's a big fucking mess."

She frowned. "Kingpin is your old... friend? Enemy?"

"Both," I admitted. "He runs the Royal Bastards MC in Nashville, but he also has his claws elsewhere. He's the reason I ended up in the Road Monsters in the first place. And we have a nasty history involving my first fiancée, Eve." I paused, my throat tightening. "Anyway, I got someone on the inside who might feed me info soon."

She searched my face. "So now what? We just wait?"

I leaned in, pressing a soft kiss to her temple. "We keep you here, keep you safe. Meanwhile, I'll wait for word. The second I know who's pulling the trigger, I'll put an end to it. One way or another."

Her gaze flicked over my mouth, then up to my eyes. "I hate being helpless."

"I know. And I'm sorry." I ran a thumb over her bottom lip, my chest aching with the need to comfort her. "Believe me, I want to fix this more than anything. I can't stand the idea of you living in fear."

She sighed, leaning into my touch. "You're too good to me, Maverick."

I shook my head, a wry laugh escaping. "Not really. I'm a mean outlaw who doesn't give a shit about anything except saving your ass. And claiming you," I added, voice turning husky.

Her cheeks warmed, but she didn't look away. "Are you going to keep me locked up in this room until then?"

I smirked. "Not locked up, but... yeah, maybe. I don't trust half these assholes not to say something stupid. The Road Monsters abide by the property patch, but some might get ideas. Tread carefully."

She nodded, chewing her lip. "Fine. But you better visit often, or I'll go crazy."

I laughed, the sound surprising even me. "Oh, I'll visit. Don't you worry."

After that, I took a moment to shower off the road grime in the tiny adjoining bathroom. The hot water beat down on my muscles, each drop reminding me of the countless miles I'd traveled in the past forty-eight hours. And yet, I felt... renewed. Like the future held some sliver of hope, all because Lexi was in it. Christ, I'm turning into a fucking romantic. But maybe that was okay.

When I emerged, wearing only my jeans, I found Lexi rummaging through a bag of takeout she must've gotten from the clubhouse kitchen. The smell of fried chicken wafted through the air. My stomach growled.

She looked up, eyes skating over my bare chest. A faint flush crept over her face, but she forced a playful smile. "Hungry?"

"Starving," I said, my voice rough. But my hunger was for more than just food. The way she stood there, half-smiling, made me want to drag her onto the bed. *Focus, asshole. She's not ready, and you're both exhausted from stress.*

She handed me a paper plate loaded with chicken, mashed potatoes, and some sort of gravy. "Eat before it gets cold," she advised, taking a bite of her own portion.

I settled on the edge of the bed, devouring the meal in grateful silence. She ate too, though she looked lost in thought, occasionally glancing at me as if to ensure I wasn't about to vanish again. After we finished, she yawned, the tension easing from her shoulders.

"You look beat," I said, setting my plate aside.

She shrugged. "I haven't been sleeping great. Worrying about you... about everything."

A pang of guilt speared me. "Then let's get some rest." I hesitated, unsure how to phrase my next question. *We've got one bed,* I thought. *Usually, I'd just assume she'd share it with me.* But given the seriousness of the situation, I wanted to be sure. "Do you, uh, want me to sleep next to you? Or do you need space?"

Her eyes flicked to the bed, then to me. A small, trembling smile touched her lips. "Stay. Please."

My heart thumped. "All right, princess."

We crawled onto the bed, me in my jeans, her in her tank and shorts. The overhead light switched off. The darkness pressed around us, but the faint glow of a single lamp in the corner kept it from being pitch black. She nestled in close, her back against my chest, letting me wrap an arm around her waist. My fingers brushed over the bandage on her stomach, reminding me of the fresh ink beneath. My mark, I thought, a savage satisfaction stirring deep inside. She's mine, for better or worse.

She whispered, "Thank you for coming back."

I buried my nose in her hair. "I'll always come back. I promise."

And in that moment, I felt redeemed, like some part of my soul that had been stained by all the betrayals, Eve, Sky, Kingpin, the miscarriages, the broken illusions, was finally washing clean. If I can save Lexi, if I can keep her alive, maybe I can start over. Maybe the open highway didn't have to be my only home. Maybe I could build something real, something lasting.

But the threats still loomed. Ralph Getty, Kingpin's possible treachery, the murky role Sky played in all this. I needed to wrap up these loose ends before they strangled me. For once, I didn't want to run. I wanted to fight. Fight for Lexi, for a shot at a life that wasn't overshadowed by ghosts.

As her breathing evened out, signaling she'd fallen asleep in my arms, I watched the shadows dancing on the ceiling. My mind churned with possibilities. Eve said she'd do some digging, so I'd wait for her call. Then I'd decide if I needed to crush the Music City Syndicate or just slice off a piece of it. *One way or another, I'll keep Lexi safe.*

I pressed a gentle kiss to her temple. *If she can survive this, maybe we can both find peace.* Maybe I can be the man she deserves, the man I thought I'd never be again. A grin tugged at the corner of my mouth, a warm sense of purpose settling in my chest. *Damn straight. Let them come. Let them try. I won't let her down.*

With that final thought, I let the exhaustion pull me under, my arm tight around the woman who'd unexpectedly reawakened my heart.

CHAPTER 50

Lexi

I woke to the sound of Maverick's husky breathing as he counted off each sit-up with quiet determination. My eyelids fluttered and I stretched, letting out a soft moan. The thin mattress of his clubhouse bed squeaked under me. I'd slept deeper than I had in days, comforted by his presence, yet still half-worried the world might collapse again.

My movement must've caught his attention because, in the next instant, Maverick's voice rumbled through the small space. "Morning, princess," he said, breath coming fast from the exertion. "About time you woke up."

I blinked, propping myself up on an elbow. He was on the floor, shirtless, sweat slicking his chest and arms. He'd been doing sit-ups with an intensity that made my stomach clench. There was something mesmerizing about the way his muscles moved. "You're up early," I murmured.

He gave a wolfish grin, finishing one more sit-up before turning to me. "Did you forget I made a promise? That once I got back, I'd *claim* you properly?"

I felt a flush creep over my cheeks. "I... I thought maybe you changed your mind. Yesterday you didn't... you know."

He pushed himself up, crossing the room in a few strides. His eyes flared with an intensity that sent a shiver down my spine. "Did you really think I'd changed my mind?" He leaned over the bed, bracing a hand on either side of me. "You're owed a special night, Lexi.

And I'm not about to do it here in this dingy-ass clubhouse. You deserve better. We'll make a reservation."

A nervous laugh tumbled from my lips. "You're telling me you want us to go to a fancy hotel to... make the property patch real?" My voice wavered, half with excitement, half with nerves.

He smirked, leaning closer. "Hell yes. I'm no gentleman, but I'm not some animal, either. I want to do this right. And if I gotta prove it to you, I can manage that. Besides..." His grin turned crooked. "I gotta put out. Otherwise, how's that patch gonna mean anything?"

A bubble of laughter escaped me. "You're ridiculous."

He grazed the tip of his nose against mine, his breath warm. "Damn right. But I'm your ridiculous now." Then he pulled back, standing upright. "I'll go grab us some breakfast. When I get back, we'll find a place to hole up for a night. Someplace nicer than this clubhouse."

I sat up, swinging my legs over the side of the bed. "That sounds... amazing, actually."

"Good. Be ready." He grabbed his cut from the back of a chair and shrugged it on. "I'll be back soon."

Once Maverick slipped out, I realized how quiet the room felt without him. I stretched again, then grabbed my phone from the nightstand. A text from Nova sat unread:

Nova: *Where are you, girl? You haven't updated me in ages. I'm worried. Chigger took off on some job. Haven't heard from him in a day.*

My heart twisted with guilt at her concern. I typed back:

Me: *I'm safe, promise. Can't tell you where, but I'm fine. Sorry for not texting sooner.*

Me: *You okay?*

The little dots popped up, then her response came:

Nova: *I guess. Bored. Missing Chigger. He said it's club business. I know better than to ask questions. Anyway, I did what you asked with your mom's remains...*

Grief pinched my chest. "Thanks for dealing with Mom," I whispered, remembering the day she died in that tent. My thumb hovered over the keys.

Finally, I typed:

Me: *Thank you for handling everything. Did you pick out an urn?*

She answered fast:

Nova: *Yes, a really pretty one with some sort of sparkly design. Not too gaudy. She'd like it.*

Nova: *How are you holding up? You better be back soon. Don't you have work on Monday?*

I almost laughed at the reminder. Work. The normal world.

I typed:

Me: *Yep, I might have to call in. But at least I'm alive, right?*

Nova's reply came with the speed of a best friend who always had the perfect comeback:

Nova: *Haha, yeah. Could be worse... you could be dead.*

Nova: *How's that tat, by the way?*

I reflexively touched the tender area on my lower stomach. It still stung, but not as intensely. *It's more the emotional impact that throbs.*

I wrote back:

Me: *Still hurts, but I'm dealing. Kinda worried about... something else hurting soon.*

Nova's next text was immediate:

Nova: *Where are you going?!*

I rolled my eyes. Of course, she'd interpret it that way. I'd already told her he said he wanted some privacy.

I typed a quick, mischievous response:

Me: *Nowhere special. Just some alone time with... him.*

Me: *I'll give you details after the deed is done, promise.*

She shot back a barrage of laughing emojis:

Nova: *You better. Good luck, Smutty. I'm sure you'll do just fine in bed, you big nerd.*

I smiled, shutting off the phone as footsteps approached outside.

The door creaked open, and Maverick stepped back in, carrying two coffee cups and a paper bag. The rich aroma of fresh brew made my stomach growl.

"Hope you like greasy bacon or sausage." He handed me a coffee. "They were out of eggs, so I got whatever was left. Just in time, I guess, the prospect in the kitchen was about to toss the last batch to the dogs."

I laughed, taking the bag and peeking inside. A couple of breakfast sandwiches, one bacon, one sausage. I raised an eyebrow, smirking. "Better than starving. Thanks."

We settled on the bed, cross-legged, devouring the sandwiches and sipping coffee. *Damn, it tasted good.* The coffee was cheap and bitter, but after days of stress, it felt like a luxury to share a simple meal with Maverick. My stomach fluttered at how domestic it all seemed.

"So," he said around a mouthful of bacon, "any ideas where you wanna go for our little getaway? Gotta be somewhere not too far from Lebanon, but nicer than a roadside motel. Possibly one with actual water pressure."

I pulled out my phone, opening a search. "Let's see... I'm sure there's a decent hotel within an hour or so. Hang on." As I scrolled, Maverick watched with mild interest. "Okay, there's some bed-and-breakfast type places, some chain hotels with decent reviews... or...oh, there's this fancy resort-spa type place about thirty miles from here. Might be pricey, but they have big tubs, a sauna, the works."

Maverick shrugged, swallowing the last of his sandwich. "I don't mind pricey if it means you'll finally relax. The MC can foot the bill."

I eyed him skeptically. "A spa resort? Kinda out of your comfort zone, isn't it?"

He leaned over, pressing a short, possessive kiss to my temple. "Princess, I'd sit in a fluffy pink robe and let them paint my nails if it meant I get you in a hot tub afterwards."

Heat rushed to my cheeks. "So we're going all out?"

He grinned. "Damn straight. Let's do it."

After scarfing down breakfast, we stuffed our minimal belongings into Maverick's saddlebag. I was glad to leave the dank, moldy smell of the clubhouse behind. The idea of a proper shower in a nice hotel room was downright thrilling. My stomach fluttered again, though, with a mix of anticipation and nerves. Tonight could be the night, the real claiming, that I'd only read about.

We walked through the clubhouse, ignoring the curious stares of a few bikers. Taz gave us a lazy wave, and Ruby, perched on a barstool, winked at me. I nodded back, oddly proud that I was stepping out with Maverick, my supposed "property patch" hidden under my shirt.

Maverick started his Harley, and I hopped on. We screeched out of there, dust flying everywhere in the heat. The wind blew my hair all over, and I could feel the engine vibrating in my legs. After all that craziness, I felt surprisingly alive. Free.

The ride wasn't long, maybe an hour. We drove past fields, farms, and tiny towns. Eventually, we spotted the turnoff for the resort, a tree-lined drive that led to a grand structure overlooking a man-made lake. It was bigger than I expected, complete with a nice-looking spa building to one side.

"Holy shit," I muttered as Maverick parked the Harley near the main entrance. "Did we just land in luxury?"

He smirked, cutting the engine. "Not exactly the Ritz, but it's nice enough."

We headed inside, the lobby gleaming with polished floors and large windows. A friendly receptionist greeted us, eyebrows hiking at Maverick's leather vest. He wandered around the lobby as I went to the counter. I handled check-in, using Maverick's cash, but she asked for a credit card. Maverick was out of earshot, so I handed her my card. My mind flashed to criminal cases I'd studied, so I knew my card was traceable. But being claimed by Maverick was worth the risk.

"It's only for incidentals." She handed over key cards with a professional smile.

The elevator whisked us to a third-floor suite that overlooked the lake. The moment we stepped into the room, I felt my jaw drop. A plush king-sized bed with crisp white linens, an oversized bathroom with a glass-enclosed shower and a whirlpool tub, and a big window framing the shimmering water outside.

I set my small bag down, turning to Maverick with a grin. "This might be the nicest place I've ever stayed."

He gave a low whistle, sliding a hand around my waist from behind. "Told you. I wanted you to feel special."

Every ounce of me fluttered. "You're spoiling me."

"About damn time somebody did," he murmured, pressing a kiss to the side of my neck. "Now, how about you grab a shower? Then we'll see how we're doing."

I laughed softly, leaning back against him. "Yeah... The shower here beats the mushrooms in the tub at the clubhouse. So, I'm definitely doing that."

He patted my hip. "Go for it, princess."

I took my sweet time in the bathroom, letting the hot water cascade over me, washing away the sweat and grime. The tile was spotless, the water pressure blissful. I even used the complimentary, fancy shampoo that smelled like lavender. God, I needed this.

Tonight would be the night. A good chunk of me was excited. I'd yearned for Maverick's touch since the day he rescued me from that creep who exposed me at the rally. But a bit of me trembled with fear. I was a virgin, and this was going to be intense. The property patch still stung on my lower stomach, reminding me of his claim. I belong to him now, in the eyes of the MC. That's no small thing.

Eventually, I stepped out, wrapping myself in a plush robe. Steam hung in the air, the mirror fogged up. My heart pounded at the thought of what might happen next. Deep breaths, Lexi. You've read a million romance novels, dirty ones. But those were stories. This was real.

CHAPTER 31

When I emerged, the room had changed. Soft lighting glowed from the side lamps. Rose petals, actual rose petals, were scattered across the bed. A small bottle of champagne chilled in an ice bucket on the dresser with two flutes set nearby. My eyes darted to Maverick, who stood by the window, wearing only his jeans. My heart did a double take at the sight of his muscled arms, knowing soon they would be wrapped around me. He turned, a devilish grin spreading across his face.

"You like it?" he asked, motioning to the bed. "I thought about your fancy romance books and figured I'd do it right."

My throat felt tight. "It's... perfect," I whispered. "You went all out."

He crossed the room and slipped an arm around my waist, tugging me into an embrace. "A man's gotta prove himself, right?"

A nervous laugh burst from me. "You're not who I expected you to be when we first met."

He chuckled back, brushing a finger under my chin. "I'm a mean outlaw, princess. But even mean outlaws can do nice things for the right woman."

"You sure you want me to be that woman?"

He ran his fingers along the edge of my robe. "I'm damn sure." Then he tugged the belt loose, letting the robe fall open slightly.

I nearly lost my breath.

"May I?" he asked, voice dripping sex.

With a nod, I couldn't hide my excitement. He slipped the robe off my shoulders, letting it pool at my feet. Air kissed my skin, and I fought the instinct to cover myself, remembering I wanted this. His eyes raked over me, obviously appreciating my body. My face got hot with embarrassment, but I was also very turned on.

"Beautiful," he breathed, gently guiding me toward the bed. "Lie down."

Unable to breathe, I did, the rose petals tickling my skin. He knelt beside me, popping the champagne and pouring two glasses. I propped up on my elbow. He handed me a glass. We clinked them lightly, the bubbles fizzling as we drank. I savored the crisp texture, never taking my eyes off him.

It felt like a dream, unreal and completely surreal. "I've never had a drink naked before."

Maverick set his glass aside, leaning over me. "Relax, princess. Let me take care of you." His voice was deep, resonant with a promise.

I thought he'd waste no time, but the biker oiled his hands, enticing me onto my belly. He started with a massage, pressing his palms firmly into my shoulders and back. A soft moan escaped me as his thumbs dug into knots I hadn't realized were there. His warmth, his steady touch, melted away my nerves. His hands did things to me, and I was close to losing it. I'd never had a real massage before. This was beyond any fantasy from my books.

"Feel good?" he murmured, leaning to brush a kiss at the base of my neck.

"So good," I breathed, eyes fluttering shut. My limbs felt heavy, relaxed. I could barely remember how to speak.

He traced his way down my back, kneading muscles along my spine. Then he rolled me gently, sliding his hands down my arms, down my stomach, avoiding the tender area where my tattoo was. He was so careful. But with each slide of his fingers, the flames of my desire grew taller, crackling and spitting.

When his mouth replaced his hands, my skin was seared. He peppered kisses across my collarbone, down between my breasts. He gently sucked on my nipples, one after the other. As if on cue, overwhelmed, I arched slightly, as if I was acting out a play I'd only read about. Was I really doing this? Yes. I felt too good, I didn't care about anything else.

The biker moved lower, leaving hot, wet kisses on my belly. I trembled, thinking of his next move. Biting my lip as his tongue slipped between my slick folds, I tried to keep in control. But when his tongue moved, I moaned his name. Maverick shot up to kiss my lips, assaulting me with the taste of my arousal. Fuck me. What I'd always thought was gross was an absolute turn on.

This biker, this glorious man tasted like the pussy he just lick, my pussy.

Looking downright primal, he undid his jeans, sliding them off. I caught a glimpse of him, my pulse sky-rocketing. I'd seen a naked man or two before in fleeting moments, even him. But this was... different. The biker was large, muscular, and entirely male, with an erect burgeoning male hood, member, manroot... I thought of every euphemism for his cock as he stroked a length to rival all others. And the hunger in his eyes was directed solely at me. I thought we'd work up to intercourse, that he'd want a blow job or something, but it seemed Maverick was going in for the kill.

"I've got you, princess," he said softly, sliding up until our bodies aligned perfectly. "I won't hurt you."

Nerves made me let out a soft, high-pitched laugh. "I'm a lawyer, you know, not some silly teenage girl. It's stupid for me to be afraid. I've *read* everything about this."

Though reading and reality were worlds apart.

He tenderly touched my cheek before giving me a sweet kiss. "It's not stupid. And I don't want you to regret this." He paused, searching my eyes. "You sure you're ready?"

A thousand thoughts collided in my head, the danger chasing us, the property patch etched on my skin, the nights we'd spent together, half in terror, half in longing. "Yes," I whispered, though my voice trembled. "I want this. I... trust you."

His gaze flared with gratitude and something much deeper. "Thank God," he murmured, brushing his lips across my jaw. "I'll go slow."

He started with sweet kisses, his mouth exploring mine. We tangled in the sheets, practically humping each other, the rose petals crushed beneath us, releasing a faint floral scent. My skin buzzed with electricity as he took a hold of my hips and truly aligned himself between my thighs. His every movement was careful, almost reverent, as the head of his dick butted against my entrance.

"Wait," I said. "What about protection?" I knew he'd had a condom in his saddlebag.

Maverick bit his lip. "I'm claiming you, princess. I'm going to fuck your pussy raw. You okay with that? We can stop."

He'd given me pause, not because of the implications, no protection, but because of how he'd said it. The raw desire and need in his voice. "No. I'm okay," I squeaked, wanting nothing more in my entire life.

And then he moved. A sharp shock of pain followed as he pressed forward.

I stiffened, gasping. "Ouch..." I hissed, eyes flying open. I hadn't expected it to hurt this much, despite all the warnings and reading.

Maverick froze, concern flooding his features. "Shit, sorry," he breathed, cupping my cheek. "Didn't mean to...."

"It's fine," I mumbled, even as tears pricked my eyes. "Just... gimme a second."

He eased back but was still there. I felt the burn still there, too, a dull ache. I was so upset, I felt like crying. This was supposed to be romantic. Damn it. I plastered on a smile, but I bet it looked fake. "I'll be okay." Fuck. I wanted him, bad.

His brow furrowed. "We can stop if you want..."

"No!" I blurted, though part of me was real tempted to call it off. The other part needed him inside of me. I'd come this far. "Just... slow."

The biker nodded, pressing gentle kisses to my neck as he moved his hips ever so slowly. Gradually, the sting lessened, I thought, until he pushed forward again. I was in agony. My body was rigid with pain. A high-pitched whimper escaped me, and instinctively, I jerked away, crawling backward. The abruptness made him slip free, and I could see the frustration and guilt in his eyes.

I was failing at this. My cheeks burned with utter embarrassment.

"Princess," he said, sitting up, voice thick with worry. "Talk to me."

I stared at him, tears hovering in my eyes. "It hurts," I admitted, choking on the words. "I know it's silly. People do this every day, but I can't..."

He exhaled slowly. "You're not silly. Your body's never done this before. It's okay."

But something about his expression shifted, a resolve hardening in those stormy eyes. "Trust me again?"

I kinda hesitated, then nodded. "Yes."

He laid me back gently. "Sometimes... you just gotta rip the bandage off. That's how it is in those books, right? The men take charge?"

My pulse kicked. "I guess so." A tremor ran through me as he positioned himself again, one large hand bracing my hip. I knew what he planned to do. He didn't plan to stop. Was I consenting to this?

"Look at me," he commanded softly. "Breathe. Let me do this. I promise I'll make it worth it."

My throat was dry. I locked eyes with him, forcing myself to relax. Then, in one rough thrust, he broke through. The biker popped my cherry. The pain made me gasp, but this time, he didn't back off. He stilled inside me, letting me adjust, his hands gripping mine above my head. Tears leaked from the corners of my eyes, but my mind clung to him, focusing on the warmth and weight of his body on top of mine, the sound of his ragged breathing.

"Oh, fuck me," he groaned, his voice laced with pleasure and concern. "God, Lexi. Fuck, princess," he rasped, voice strained. "You feel. God, you feel so goddamn good."

I couldn't form words. He felt so goddamn big. And I was too full. However, I couldn't speak it. I let the sensations wash over me as I struggled for air, the initial shock ebbing. Slowly, a tingling warmth replaced the sting. But he moved, and I felt a raw friction that teetered between pain and something deeper.

"M-Maverick..."

He dipped his head to kiss me, swallowing my moan as he began a careful rhythm. Each thrust drew a stifled cry from me, until gradually, my cries shifted from those of pain to a wobbly sort of pleasure. My entire body felt lit from within. The fire was inside. Sensations I'd only ever read about burnt me alive.

"Good?" he panted, brow furrowed with concentration.

My tears mixed with a half-laugh. "Yeah... it's... oh God..." My words dissolved into a gasp as he angled himself differently, hitting a spot that made me see stars. The ache was still there, but overshadowed by wave after wave of something new, something exhilarating.

Maverick's grip tightened as he moved faster, reminding me of the fierce, possessive men in my novels when they claimed their women. A strangled groan left my lips, my body bowing up to meet his. The bed creaked beneath us, rose petals crushed to bits. The scent of them mingled with the musk of sweat and sex.

This was happening. The realization made my head spin.

"Lexi," he growled, burying his face in the crook of my neck. "You're mine." His words vibrated through me, a benediction of sorts. I held his back, a surge of heat coiling low in my pussy.

My mind went hazy as our sex built to a climax.

Somewhere in that frenzy, he pressed his forehead to mine. "You're mine now. *Mine*. You hear me, princess?"

"Yes," I gasped, tears streaming down my face. Not from sadness, but from the overwhelming storm of sensations and emotions. "I'm yours."

"Property patch or not," he growled, each word punctuated by a heavy thrust that nearly done me in. "You belong to me... I belong to you."

"Always," I whimpered, meaning it in that moment with every fiber of my being.

A heartbeat later, he surged his dick into me harder than ever before. Despite the lingering sting, a rush of pleasure crested within me. Then, a wave of pleasure, like a deafening clap of thunder, slammed into me, a soundless roar that forced a cry from my throat.

The biker growled in response, gripping my hips as he sped to his own release. His body shook against mine, his muscles taut as he claimed me in the most primal way, his hot mess spilling into me.

It was done. No going back now.

For a few moments, we lay there, panting in unison, sweaty and tangled. My heart hammered so loud I thought it might burst. A swirl of emotions stormed inside me. Relief, triumph, soreness, warmth, a strange sense of pride. And more than that, love.

I'd done it. We'd done it.

Maverick whispered, "I love you." Echoing my own feelings.

If I could speak, I'd say it right back.

His chest rose and fell against mine. I turned my head, nuzzling into the crook of his neck. His skin smelled like sex and roses. I let out an unstable laugh, half delirious from the rush.

"That was..." I started but couldn't find a word.

He pressed a kiss to my temple, still catching his breath. "Yeah... it sure was." Then he eased out of me. A fresh wave of soreness spread between my thighs, but it wasn't as sharp as before.

"Sorry," I mumbled, cheeks flushing at the memory of me running from him mid-act. "I kind of freaked out."

Maverick cupped my face, forcing me to look at him. "Don't be sorry. It's your first time. I just," He exhaled. "I didn't want to hurt you."

I managed a smile. "It was worth it," I whispered, and I meant it. Even with the pain, I felt... liberated, somehow.

I had trusted him to see me at my most vulnerable, and he didn't let me down.

He let out a quiet laugh. "Thank you for trusting me, princess." Then, with a smirk, he murmured, "I guess this means the property patch is official. You're really mine now. No going back."

My stomach flipped at the possessive edge to his voice, though it sent a thrill through me. I might've bristled at being called property once, but here, wrapped in his arms, I found it oddly comforting.

He wants to protect me. Cherish me. Right now, that's all I can ask for.

He carefully shifted onto his side, drawing me against his chest. I curled into him, listening to the steady beat of his heart. The afterglow pulsed through my limbs, mingling with the ache and the swirl of emotions. When did my life become a romance novel? A small grin tugged at my lips. Maybe it always was, and I just never realized it.

"Sleep, princess," he whispered, pressing a final kiss to my hair.

Exhaustion dragged me under. For once, no nightmares hovered at the edges. Instead, I drifted into a deep, satiated slumber, lulled by the warmth of Maverick's body and the beating of his heart. My unlikely hero, my biker, my mean outlaw who'd just shown me more tenderness than I ever knew possible.

CHAPTER 32

Maverick

I lay on my side, staring at Lexi's sleeping form in the soft glow of the hotel lamp. The night felt still around us, the hush of the upscale room almost unreal compared to the rough roads and clubhouse bunks I was used to. My heart still thundered from what we had done only moments earlier. Every breath she took reminded me that this wasn't a dream. Or if it was, I never wanted to wake up.

I had taken her as gently as I knew how, but with a hunger I couldn't leash. It had started right after we checked into the resort, a place far more polished than any outlaw biker like me should have deserved. I scattered those rose petals, popping cheap champagne, determined to give her something sweet, something special, because she was worth more than the dingy clubhouse mattress or the back of my Harley. She needed softness and a hint of romance, even if I had to fake being that guy.

Perhaps I was that guy for her.

When she stepped out of the bathroom in that plush white robe, hair damp and curling around her shoulders, I almost forgot how to breathe. *Fuck,* I had thought, *she's so beautiful.* My entire chest ached. I never felt that way before... not with Sky, not with anyone. Lexi was different. She looked at me like she trusted me, like the rest of the world's danger didn't exist for one fleeting night.

And she trusted me with her virginity, something I won't lie and say it didn't turn me on one hundred times more. My princess would be all mine, only mine. My dick throbbed as I saw every new inch of her skin. She trembled, but the desire in her eyes was stronger than her fear. God, I wanted to devour her, but I forced myself to take it slow.

I had guided her to the bed. I reached for the small bottle of massage oil I'd found in the courtesy basket, warmed it in my hands, and coaxed her onto her stomach. It took everything in me not to go for her plump ass first.

My palms skimmed across her back, pressing out knots I hadn't realized she carried. She moaned, the sound muffled by a pillow. My pulse was deafening, but I kept focusing on her comfort as I explored her soft curves. If this was her first time, I refused to let anything overshadow it.

Eventually, I helped her turn over, marveling at how she looked. A work of art, like one of those Greco-Roman paintings, a goddess splayed against the rose petals, hair fanned around her. Her large natural breasts gave way to a soft feminine belly showing my property patch. Between her thick thighs, her snatch was void of any hair. And I knew it had been untouched. Her skin was as breathtaking as marble. I slid my hands down her waist, careful to avoid pressing too hard near the fresh tattoo as I gave the front of her body as much attention as I'd given the back.

My cock throbbed in my jeans, almost painful.

Keeping them on, I took my time and kissed every inch of her tender skin. My head bent to her thighs and my tongue swept her wet folds, lapping up her honied desire. She moaned my name, and I rushed up to kiss her, making her own sweet wetness mix with the champagne dryness. That was when I felt her melt under me, her arms wrapping around my neck.

Straining back, I lost my pants, watching her eyes capture the moment. Her sly grin, her eyes twinkling with want as she took in my enormous cock, was fuel for my fire.

She looked strained for a moment, but I murmured, "I've got you, princess," and she relaxed. We kissed, things heated up fast, and my brain kinda short-circuited. I could only think with my dick. My cock ached for her, and I pressed it against her clit. She whimpered, half with anticipation, half with nerves, I could tell.

Hell, yeah, I was going to fuck her raw. She was mine, and I planned to enjoy her untouched pussy to the fullest extent. I tried to be gentle at first, guiding myself slowly. Goddamn, I was about to explode already when I charged into her hot vice. She gasped, tears gathering in her eyes. Though busting her cherry was my cock's singular mission, the thought of hurting her made me uneasy.

"I'm sorry," I whispered hoarsely, ready to withdraw. But she insisted she wanted this. Her voice trembled yet was resolute. She'd read enough biker romances to guess how it sometimes went, fast and rough. I asked if she truly wanted me to do it that way, and she gave me a panicky nod.

I was one lucky son of a bitch. So, I did, in one sharp motion, crushed my rigid dick into her soft tight cunt. She cried out, and the sound shredded me. I clutched her hands over her head, covering her face with kisses, trying to absorb her pain. For a moment, I felt her quivering as she caught her breath as she squeezed my hands almost as hard as her snatch was squeezing my cock. Then her grip on my hands eased. The pain was receding, giving me permission to move, and the moment I sensed her wetness softening around me, I lost all control. The outlaw in me took over, and I laid claim to her pussy as though she were the last tether to my humanity.

Perhaps she was.

Our bodies found a fierce rhythm, the bed creaking under us, petals scattering to the floor. Her eyes shimmered with tears and something else. Trust. Maybe love. I rasped her name, cursing as pleasure knifed through me. She was mine. Sure, it was etched on her body, but I was etching it into her mind and soul. When we finally exploded together, it left us panting in each other's arms.

I couldn't help but whisper the words I felt so deeply. "I love you."

Afterward, she curled against me, her body spent and shuddering. I had half a mind to go again, to sink into her pussy for the rest of the night. Hell, the rest of my life. But I made myself let her rest.

You've got all the time in the world, I told myself as I imagined tying her small wrists together. Would that scare her? I watched her drift off, face pressed to my chest, and wondered how someone so good could ever want me. Yet there my princess was, breathing softly, trusting me.

I recalled every detail of that night as I lay there. And as soon as I woke, the night replayed again. Normally, I would have loved to wake her with slow, lazy kisses, see if she'd let me slip inside her again. But the world had other plans.

My phone buzzed on the nightstand. I eased out from under the sheets, careful not to jostle Lexi. I snagged my phone and saw the number, *Eve*. My heart sank. There was only one reason she would contact me, something to do with Kingpin, or possibly the twisted threads that connected me to my ex, Sky.

I opened the message.

Eve: *You need to come to Nashville now. Meet me at Bootsie's.*

"Fuck," I muttered under my breath, typing a quick response:

Me: *Okay, I'll come as soon as I can get away.*

My mind spun. So much for a slow morning.

Me: *Does Kingpin know anything?*

Eve: *I haven't told him a thing.*

Damn, Eve was dense sometimes. I typed back, clarifying:

Me: *I'm asking about Getty and Sky? What did you find out?*

Staring at the three dots for too long, I set the phone aside to go to the bathroom and splash some water on my face. I told myself I'd figure out how to break the news to Lexi gently.

She was not gonna like that I'd to leave her again so soon, but this was how it went in my world.

When I stepped back into the room, Lexi stirred, sitting up in the sheets. Her dark hair tumbled around her shoulders, and a flush crept into her cheeks as she realized we were still both naked from the night before. My dick instantly hardened thinking about the second time, I wouldn't have to be so gentle. Biting my lips, I looked to the tie on her robe, knowing I could secure her with it.

Lexi's gaze flicked from my cock to my phone, which I'd dropped on the little table beside her.

She reached for it, then froze, meeting my eyes. "I'm sorry," she said quickly. "It lit up with a text, and I already glanced at it."

Fuck, the burner phone wouldn't lock like my smartphone. My dick going limp, I felt a pulse of dread. "No, it's fine," I assured her, stepping closer. "Just... let me see."

She held it out to me, a frown on her face. "Eve texted again," she said softly. "Says something about your ex not leaving you by choice, that she was blackmailed."

My chest twisted as her words hit me. I read the screen, scanning Eve's message:

Eve: *I don't think your wife ever wanted to go with Ralph willingly. Kingpin got a weird text and the girl's mother confirms it. Ralph blackmailed Sky to tell everyone she was leaving you for him. She's in danger.*

Sky didn't leave me on purpose? She always gave me a load of excuses, that we'd grown apart after losing our baby, that she wanted a man with power, that she couldn't stand my drinking, my anger. But if Eve's intel was true, maybe Sky had lied to protect me or her child. A mess of old wounds instantly reopened, and I struggled to keep my expression neutral.

I typed back:

Me: *Are you sure?*

Eve replied:

Eve: *Kingpin seems to believe it. Her mom is beside herself.*

I cursed under my breath. I'd spent so long hating Sky for betraying me.

Me: *You're telling me she was forced?*

Eve: *Get here as fast as you can.*

Me: *I'm coming.*

I wanted to throw my phone across the goddamn room.

While I was reeling, Lexi asked quietly, "So, your ex is in danger? She didn't leave on purpose? What does that mean?"

I wobbled my head, numb. "That's... what it sounds like. If the mob blackmailed her, she might've had no choice." My voice sounded as hollow as a felt.

Lexi's eyes flickered with hurt. "Isn't Eve also your ex?" She emphasized the name.

"Yeah, I told her to let me know what she found out."

Lexi blinked like she couldn't believe I had any contact with my ex. Until the other day, I hadn't. "Eve said, *your wife*. Are you still married?" she asked, her voice rising.

I hesitated, forcing myself to meet her gaze. "Legally, under our old fake IDs from Alaska, yeah. Savannah Black and Owen Black are still married. But we aren't those people anymore."

She chewed on her lip. Then she rose from the bed, gathering her clothes. She didn't say a word, just disappeared into the bathroom. The door shut, and I heard the lock click, a quiet finality in the sound.

Fuck. I wanted to chase after Lexi, explain, but I couldn't. What the hell would I even say?

I yanked on my jeans, my mind churning with guilt and confusion. I still cared about Sky, even if I tried to bury it. But Lexi... Lexi was the one I wanted, the one I loved, or damn close to it. After everything I'd been through, she was the fresh start I never believed I'd get.

Lexi exited the bathroom fully dressed, with her bag slung over her shoulder. She avoided looking at me, but I caught the shimmer of unshed tears in her eyes. I wanted to hold her, to promise this wouldn't ruin us, but I sensed she wasn't ready to hear it. Instead, I jammed my shit into my saddlebag, muttering curses under my breath.

"I'm taking you back to the clubhouse," I finally said. "You'll be safe there. I have to go to Nashville."

She gave a stiff nod. "Okay."

"It doesn't change anything between us," I tried, hating the desperation in my tone. "You're mine, Lexi. And I'm getting to the bottom of who put a target on you."

She dropped her eyes. "What about your wife?" she whispered.

I had no answer for that. Instead, I tightened my jaw and led the way out, checking out of the lodge in stony silence. We rode back to the Road Monsters MC compound, under storm clouds. I could feel her clinging to me, but not with the same warmth as before. It was a duty now, not an embrace of trust.

At the clubhouse, I helped her off my Harley. She kept her helmet pressed to her chest, her gaze distant. Neither of us were speaking after the long ride.

"I'll call you," I mumbled.

She just nodded, blinking fast. My gut twisted as I turned and revved the engine, tearing out of there before I changed my mind.

Fuck. I was messing everything up. But I had to see what the hell was going on with Sky, especially if she was behind the threat to Lexi.

The highway to Nashville blurred under my wheels, my thoughts cycling through old memories of Sky's laughter, the miscarriage we endured, the day she vanished. And now Lexi, the woman who let me into her life, and her body, despite all the danger.

How the fuck do I fix this?

CHAPTER 33

I hit the city by nightfall, ignoring the pang in my chest. The lights of Broadway felt like a neon prison. I texted Eve from my burner phone, letting her know I was in town. Her reply came quick:

Eve: *I'm at Bootsie's. Out back in the alley.*

A place I knew well, too well. Where Eve and I first met. I parked my Harley on a side street. This was all too familiar, like some twisted time loop.

I slipped into the alley behind the bar, expecting to see Eve's blonde hair. Instead, I found Kingpin, tall, imposing, black beard, and that ridiculous looking fringe jacket. Not to mention, he bristled with quiet rage. He wasn't alone. With his red hair, Irish stood to one side, cracking his knuckles, and Villain lurked in the shadows, knife glinting in his belt. Man looked like Prince Charming but was pure evil.

Shit. Before I could bail, Kingpin lunged, fingers crushing my throat against the alley wall.

He sneered. "What the hell are you doin' in my wife's phone, Pig?"

I gagged, vision flashing red. "Eve, texted, me," I choked.

Kingpin let go enough for me to gasp.

"Let's just say my wife lost her phone. I found your number in it, decided to see if you'd show. You just can't stay away, can you?" He was snarling. "You think I was born yesterday?"

I coughed, rubbing my bruised throat. "Where's Eve? You said..."

"She's not here," he snarled. "I needed to know if you were meeting her for some other reason. Or about *Sky*." He paused, studying my face.

"Of course, it's about Sky," I strangled out.

"Turns out it is, so that checks out," he admitted, letting my neck go.

"The stuff about her being blackmailed... is it real or not?"

He finally let me stand properly, stepping back. "Oh, it's real all right. Her mom claims Sky's the one who lured Grinder into killin' Dirty Diana. Says she wanted to get our attention."

"Fuck, she got our attention, all right. What about Diana's daughter?"

"Getty's daughter, you mean. Apparently, the mobster had a secret. He'd been taking care of Diana and her daughter all these years. Ralph got rid of his uncle and his cousin but didn't know there was anyone else standing in his way until he got into Alexander's files."

"Did Sky know that you got me involved?"

Biker's hand twisted his neck. "No clue. But Diana was running her mouth on me, too, remember. Why I got involved in the first place. Anyone hearing her talk about me would know, I'd want to shut that whore's mouth. Her and I weren't exactly on good terms any more. Maybe they planned to blame Diana's death on me."

"But if Sky's been forced to stay with Ralph..." I started, trying to connect dots.

"Could be Ralph is blackmailing her. Could be she's tired of him. Or maybe she's screwing us all over. Who the hell knows?" Kingpin belted out in frustration.

I ground my teeth. "If there's a chance Sky's in danger, we gotta help her."

Kingpin barked a laugh. "We don't know if she's in danger. Sky's a fuckin' nutcase. She might be playing us. The only reason I'm not killing you on sight is because of your old ties to her. That, and maybe she's telling the truth about needing out. And this is a favor to Maddie, not you, not Sky... But we can't risk the Syndicate starting a war in Nashville, either. So, if she wants to run, you gotta take her somewhere else. She can't be near *my* wife or my kids. That's final."

"So, Eve doesn't know?"

Kingpin narrowed his eyes. "That's none of your goddamn business."

Relief and anger surged through me as I processed his proposal. "Fine. Let's do it."

He motioned Irish and Villain to stand down, then lowered his voice. "We already got a plan. Maddie, Sky's mom, arranged a meeting tomorrow. My men will snatch Sky, see if she wants out. If she's serious, we'll bring her to you. Then you take her wherever the hell you want. Out of state. Out of my hair. I'm washing my hands of the woman."

My guts roiled. Take her where, the same place as Lexi? The same place my new woman is holed up with heartbreak? I swallowed. "All right."

He eyed me, crossing his arms. "You sure you're not still sweet on her? Because if you are, I don't want you half-assing it. You can't trust her. This is about business now."

I pressed my teeth together. "Don't worry. I'll handle it."

Kingpin smirked. "Good. We'll see. You better not let your dick do the thinking. You got a new girl, right? I heard the chatter about you and Diana's daughter. Hope she's not like her mom. Woman couldn't keep her mouth or her legs shut."

Rage and embarrassment flashed through me. "Shut the fuck up, Kingpin."

He grinned, but it didn't reach his eyes. "We're done here. Let's grab a drink."

I muttered curses but followed him inside the bar to hash out final details over some expensive Tennessee whiskey, on him. My head was about to explode.

We made the plan. Sky would meet Maddie at a diner off I-65. Kingpin's men would watch from unmarked vans. If Sky showed signs of wanting out, Maddy would give a signal, and Villain and Irish would intercept her. But I would be the one to take her away. No reuniting with Kingpin, no returning to Nashville. Ralph Getty and the Music City Syndicate would tear the state apart if they realized we had her. We had to move fast.

The next morning, I parked behind a rundown gas station near that diner. I felt queasy remembering I'd left Lexi behind in Kansas.

She was alone and hurting while I tried to figure out if my ex needed rescuing. And Lexi wasn't taking my calls. However, I knew from talking to Sarge she was still at the Road Monster's clubhouse, though. Safe and sound.

Fucking hell. But if this was the only way to save Sky and Lexi, I had to do it.

Villain kept me posted over text. Sky arrived in a black SUV, stepped out, and approached Maddie. But they went inside to eat. Not until they finished and stepped out did Maddie flash a peace sign, the signal. Irish and Villain swooped in, cornering them in an empty lot. I lingered, nervous as hell, until Villain called me over, meaning she wasn't resisting.

I found Sky pinned near a dumpster, Maddie off to the side, looking terrified. Sky's eyes locked on mine. She looked older, harder. Fuck, it hadn't even been a year. There was a flicker of relief in her gaze.

"Hallow," she breathed. "You're here. Finally."

I swallowed, forcing a nod. "Yeah. If you want out, I'll help you."

She looked at Maddie, tears gathering. "I've been blackmailed by Ralph. He threatened my child. I had no choice. I had to keep you away, so he wouldn't hurt little Ralph."

"Little Ralph?"

"You think Ralph will let his son be called Bo or Caden?" she said, explaining the child now had a third name.

Caden. I'd tried hard not to think of the kid I'd been raising with her as my own when she up and left me, taking him with her. "Where is he?"

"Still with Ralph and the family. Adam," she called me my real name. "Ralph will never let him go. Our son is lost to his real father. But I can't take it anymore."

A tangle of guilt and anger coiled in my gut. So maybe she never truly left me by choice. I tried to keep a blank face from the emotions that were giving me whiplash. "Then come with me. We'll figure it out."

Sky didn't argue. She just sobbed once, then threw her arms around me. I stiffened, memories flooding back. I was totally confused.

Lexi, I'm sorry, I thought silently, stepping away from Sky.

We hurried to my Harley, ignoring Maddie's sobs. She would stall anyone who came looking. If Ralph's men showed, Irish and Villain would handle it. I gunned the engine, and Sky hopped on, her arms around my waist like old times. It was like a dream. Or a nightmare. I was a bit fuzzy on the difference. Shaking, she buried her face in my back.

Then I tore out of there, heading north, away from Tennessee, away from the chaos. My mind spun with old regrets, longing, and raw fury at Ralph. If he truly blackmailed her, forced her to leave me, fuck him. I wished him dead. But overshadowing all that was Lexi's face, her tearful eyes when she had asked about my "wife."

Damn it. Her safety was my responsibility, too. I saved Sky, but was it nostalgia, guilt, or love? Couldn't say.

I rode for hours, Sky silent when we stopped briefly, except for her soft, uneven breathing. Every mile brought me closer to Kansas and Lexi. But how the hell could I explain it?

Hey, princess, this is my ex, the one I used to plan a future with, who might or might not still love me. I felt sick. *My ex, who set your mom's murder into motion, all to get my attention.*

But I had no other option. Kingpin had made it clear. Sky couldn't stay in Tennessee, not with the mob breathing down everyone's necks. My old illusions about Sky's betrayal lay in ruins, replaced by something more complicated. If she'd been forced to leave me. That meant I never gave her a chance. I never once doubted her leaving, but on her own accord. Fuck, I'd abandoned her too.

And where did that leave Lexi, the woman who just gave me her virginity, who was now reeling from the news?

The horizon stretched before me like a question I had no answers for. Sky clung to me, her tears soaking into my cut. And all I could do was grit my teeth, tear up the asphalt, and pray that I could salvage something out of this nightmare without losing Lexi in the process.

CHAPTER 34

Lexi

I could practically feel the storm brewing the moment they rode up to the clubhouse gates. After all the heartbreak and chaos, the last thing I expected was to see Maverick and Sky rolling in together. Yet there they were, her arms wrapped around his waist on his Harley, dust swirling around them as they rumbled onto the gravel lot of the Road Monsters MC compound in Kansas.

My heart twisted with a combination of dread and anger. Just days ago, I'd given Maverick my virginity, trusting him with my body and soul. Now he had arrived with his wife, the woman he'd once told me had left him, but apparently was still legally tied to him, or some version of him. I'd tried to remain calm, to remind myself that he'd gone to help her only because she was in danger. But seeing them together, leaning so close, nearly broke me all over again.

I stood at the edge of the clubhouse yard, arms crossed tight over my chest. My chest felt void. *So, this is it,* I thought bitterly. He rescued her, after all. Good for him. All around us, bikers milled about, some shifting in curiosity, others watching for a potential fight. After all, the MC had reason to be on guard. While Maverick was gone, I learned one of the reasons the bikers had been so weird about me being here was because they knew I had a target on my back. My presence was putting them all in danger.

Maverick killed the engine. In that fleeting moment of silence, he looked around, his gaze scanning for me. He found me near the steps of the porch and dismounted, helping Sky off the bike. Even from a distance, I noticed the way his hands lingered protectively at her waist. A knife of jealousy twisted in my chest.

I tried to harden my expression. *Don't let him see you cry, Lexi.* But when his eyes locked on mine, I saw a flicker of guilt cross his face. Sky looped her arm around his, her features still drawn with what might've been worry or exhaustion. Her dark hair was pulled back, revealing a scarred face. *What had happened to her?* I gasped at the sight. She was so thin, her face sunken in. She looked... used up, like someone stuck a straw in and sucked out whatever had been inside. But also she was, one hundred percent, intimately connected to my biker in a way that made me feel like an outsider all over again. What was worse, the tattoo on his arm, of a beautiful sad woman had come to life.

Sarge, standing nearby with a watchful glare, cleared his throat. "You're back," he rumbled to Maverick, tone flat. "And you brought... company."

Maverick nodded. "Yeah. We had some trouble on the road. I need to keep her here for a bit, Sarge. Just until we figure out the next move."

"And who is she?" Sarge asked, eyeing him with suspicion.

"My wife," Maverick said simply, his voice so cold.

Sarge's gaze flicked to me and then to Sky. "Huh. If you say so. Better keep a tight leash, brother. The rest of the club ain't exactly fans of extra drama."

Maverick just grunted in acknowledgment. He exchanged a few clipped words with Sarge that I couldn't quite make out, and then he started toward the clubhouse door, Sky in tow. My place, effectively... because he'd put me here, told me I was safest in these walls. Now he expected me to share the space with his wife?

A swirl of anger bubbled up, forcing me to close my eyes and inhale slowly. Stay calm. Listen. But I couldn't quell the ache in my chest. Before I could approach them, Maverick gently deposited Sky on a bench by the side entrance and said something in a low tone. She nodded, leaning her head back against the wood. He rubbed her shoulder, whispered something. My stomach clamped so hard I thought I might be sick.

At last, Maverick seemed to make up his mind and strode over to me. I stiffened, refusing to budge, even though every nerve screamed at me to run away or maybe to fling myself at him. This biker had turned my world upside down. His dangerous world had killed my mother, but he had forced me to realize I could love... love him, an outlaw biker, man from my fantasies. And then he'd left for reasons I tried to understand but cut me deeper than I'd ever experienced.

He stopped a couple of feet away, close enough that I could smell the leather and dust on him. "Lexi," he hissed.

I looked up, hating how my heart sped at his voice. "Maverick," I answered, my tone clipped.

He swallowed hard. "I'm sorry. I know this is a mess."

I let out a brittle laugh. "A mess? That's an understatement. I thought you were in love with me," I almost screamed. "I gave you everything, and now you show up with her."

His eyes flicked with pain. "She's in danger. She needed a place to hide."

"She's your wife." I spat the word. "You never mentioned that before."

He opened his mouth, then closed it, a muscle ticking in his jaw. "Technically, on paper, yeah, but we separated a long time ago. It's complicated."

"And that's supposed to make it, okay?" My voice cracked. "You told me you were done with her."

"I was. But... I can't just let her die, Lexi. She's got a kid. I care about him, too. Ralph threatened him."

"Of course," I muttered, cutting him off. "Naturally, we're adding a child to this fiasco. Why not? Is it yours?"

"No. Lexi," he pleaded, reaching for my arm. I jerked away. "I'm not abandoning you. I swear. I just... had to do what was right."

I stared at him, tears stinging my eyes, half from anger, half from heartbreak. "Do whatever you want. I'm nobody to you, apparently."

"That's not true," he growled. "You're mine."

I nearly laughed in his face. "Am I? Because it sure looks like she's yours, too. Bet if I stripped her down, we'd have matching tattoos." Without waiting for him to respond, I spun on my heel and stormed into the clubhouse. My chest felt like it was ripping open.

Damn him. If he wanted to say more, he'd have to chase me down, but I doubted he would, given how he needed to comfort his precious ex.

Over the next hour, I paced around the common area, uncertain if I was angry or devastated. Bikers came and went, some casting curious glances my way, but I ignored them. Eventually, I caught sight of Maverick leading Sky deeper into the building, presumably to talk privately or to set her up like he did me. She still looked shaky, gripping his arm for support. I wouldn't feel sorry for her. I couldn't.

Something in me snapped. I followed at a distance, determined to see what was really going on. They turned down a side hallway leading to a small office-like room used for storing documents or MC records. I inched closer, pressing my back to the wall just outside the door.

I heard muffled voices. *Should I do this?* Probably not. But I needed to know the truth. I inched closer until I could make out their words.

Sky, her voice quaked: "Thank you for bringing me here. I... I didn't know if you would, after everything."

Maverick, so softly: "Yeah, well, guess I'm still a damn fool. Why didn't you tell me before now you were forced to leave? You let me believe you just hated me."

Sky: "Ralph threatened to kill my child if I didn't leave you. If I didn't help in his scheme to seize power. I swear, I never wanted to. But then... then I figured you moved on, or wouldn't believe me, or... with everyone involved that got hurt, like Eve. I was scared. I was scared Kingpin would kill me for my involvement. Ralph promised he could keep me safe."

Maverick, a pause, harsh exhale: "We lost our baby, we were at each other's throats. I thought you hated me, Sky. Maybe I hated you, too. So, when you left, I believed it. When we rescued you before, I had hope. When I saw you killed Alexander Getty and watched you leave with Ralph, I hurt like I never had before. But now I find out it was all a lie."

Sky: "Maybe we can fix it now?"

She sounded so hopeful. My stomach dropped.

Sky: "I mean, I'm not asking you to pick me over... her... but we share so much history. I love you. I never stopped loving you, Adam.

She called him his real name, his middle name. Hearing that intimacy about killed me. He didn't say anything.

Sky: "I just want a safe place, maybe a chance to start fresh."

Maverick: "I won't abandon her right now."

Right now?

Sky: "I understand. It's just... God, seeing you again... I'm sorry, baby."

Her voice wavered, like she might be crying.

Maverick: "Shhh, it's all right. You're safe now."

A lump formed in my throat. This was worse than I imagined. He *did* care for her, deeply. Or at least felt some sense of duty. I heard the rustle of fabric. Maybe him putting an arm around her.

Maverick, so softly: "I promise I'll protect you. Even if it kills me."

It was as if Maverick's words killed me dead. I couldn't listen anymore. My vision blurred with tears, and I pushed away from the wall, stumbling back into the main hall. He promised to protect me too, I thought bitterly. But apparently, Sky's safety trumped everything. A sob wrenched from my throat. I refused to cry in the hallway like some abandoned child. So, I did the only thing that made sense, I headed for the bar in the common room for a drink or maybe six.

CHAPTER 35

The bar area was already lively, a handful of bikers shooting pool, a couple more laughing over beers. The bartender was a redhead in her late twenties who wore a battered Road Monsters' cut with a "Property of Taz" patch on the front. As I came closer, she glanced up, polishing a glass.

Her eyes flicked over me, picking up on my distress. "You look like you've been run through the wringer," she commented, noticing my tears.

Sniffing, I forced a laugh. "You have no idea. Give me something strong. Whiskey. Neat."

She set the glass aside, nodding. "Sure, honey." She poured a generous shot, sliding it over. "Name's Pep."

"Lexi," I replied, tossing back the whiskey in one gulp. It burned down my throat, but I welcomed the distraction.

"Easy there," Pep remarked, arching a thin red brow. "You keep chugging like that, you'll be on your ass in no time."

I shrugged. "Better than... dealing with *this*."

She didn't ask for details. Instead, she poured me another shot, slower this time. "I get it. Sometimes you gotta numb the pain. God knows I did when I first hooked up with Taz. Man's an ass half the time, and he can't keep it in his pants, but God I love him." She laughed. "I know all about you. Apparently, Maverick and you gave him quite the show the other night. After he got that ink in you, he was aching to get into me."

"Maverick," I repeated his name with distaste.

"What's your story, if you don't mind me asking?"

I watched the amber liquid, swirling it absently. "I fell for a biker. Then his ex shows up, his wife, and I find out he's still got feelings for her. Now I'm stuck here, watching them cling to each other while I... lose my mind."

She nodded sagely, leaning on the bar. "Biker life can be a real bitch. I was an army brat, you know. My dad drank himself to death, my mom ran off. I swore I'd never depend on a man. Then I met Taz, and next thing you know, I'm wearing his patch, running this compound with him. Not a month goes by that I don't have to run off one of his ex whores." She sighed, but there was a fond smile in her eyes. "Point is, it's messy. Always is, especially with old flames and clubs in the mix."

I sipped this time, letting the warmth settle. "Yeah. Messy is an understatement."

Pep studied me. "You love him?"

I hesitated, then gave a pained nod. "Yeah. God help me, I do," I said, channeling her words.

She patted my hand. "Then hold your ground or walk away. Those are your only real choices in the biker world. Standing in the middle will tear you apart."

Her words hit me like a punch to the gut. "I... guess you're right."

Hold your ground or walk away.

Music cranked up on the old jukebox, some hard rock track that rumbled through the bar. A few bikers started hollering, pulling random girls, friends or club girls, onto the makeshift dance floor in the corner. I watched them, finishing my whiskey. A strange numbness flooded me. Why not let loose? I can't do anything else right now.

I shoved the glass at Pep. "Another, please."

She narrowed her baby blue eyes. "You sure?"

"Positive."

She poured, and I drank, letting the burn dissolve my heartbreak. Before long, a haze of alcohol blurred my edges. I found myself drifting toward the dancing crowd. A tall biker with a shaved head beckoned me over, grinning. His name patch read Dogma. Normally, I'd have avoided a tough looking guy like him, one covered in gold chains, looking like he stepped off the cover of a gangsta rap album, but tonight, I didn't care. Bad boys were apparently my thing now. The biker was as gorgeous as Maverick, in his own way. Hell, I needed an escape from the pain stabbing my heart.

Dogma placed a hand on my waist, spinning me into a clumsy dance. My cheeks flushed at the closeness, but I forced myself to smile, ignoring the voice in my head screaming that Maverick might see. Let him, I thought. He had Sky, so why couldn't I have a harmless dance?

We stumbled to the heavy beat, Dogma's hands slipping lower than I liked. I shot him a warning look, but I was too buzzed to articulate it. He laughed, leaning in. "You got a name, shorty?"

"Lexi," I mumbled, pushing his hand up a bit. "Keep it above the belt, buddy."

He chuckled. "She bites."

Then I heard an all-too-familiar snarl behind me. "Get your fucking hands off her."

My heart lurched as I turned to see Maverick standing there, fists clenched, rage blazing in his eyes.

Dogma smirked, keeping his hold on my waist just to provoke him. "Who you think you're talkin' to?"

"I'm the man who's gonna break your jaw if you don't back off," Maverick growled.

I felt an odd thrill at his jealousy, but also a swell of fury. He dares to be possessive now? After comforting his wife in front of me?

Dogma shrugged. "Didn't know you pissed on this one. She lookin' mighty hard up. She came to Dogma, probably because she heard this long dick will set her right."

Maverick lunged, grabbing Dogma's cut. Dogma responded by shoving Maverick's chest. Within a heartbeat, a scuffle broke out, fists flying, curses echoing. Several onlookers rushed to intervene. My pulse roared with panic. Oh God. I stumbled back to avoid the swinging arms.

"Stop it!" I shouted, but they ignored me. Maverick socked Dogma in the jaw, sending him sprawling into a table. Dogma spat blood, anger flashing, and tackled Maverick around the waist. Chairs crashed. The music cut off abruptly as someone yanked the jukebox plug. Bikers crowded around, some cheering, others yelling to break it up.

At last, Taz and Pep jumped in, along with Sarge, dragging the two men apart. Maverick's lip bled, and Dogma sported a bruised cheek.

"Cool it, assholes!" Sarge barked. "We don't need this shit right now." He shot me a glare, like I was partly to blame for the commotion.

Maverick shook Taz off, stepping toward me. His chest heaved, his anger pouring off him.

"What the fuck, Lexi?" he hissed, voice trembling with rage. "You letting random bikers touch you now?"

I bristled, matching his glare. "You got a problem with that? I thought you had your hands full with *Sky*."

He wiped blood from his mouth, eyes flashing. "Don't you bring her into this."

"Why not?" I snapped, thrusting a finger at his chest. "You brought her here. You told me you loved me, then come waltzing in with *your wife*. You have zero right to act jealous."

The room went silent like I had committed some crime. Some people drifted away, muttering about not wanting to witness personal drama.

Maverick exhaled, shoulders sagging. "Lexi, it's not like that."

"It sure looks like *that*," I said, voice quavering. Tears threatened to fall. "When you find me dancing, you lose your shit. But you're comforting your wife, promising to keep her safe. What am I supposed to think?"

He tried to reach for me, but I stepped back. "Damn it, Lexi, you're mine. I told you that. I can't let you throw yourself into another man's arms, especially not some random asshole."

"Says the man who spent half the day hugging *Sky*, whispering sweet nothings," I fired back. "You can't have it both ways."

His eyes darkened. "She needed me. She's in danger."

I let out a sharp laugh, ignoring the curious stares from the remaining onlookers. "And I'm not? I almost got killed. My mother *did* get killed. And yet you run off to save your precious wife while leaving me behind. Then you bring her into my safe space and expect me to just... *accept* it?"

He opened his mouth, nothing coming out. Finally, he rasped, sounding exhausted, his anger draining. "I'm trying to protect everyone. You don't understand."

"Get out," I said firmly, swallowing the sob threatening to rise. "Just... get out of my sight. I can't deal with you right now."

Pain flickered in his expression. He hesitated, as if he might fight me on it. But something in my eyes must have convinced him. He turned and stalked away, shoulders tight, blood still trickling from his split lip. My chest felt too tight to breathe.

I barely remembered stumbling back to my room. I locked the door, leaning against it, tears streaming silently. This entire world was too chaotic. Bikers, wives, blackmail, mob hits... *I'm done.* I just wanted to vanish.

But Maverick was waiting for me. He was in the room, and he had a belt in his hands. "How dare you disrespect me in front of my brothers."

My eyes darted to the belt. "What the hell do you think you're going to do with that?"

Twisting me around, he had my arms bound behind my back in a flash. I guess he was a cop before, but I was still shocked.

Maverick pressed my face against the door, whispering into my ear. "You're mine, and you'll respect that fact in this clubhouse and out." His hands ran down my body. I could feel his erection hard against my ass. And he reached around, started to undo my jeans.

Was this supposed to turn me on? I started crying. Hard and fast tears fell.

Maverick let go of me like I was on fire. He backed off and had me untied just as fast as it happened. "I'm sorry, Lexi. I never. I just wanted to make it up to you."

"Just go be with Sky. She needs you," I cried out.

"Fuck that," he roared.

But I turned from him. "Just leave," I shouted.

He unlocked the door and slammed it behind him.

With trembling hands, I yanked out my phone and dialed Nova. It rang twice before she answered.

"Lexi? It's past midnight. What's going on?" Her voice was groggy.

I pressed a hand to my mouth, trying not to cry. "Nova, I'm... the biggest fool. I left everything to hide here, ended up losing my virginity to a biker who was married the whole time. He's with her right now, in the same place. She's... she's basically never leaving. I can't do this."

"Whoa, slow down." Nova's tone sharpened. "He's *married*? I thought you said he was divorced or separated."

I let out a shuddering breath. "It's complicated. Either way, I can't stand it anymore. I need out. Will you come get me? Take me to your place in Texas or anywhere that's *not* here."

Nova paused. "Chigger's around. I can ask him to help. We can drive up tomorrow night if you need. You sure this is what you want?"

"Yes," I whispered, tears burning my cheeks. "I can't stay here, watching him with her. Just... please hurry."

Nova agreed without hesitation, promising to call me back with logistics. I hung up. *Good.* I just needed to survive one more day, then I'd be free of this heartbreak. *I'm done waiting for a man who can't decide between me and his wife.*

That night, I barely slept. Every time my eyelids fluttered shut, I saw Maverick's anguished face, remembered his touch, the way he'd made me feel so secure and cherished. Now it all felt like a lie. So I tossed, turned, and cried until exhaustion claimed me.

I didn't leave my room the whole next day, drinking water from the faucet in the bathroom. Maverick banged on the door, he texted, he called, but I wouldn't show my face. I blocked his number.

"I can hear you breathing, Lexi. That's good enough for me," he would say through the door. "I'm sorry," he repeated over and over, but I blocked him out.

I didn't leave until I got the word from Nova. True to her word, she rolled up with Chigger in the late hours, using a battered pickup to avoid drawing attention. I'd quietly packed my few belongings, sneaking through the clubhouse halls while most of the bikers were busy partying or off duty. I didn't see Maverick or Sky anywhere. Fine by me.

Chigger was at the wheel, and he gave me a nod. "Let's go, girl. Don't need any drama."

Nova got out and hugged me tight, eyes filled with sympathy. I felt a pang of guilt at bailing on the MC, but I reminded myself, I owed them nothing. Maverick made it clear where his priorities lay.

We snuck out, slipping past the dozing prospect at the gate. My heart pounded, expecting Maverick to appear, to fight for me. He never did. *So that's that.*

I climbed into the back seat, letting the truck rumble off into the darkness. Each mile away from the clubhouse felt like a weight lifting, but also a crack forming in my heart. By the time we crossed into the next state, tears silently streamed down my cheeks.

"I'm so sorry, Lex," Nova murmured as she turned and placed a comforting hand on my arm. "It'll be okay. You'll crash at my place until you figure out your next step. Maybe go back to work, normal life."

"Yeah," I whispered. "Normal life."

But deep down, I wondered if any normalcy could erase the memory of Maverick's kisses, his rough hands on my skin. *You'll be okay,* I told myself. *He's got his wife. You have your pride.*

It had to be enough.

CHAPTER 36

Maverick

I was awakened abruptly. My body still ached from my scuffle with my brother, Dogma, the other night. I groaned, sitting up on the small cot in the room I'd taken over after Lexi kicked me out. *Fuck*, my head pounded. I'd spent the night replaying our fight, drinking myself to death, cursing myself for being such a mess.

Finding out Sky still loved me didn't do anything to erase my love for Lexi. As I fought with Lexi all day, I avoided talking more with Sky. I didn't know how I was going to handle that situation. I didn't want to break Sky's heart, but I wouldn't abandon Lexi for her, either. In my heart, my old memories with Sky battled my fresh times with Lexi, and Lexi won every time. But guilt gnawed at me. I didn't love Sky like I loved Lexi, not anymore. It wasn't her fault, but it was the truth.

The sound that woke me grew louder. Shouting and boots pounding on concrete became clearer. I heard Sarge's voice bellowing in the hallway. "Mobsters! Fuckers at the damn gate! Everyone, arms up!"

Grinder. The name shot through my mind like a bullet. He was the bastard who'd killed Diana for Getty. Now, apparently, he'd tracked Lexi to the Kansas clubhouse. I grabbed my gun from the nightstand, shoving aside the blanket, ignoring the sharp protest in my ribs. Fear lanced me. Lexi. If Grinder's men were here for her, that meant they wanted her dead for being Alexander Getty's heir.

As I stepped into the corridor, chaos erupted. The clubhouse was crawling with men wearing slacks, obviously not our typical biker rivals. Several of them brandished handguns, exchanging gunfire with Road Monsters with hunting rifles who were ducking behind pool tables or door frames. My survival skills kicked in full force.

I spotted Sarge crouched behind the bar, shouting directions at Taz and Tank. Shots rang out, wood splintered. "They're looking for the Getty girl!" Sarge hollered. "Where is she?"

I bolted into the main lounge, returning fire at two mobsters creeping in from the windows. Bullets whizzed overhead. Shit, this was a warzone.

In the midst of the smoke and shouting, I spotted a figure in the corner. Sky. My blood ran cold. She looked far too calm, standing amid the carnage. Our eyes met, and a twisted smile curled her lips. What the hell?

Suddenly, two goons advanced on me, so I dropped behind a sofa, firing at them. One went down, the other retreated, cursing. Gunpowder stung my nostrils. I risked a glance back at Sky. She was backing away from the chaos, heading for the side exit. What's she doing?

I dashed after her, weaving through overturned furniture. Bikers were hollering, some wounded. The mobsters kept pressing in from the doors, and I had to retreat. However, they seemed confused, likely expecting fewer opponents.

Where's Lexi? Fear gnawed at me. She had to be in her room. I reached the corridor leading to her quarters, only to find it empty. We'd argued, and she'd locked me out, but now the door was open. Strange. Maybe she's out front? I went to find out.

Suddenly, Sky stepped into my path, flanked by two armed men. My heart slammed. She wasn't cowering or begging for help. Instead, she looked triumphant.

"Sky, what the fuck?" I snarled, raising my gun. The two men aimed theirs back, so it was a standoff.

Her lips twisted. "I led my men right here," she said coldly.

Her men?

"Ralph wanted Diana dead once he found out she'd been extorting his uncle for two decades. But I told him the real threat is her daughter, Lexi. She's Alexander Getty's legitimate child, the only one who could threaten our son's inheritance. Sorry, but she has to die."

Rage exploded in my chest. She used me. "Kingpin was right. You played us?" My voice trembled with fury. "You let me believe you were blackmailed, that you needed rescuing."

She shrugged, eyes hard. "I *was* blackmailed... once. But it's different now. I made a choice. And I realized I can have more power at Ralph's side if Lexi is out of the picture for good. You made it too easy, bringing me here."

I ground my teeth. "You bitch," I spat. "You threatened Diana and started the rumors about her secrets, just to get Kingpin's attention. Why?"

She laughed. "I didn't do a damn thing to alert him or you. Diana got scared and started throwing Kingpin's name around, threatening to tell his secrets, hoping he'd save her. She put her trust in the wrong man."

"Now you're after Lexi?"

"And you're protecting her? You're as much as a fool as Kingpin."

"She's done nothing to you. She doesn't want your man or your shit life."

Sky laughed bitterly. "She *exists*. *She's blood*, Maverick. That's enough. We'll find her eventually and eliminate her."

Eliminate? I was struck by how cruel Sky'd become. My mind whirled. If Lexi was still inside, the mob would shoot her on sight. "Where is she?" I growled, trying to maintain composure. "Sky, if you've touched her..."

A bullet ricocheted off the wall near my head. One of Sky's men fired a warning shot. "Enough talk," he hissed. "Kill him, Boss?"

Sky hesitated. A ghost of old sentiment flickered in her eyes. "No," she said softly. "I owe him at least a mercy. Let's go." She jerked her head, and the two men flanked her as they retreated down the hall. Another wave of goons covered their escape, exchanging gunfire with Taz and Sarge.

I snarled, popping off two shots at the men who were covering her. One bullet grazed a mobster's arm, making him stagger. Before I could line up a fatal shot, a different thug fired, clipping my shoulder.

Pain seared through me, knocking me back. I cursed, pressing a hand to the bleeding wound. Fuck. Not again.

By the time I steadied my gun, Sky and her entourage had disappeared through the side exit. A wave of fury and betrayal surged. I should chase them... kill her for what she's done. But my vision blurred from the pain. The corridor raged with gunfire as more Road Monsters closed in.

Finally, after what felt like an eternity, the mob's assault fizzled. They must have realized Lexi wasn't here, that this was a dead end. The survivors retreated, leaving half the clubhouse in ruins. I collapsed against the wall, breathing hard. Taz rushed over, calling for help. My shoulder burned, blood trickling down my arm.

"Shit, Mav, you good?" Taz growled, crouching beside me.

I nodded weakly. "Just a graze." My mind spun with the terrifying revelation that Sky had orchestrated everything. "Where's Lexi?" I croaked, heart pounding. "Is she safe?"

Taz frowned. "She left. I saw her sneaking out with Nova and Chigger earlier. She's not here. You lucked out, brother."

Relief and sorrow flooded me. So she was gone, not caught in the crossfire. *Thank God.* But also... *She's gone.* She left me, didn't even say goodbye. Maybe she'd blocked my number, too, which explained why she wasn't answering.

I stumbled to my feet, pressing my palm to the wound. Sarge was yelling for men to gather the injured. A few bodies lay on the floor. Getty's who hadn't made it out alive. One of them jerked, but there was no saving him, his brains half out. I put a bullet in him as mercy, thinking about how Sky spared me.

The next time we met, I wouldn't repay the favor.

I pulled out my phone, ignoring the pain in my shoulder as Taz tried to patch me with a rough bandage. Dialing Lexi's number. *Call ended.* It didn't even go to voicemail, just a dead line. *She blocked me.* My lungs tightened.

I dialed Kingpin next, hands trembling with anger and heartbreak. He picked up on the third ring. "What?"

"Sky fucked us," I spat. "She led Getty's goons right to Lexi's location. Good thing Lexi already left, but half our guys are injured. Sky got away with the mob. She's not blackmailed. She's working with them."

Kingpin cursed, "Fucking wacko, bitch. I suspected she might be lying, but not to this extent."

I inhaled sharply. "Now I gotta find Lexi and fix this shit. Sky's on the loose, and she's gunning for Lex. You better watch your back, Kingpin. Sky might come for you and Eve, too."

He grunted. "If she tries, she'll find a bullet waiting. As for Diana's secrets on me, they probably died with her. No use shaking down the daughter any longer."

"You expect me to leave her for dead?"

"I never said that. You think I want Ralph Getty to win? You do what you need to do. Getty's true heir. Maybe she'll come in handy in the future."

"Fuck you, Kingpin. I won't let you use Lexi in your twisted game."

"Not even if it keeps her breathing? Keep me posted." He hung up abruptly.

I shut my eyes, letting Taz finish taping a makeshift bandage to my shoulder. My mind swam with guilt. Lexi had been right. I should've listened to her. I was a fool to trust Sky. I sank onto a broken chair, blood dripping down my torn sleeve. I might've just unleashed more hell on Lexi.

Shoving aside the agony, I stood. "Taz, get Pep to patch me up better. I gotta go find her."

He lifted a brow. "You're insane. You need rest."

I glared. "I'm not letting Lexi face this alone. The mafia is after her, and Sky's out there, after her. She has no clue how deep the threat runs."

He sighed, muttering curses, but complied. Ten minutes later, I left the clubhouse with a fresh bandage, my gun loaded, and my bike roaring. My shoulder screamed in protest, but I ignored it. Lexi had to be with Nova somewhere in Texas. That's where I'd start searching. I wouldn't rest until I found her, no matter how many states I had to cross. Because, by God, if she hated me forever or never forgave me, I still needed to keep her alive.

Hold on, princess, I thought, tears threatening to blur my vision. *I'm coming.*

CHAPTER 57

I roared into the sleepy suburban street just after sundown, my Harley echoing in the quiet Texas neighborhood. A thick knot pressed at the back of my throat. The house at the end of the cul-de-sac had its porch light on, a welcoming glow.

Nova's place. That's where Chigger said he'd taken Lexi, where she'd run to escape the drama of the clubhouse. He gave up the address after I threatened his life. I told myself I came here to protect her, to keep her from Sky's betrayal and Ralph's mob threats. But deep down, I knew I was here to beg forgiveness.

I could take her away, protect her. We could be together on the run. I was a nomad, and she could be my ol' lady. Live at the clubhouse in Kansas or another safe house. Maybe Lexi could do legal work for the club. It was perfect. I'd get rid of the threat and maybe we could have a real life together. Maybe I'd make a deal with Sky and Ralph. I knew Lexi would never want to be the head of a crime family. I was sure I had something they wanted. Like my knowledge about Kingpin's ties to the Road Monsters MC. But would I betray the old bastard that, despite our bad blood, was in my corner?

A plan forming in my head already, I parked along the curb behind Chigger's truck, noticing two unfamiliar vehicles up ahead, a big black SUV with tinted windows and a sleek foreign sedan that cost more than everything else. Reeking of money and danger, they stuck out like a sore thumb in this modest neighborhood.

No fucking way that was a coincidence.

I killed the engine and slid off, swallowing the pain from my freshly bandaged shoulder. The bullet graze from the shootout still throbbed, but the prospect of having Lexi again coated my nerves in steel.

Chigger emerged from behind a tall hedge, scowling. He wore his cut over a wrinkled Anthrax T-shirt, arms crossed.

"Brother," he said, glancing around. "You sure you wanna do this?"

I narrowed my eyes. "You know damn well why I'm here. Where's Lexi?"

He grimaced, eyes flicking toward the house. "Inside. But things got complicated. She's... not alone."

My gaze darted to the black SUV. "Syndicate?"

Chigger shook his head. "Not exactly. Or maybe. I... look, some suits came by. Lexi walked in with them. She's... dealing with 'em. That's all I know. You probably shouldn't go in there if you want to keep breathing."

The hairs on my neck prickled. Suits. In my world, that meant lawyers or high-powered mob types. Possibly both. "I don't care. She's in danger."

He stepped in front of me, tone urgent. "She's hammered out some arrangement or deal, man. She said she's done with the club bullshit, done with you, all of it. She's got lawyers, or some kind of fixers. They were all cozy in the living room earlier. I'm telling you, she's making a choice."

My jaw clenched. "I gotta talk to her. She doesn't know about the shootout. She doesn't know Sky was behind it." My voice nearly cracked. Sky, that lying snake. Anger flared at how I'd let her slither into my life again, risking Lexi in the process.

Chigger squeezed his eyes shut. "You sure? Because from where I'm standing, Lexi's had enough heartbreak. She's safe now, apparently, or about to be. Don't stick your dick in, man."

My nostrils flared. "Safe from who? The same mob that wanted her dead last week? That's bullshit, and you know it."

He shifted uncomfortably. "Hey, I'm on your side. But if you go in there guns blazing, you might screw up whatever negotiation she set up with these people. I guess they're some branch of the... I dunno, Marciano or something. Heard the name a few times."

Marciano. A name whispered in the underground, some cousin or affiliate of the bigger players like Ralph Getty. Otherwise known as Grinder. Man who had her mother killed. Man working for Sky. Fuck. My heart pounded as images of Lexi tangled with mobsters flashed in my mind. She wouldn't do that unless she saw no other way.

And maybe since she believed I'd chosen Sky over her. Maybe she felt forced to protect herself.

Pain forgotten, I gasped for air. "I can't just walk away."

Chigger studied me for a long moment, then sighed. "I figured you'd say that. Fine. But watch yourself. There's at least two goons in there, armed to the teeth. And some stiff in a fancy suit who's all up in Lexi's space. They've been inside for half an hour, talking shit I couldn't catch."

Jealousy flared at the thought of some man comforting Lexi. No. She's mine. I pushed past Chigger, ignoring his hissed protests. "Stay out here if you want. But I'm going in."

He spat on the ground. "Your funeral, brother."

I strode up the driveway, my boots scuffing on the concrete, the porch light gleaming off the black SUV's tinted windows. A silent threat, lurking. The sleek sedan's door was unlocked. I opened it to see some expensive bag on the passenger seat. Lawyer, probably. A wave of resentment brewed. Lexi was stuck dealing with these sharks because I'd failed to keep her safe.

No more waiting. I threw the front door open, stepping into a modest living room. The scent of air freshener and scented candles assaulted me. The overhead light was off, but I instantly spotted Lexi at the small kitchen table, back turned to me. She wore a skirt and a loose blouse, her hair up in a neat bun. Dressed like she's going to work. Even from behind, I could sense her fear.

Across from her sat two men, both in dark suits. One was broad-shouldered, buzz cut, probably a bodyguard type. The other looked older, graying temples, entitlement in his posture. But my gaze snapped to the man with his arm around her shoulders. A slick, handsome prick in a tailored suit, tie undone just enough to look casual. He was leaning in as Lexi quietly wept, signing something on a stack of papers.

My blood ran hot. That was my woman, and some asshole was touching her, comforting her. In one stride, I stepped forward, my voice echoing in the cramped space. "What's going on here?"

They all turned when I walked in. The older bodyguard type tensed, sliding a hand under the table. A flash of metal told me he was ready to draw a gun. The second goon, broad-shouldered, scowled, shifting as if to stand. The pretty-boy suit tightened his grip on Lexi's shoulder, and she stiffened.

"You should leave," the pretty boy said, voice smooth as oil. "You're not needed."

I ignored him, locking eyes with Lexi, who stared back through teary lashes. Her face was blotchy, heartbreak carved into every line. I felt sick. "Lexi," I said, "Are you okay? Why are these men here?"

She lifted her chin, trying to hide her tears. "I'm... I'm fine," she managed. But her voice trembled. "Everything is settled now." She gestured to the papers, hand shaking. "I'm signing a contract."

My hands curled into fists. "What contract?"

The older goon glowered, pushing his jacket aside to reveal a holstered pistol. A warning. But I was too furious to care. I took another step forward. "You can't do this, Lexi. You can't trust them."

The pretty-boy suit stood, moving around the table to block me. He was about my height, but thinner, with well-groomed hair and an expensive watch. She said his name.

Mark? That name from when she told me about her law firm stabbed my memory.

"You're not her attorney," Mark said coldly. "And you're certainly not her friend, from what I hear. This is a private legal matter. Everything's settled."

"A private legal matter involving Marciano, right?"

Lexi spoke up, voice thick with tears. "I agreed not to stake any claim to the Getty family empire, if Alexander Getty really was my father. Marciano and his associates will leave me alone. They'll keep me safe from Ralph. It's all here in writing." She gestured vaguely at the documents.

Safe from Ralph Getty and Sky, who'd just tried to kill her, but she didn't know that. The irony stung. "Grinder wants to use Lexi as leverage? Are you fucking insane?" I could protect her better than any mafia scumbag, if she'd let me. "Lexi, that's a lie. They'll never keep you truly safe. They'll twist this into controlling you. I can keep you safe."

The older goon cleared his throat, leaning forward. "We're not here to harm her. We have an arrangement with her law firm. Ms. Bryan is a valued employee," His tone dripped with condescension.

The pretty boy nodded, giving Lexi a side hug that made my stomach churn. "Yes, and once everything's processed, she won't need bikers or guns. She'll have corporate protection. She won't need to go anywhere." He winked, which nearly made me lunge across the table.

Lexi's eyes brimmed with fresh tears. She spoke softly, "Maverick, I can't keep running. I can't handle more shootouts, more betrayal. At least here, at home, in Texas and at Martin & Sons, I know what I'm dealing with."

My voice dropped to a growl. "I don't trust these men to keep you safe."

The older man stood, smoothing his suit jacket. "We'll manage Maverick, or whatever your name is now," he said, letting me know he knew who I was. A threat. "This is done. Good day." He gave Lexi a nod, then motioned to the other goon. They collected the papers with minimal fuss.

Lexi turned away, burying her face in the pretty boy's chest, sobbing softly. My gut twisted with rage and hurt. That bastard, Mark, stroked her hair, shooting me a smug look.

"Everything's settled," Mark said, his tone dripping with finality. "No more bikers or running. She can get her life back. She'll be at the office soon enough, right, Lexi?" He winked at her, trying to be charming. I was enraged at how close he was to her.

I wanted to throw the table aside, smash the pen, burn those fucking papers. But the guns under the suits' jackets told me that would end badly. And the haunted look on Lexi's face... Maybe I'd just make it worse.

A beat of silence lingered, then Lexi managed a whisper. "Thank you, Mark. And, thank you, Mr. Russo," she added, addressing the older goon. "I appreciate this."

Appreciate? These men killed her mother. She was handing over her freedom to some twisted mob-legal alliance, all because I couldn't protect her.

She didn't even look up from Mark's shoulder. The men at the table gathered their things, the pen, the contract. The older man's phone buzzed, and he muttered something about "Mr. Marciano expecting an update." They started out, and Mark angled Lexi with him, a protective arm around her.

Once they were out the door, Lexi's eyes met mine. "It's not all bad. They're paying me hush money. I'll be under their watch, not the Gettys. I can go back to my life, my job... maybe in a few days." She swallowed hard, blinking tears away. "You... you should go."

My pulse pounded so loud I could barely think. "Lex, you don't have to do this. If you come with me, I can help you."

She shook her head, a quiet sob escaping. "No more clubs. No more... us. I can't trust anything anymore. Especially you."

"Let me explain," I started, wanting to pour my heart out.

She held up her hand. "Don't you think you've caused enough trouble?" Her gaze flicked to my bandaged shoulder. "I see you're hurt. Another shootout, right? That's exactly why I can't do it."

A crushing weight settled in my chest. She was given up on me. The revelation nearly buckled my knees. I wanted to scream about Sky's betrayal, about how she'd set me up, how none of it was my intention. But the fear in Lexi's eyes told me I was too late. She believed I was responsible for her heartbreak, and maybe I was.

"Lexi, you wear my brand, remember?"

She shrugged. "It served its purpose. I can get it removed, remember?"

I wanted to drop to my knees and tell her Sky deceived me again. That she was simply leading the mob to Lexi to kill her. But I swallowed the words. I couldn't admit I put her in so much danger. Especially in front of her hero, Mark. And if I told her I wasn't with Sky, would it even change anything? Instead, I nodded stiffly. "If you're safe, that's all that matters," I forced out, bitterness coating every word. "I'll... I'll be on my way, then."

"I'll see him out," Mark said coolly, jerking his chin at me. He was acting like he owned the place.

Lexi gave a trembling nod, wiping her eyes. "Maverick..." Her voice cracked. Then she just trailed off, turning away, letting Mark guide her further into the kitchen. My entire chest seized as he positioned her safely away from me, like he thought I might grab her and run away.

I wouldn't lie. The thought had crossed my mind.

Mark escorted me to the front door, stepping onto the small porch. Outside, one goon lit a cigarette, leaning against the big SUV. The other opened the driver's side door, talking quietly into his phone. Mark turned to me, arms folded. I noticed the flicker of triumph in his eyes.

"You see," he said softly. "Lexi's in good hands. She doesn't need your brand... of justice anymore."

My jaw was clamped shut. "You might think you're saving her, but these mob connections aren't a guarantee of safety. If you or these suits hurt her, if Marciano pulls some shit, I'll kill you." My voice trembled with barely leashed rage.

He gave a thin smile. "Maybe you don't know who I am. Mark Martin, of Martin and Sons. The, Matthew Martin's son."

I snorted. "Who's he, the Pope? I don't give a goddamn. You're no one in my world. You hurt her and you'll be dead."

He smirked. "I wouldn't hurt her or lie to her like some lowlife thug." He was digging at me. "She's a valuable asset to the firm. We look after our own. And Marciano finds her... interesting. But that's not your concern. She's out of the Getty crosshairs now. That's the best outcome, right?"

I studied him, hating every inch of that smug face. "She's more than an asset. She's a woman who's been through hell. Keep that in mind. And watch your back. I'll be watching you."

He shrugged. "Don't worry. I'll take good care of her, better care than you did, apparently." He stepped closer, voice dropping. "She's done with bikers, but if you come around messing up her arrangement, you'll just drag her deeper into trouble. Get her killed. Think about that."

My fists clenched. Chigger hovered a few yards away, eyes flicking between me and Mark, ready to intervene if I lost my shit. I forced a measured breath. "If I hear a whisper that she's in danger, from you, from Marciano, from anyone, I'll come back and burn your entire operation to the ground. You got that?"

Mark's expression stayed cold, but a flicker of caution showed in his eyes. "Understood. Let's hope it doesn't come to that. For her sake."

With that, he turned and strode back inside, presumably to rejoin Lexi. My chest ached, imagining him wiping her tears. That should be me. But apparently, my world had no place in her life anymore.

I glanced at Chigger, who exhaled a long breath. "You done here, brother?"

I nodded slowly, hands trembling at my sides. "Yeah, I guess I am."

"Wanna blow off some steam? We could knock that stiff's teeth in," Chigger suggested grimly.

I declined with a headshake. "She'd hate me more. Doesn't matter. She's safe, or so they claim."

Chigger grimaced, glancing at the SUV. "You buying that?"

My mouth twisted. "No. But if Lexi's decided she trusts them more than me, not much I can do." The words tasted like acid. "Let's get out of here."

He bowed, and we went back to our bikes. I felt like I was dragging my feet. I looked back once at the house, half-hoping to see Lexi run out after me. Of course, she didn't. The porch remained empty. The black SUV's door slammed, one of the goons climbing behind the wheel, a silent reminder that the mafia's tendrils had claimed her now.

My Harley roared, and I nearly cried. I lost her. She'd told me to my face, no more clubs, no more me. The distressing noise she made the other night when I tried to force her to be with me echoed in my ears. I couldn't make her hate me more than she already did. My heartbreak seared deeper than any bullet wound. But I couldn't force her to see reason. If she believed she was safer in the suits' arms, who was I to stop her? My entire life was a rolling disaster, and like every woman before her, Lexi wanted off the ride.

As we pulled away from the curb, the house lights faded in the rearview mirror, leaving me with a hollow ache in my chest. Sky tricked me. Lexi hates me. The Syndicate probably wants me dead. There was only one path left. Keep riding. Keep breathing. I'd lick my wounds and plan my next move.

I sped down the street, ignoring Chigger's concerned glances. The night wind slapped my face, but it couldn't numb the agony ripping apart my insides. You're free, Lexi, I thought bitterly. Free of me, free of this life. If that was what she truly wanted, I wouldn't stand in her way.

CHAPTER 58

Lexi

I stared at the battered Road Monsters' clubhouse, my heart in a knot after I slipped into Chigger's truck. Nova was already in the passenger seat, twisting around to watch me with concern. The engine idled, rumbling softly. I clutched my duffel bag tighter, nerves rattling like loose marbles in my gut.

I was done. Done with the violence, done with the heartbreak, done with the entire MC world. But leaving meant leaving him, and my heart couldn't decide which hurt more, staying in the same building as him and his wife, or walking away to protect my sanity.

A coil of anguish tightened in my chest, remembering the night we shared, the sweetness, the absolute surrender, our sweat drenched bodies. I understood every description in the erotic romance novels, even the poorly worded, cringy ones.

It was never hard to put into words how Maverick made me feel. He made me feel truly alive for once in my life. But even with all the passion lingering, it seemed like a lifetime ago. I was sneaking out with Chigger and Nova, running from danger and heartbreak all at once.

The moment Chigger put the truck in reverse, my pulse jumped. This was it. I was leaving the only place that tethered me to Maverick's world. Fear fluttered in my stomach, but then there was relief washing over me. I was doing the best thing.

We pulled onto a dusty road, the clubhouse fading in the side mirror. Silence thickened inside the cab. Nova tapped her foot anxiously, fiddling with the radio until static buzzed. She finally gave up, flicking it off. I hunched in the back, arms folded around myself, trying not to think of the dark haired biker who'd said he loved me but let his wife under the same roof where I was supposed to be safe.

Chigger cleared his throat. "So... we'll head south, drive through part of Oklahoma, cut across. Should get to Nova's place in Texas by morning if we rotate driving. I would drive the whole stretch, but we just made the trip up." He cast a glance at me through the rearview. "You cool with that, Lexi?"

I forced a nod. "Yeah. Thank you." My voice sounded vacant, even to my own ears. "I'll drive the whole thing if I have to."

Nova rotated in her seat. "You sure about this? We can find another route if you need to... I don't know, avoid certain highways."

I knew she was hinting at whether I needed to dodge potential dangers. The mob out to kill me. A numb chill spread through me. I would rather die than stay and see Maverick with another woman. "No, it's fine. Let's just go. The sooner we're out of here, the better."

No one argued. The truck lurched onto the highway, picking up speed. Soon, the Kansas plains stretched out, distant lights flickering. We fell into an uneasy silence, and I dozed intermittently, waking to the hum of passing vehicles, the glare of Truckstop lights, and my complicated emotions. Every time I jerked awake, the pain of betrayal stabbed me anew.

Maverick had called me his, claimed me as property, then turned around and whisked his wife, Sky, into the clubhouse saying he would protect her, *even if it killed him*. How could he? The memory made my chest ache so fiercely, I had to bite back tears.

By the time we reached Nova's neighborhood in Texas, the sun had climbed halfway up a pale sky, casting everything in a hazy glow. My head pounded from too little sleep and too many tears. She parked outside a modest one-story house with a small yard, potted plants on the porch. Nova sighed wearily.

"Home sweet home," she muttered, pushing open the passenger door.

I felt horrible that I hadn't drove at all. With the help of energy drinks, her and Chigger drove all night. I slid out, wincing at how stiff my legs were. The air was warmer than Kansas, thick with humidity. Chigger hopped down, stretching his arms with a grimace.

"I'll let you two settle in," he rumbled, hauling out the bags. "I'll be around, keepin' an eye out for trouble. The Syndicate or any one, they won't get close without me seeing."

Nova unlocked the front door. The interior was familiar, cozy, with mismatched furniture, a pile of laundry on the couch. She flicked on a fan, gesturing for me to sit. "Don't mind the mess, I wasn't expecting company. Or a meltdown."

I managed a tired smile, sinking into the worn cushions. This was better than the MC clubhouse, at least. The faint scent of coffee drifted as Nova resumed her typical morning routine. Meanwhile, Chigger lingered near the door, scuffing a boot on the floor.

"Hey," I said softly. "Thank you for helping me, both of you."

Nova gave a dismissive wave. "You're my best friend. Of course I'd help."

Chigger nodded. "Maverick's... well, he's complicated. I know you're upset, but he's not all bad."

My stomach churned. "He brought his wife around, Chigger. The same woman who... apparently tried to kill me? Or at least wanted me dead. Hard to keep track anymore."

His mouth opened, then shut, scowling. "I... yeah, I get it. Listen, I'm just sayin', no matter what, Mav is probably furious with me for helping you leave. But I'd rather have him pissed than you leave on your own, see you get whacked by the Syndicate."

Nova said, "I didn't want to think of you crying yourself to sleep while he's busy with Sky."

Pain flared in my chest again at the mention of it. "That's exactly what happened," I whispered. "He made me his property in the most humiliating manner. Feeling me up in front of that tattoo artist. Then turned around and brought his wife to the same damn place. I guess he thought I'd be okay with it. I wasn't."

Chigger grimaced. "For what it's worth, I'm sorry. If I'd known how messed up it was, I would've done... something. Said something to him."

Nova cleared her throat. "You did what you could, Chigger. Now go keep watch. We're safe inside. Lexi and I need some girl time, anyway."

He massaged the nape of his neck. "Sure. I'll be around. Holler if you need me." With that, he gave a curt wave, then slipped outside, presumably to keep an eye on the street.

At least one biker is looking out for me, I thought bitterly.

Nova shut the door, locking it. She turned, shaking her head in exasperation. "Men, huh?"

A broken laugh escaped me. "Right. Men."

"Bikers," she said, one upping me. Then she set about rummaging in the kitchen, calling over her shoulder, "You want ice cream or wine first? I have a feeling we need both."

I sank against the couch cushions, fatigue sapping my limbs. "Let's do both, together, if possible. Breakfast of champions."

Her face lit in a weary grin. "Got it."

Within minutes, she returned with two pints of ice cream, a half-empty bottle of cheap red wine, and a couple of mismatched spoons. We settled cross-legged on the rug, using the coffee table as a surface for the glasses.

I took a spoonful of chocolate ice cream, savoring the sweetness as it melted on my tongue. It dulled the bitterness inside me by a fraction. Nova poured us each a glass of wine, swirling it with the practiced ease of someone who'd faced heartbreak many times.

"So," she prompted gently. "Wanna really talk about it? Now that Chigger isn't listening."

A lump rose in my throat. "I... I guess. I just can't wrap my head around it. Maverick claimed he loved me, we, we were intimate... He fucked me at least even if it felt like we were making love. It was like a fairytale, straight out of one of our romance books, Nova. We were at a fancy resort, like I meant something to him. Rose petals, Champaign, a real celebration. The sex, I don't even want to think about how he made me feel... Like I was valuable, wanted. Hell, he whispered he loved me, Nova. Then he gets a text from an ex and all hell breaks loose. He shows up with another ex, still his wife, calls her a victim, tries to protect her from the mob, too. Knowing she set the dominos in motion. The deadly dominos that killed my mom and wants to kill me. I can't... My brain is fried. My heart..."

Nova reached over, squeezing my shoulder. "I'm so sorry. That's so messed up." She paused, spoon in her mouth. "That must've been a terrible shock, seeing them together."

Tears pricked my eyes. "It was. And the worst part is... part of me still wants him to show up, fix everything. Grovel at my feet and beg me to forgive him. But that's not how this works. Not in the real world. He's married, Nova. Married. Whether or not it's real, he called her his wife right in front of me." I took a jagged breath, recalling the anguish when I'd heard him say those words. "And I can't handle it. I can't handle being second best, or in constant danger. Maybe I was naive to trust him at all."

Nova sighed, gulping down a mouthful of wine. "You're not naive, just... you fell in love with an outlaw. I get it. Chigger's a complicated guy, too. Sometimes we see the good in them, even if it's buried under layers of crap."

A hush lingered. I sniffled, hiding my face in my hands. "I wish it wasn't so complicated."

She patted my knee. "Same, girl. But maybe it's for the best. You'll heal, move on. Right?"

I nodded dully, not sure if I believed it. "And what about you? You and Chigger, you seemed... close."

A wry smile tugged at Nova's lips. "He's sweet, all right. The sex is... amazeballs. Like, I can't even describe. But it's not serious. He's always got women blowing up his phone, always secretive about the MC. No talk of me being his anything." She shrugged. "I guess that's what I want, though. Just fun, no strings."

"Are you sure?" I asked softly, seeing the flicker of hurt in her eyes.

Her smile wobbled. "I'm not sure of anything. But I can't keep hoping for more with a biker. He's never said he wants more. So maybe I should just enjoy the ride, pun intended."

We both laughed bitterly, wine warming our bellies, ice cream sweetening our sorrow. For a moment, we just ate in silence.

After we'd downed half the wine and devoured most of the ice cream, exhaustion hit us like a freight train. Nova suggested we crash in her bed for a nap. "I only have one bed, Smutty, but we can share. Unless you want the couch?"

I was too drained to argue. We laughed about the one bed trope. "Your bed is fine, Slutty. But don't try to ravish me." So we curled up under a worn quilt, sobbing quietly about men and heartbreak until sleep claimed us.

A few hours later, I jolted awake to the shrill ring of my phone. My head throbbed from crying and the wine. Next to me, Nova mumbled something, rolling over. I scrabbled for my phone on the nightstand.

"Hello?" I croaked.

A clear male voice came through: "Lexi? Where have you been? I tried emailing you all morning. This is Mark."

I blinked, confusion swirling. "Mark?" Then it clicked. Mark from my law firm. My boss. Crap. "I'm sorry, I've... been out of town. Kinda dealing with personal stuff."

He let out a mild laugh. "I can imagine. Heard your mother passed away, right? Are you okay? Do you need more time off?"

My chest tightened. "Yeah, um, my mom... she was actually murdered. So it's complicated. I might need more time."

He exhaled sharply. "Murdered? Lexi, God, I'm so sorry. Do you... do you need legal help with that?"

A hysterical laugh bubbled up. "You're a lawyer... That's what I wanted to ask. There's a chance someone wants to kill me too. Should I go to the cops or... is that a bad idea?" My words spilled out, half delirious from stress.

"Whoa, slow down," Mark said, tone shifting to professional seriousness. "There's an attempt on your life? If you suspect police corruption or something, maybe we should handle it differently. I have... connections. Let me see what I can do. Where are you right now? I can come see you."

Alarm bells tinkled. "No, I... I'd rather not say my exact location," I stammered. "But I'd appreciate any help. The man behind my mother's murder is a big deal in the underground, calls himself Grinder or Getty. Hard to keep track. I'm not sure who's who. Either way, it's the mob, and I'm terrified."

Mark hummed thoughtfully. "Mob involvement is a whole different game. Don't go to the cops yet. You're right. Some dirty cops could easily tip them off. Give me a couple hours, I'll reach out to some folks. We might arrange a protective order or something more... clandestine. You trust me, Lexi?"

I shut my eyes, tears threatening again. Did I trust him? Maverick's an outlaw, and that ended in heartbreak. Mark was my boss, someone from a far more civilized world, presumably. "Yes, I guess so. Please, do what you can. I'm desperate."

He sighed softly. "All right. I'll call you back soon. Keep your phone close. And I need your address."

I rattled off Nova's address, and we hung up. My stomach churned with uncertainty. Telling Mark might be a huge mistake. But I was out of options. I needed to protect myself, and maybe my normal job was the one safe link to a stable life.

I rolled over, seeing Nova stir. "What's up?" she mumbled groggily.

I sighed, flopping onto my back. "My boss. He wants to help. He's got connections or something. I told him everything. Maybe too much."

Nova sat up, eyes puffy from the nap. "Everything? Lexi, that might be risky. Lawyers can have shady ties too. Especially if the mob's involved."

I shrugged helplessly. "I know. But I can't keep living in fear. He's a partner at a prestigious law firm. Mark and his father run it. I haven't worked there long , but they hired me right out of school. They have a ton of big clients. I'm sure they can handle this better than me running to random safe houses with bikers."

Nova chewed her lip. "I guess. Just be careful. Last thing you need is a double-cross."

CHAPTER 39

Worrying that I may have just gotten myself into more trouble, we got up and poked around the kitchen for something to eat. My appetite was gone, but I forced down some toast. Chigger stuck his head in once, reporting that everything was quiet. The day wore on in a stressed out silence, me jumping at every little noise from outside.

By late afternoon, Nova glanced at her phone, cursing. "Crap, I have to get to the office. I'm behind on a case. I can't lose my job over this. You'll be okay if Chigger stays, right?"

I nodded wearily. "Yeah, I guess so." Chigger was loyal, but I just wanted to be alone. At the same time, I needed the security. "Go. I'll be fine."

Nova squeezed my hand, grabbing her purse. "Text if anything happens. And if Mark shows up, make sure Chigger doesn't kill him, okay?"

That forced a snort of amusement from me. "Noted. I'll let him know we need him alive."

She smirked, then softened. "Be safe, Smutty. We'll figure something out. I promise."

I mustered a sad smile. "Thank you, Slutty."

And then she was gone, leaving me to pace the living room, phone in hand, expecting Mark's call. What if he can't fix anything? What if he's corrupt, too?

The phone buzzed right on cue. A text from Mark:

Mark: Be there in 30. I've got a solution, trust me.

Solution? My head spun with possibilities. Did that mean he'd found a way to neutralize Grinder? Doubtful. I set about freshening up, showering quickly, combing out my hair. For some bizarre reason, I raided Nova's closet and changed into a skirt and blouse, the kind of professional attire I'd wear to the firm. Maybe it was a desperate attempt to feel normal or not embarrassed myself further in front of my boss. I even pinned my hair into a neat bun, slid on my black heels.

The reflection in the bathroom mirror showed a haunted woman with red eyes, but at least I looked put-together.

Just as I finished, the doorbell rang. I hurried to the living room, seeing Chigger open the door. Mark stood on the porch, alone, briefcase in hand, a stylish black suit hugging his tall, lean frame. He had a confident stance, short brown hair slicked back, sharp green eyes. I'd always found him handsome for a slightly older man but never considered him more than a friendly colleague or boss. Now, with everything going on, he looked almost... threatening in that expensive suit.

"Mark," I greeted, stepping forward. "You came."

He flashed a smooth smile. "Of course. We're... friends, right? I told you I'd help." He cast a quick glance at Chigger, who hovered protectively. "Mind if I come in?"

Chigger grunted, crossing his arms. "I'm watchin' you." He shot me a questioning look, and I nodded, letting Mark inside.

Mark stepped in, taking in Nova's modest living room with mild disapproval. "Interesting place. Cozy," he remarked. Then he turned to me, pulling out a folder from his briefcase. "I brought some documents for you to sign. We need to formalize an arrangement."

I swallowed. "What arrangement?"

"Before we talk about that, you need to tell me everything," he said, with the tone he uses at the office when shit was serious.

After I shot a look to Chigger, I let everything flow from me. I told him all about my crazy week. About finding mom dead, the bikers protecting me, the shootouts, the hiding, and about Maverick bringing the women who may have been behind it all right to my doorstep. I left out the more private parts, but didn't hide the fact that I'd been falling for the biker, and that he broke my heart. I tried to, but the tears streaming down my face would betray me.

He pulled a handkerchief out of his coat and pressed it into my hands as he guided me toward the small kitchen table. "You said the man behind your mother's murder might be called Grinder. His name is Marciano. Well, I can personally confirm Marciano is definitely the one controlling that faction you spoke of. He's... a client of ours. My father's firm has represented him in certain transactions for many years. So, I reached out discreetly. He's willing to provide you protection from the Getty side of the family, in exchange for a few conditions."

"Conditions?"

Before Mark could answer, the door burst open. Two men in dark suits, guns in their hands, strode in like they owned the place.

I jumped out of my seat. Chigger cursed, reaching for his waist. But one of the men flashed his piece threateningly, making it clear he'd shoot if we resisted. My blood ran cold. This is happening all over again?

Mark wrapped an arm around me, an oddly possessive gesture. "Easy," he murmured, as I tensed. "These are Marciano's men. They're here to make sure we finalize the contract peacefully."

I stared at him in horror. "You brought armed thugs to a house in the suburbs?"

He shot me a level look. "It's the mob, Lexi. They don't do polite house calls. This is the best I could do. Please sit."

The two goons took positions by the walls. One had the dead-eyed stare of a career killer, the other was scanning the house for threats. Chigger hovered in the corner, outnumbered and outgunned.

I was so upset, I could barely see straight. This was so messed up. "So... what do they want me to sign?"

Mark slid the folder onto the table. "A contract stating you won't stake any claim to Alexander Getty's empire, or affiliate with any group who might. In return, Marciano ensures you're left alone, protected, from Ralph or any Getty associates." He paused, lowering his voice. "He's also willing to pay you a considerable sum to keep quiet about your lineage unless he says otherwise."

I stifled a sob. "He's using me to get leverage?"

Mark shrugged.

"My mother died at their hands, and now I'm supposed to... sign away my rights and for dirty money?"

One of the goons spoke up. "You either sign, or your friend here, and any biker scum you know might meet an early grave. We clear?"

I glanced at Chigger in alarm, but Mark tightened his grip on my shoulder.

"Let Chigger go, and I'll sign."

They waved him out of the house with their guns.

"Lexi," Mark whispered, meeting my eyes. "This is the only way. They'll kill you and everyone you care about if you don't. I tried to get a better deal. This is it."

Shuddering, I sank into the chair, tears spilling. "Fine. Give me the pen," I managed, my voice shaking like a leaf.

Mark nudged the pen toward me, flipping to the last page. My thoughts whirled. Maverick would want me to fight. But Maverick was nowhere to be found. He had his own problems. And he'd effectively broken me. Besides, he had his wife back, the woman who had been tattooed on his arm. I had learned so much, like Sky had a son that Maverick loved, too.

If anything, I was a roadblock for him. I stood in the way of having his wife back, his lost love, a family, even. And we barely knew each other. He said there had been countless women. I figured I was just one of the many. Many one-night stands. God, there had even been another woman who he took to the Road Monsters' clubhouse. Thinking of it, it all became so clear. I was nothing to that biker. Maybe this was my only chance at living peacefully.

I scrawled my signature on the first page, tears dropping onto the paper. The goons nodded. One of them pulled out a phone, texting someone. "It's as good as done," he muttered to the other. They holstered their guns, tension easing.

Mark rubbed my back, a gesture I found both comforting and intrusive. But it did nothing to erase my grief and anger.

I was signing my life to these monsters, but what choice did I have?

Mark pointed to more pages for me to initial, but suddenly, the door slammed open again, and my heart leaped into my throat. Maverick.

My gaze snapped to him, battered and furious, shoulder bandaged, eyes wild with panic.

God, how did he find me?

CHAPTER 40

Seeing him broke my heart. For a split second, I wanted to run to him. But the memory of his betrayal, of Sky, came crashing back. No. I stayed there, shaking like a leaf. Not to mention, they were gonna kill him if I made a move.

He took in the scene, me with Mark's arm around me, two goons stashing weapons under their jackets, a contract on the table. His face contorted with rage and heartbreak. "What's going on?" he demanded, stepping forward. "Lexi, are you okay?"

Mark stood, blocking him. "You need to leave," he said smoothly. "This is private legal business. Everything's settled."

Maverick glared, ignoring Mark's stance. "I'm not going anywhere without an explanation."

I inhaled shakily. "It's... it's fine now. I signed a deal with Marciano's men. They'll protect me from Ralph and the Getty clan. I don't need you or the MC. This is better."

One of the goons flashed his gun under the table, a silent warning for Maverick not to intervene. My stomach twisted at the cruelty of it all.

Please, don't get yourself shot, I pleaded silently to Maverick.

I saw him notice the flash of metal. He looked at me, heartbreak etched across his face. "You can't trust them."

Tears welled again. "I can't trust anyone, Maverick," I whispered. "Not after everything I've seen and... learned." My voice shook. I was talking about him, about how he let his wife into the clubhouse, endangered me.

A flicker of pain crossed his eyes. Mark gave a condescending shrug. "It's done. She's under Marciano's protection now. That's better than your half-assed nonsense, right?" He turned to me, giving me a side hug. "No more running, no more bikers. Just a stable life again. You can come back to work soon, kid." He winked, his face too close, his tone too familiar. I felt nauseated. But I let it happen, to keep the peace.

Maverick's fists tightened, his jaw twitching. My heart pounded, seeing him on the verge of exploding.

My tears spilled freely now. The goons gathered their documents, murmuring quietly. One gave me a nod, as if to say they were done here.

For a moment, I thought Maverick might fight them all, damn the consequences. But then his shoulders sagged, and he whispered, "If you're safe, then I guess that's all that matters. I'll go."

He was leaving. He wasn't even fighting for me. A wave of heartbreak and relief mingled. Maybe it was better this way. No more illusions.

Mark escorted him outside, the door closing behind them.

Mark returned a minute later, alone, a crease his brow. He set the briefcase on the table, glancing at me. I wiped my tears hastily, not wanting him to see me so vulnerable.

Mark exhaled, loosening his tie even more. "Well, that was awkward. I'm sorry you had to see him again."

I swallowed. "Maverick came here to… never mind. It doesn't matter. He has a wife, so I guess it's over anyway." My chest ached at the memory.

Mark studied me. "Yes, well, from what I gather, that relationship is complicated. But so is the rest of your life. You are, apparently, Alexander Getty's daughter."

I pursed my lips. "I… guess. I never met him. So I have no clue."

He nodded thoughtfully. "He was very powerful, well connected. We handled some of his finances in years past. Now, Marciano's stepping into that space. Anyway, I see the resemblance now."

A bitter laugh escaped me. "I don't. I got no fatherly support from him. My aunt raised me, and my mother was always drifting around. He never reached out."

He shrugged. "Yet somehow, you ended up in the best schools, working at my father's prestigious firm. Hardly a coincidence."

My stomach lurched. "What are you implying?"

His lips curved in a smirk. "I suspect your father funneled money your way, or at least ensured you had opportunities. Why else would we hire a nobody fresh out of law school?"

My blood boiled. "A nobody? I scored top marks, I worked my ass off."

He lifted his hands. "Not insulting you, just pointing out that my father doesn't hire novices without reason. Maybe he owed your father, or he nudged him. It's all speculation. Doesn't matter now."

I swallowed fury, a swirl of confusion hitting me. Could my father's blood-soaked money have paid for my tuition? Could the firm have taken me on as a favor to the mob? "I can't deal with this right now," I muttered, dropping into a chair, burying my face in my hands.

Mark stepped closer, voice turning smooth again. "Lexi, all I'm saying is, you're not as random as you think. The Getty name might follow you your whole life, unless you stay under Marciano's wing. And under my watch."

My shoulders hunched. "Your watch?"

He flashed a confident grin. "Someone has to ensure those men keep their word. And it won't be hard, considering I will see you at the office. Not that I haven't noticed how beautiful you are, before, but that's a separate matter." He wagged his eyebrows suggestively.

A flush of disgust and unease prickled my skin. Is he hitting on me? Now? "So now that I'm important, you're interested?"

He laughed softly. "I've always been interested, but you seemed aloof. Too innocent. Also, mixing business and pleasure is tricky. But these circumstances changed everything. We can get to know each other, see how we handle this... arrangement."

I folded my arms. "I'm sure I don't want that."

He just shrugged, stepping back. "We'll see, Ms. Bryan. For now, I'll let you settle. I'll see you at work soon. Don't forget, the big project with Mendez & Associates is due next week."

I scowled, offended by the abrupt shift to everyday business. "Sure. I'll be there," I snapped. "You can see yourself out."

He gave a mock bow, then headed for the door, making a quiet phone call.

I just signed away my autonomy to these scumbags.

Mark paused in the doorway, glancing back. "Lexi, you may not fully grasp my world, but you belong in it more than you realize. It's in your blood."

My throat constricted. He left, the door clicking shut. I stood there, alone in the quiet living room, trembling. In my blood? The thought made me ill. I wanted no part of a mob life. But that's apparently the world I was born into.

A sob tore from my chest. I collapsed onto the couch, tears streaming, mind whirling with heartbreak over Maverick's abrupt departure. Part of me raged that he hadn't fought harder, hadn't thrown me over his shoulder and declared he wouldn't let these assholes touch me. But another part whispered that I'd forced him away. I told him to back off. I told him I was done.

He listened.

Now, no one was left to help me. Nova was at work, Chigger had vanished, maybe he got spooked by the suits?

I was truly alone.

Burying my face in a cushion, I let out a muffled scream, the night's shadows long across the floor. No one came. No one cared. This is my reality now, hush money, mafia deals, and heartbreak.

I must've drifted into a restless doze on the couch because the next thing I knew, I heard the front door open. Streetlights streamed in, revealing a tall figure in the threshold. My heart lurched, hoping maybe it was Maverick after all. But the shape was slender. Nova.

"Lex?" she called softly, flipping the light switch.

I blinked, straightening. My eyes felt swollen from crying. "Nova?" My voice cracked.

She set her bag down, frowning. "What happened? You look worse than before."

I gave a hollow laugh. "Mark came by. And some mob goons. I signed a deal. Maverick showed up too."

Nova's eyes went round. "What?" She hurried over, kneeling by the couch. "Explain. All of it."

So I did, haltingly, voice vibrating. I told her how Mark was apparently some big shot at the firm, with direct lines to Marciano, who might be Grinder, or at least part of that network. He'd arranged a hush money contract to keep the mob from killing me. Maverick tried to intervene, but I shut him down. Then Mark flirted, insinuating I was special because of my father's lineage. Nova's jaw dropped further with each sentence.

"Holy. Shit," she breathed. "That's insane. Lex, you basically sold your soul to the devil."

I buried my face in my hands. "I know. But I saw no other way. They threatened to kill me, you, or Chigger, everyone I care about. Maverick, too. I couldn't let that happen."

Nova plopped onto the couch beside me. "Damn. This is all so messed up. But... maybe it's safer, right? They said they'd protect you?"

A shaky exhale left my lips. "They said so. Mark claims it's the best solution. But at what cost? I'm effectively a puppet for them, bound to never claim the Getty name or do anything they don't like unless they want to use me."

She let out a low whistle. "That's heavy." Then she hesitated. "And Maverick... how did he take it?"

A hollow ache clenched my chest. "He saw Mark holding me, realized I'd chosen this route. He left. Didn't fight, didn't push. He just... walked away."

Tears threatened again, but I forced them down. "Maybe it's for the best," I whispered. "He has a wife. She nearly got me killed."

"Are you sure he wants to be with her after all that?"

"He... he didn't deny it. So, what am I clinging to, anyway?"

Nova rubbed my back. "I'm so sorry, Lex. You loved him, didn't you?"

I swallowed. "Yeah, I did. Part of me... still does." My voice broke. "But it's over. He's an outlaw and I'm... apparently a mob princess who just sold out to a rival family." The absurdity of that statement made my head spin.

Nova gave a shaky laugh. "What a pair we are. You with your hush money from some gangster, me messing around with a biker who barely acknowledges me. We need a new approach, huh?"

I managed a watery smile. "We do. I might as well go back to my normal life, deal with the aftermath. Mark says I can return to the firm in a few days. Once the dust settles."

She nodded, then her eyes brightened with an idea. "You know what? Why don't we get a better place together? A proper, safe apartment in the city with security. I can help pay rent, and you'll be closer to the firm. We can keep watch for each other."

A wave of relief washed over me. Living alone seemed scary now. "That might be good," I admitted. "This place is fine, but it's out of the way, and I'd be isolated if anything happens."

She beamed. "Exactly. We're better off with each other than random men who break our hearts, right? We're not damsels in distress from those romance books, waiting for some alpha male to fix everything. We're high-powered women with futures."

I inhaled, a spark of determination flickering. She's right. "Let's do it. We'll start looking tomorrow for something downtown, near my firm."

Nova grinned. "Yes! Finally a roommate after all these years. Remember in college, we joked about getting a swanky place with a city view?"

I recalled how I'd turned her down back then, wanting my own space because all the men she'd have over. "Yeah, I remember. This time, I won't say no. Let's do it."

We exchanged a weary hug, relief mingling with sorrow. My mind still buzzed with thoughts of Maverick, his stormy eyes, the bandaged shoulder, how he told me I was his. Now he was gone. But if I was truly forging a new path, maybe I needed to bury that memory once and for all.

Nova rose, yawning. "It's almost midnight. Let's get some rest. Tomorrow, we'll do serious apartment hunting. A new start."

I nodded, standing. "A new start," I echoed numbly.

Still, as I followed Nova to her bedroom, the weight in my chest remained. My body felt like a shell, numb after so much heartbreak. The hush money, the contract, the mob's threats... all swirling in the background. But above it all, the ache of losing Maverick overshadowed everything.

Even if he had a wife, even if he'd put me in danger, part of me longed to see him charge in again, fight for me, prove me wrong.

But he didn't.

And that fact tore me to pieces.

Lying awake, staring at the dark ceiling, I pressed my hands over my heart, wishing the pain would fade. Nova breathed softly beside me, half asleep.

I'm a battered soul, pinned between the underground and heartbreak. Maybe I should write a book?

The night yawned on, silent except for my soft tears. Eventually, exhaustion took me. My final thought before drifting off was a fervent wish, that the hush money was enough to keep me alive, and that maybe, in another lifetime, Maverick and I could've had something real.

But not this lifetime. Not anymore.

CHAPTER 41

It amazed me how much life could change in just a few weeks. One month, to be precise, after I'd signed that contract. There was no more frantic packing, no more scouring for hidden mob threats in every shadow. Nova and I had moved into a new condo, perched high in a downtown tower with floor-to-ceiling windows offering a panoramic view of the city skyline. The rent was exorbitant, but between my hush-money settlement from Marciano and Nova's decent salary at her law firm, we could afford it. And if I was being honest, it soothed my nerves to look out over the sparkling city lights each night, reminding myself I was in a world far removed from any dingy biker clubhouse.

I stood before the mirror in my bedroom, sleek white walls, minimalist décor, plush gray rug over lustrous floors, rummaging through my jewelry box for the perfect necklace. Outside, dusk settled over the skyline, the last rays of the sun glinting off the steel towers. My reflection showed a woman in a fitted black cocktail dress, hair done in loose waves. I cocked my head, assessing the look. *Mark would approve,* I thought. He liked me in classy attire, something that whispered "professional" even outside the office.

But something else nagged at me. A subtle, insistent worry I'd been ignoring for days. *I still haven't started my period.* The stress of the last few months could explain it, maybe. But a tiny voice in my head kept insisting it was something more. I tried to push the thought aside, focusing on the glimmer of the gold necklace I'd just fastened. *Don't jump to conclusions,* I told myself.

Nova's voice carried down the hall. "Lexi, I'm heading out real quick!" She popped into my doorway, wearing leggings and an oversized T-shirt, phone in hand. "Just need to grab something from the store. Be back in ten."

I eyed her suspiciously. "At this hour? Don't you have a date with your new fling tomorrow morning?"

She rolled her eyes. "He's not a fling, he's... well, maybe he is." She shrugged, tapping her foot nervously. "Anyway, I'll see you soon. You sure you're okay for your big date with Mark?"

I pressed my lips together. "I guess so. Everything's planned. We're going to that fancy new restaurant near the art museum. Then probably back to his place."

Nova gave me a pointed look, but said nothing. She walked up to me, rested a hand on my arm. "You're good, though, right? Because I know you haven't exactly..."

I swallowed. "I'm fine. He's... I mean, Mark's not a bad guy. It's been a month, and he's been respectful enough." Guilt swirled in my gut. I'd let him kiss me, but never more than that, despite his gentle hints that he wanted more. *He's not Maverick,* a voice in my heart whispered, but I shoved that down.

Nova nodded slowly. "Okay, but if you need me...."

I forced a bright smile. "I'll be fine. Really."

She squeezed my hand. "Right. I'll be back soon." And with that, she disappeared down the hallway, the front door clicking shut behind her.

I turned back to the mirror, smoothing my dress, trying to dismiss the persistent ache of memory. *Maverick.* I hadn't heard from him at all since that day I signed the contract. Maybe he'd gone back to his *wife*, or maybe he was just living as a nomad, drifting on highways. It shouldn't matter. We'd ended in heartbreak. He'd brought me danger on two wheels, and I chose safety.

Yet my heart still twinged whenever I let my mind linger on him too long. I forced myself to focus on Mark. He was stable, kind, and apparently ready to shield me from the underground. Sure, our relationship was mostly dinners, subtle flirting, and occasional make-out sessions but no deeper confessions of love. Perhaps that's what I needed. A calm, rational partner who'd keep me out of the crossfire. *Right?*

I sighed, banishing thoughts of Maverick, and stepped into the living area. Our new condo was all angles and glass, the furniture modern and white. Nova had insisted on an open floor plan, so the living room flowed into a sleek kitchen with granite countertops. Tall windows framed a breathtaking cityscape that stretched for miles. *This was a dream home, the kind I used to fantasize about in law school.* It should've felt perfect, but I couldn't shake the sense of emptiness.

Before I could sink too far into melancholy, Nova burst back in, panting. She held up a small plastic bag. "Got it," she announced, breathless.

I frowned. "What?"

She shoved the bag into my hand. Inside was a pink rectangular box. A Pregnancy Test. My heart stuttered. "You... how'd you know?"

Nova's cheeks flushed. "You know we've been synced up for ages. And you dropped hints all week. You kept saying you were exhausted, and you were freaking about your missed period. I thought you might as well be sure, right? Especially before your big night with Mark."

A cold sweat broke out along my spine. "I'm probably not pregnant," I whispered. "It was just one time with that biker." I wouldn't use Maverick's name. "And I'm not planning on sleeping with Mark tonight."

She folded her arms, eyes sympathetic. "Lex, I'm not judging, but you said you didn't use anything. I know you weren't on birth control."

"What reason did I have to be?"

"So, you agree. It's not impossible."

I forced a laugh. "Right, okay. Let's... let's do this." My hands trembled as I took the box and headed to the bathroom. The sleek white tiles glared under harsh lighting. My reflection in the mirror looked so pale, and my eyes were wide open, like a deer in headlights. *How was this happening?*

I read the instructions twice, then did what it said, nerves stretched as a bowstring. Nova hovered outside, occasionally calling, "You okay in there?"

No, I thought, *I'm definitely not.*

I set the test on the counter, waiting the required two minutes that felt like an eternity. I half-expected Nova to burst in. Finally, I mustered the courage to look.

Positive.

My stomach dropped. I bit back a cry, stumbling to unlock the door. Nova rushed in, seeing the expression on my face. "Oh, Lex," she murmured, drawing me into a tight hug.

"It's... I'm pregnant," I choked out, tears slipping free. I couldn't believe it. Or maybe I could. That night had been intense, emotional, unprotected. *Of course.* But the reality still blindsided me.

Nova stroked my hair. "What are you going to do?"

I stared past her shoulder, mind spinning. *What could I do?* I hadn't heard from Maverick. Maybe he was content with Sky, or maybe he was long gone. My anger and heartbreak reared up, overshadowed by a sudden, fierce protectiveness for the tiny life inside me.

"I guess I'm keeping it," I said, resolute. "But I don't know how I'll manage. That biker... he's gone. He might be with that..."

My knees buckled. I sank onto the edge of the tub, tears blurring my vision. *Pregnant. With Maverick's baby.* The realization slammed into me like a freight train. I thought I'd lost everything connected to him, but this damn tattoo. Apparently not. Something of his still lived inside me.

Nova gently guided me back to the living room, handing me a glass of water. I stared at the floor, the test still clutched in my hand. *What am I going to do?* Maverick was gone. Meanwhile, I'd begun seeing Mark, the far safer choice. But now? *A baby changes everything.*

"Lex, talk to me," Nova urged. "How do you feel?"

I laid a hand on my stomach. "Terrified. Confused. I can't believe this is happening." My eyes stung with fresh tears. "He's not here. He's... I don't even know where. And I'm carrying his child."

Nova's face softened. "He doesn't know, obviously. Are you going to tell him?"

I shook my head fiercely. "Why? For him to show up with that psycho wife again? No, thanks. Besides, he's never even tried to contact me. Maybe he's happy in his messed-up world. I doubt he'd want to raise a baby with me, anyway."

She grimaced. "But a father..."

My chest twisted. "I can't do it alone, Nova. I don't want to. But maybe... maybe Mark can step in?" The words tasted strange on my tongue. "He's stable, wealthy, connected. If I'm pregnant, maybe it's better to have a father figure around. Right?"

Nova's eyes widened. "You'd pretend it's his baby? Or you'd actually... what, seduce him into fatherhood?"

I winced. "I don't know. I'm panicking, okay? He wants to get closer. Tonight might be the night we... go further. You thought so yourself. I could pass it off as his, eventually. Or just let him believe I was pregnant from him, if he never questions the timing." My face burned with shame. "God, I feel awful even thinking it."

She sighed. "It's a big decision. Don't do anything rash, Lex."

Tears spilled again. "I'm so lost. I just want some semblance of normal. And I guess Mark offers that."

We clung to each other for a while. My phone dinged, reminding me I needed to finish getting ready. Mark would pick me up soon. I pushed the pregnancy test deep into a drawer, trying not to think about the momentous truth it confirmed.

CHAPTER 42

Mark arrived in a sleek black town car, courtesy of the firm's private driver. I rode with him to an upscale restaurant near the art museum. Candlelit tables, plush red booths, a hushed ambiance that made even the clink of silverware sound elegant. He guided me in with a hand at the small of my back, offering a polite but warm smile.

Everything about him was polished and controlled.

We settled into a corner booth. The soft glow of chandeliers bathed his neatly parted hair. A waiter appeared, rattling off specials. Mark ordered a bottle of fine wine for himself. I discreetly asked for water, citing an upset stomach, and we perused the menu. My appetite was nonexistent, but I managed to nibble some bread.

"You look stunning," Mark said, his eyes sparkling. "That dress suits you perfectly."

I mustered a small smile. "Thank you."

He reached across the table, lightly brushing his fingers against mine. "How are you feeling this evening, Lexi? Any... trouble with Marciano's men?"

An icy chill ran through me. He always did that, bringing up the mob so casually. "No trouble. I've been left alone, actually."

Aside from the ominous knowledge that they're only leaving me alone because I signed my freedom away.

He nodded, a satisfied smile on his face. "Good. I want you to be able to focus on your career. I've recommended you for that big corporate case next month. We'll be working side by side, if you're interested."

I swallowed. "Oh. That's... good news." If I could keep this pregnancy under wraps.

The waiter arrived with our orders, mine delicate salmon, Mark's a rare steak. As we ate, Mark steered the conversation to the firm's upcoming deals, dropping hints about potential promotions. He even joked about me possibly joining him and his father on some high-profile client negotiations.

Meanwhile, my mind was a drift.

I was pregnant with the baby of a man I once believed could be my future, and here I was playing perfect date to my boss, which would be a problem in itself if Mark didn't also own the firm with his father.

After dinner, he led me to a small private lounge tucked behind the bar, ordering dessert drinks. I declined the rum cocktail, opting again for water. He didn't question it. We talked about law school memories, sharing anecdotes about clueless professors and late-night cram sessions. He laughed easily, leaning in closer with each exchange, his knee brushing mine under the table. He was charming, in that smooth, practiced way.

I kept seeing Maverick's face in my mind, sudden flashes of his crooked grin, the rough stubble on his jaw, the warmth of his calloused hands. Every time I compared him to Mark, my stomach rocked with guilt. Mark was refined and considerate.

Maverick was raw, passionate. And gone.

"You okay?" Mark asked softly, noticing my distant gaze.

I forced a smile. "Yeah, just tired."

He offered me his hand. "Then let's head to my place. I have a big comfy couch, if you want to crash, or a bed." His tone teased. "Up to you."

My heart fluttered. This is it, I realized. He was inviting me to cross that line. Should I do it? Some part of me insisted I needed a stable partner if I was carrying a baby. Another part screamed it was wrong, that I still loved someone else. But that someone else had vanished into the wind.

He's not here, and I'm alone.

"All right," I said quietly. "Let's go."

Mark's mansion sat in a gated community on the upscale side of town. Massive wrought-iron gates swung open at our approach, revealing a winding driveway lined with sculpted hedges. The house itself was a three-story modern affair, all glass and concrete, with an interior courtyard lit by artfully placed spotlights. My mouth went dry.

This was wealth on another level, like something out of Luxury Living magazine.

The car pulled into the circular driveway, and the driver let us out. Mark opened my door, taking my hand to help me out of the back. The front door opened onto a marble-floored foyer, high ceilings, a sweeping staircase with a glass banister. Modern art pieces stood on pedestals. The entire space felt cold, echoing our footsteps.

"Welcome," he said, dropping his keys on a sleek console table. "Make yourself at home."

I hovered near the entry, strangely intimidated. This place was too perfect. "It's... beautiful," I managed.

He smiled, shrugging off his suit jacket. "Thanks. My father's taste, mostly. But I've added a few touches." He gestured to a grand piano in a side alcove, a bar cart gleaming with top-shelf liquor. "You want something to drink?"

I hesitated, remembering my newly confirmed pregnancy. "Uh, no, I'm still not feeling... up to it."

He gave me a curious look but didn't push. "No worries. Let me show you around."

We moved through an open-concept living area with floor-to-ceiling windows overlooking a landscaped backyard with an infinity pool. White leather couches sat around a minimalist fireplace. It reminded me of a high-end hotel, lacking any personal warmth. Then again, maybe that was what Mark preferred.

"You're quiet," he remarked as we strolled upstairs.

I forced a laugh. "Sorry. Just taking it all in. It's... a lot. And, I guess, to be honest, I'm nervous about being here. With you. All alone."

A knowing smile, he took my hand, guiding me into a large bedroom dominated by a king-sized bed with a gray upholstered headboard. Windows lined one wall, showcasing the courtyard below. He flipped a switch, dim recessed lighting glowing around us.

"Better?" he asked softly, drawing me to the bed.

I swallowed, nerves tangling in my belly.

I could do this. If I intended to pass off this pregnancy, or even maintain a semblance of normalcy, letting Mark close might be my path. But did I really want it?

He leaned in, kissing me gently. His lips were soft, his movements measured, polite, as always. Nothing like Maverick's demanding urgency. I shuddered, forcing myself to focus on Mark, on his pleasant cologne and controlled caresses.

He whispered, "We don't have to rush, if you're not ready."

I bit my lip, heart pounding. "I want to," I lied. Or maybe I partly wanted to, needed to. My mind flared with images of Maverick, but I pushed them away.

He left. This was my life now.

Mark smiled, sliding his hands along my sides. He unzipped my dress slowly, laying it aside. I tried to relax, letting him see me in my lace underwear, conscious of every flaw I imagined. He didn't seem to care, eyes gleaming with admiration. "You're fucking gorgeous," he murmured, pressing light kisses down my neck. "But what's with the tattoo?"

"That biker forced me to get it."

"Property of Maverick. He didn't force you to do anything else, did he?" Mark looked properly concerned.

"No, he didn't. Thank goodness," I said. It was the truth, even if that wasn't what he was asking. I let him think I never had sex with the biker.

"But you've been with a man before."

I bit my lip. "Yeah, just one, just once. It seems like a lifetime ago." That was all too true as well.

"Then I'll be gentle."

The bed felt firm under me as he urged me onto it, carefully removing his tie, then his shirt. His body was lean, not particularly as muscular as the biker, but fit enough from time in the gym. He moved with polished confidence, as if everything he did was scripted in a textbook on seduction. I kept my eyes closed, letting him undress me further. A pang of guilt twisted my gut.

This wasn't passion. It was a transaction. But I obliged myself to let go, to respond, soft moans, gentle touches.

He tried to please me, murmuring sweet nothings, asking if I was comfortable, if I liked it. I tried to pretend I was into it. But the ache in my heart rendered it all meaningless. My mind drifted to a rougher, more urgent lover who'd once pinned me under him with raw need.

Stop thinking about Maverick, I screamed internally.

When Mark finally entered me, it was slow, careful, almost clinical. He groaned softly, pressing kisses to my shoulder. I clung to him, going through the motions, hoping maybe it'd spark something real. But the spark never quite came. My body responded in a mild wave of pleasure, but my soul remained numb. *He's not Maverick. Not my biker*. The refrain haunted me, even as I moaned and arched for Mark's benefit.

Afterward, he curled an arm around me, panting lightly. "You okay?" he asked, brushing my hair back.

I nodded, throat tight. "Yes. Thank you." Thank you? My stomach lurched at how formal it sounded, but what else could I say?

He smiled, snuggling me against his chest. I stared at the ceiling. *It's done*, I thought. The final line had been crossed. Now maybe I could pass off the baby as his. Guilt and sadness warred in my chest. I willed myself to sleep, pushing away the image of Maverick's face that threatened to break me all over again.

Time blurred. Mark and I fell into a routine of office flirtation and regular dates. I kept sleeping with him, though my heart never truly engaged. My body finally was, and my heart would open to him eventually. At least the arrangement seemed stable, no gunfights, no betrayals, just the everyday drama of big law. My belly started to feel strange, a faint swell I hid under looser blouses.

Finally, I couldn't dodge the truth any longer. I was definitely pregnant, and I needed to tell Mark before he suspected something else. I couldn't go to a doctor and leave a trail until he knew. The day I decided to break the news, we were in his office, a spacious corner suite with a view of the city, a much better view than my apartment had. He was wearing an impeccable navy suit, flipping through a contract. I stepped in, closing the door behind me.

"Got a minute?" I asked, trying not to wring my hands.

He glanced up with a smile. "For you, always. What's on your mind?"

I drew a shaky breath, taking the seat across from his massive desk. My hands twisted in my lap. "I, uh... I need to tell you something. It's serious."

Concern flickered in his eyes. "Everything okay? Is Marciano pressing you for more?"

I swallowed. "No, not that. It's... I'm pregnant." The words dropped like a stone in a still pond.

He froze, blinking. "Pregnant?" Slowly, he stood, coming around the desk. "You're sure?"

I nodded, my eyes watering up for all the wrong reasons. "Positive. I've taken a test. I... I haven't been to a doctor yet, but I'm certain." I exhaled erratically. "And before you ask, no, I don't want to get married. I'm not trying to trap you."

Mark's face shifted from shock to something softer, almost relieved. "So you're not... you don't want me to propose?"

I managed a hollow laugh. "No. I'm not ready for that. Marriage is a big step, and we barely know each other. I just... thought you should know. Since we've been... involved."

For a moment, he stared at me, his expression inscrutable. Then he reached out, brushing his thumb across my cheek. "Lexi, I'm... I won't lie, I'm surprised. But I'm also happy, in a strange way." He paused, lips curving into a small smile. "You're carrying my baby?" The question lingered in his tone.

I swallowed. "Yes. We've been sleeping together for a month or so. It makes sense. I'm sure it's yours." The lie tasted bitter. But I stuck to it. "You could ask the mob if they've seen me with anyone else." He didn't need to know the truth, that Maverick had fathered this child a month before I ever let Mark into my bed.

Mark's shoulders relaxed, and he moved closer, laying a gentle hand on my abdomen. I resisted the urge to flinch. "Nonsense. I know you haven't been with another man. I'm just, I'm stunned. It's hard for us, men in my family. That's why I have a twin brother. You've met Max. My mother had to do IVF... I'm not demanding marriage," he said softly. "But I do want to be a father, if you'll let me. We can figure out the details as we go. I won't push you away or make you do this alone."

Tears welled, half relief, half guilt. "Thank you," I whispered. "I appreciate it."

He smiled, guiding me into a loose hug. "I'll do whatever it takes to win your heart, Lexi. We can keep it discreet at the firm for now, if you prefer. No sense stirring gossip."

I nodded numbly, leaning into his chest. "Yeah, let's keep it quiet. I just... I need time to process."

Time to bury the memories of the biker who truly fathered this baby.

He held me a moment longer, stroking my hair. Outside the window, the city glimmered, oblivious to my tangled secrets. As he whispered reassurances about co-parenting and we talked about setting up prenatal appointments, I felt tears slip down my cheeks, silent, salty reminders of a past that refused to be erased.

"I'm just so happy," I said, explaining the tears away.

I was carrying Maverick's child, passing it off as Mark's. A fresh ache bloomed, but I let Mark's gentle words soothe me. Because what else could I do?

CHAPTER 45

I smoothed my hand over my swollen belly, feeling the gentle curve that had finally become obvious in the last month. Four months pregnant. N*early halfway*. The doctor had said with a smile. Every day, I felt the slightest bit heavier, my balance shifting. I'd catch glimpses of my reflection in shiny office doors or mirrors and think, *That's me*. A soon-to-be mother, forging through life at a prestigious law firm that, ironically, had ties to Marciano and the mob.

I stood in my cubicle, tapping a pen against my notepad. Outside the tall windows on the twentieth floor, the city sparkled under the afternoon sun. My desk was cluttered with case files, Post-it notes, and a half-eaten sandwich I couldn't stomach finishing. The baby had me craving odd things, but mostly I just felt nauseated at random times. I took a breath, steadying myself.

My baby, the baby that belonged to *Maverick*. The biker I hadn't heard from in months. The real father who probably believed I'd moved on. *Well, I had,* in a way. Mark, my boss, had swept me into his orbit, wooing me with fancy dinners and lavish gifts, calling me *his girlfriend*. He'd been surprisingly sweet, pulling out chairs for me, offering foot massages when I complained of swollen ankles, insisting I rest at every opportunity. At least once a week, we'd end up at his mansion or my apartment, having dinner, sipping tea, or, before I was too nauseated, making love in that hollow, mechanical way that never quite replaced what I'd felt for Maverick. But it was *comfortable*. Safe.

Yet guilt gnawed at me. He believed this growing bump was *his* child, that we'd somehow conceived it in those early times we fooled around. I'd lied by omission, letting him think it was possible. I told myself it was for the baby's sake, to secure a father figure in case Maverick was truly gone forever. But the mass on my conscience grew each day, matching the bulk of my stomach.

Worse, I'd noticed signs that Mark intended to propose. He'd dropped hints about "the future," and how "wedding should be small, intimate." I'd pretended not to understand. But a few days ago, rummaging in his desk for a pen, I stumbled upon a black velvet box. Tiny, discrete, but undeniable. My chest had seized in panic. *I can't do this*. How could I marry him under the pretense that he was the father, when I carried that biker's child in my womb?

I set down my pen, exhaling shakily. *I have to tell him. Tonight.* Or maybe right now. The day's tasks weighed on me, but I couldn't focus on legal briefs or depositions.

My phone buzzed. I glanced at the screen. *Nova*. Perfect timing. I grabbed it, ducking into the hallway, then slipped into the ladies' restroom for privacy.

"Nova?" I whispered, pushing the door closed behind me.

Her voice crackled through. "Hey, Lex. Busy?"

"I'm at work," I said softly, leaning against the counter. The fluorescent lights hummed overhead, reflecting off the polished sinks. "But I'm free enough to talk."

Nova sighed. "Just checking on you. You never texted back after that appointment."

I closed my eyes, imagining the latest ultrasound, how I saw the baby's tiny limbs, the flutter of a heartbeat. "Everything's normal. The baby's healthy, measuring fine." My throat tightened. "I'm four months in, Nova. But it's actually five. And I'm living a lie."

She made a sympathetic noise. "I know. Mark's still clueless, huh?"

I nodded, though she couldn't see. "Totally. He's doting, sweet, treating me like a queen. I can't take it anymore, feeling all this guilt. I think he's going to propose soon. I actually saw a ring in his drawer. I can't let it get that far."

Nova sighed. "So, what's your plan? Tell him the truth?"

My stomach twisted at the thought. "Yes. I have to. I can't marry him, letting him believe he fathered this baby. He deserves honesty, even if I'm terrified of how he'll react."

A pause. "Yeah, you gotta do it," Nova agreed. Then her tone turned cautious. "By the way, I ran into Chigger the other night. He was skulking around the bar where I was meeting a friend. Looked anxious. Told me he'd... well, asked if you wanted him to pass any message to Maverick."

My heart lurched, unexpected hope stirring. *Maverick*. But just as quickly, anger and sorrow swelled. "No," I said firmly. "Don't say a word. He left me. He never looked back. Why would he care that I'm pregnant? He didn't fight for me, or even check in. So, no. Let's keep it quiet."

Nova hesitated. "All right, Lex. If that's what you want."

"It is," I lied, voice wavering. "Look, I gotta go find Mark before I lose my nerve. Wish me luck."

"Good luck," she whispered. "Text me if you need bail money."

A strained laugh slipped out. "Let's hope not. Bye, Nova."

I hung up and stared at my reflection in the mirror. My belly curved under my blouse and pencil skirt, a gentle swell that was impossible to hide now. *This is it.* I had to be honest, or I'd never forgive myself.

I left the bathroom, heart hammering. My heels clicked on the polished floors as I navigated the maze of cubicles and offices in the firm's main suite. The place smelled of coffee, paper, and expensive cologne, the usual. A few paralegals nodded as I passed, offering polite smiles. They probably thought I was lucky to be dating a senior associate who'd eventually inherit the firm. I felt sick.

Mark's corner office had frosted glass walls, a mahogany desk, and a stunning view of the city. The blinds were drawn. My pulse spiked as I noticed the door was closed. *He's probably on a call.* But I needed to do this, so I rapped softly.

No response. Strange. Usually, Mark shouted a come in or told me to wait. Hesitant, I turned the knob and stepped inside.

I blinked in the bright light, and my stomach did a flip. Behind Mark's desk, I caught a glimpse of bare legs and an unfamiliar skirt hiked up. A woman was kneeling there, hidden mostly by the desk's wooden panel. Mark's chair was pushed back, his suit pants around his thighs. *Oh, my God.*

For a moment, my brain refused to compute. Then it crashed in horror. Mark's head jerked up, eyes wide, face flushed. The woman whipped her head around, hair disheveled, cheeks burning. *He had a woman under his desk. A blow job at the office.*

I froze, a wave of revulsion and shock crashing over me. This man was supposedly my boyfriend, the father of my unborn child, in his mind, and he was cheating on me in broad daylight. A nauseating swirl warped me.

"Lexi," Mark gasped, leaping up from his chair, fumbling to pull up his pants. "What are you? This isn't what it looks like."

The woman scrambled to her feet, face bright red, tugging down her skirt. She'd been getting hers, too. Rebecca, a young college intern, cast me a mortified glance, then brushed past me in a flurry of stiletto clicks, darting out the door. The scent of cheap perfume trailed her.

I stood rooted, anger and disgust roiling. "Really, Mark?" I rasped. "Not what it looks like? Because it looks like you're getting off with someone else in your office. Aren't we supposed to be dating?" My voice trembled with fury.

He ran a shaky hand through his hair, struggling with his zipper. "God, Lexi, calm down. It's just a fling. You know how things are. I was stressed, needed... release."

Disbelief speared me. "Stress relief? You do realize I'm pregnant with your so-called baby, and you're screwing around behind my back?"

He huffed, straightening his shirt before he flew to the door to shut it and lock it. Of course, he doesn't want anyone to hear. "Lexi, we never had an exclusive talk. We're not married yet."

My throat burned with rage. He called me his girlfriend. "You think that justifies it? You were prepared to propose, for fuck's sake."

He paused, confusion flicking across his face. "You... you knew about the ring?"

I snorted bitterly. "I'm not blind. I saw it. But guess what, Mark? I was actually coming here to..." I cut myself off, seething. Then I decided to reveal the truth. Tear the bandage off. "To tell you, the baby isn't yours," I spat, chest tight. "It's someone else's. I lied. I'm sorry. But I can't do this charade anymore."

For a second, the room fell deathly silent. Mark's eyes narrowed, emotion flickering, shock, then anger. "You're joking," he said, voice dangerously low. "You told me we'd conceived early on. You let me treat you like, like a mother of my child."

Tears stung my eyes. "Well, if this is how you treat the mother of your child, I'm glad that's not me. I'm sorry. But after seeing you with that woman... *I'm done.*"

He took a breath, cheeks flushing red. "You're done? *You're done?*" His voice rose. "After everything I've done for you, after I protected you from the mob, you're just going to walk away? The father of that brat is some random man, isn't it? Do you even know who?"

My jaw clenched. "He was...someone from before. Look, you're the one cheating, so don't act high and mighty."

Mark's face twisted in fury. "You think I care about that? I told you I needed an heir. I was prepared to give you everything, to make you my wife, to share the firm's future with you. You benefit from my father's connections, from Marciano's protection. And now you tell me it's *not* my child?" He barked a humorless laugh. "Too bad. I'm not letting you off the hook that easily."

A chill crawled up my spine. "Excuse me?"

He marched around the desk, looming over me. "You *will* marry me, Lexi. You *will* pass that baby off as mine. Because if you don't, I can call in Marciano, have them revoke your precious agreement, and see how you like it when the Syndicate sets its sights on you again. Or, better yet, watch your friend Nova suffer. You want that?"

My blood ran cold. *He's threatening me.* "You're insane, Mark," I breathed. "I won't be forced into marriage. This baby isn't yours."

He sneered. "I don't care whose it is. I need an heir for the firm. *You* need a father for your kid. It's a win-win." He gestured around, voice trembling with suppressed rage. "You enjoy the power, the safety, the money. Just keep your mouth shut about the paternity. We'll be the perfect couple. And if you refuse, well... I have the mob on speed dial."

My heartbeat thundered in my ears. "You're disgusting. You want me to lie for the rest of my life, say this baby is yours, so you get your big inheritance or whatever?"

His eyes gleamed. "That's right. I was trying to be nice, but you forced my hand. You'd better cooperate." He reached into his desk drawer, pulling out a small velvet box. *The ring.* He let out a twisted chuckle. "Now's as good a time as any."

Before I could protest, he dropped to one knee in front of me, eyes glittering with a mix of desperation and malice. The ring glinted in the office lights.

"Lexi," he said, voice dripping with forced sweetness, "will you marry me?"

A strangled laugh escaped me, half-sob. *"You can't be serious."*

His eyes were icy. "I'm quite serious. Or do you want your life destroyed? Your friend's life? You want to carry a bastard child with no safety net? We both know the father's not around. It's that biker, right? He doesn't care about you. You told me yourself he left."

I felt a sharp pain in my chest. *Maverick.* Anger and heartbreak collided. He did leave me. But that didn't excuse Mark's vile behavior. Still, the cold reality was that Marciano held my life in his hands. If Mark told them I'd broken faith, they'd come after me. *Fuck.* I swallowed hard, tears burning.

I stared at Mark's face. He was the devil I knew, versus a mob that wanted me dead. My baby's safety overshadowed my pride. *What choice did I have?* My lip trembled. "You're forcing me," I whispered.

He straightened. "No, I'm giving you an option. Accept, and enjoy a secure life. Refuse, and… well, we'll see how a mob boss handles betrayal. Not as well as me."

My vision blurred with tears. *I have to protect my baby and Nova. Maverick's* name pounded in my chest, but he was nowhere around. No cavalry to rescue me. *Damn it.*

I drew a trembling breath, voice barely above a whisper. "Yes," I said, choking on the word. "I'll marry you."

Mark's smirk reeked of victory. He stood, slipped the ring onto my finger. It felt cold and heavy, a prison shackle. My gut churned with revulsion.

"Good," he said quietly. "We'll announce our engagement soon. We'll plan a wedding that suits our image. You'll publicly confirm the baby is mine. Another announcement in the paper." He paused, glancing at the desk where that other woman had been just minutes ago. "And next time, knock, okay?"

I stared at him, tears finally spilling over. I hated him at that moment. Yet I was trapped, cornered by my own lies. Wordlessly, I shoved past him, staggering into the hallway. My entire body shook with rage, grief, and terror. I felt the ring's weight on my finger, like a chain tethering me to a future I didn't want.

I'd said yes. Because I had no choice. If I refused, Mark would unleash the mob. He'd said it plainly. *God, what have I done?* The baby kicked faintly, a flutter I barely recognized. I pressed my hand to my belly, tears blurring my vision. *I'm so sorry,* I thought silently to my child. *So sorry.*

As I fled the office, ignoring the curious stares of coworkers, one thought burned through me. I had to survive. Even if it meant being engaged to a cold, manipulative lawyer who'd cheat on me and treat me like property. Ironically, he was no better than the biker I'd run from. *All men who wanted ownership.* That's all I was to Mark, a tool to secure his inheritance or his firm's future.

But there was a flicker of defiance in my heart. *I'm not done fighting.* My child deserved better than a forced marriage based on lies. One day, I'd find a way out. But for now, I'd have to bide my time.

Tears streamed down my cheeks as I stepped into the elevator, the ring shining mockingly on my hand. I stared at the reflection in the polished metal doors, a pregnant woman, terrified and trapped, wearing an engagement ring that symbolized everything she loathed. The baby shifted again, as if sensing my distress.

I wrapped an arm around my belly, sucking in a shaky breath. *I can't let Mark or Marciano break me.* Even if Maverick was gone, even if my life was tangled in lies, my child would be born, and I would protect them at all costs. *I just have to keep going.*

But as the elevator descended, I couldn't stop the tears. Maverick's face haunted my every breath. If he knew... if he'd cared... maybe none of this would be happening. Or maybe I was delusional.

The elevator dinged, doors sliding open onto the lobby's marble floors. I wiped my cheeks, forcing my posture upright. People might see me, wonder about my tears. *No more tears,* I told myself, stepping out. *I have to be strong for my baby.*

CHAPTER 44

Maverick

I'd never imagined returning to California would feel so damn hollow. The roar of bikes, the swirl of smoke in the air, the pounding of heavy rock from huge speakers around the rally grounds. It should've been invigorating, reminding me of better times. But I felt only a dull ache in my chest as I navigated my Harley through the throng of tents and scattered bonfires.

I was supposed to meet up with Chigger near the mud wrestling pit. He'd texted me a couple hours ago, telling me they were already getting wasted, that Nova was with him. Nova. I hadn't heard that name in a while, and it stirred up too many memories. Memories of someone else, a woman with green eyes who once tore me apart in the best and worst ways. Lexi. I tried not to dwell on it. Because it'd been a year, maybe more. She's probably living her life with that stiff from her office. Maybe I hadn't truly let go, but I'd forced myself not to care.

The Kings of Anarchy MC rally sprawled across a dusty field in Anarchy, California, a place that attracted every outlaw within a thousand miles. Tents in vibrant colors lined the perimeter, bikes parked in a chaotic row, each with custom paint or gleaming chrome. Bikers roamed with plastic cups of beer, some spectators perched on makeshift bleachers watching the mud-wrestling matches. The mud pit itself was a sloppy, churned-up mess, cheering onlookers shouting as half-naked volunteers flung each other around.

Typical MC event. Part of me used to love this shit, the lawlessness, the raw sense of freedom. Now it felt more like going through the motions. The only reason I came was because the Road Monsters' leadership told me to. I'd ridden here with the Kings of Anarchy Maine chapter, presided over by Solo, friend I'd made while doing dirty work up in New England.

Maine. I went there following another Road Monster, named Monster and his young family. My lips curled in a half-smile remembering that place, endless pine forests, rocky coasts, the smell of salt in the air. The KOAMC in Maine had offered me something akin to camaraderie after I left everything behind. I'd done jobs for them, jobs I wouldn't talk about in polite company, but it put money in my pocket and gave me a reason not to think about Lexi for a while. Now, here we were, across the country, meeting with the West Coast Kings. And I was still a damn nomad for the Road Monsters, taking orders from shadowy Aces who never showed their faces.

I spotted Ophelia just ahead, walking with a swaying confidence that turned too many heads. She was gorgeous, with waist-length black hair and a fierce gaze, the kind of woman who'd stir a crowd. But she never batted an eyelash at my attempts to flirt, which, ironically, made me keep noticing her. Her standoffish nature reminded me I was alive, but it wasn't real attraction, just a passing curiosity. The truth was, my heart was still in a thousand pieces. Ophelia gave me a cursory glance, then turned away. Fine by me. I've got other shit to worry about.

I trudged to the mud-wrestling ring, scanning the rowdy crowd. The stink of beer and sweat drifted on the hot breeze. Suddenly, I spotted a tall figure with a battered cut and sandy hair, arm slung around a petite woman with long blonde locks. Chigger and Nova. They sat on a couple of wooden crates, plastic cups in hand, cheering at the muddy spectacle. A bleacher made of old pallets loomed behind them.

I shoved through the spectators, ignoring a few shouts and stumbles. Finally, I reached them, planting myself with a grunt.

"Well, look who it is." Chigger drawled, lifting his beer in greeting. His cheeks were flushed as he was clearly hammered. "The man himself. 'Bout time you got here, brother."

Nova gave me a polite nod. She looked... prettier without Lexi sitting next to her. "Hey, Mav," she said, sipping from her cup.

I let out a low grunt, dropping onto a crate beside them. "Yeah, I got delayed. Solo took a scenic route through half the desert." I slid a glance at the mud pit, where two women in bikinis grappled to the whooping delight of the onlookers. Not my scene, not anymore. I took the cup Chigger offered me, half-filled with warm beer. "Thanks."

He clinked his cup to mine sloppily, spilling a bit on his cut. "So how's Maine, man?" he slurred, leaning in. "Heard you been up there for a while, helpin' the KOA sort out some turf trouble."

I shrugged, forcing a semblance of interest. "It's all right. Cold as hell. Trees everywhere. Did some grunt work for Solo. I actually liked it, reminded me of Alaska in a weird way. Peaceful, when it's not chaotic, if that makes sense."

He snorted. "Sounds like you're still wandering. Always on the run, Maverick." His tone wasn't accusatory, more drunkenly observant.

I tensed, flicking my gaze at Nova, who watched the mud-wrestling but was clearly listening. "Yeah, well," I muttered. "It's a nomad's life." Trying to avoid thinking about Lexi. But I didn't say that out loud.

An awkward silence settled among us, broken only by the crowd's hoots every time a mud-slick body got slammed. I sipped my lukewarm beer, my mind drifting. Maybe I should ask about Lexi, but I'd told the Road Monsters to keep me informed only if she was in serious danger, no details. I'd clung to that to keep from obsessing. But something in me stirred. Perhaps I should inquire anyway. Before I could speak, though, Nova coughed.

"I'm gonna go... find some water," she said, sliding off her crate. "You two catch up."

I nodded, though suspicion flickered in my gut. Chigger was hammered, maybe she didn't want him blurting something? She ambled away, quickly disappearing in the throng.

Chigger watched her go, swaying slightly. "That woman... phew," he muttered. "She's a handful, but man... I love that handful." He made a motion of grabbing hold with two hands. Then he cackled, draining his beer. "Been seein' her on and off, you know. She's got baby fever or some shit."

My stomach tensed. Baby fever. The words pricked at some old wound. Don't go there, Maverick. But I forced myself to keep it together. "Yeah? So, you two are serious now?"

He shrugged, grinning drunkenly. "Nova wants a baby, I think. I might be the prime candidate since she's letting me raw dog her day and night. That or she's just horny. Speaking of babies..." He paused, chuckling. "You hear about Lexi?"

My heart missed a beat. "Lexi?" I repeated, suddenly gripping my cup too tight. "No. Why?"

He shot me a confused look, then burst out laughing. "Shit, man, guess you don't keep in touch, huh? I ought to thank her."

"Why?"

"She's why I'm getting all this good pussy from Nova. Her letting me jizz in her like an old sock."

"Lexi? Why her?"

"She's good, had a baby, I heard. Married that suit from her office, I guess."

Everything around me seemed to go muffled, the roar of the rally receding. Lexi had a baby? Pain lanced through my chest, fierce and undeniable. So she moved on, started a family. My head spun. Of course she had. She deserved that. But an odd jealousy coiled in my gut. I can't believe no one told me.

I forced a calm tone. "She's... married? That quick?"

He shrugged. "A year's not that quick. Nova says the kid's about three months old. She's doin' well, fancy house, that sort of thing."

Three months old. I did the math in my head. A year ago, we parted ways... She was pregnant then, or soon after. My mind leapt to the night we had together, the primal, undeniable pull. I'd gone in raw, no protection. I didn't even know if the girl was on the pill. A virgin, she probably hadn't been. Fuck. *Could that baby be mine?* The timeline certainly fit. But she never told me. No one told me. Fuck. My vision blurred with rage and hurt.

I cut my gaze to where Nova had vanished, wishing I could corner her for details. Chigger kept rattling on, oblivious.

"Yeah, man, she's out there living the high life with that stiff in his monkey suit. Remember him. Mark, I think. From that fancy law firm." He belched, adding, "Nova's got baby fever from seein' Lexi's kid, I bet. She's got all the pics and has to show me. She's all 'ooh, so cute!' Then she's riding my hog without a helmet, if you get my drift.

"Shit, well, I guess that's how it goes. Baby fever," I responded, but rage bubbled up, a dark swirl of betrayal. A baby. My baby, maybe. They all just... let me wander for a year, clueless. My hands shook. "You're telling me Lexi just had a baby, right around now, and you never said a damn word?"

Chigger, drunk as a skunk, blinked. "Uh, man, I didn't think it was your business. She's married. The baby's that stiff's, right? She probably conceived it after she left the clubhouse. That's how it lines up, yeah? Did want you to think bad of her, getting right in another man's bed."

I clenched my jaw so tight it hurt. "I'm not an idiot, Chigger. The timeline means the baby could be mine."

He frowned. "You sayin' you got her pregnant? Shit, you told me you didn't want updates. And she's publicly claiming it's the suit's kid, I think. So maybe not yours."

My eyes scanned the crowd, spotting Nova returning, expression tense as if she sensed the confrontation. My gaze locked on her. She paled. She knew. She fucking knew.

"Nova," I growled as she approached, ignoring Chigger's drunken slur. "Tell me the truth. That baby... is it mine?"

Her eyes widened, color draining from her face. She clutched her phone. "I... Maverick, this isn't the time or place."

I snatched her wrist, not too roughly, but firmly. "Show me. Chigger said you got pictures. Why did no one tell me?" My voice trembled with raw pain.

She whimpered. "Because you said you didn't want details, and Lexi didn't want..."

"Show me," I insisted.

Nova hesitated, then she tried to step back, pressing her phone to her chest. "Don't do this here."

But I was done being polite. I yanked the phone from her grip, ignoring her protests. Swiping through her messages, I found a chain with Lexi's name. My heart hammered as I scrolled. Mentions of the baby's birth, how sweet he was, pictures of a tiny infant wrapped in a soft blanket. I stopped breathing. One photo loaded, a baby with dark hair, greenish eyes.

    Fuck.

CHAPTER 45

My breath caught in my throat. He looked so much like me. Something in the shape of his face or the faint scowl on his brow. *Or maybe I was imagining it.* But it struck me like a sledgehammer. *That's my kid.* I dropped Nova's phone, chest heaving.

She stooped to pick it up, tears in her eyes. "Maverick, wait..."

But I couldn't listen. My entire world just flipped. *A son, or a daughter? A baby, anyway.* My baby. And Lexi married some asshole lawyer for the mob, passing the child off as his? *Rage roared in my veins.*

I stormed away, pushing past the crowd. Nova called after me, stumbling with Chigger in tow. I heard Chigger slur something like, "Shit, Mav, calm down!" But I couldn't stay calm.

I reached my bike, fingers trembling as I yanked on my helmet. *I had to go to Texas, find her, find that Mark asshole.* Confront them. The idea terrified and infuriated me. *How could she not tell me?*

Ophelia suddenly stepped into my path, eyes glinting, lips parted. "Maverick," she purred, "I was wondering if you need some where to park tonight."

"Get lost," I snapped, my voice rough.

She drew back, offended, but I couldn't care. My life had just imploded. *I had a child I never met.* That overshadowed any fleeting attraction to a coldhearted woman.

She scoffed, stepping aside. I threw my leg over the Harley, jamming the key in the ignition. The engine roared, echoing my rage. *Fuck the rally, fuck the Road Monsters' orders.* This was personal. I had to see Lexi, face her, demand answers.

Nova's voice rose behind me. "Maverick, wait! You can't just..."

But I peeled out, gravel spraying under my tires, tears burning at the corners of my eyes. The setting sun cast long shadows across the dusty field as I sped past tents and bikers. No one dared stand in my way. By the time I hit the highway, my mind was a tangled storm of fury, betrayal, and a fierce protectiveness I never anticipated experiencing again.

I floored it, heading east, and didn't bother packing or saying goodbye. I had no plan except *confront Lexi in Texas*. Find out how she could hide my child. Part of me dreaded she might deny it, but I knew in my gut that baby was mine. The baby had my eyes, or something close enough. *The timeline doesn't lie.*

As the miles passed, the desert wind slapped against my face, stinging my eyes. I let the roar of the bike fill my senses, fueling the adrenaline. My shoulder twinged from that old bullet's graze, reminding me of the last time I saw Lexi. But the pain even when it was fresh was inconsequential compared to the searing anguish in my chest.

A year of emptiness, I'd tried to forget her, convinced myself she'd moved on. And she had. Apparently with Mark Martin or whatever his name was. Married him, lied to him, or maybe both lied to each other, and now they were raising *my* child.

My hands gripped the handlebars, knuckles white. *This ends now.* I needed the truth from Lexi's lips. If I had a son or daughter, I'd do whatever it took to claim them. I wasn't sure if that meant violence, or deals, or more heartbreak. But I sure as hell wasn't going to let some stiff in a suit raise my kid as his own.

The sun dipped below the horizon, and I kept riding. My phone buzzed in my pocket, likely Nova or Chigger, but I ignored it, fueling up only when necessary. *No more waiting.* Texas was a hell of a distance away, but I had rage and heartbreak on my side. I'd ride through the night if I had to, until I reached her.

The woman I couldn't forget, who'd stolen my heart and apparently hidden my child. God, I was furious, but underneath that wrath lay a twisted hope, maybe she still loved me. Maybe she'd only married Mark to protect the baby from the mob. *Too many maybes.*

The bike thundered beneath me, each rumble echoing the anger pounding in my skull. My tears dried in the wind, replaced by grim determination. *Hold on, kid*, I thought to the child I'd never met. *Daddy's coming.* And if Mark or the mob tried to stand in my way, they'd see just how far a desperate outlaw would go for his blood.

I gritted my teeth, focusing on the endless stretch of blacktop ahead. *Texas, I'm coming.* And God help anyone who tried to stop me.

Finally the Texas sun beat down on the back of my neck, scorching me through my worn leather cut, but I barely felt the heat. My pulse hammered as I leaned against a brick planter across the street, eyes locked on the outdoor patio of some high-end restaurant. Bright umbrellas shaded well-dressed patrons enjoying salads, iced tea, or whatever the hell fancy people sipped in summer. I'd never been one for places like this, too clean, too proper, but there I was, skulking like a damn stalker, watching her.

Lexi. She sat at a small bistro table near the railing, wearing a light yellow sundress that flowed over her curves. A stroller rested beside her, the canopy tilted to shield the baby inside from the midday sun. *My baby,* I thought, heart throbbing. The child I'd learned existed only days ago, a child she claimed belonged to that lawyer she married. But I knew better, from the timing, from the photo, from Nova's scared face.

She sipped some fruity-looking drink, occasionally bending over the stroller with a gentle smile. Even from this distance, I saw how her face lit up, pure maternal adoration. A knot formed in my throat. *That could've been me, sitting beside her, holding our child.* Instead, she'd married that bastard Mark. I bit the inside of my cheek hard enough to taste blood.

A sleek black sedan slid up to the curb. *Speak of the devil.* Mark stepped out, all pressed slacks and polished shoes. He strode onto the patio, glancing around like he owned the place, then leaned down to kiss Lexi's cheek. She gave a faint, forced smile, turning her face away a second too late.

Maybe I was imagining the awkwardness. Maybe I just needed to believe she wasn't truly happy with him. My chest burned as he placed a hand on her shoulder, murmuring something that made her nod. *So this is the father figure she wants for my kid?*

I dug my nails into my palms, telling myself not to charge across the street. The crowd bustled around me, businessmen, women in heels clicking on the concrete, tourists snapping photos of downtown Dallas. None of them noticed the raging outlaw with a bullet scar on his shoulder, disguised in aviators and a battered baseball cap, seething with jealousy.

When the waiter arrived at Lexi's table, Mark ordered with a confident wave of his hand, probably selecting the priciest item on the menu. Lexi fiddled with the baby's blanket, distracted. My heart squeezed at the sight of her.

A whimper from the stroller made Lexi lean over, gently cooing. She lifted the baby out, her movements careful. I caught a glimpse of a tiny face, big eyes. *That's my child.* My heart skipped a beat. *That's my blood.* I nearly lost control, half a step forward before my rational mind roped me back. This wasn't the moment to blow everything wide open, not on a busy downtown street.

Finally, Mark hailed the waiter for the check, tossed a card on the tray. Lexi stood to rearrange the stroller, and he bent down to give her a quick kiss again. She didn't seem to resist *too* much, but she didn't melt into it either. The baby fussed, and they hurried off, disappearing into that black sedan. I followed with my gaze until the car merged into traffic, lost among the sea of vehicles.

My chest ached with every breath. *A year*, that's how long I'd let slip by. Now she was living the high life with that suit. Married, apparently. A baby in tow. My baby? Everything in me roared that I needed to confront her *now*, but I forced myself to wait. I had to plan, not just charge in like a savage.

I exhaled, stepping away from my vantage point. If I hurried, maybe I could tail them, find out exactly which mansion Mark stashed her in. Because one thing was certain, I wouldn't let some arrogant prick raise my kid as his own.

CHAPTER 46

Lexi

I cradled my son. *Mark Adam Martin*, or so the birth certificate read, against my chest, bouncing him gently as I paced the marble foyer. My footsteps echoed in the high-ceilinged mansion, the same echo that made me feel alone no matter how large the place was. The baby whimpered, fussing from the heat, or perhaps picking up on my nerves. I pressed a kiss to his downy hair, tears pricking my eyes. *God, you look so much like your real father.*

Mark was at some late meeting, or so he claimed, leaving me with the baby in this cavernous house. I'd grown accustomed to the staff milling around, housekeepers, a chef, a couple of discreet security men, but it never seemed homelike. It was more like a gilded cage. A cage I'd chosen for the sake of survival.

My phone buzzed on the coffee table. I gently lowered baby Mark into his bassinet, ensuring he was settled, then hurried to snatch the device. A text from Nova:

Nova: *Maverick knows.*

Nova: *He saw the picture. He's on his way.*

My heart slammed against my ribs. *He's on his way. Maverick.* Panic and longing warred in my chest. For a moment, I couldn't breathe. I typed back with trembling fingers:

Me: *What? He's here in Dallas? Nova, how?!*

Nova responded almost instantly:

Nova: *He was at that rally. Chigger got drunk and spilled everything. He scrolled my phone, saw the baby pics. I'm so sorry.*

My eyes brimmed with tears. *Damn it, Chigger.* Fear spiked. If Maverick confronted Mark or the mob, someone might die. My entire world threatened to crumble. I typed back:

Me: *He can't come here! Mark has threatened me before, plus the mob is still watching. If Maverick storms in... oh God.*

Nova's next text came quickly:

Nova: *I know. He's furious, Lex. He's sure the baby is his. I thought he just stormed off, but Chigger just said he left for Dallas that night. A couple days ago.*

A sob escaped my throat. Of course the baby was his. But I'd told everyone it was Mark's or at least implied it.

"Shit," I whispered, pacing. *What do I do now?*

Me: *I don't know how to keep him away. I can't let him get shot or... Mark's father has connections, you know. They'll kill him.*

Nova: *Just keep your head. We can figure this out. Maybe call me if he shows up. Good luck. I'm sorry.*

My hands shook so badly I almost dropped the phone. Baby Mark let out a soft cry from his bassinet, and I hurried back to rub his little belly, fighting tears. "It's okay, sweet boy," I murmured. "Everything's fine."

But it wasn't. Nothing was fine. Mark wanted me to keep up this facade indefinitely, pretending the baby was his. If Maverick clashed with him, there'd be blood. The entire reason I'd agreed to this hellish arrangement was to protect Maverick, Nova, Chigger... everyone. *Damn it, Maverick,* I thought, tears rolling down my cheeks.

Why did you have to come back now?

The doorbell rang. I froze, heart in my throat. The baby whimpered again, maybe sensing my terror. I glanced at the clock, eight-thirty in the evening. Could that be Mark? Usually, he let himself in. Maybe it was a package or... *Maverick.* My pulse raced.

The housekeeper, Mrs. Delgado, quickly approached from the side hallway. She gave me a questioning look. "Should I get it, ma'am?"

I swallowed. "Yes, but let me see who it is."

She nodded, stepping toward the grand double doors. I trailed behind, baby fussing in my arms. The door opened to reveal none other than the biker, standing on the porch, eyes dark with anger and something deeper. My knees almost buckled. He wore a worn leather jacket, dusty torn jeans, his hair unruly from the ride. My throat went dry. God, he looked the same but lines of pain were etched around his eyes.

"Lexi," he said, his eyes everywhere at once.

Mrs. Delgado peered at me for direction.

My mind screamed *Send him away*, but my heart fought it. I cleared my throat. "It's okay. I'll handle this."

She hesitated, then bowed slightly and retreated down the hall. Maverick stepped inside before I could say otherwise, boots echoing on the marble. My chest pounded, baby Mark squirming in my arms. The door clicked shut behind him, sealing us in the foyer, a place too lavish for an outlaw like him. He looked around with a sneer.

"So this is your new house?" he muttered, gaze flicking over the marble floors and ornate fixtures.

I cradled the baby closer, my voice trembling. "You can't be here. If Mark finds you..."

His brow furrowed. "I don't give a damn about Mark. I'm here to see my kid."

A shiver ran down my spine. *He's not wrong.* But fear roiled in my gut. Mark had powerful allies. They could kill Maverick if they caught him here. "Mark already knows you might be the father," I lied. Mark one hundred percent knew it for a fact. "He doesn't care. But I do. If he comes home now, he'll kill you."

Maverick's eyes narrowed. "Then we'll see who ends up dead." He stepped closer, voice low with anger. "You're leaving with me. Pack your shit, give me the kid. Let's go."

My heart twisted. "No. I can't uproot my life. I have to keep the baby safe. And you're married, Maverick. Aren't you?" The bitterness seeped out of me. "Sky, your wife, did you bring her along for the ride?"

He flinched, pain flashing in his eyes. "No. She betrayed me, Lexi. She tried to lead the mob right to you. That's how I got shot in

Kansas. She wanted you dead, maybe to protect her own child's claim to the Getty empire or some bullshit. She's gone, all right? She and I are finished. Had been since the day you signed that contract."

A wave of confusion and regret hit me.

All this time, I assumed he chose her.

"I... I didn't know," I said, throat constricting. "I thought you were off living happily. That's what I was told." My voice cracked. "Mark told me if I didn't marry him, he'd have the mob come after you again. He threatened Nova and Chigger. I couldn't risk it." I lowered my gaze, tears slipping down. "I had to let him claim the baby, pretend it was his."

He exhaled, anger warring with hurt in his dark eyes. "And you never even let me know?" He stared at the infant in my arms, who squirmed under our strained voices. "We made this kid. You lied to me."

Guilt swamped me. "I'm sorry. I believed you were gone, that you had a wife and no place for me. Then the mob threatened everyone I cared about. I didn't see another way."

He clenched his fists. "Well, I'm here now. Let's fix this. Come with me. I'll protect you both. *I promise.*" His voice grew desperate, stepping closer until we were mere inches apart.

My heart ached, wanting to fling myself into his arms. But reality intruded. Mark's threats, the constant watch by the mob, the hush money, the entire precarious arrangement. "No," I whispered. "I can't. I have to keep my baby safe."

He stared at me, anguish etched on his face. "You think I can't keep her safe? I'd die for you both."

Tears dripped onto my cheeks. "And that's exactly why I won't risk it. You could die. And then who's left to protect the baby? Marciano's men might kill me for breach of contract." I forced a bitter laugh. "I'm not free, Maverick."

He growled under his breath, glancing around, probably half-expecting Mark's security to bust in. "At least let me see the kid," he snapped. "Let me hold her?"

A pang shot through me, remembering the child's official name: *Mark Adam Martin*. *Adam*, like Maverick's real name. Mark didn't know why I chose it. But I was too terrified to hand him over. Mark had cameras in half the rooms. *He might see.* "It's a boy," I choked out. "Named him... Mark Adam."

Maverick's face twisted at the mention of "Mark." Then he winced, as if hearing "Adam" gave him a spark of recognition. "Goddamn it," he rasped. "You named him Adam? That's, that's my middle name. You do realize that, right?"

I nodded, tears threatening again. "I know. I had to pretend Mark was the father, but... I guess I tried to honor you somehow." My throat burned. "You can see him, just... for a second. Then you have to go."

He let out a shivering breath. "Fine, let me see my son."

I cradled the infant carefully so Maverick could look. He reached out hesitantly, but something in my eyes must've warned him off, and he let his hand drop. We stood there, side by side, staring at the tiny face. The baby blinked up at Maverick, wriggling a fist in the air. A muscle in Maverick's jaw twitched, raw emotion shining in his eyes.

He recognized himself in that child. The resemblance was too strong to deny.

Finally, Maverick sucked in a breath. "He's... perfect," he whispered. "We made a perfect kid."

My heart cracked wide open. "Yes," I murmured, tears streaming silently. "And now you've seen him, so please go. For your own safety and ours. Just go."

He blew air out his nose. "You can't be fucking serious. I'm not leaving my kid with that bastard you married."

I brushed past him, baby in my arms, guiding him gently toward the door. "I'm sorry," I croaked. "But I can't risk Mark's wrath. He might call Marciano, and the mob would slaughter us all. If you really care, you'll keep your distance."

He spun me around, eyes flashing with anger. "I can't do that."

I trembled, tears burning my eyes. "You have to."

He hesitated, rage and heartbreak raging behind his expression. Then, with a muttered curse, he stepped back, nodding. "I'll find a way, Lexi," he said, like it was a promise. "I won't let you suffer under that prick."

I shook my head miserably. "I'm happy here," I lied, hoping he'd believe it. "Mark is... good to me." The words tasted like ash. "Just... go."

Slowly, Maverick walked to the door, pausing once to cast a final look at me and the baby. His eyes shone with sorrow. Then he turned the knob and slipped out into the night, leaving the mansion silent.

The moment the door clicked shut, my knees nearly buckled. A wide-eyed butler stepped forward from the shadows. "Ma'am, are you all right?" he asked softly.

I clutched the baby, tears choking me. "I'm fine," I snapped automatically, then softened. "I'm sorry. It's just... a friend from my old life. He had no business being here."

The butler nodded politely, but his gaze flicked to the door. "Should I inform Mr. Martin that you had a visitor?"

Mark's staff is always watching. I swallowed. "No need. I'll... I'll tell him myself. Thank you."

He bowed, stepping away. I realized how close I'd come to chaos. If Mark had arrived during that confrontation, Maverick might be dead. Or Mark might have forced me to watch him kill him.

Either way, I have to maintain this façade.

Tears welled as I turned, heading back to the grand living room. The baby fussed again, picking up on my turmoil. I sat on the plush couch, rocking him gently, staring at the massive windows that overlooked a dark, manicured lawn.

I was trapped. Maverick's sudden reappearance tore open old wounds, reminding me of the illusions and the lies. But I had to act as though I wanted this life with Mark. I'd do anything to keep my child safe, even if it meant crushing my own heart.

As I buried my face in baby Mark's tiny shoulder, I realized that even though I'd pushed Maverick away, a part of me clung to the hope he'd find a way to free us from this living nightmare. Because no matter how many times I said I was "happy," I couldn't ignore the ache in my chest that whispered, *You still love him.*

But until then, I'd lock my heart behind these mansion walls, pretending everything was fine. Pretending Mark Adam Martin wasn't truly Mark *Adam Hart.*

CHAPTER 47

I watched the front doors of our mansion swing open as Mark strode in, precisely at ten o'clock, a mere ten minutes later than he'd texted. My heart did its usual uneasy flutter, equal parts dread and resigned acceptance. The baby, tucked in my arms, let out a soft coo, unaware of the trouble filling the foyer.

"Lexi?" Mark called, his voice echoing off the marble. He stepped into view, immaculate as always in a tailored charcoal suit, tie loosened just enough to appear casually refined. His gaze flicked over me, then over the baby. "Who was at the door earlier?" he asked, setting his leather briefcase on a polished hall table.

Of course he'd ask. The security staff probably mentioned a visitor. My mind flashed to Maverick, the raw desperation in his eyes, the way he looked at our son, his son, before I practically forced him out. I was still shaken up by it.

There was no use lying. Mark would see him on the video. I summoned a steady breath. "It was... Maverick," I said quietly, choosing honesty.

His expression hardened, though a spark of interest flickered in his eyes. "He showed up here?" He stepped closer, brushing his hand over the baby's head. "And you sent him away?"

"I told him the baby isn't his, and that I was happy here." The lie caught in my throat, but I forced it out. "I handled it."

Mark visibly eased. "Good." His lips curved in a triumphant smirk. Then he leaned in and pressed a perfunctory kiss to my cheek.

The scent of his expensive cologne washed over me, and under it there was another scent, more feminine. Nauseatingly sweet.

"He left," he murmured. "So, you did well."

My cheeks burned with anger and shame, but I kept a placid smile plastered on my face. He gave my waist a possessive squeeze, then pulled back. "I'll be out late tonight," he added, removing his tie and draping it over a marble bust near the hallway. "Don't wait up."

I stifled a bitter laugh. We both knew what that meant. He'd been discreetly seeing other women for months, some fling or multiple flings, though he never bothered to hide it much after I'd caught him in the act at the office. Our marriage was nothing but a front, our bedroom arrangements purely for show. "All right," I whispered, adjusting the baby's blanket.

He gave me a final nod, then swept through the hall, calling out for the driver. The front doors banged shut behind him, leaving me in the echoing stillness.

I stared down at the baby's eyes, big and bright with innocence, my heart aching. This was how life had been since I married Mark, empty, routine, ruled by fear. If Maverick hadn't appeared earlier, I might've stayed numb. But his visit cracked open something inside me, a longing for the biker I once trusted more than anyone else.

Yet I'd told Mark I was happy, just to protect my child from more mob threats. The same twisted sense of duty had forced me to keep Maverick away. *I'm sorry,* I silently told my son. *It's the only way I know how.*

Afterwards, the days blurred. Mark came and went, sometimes doting on the baby, other times ignoring us entirely. Every coo, gurgle, and smile from the baby reminded me so much of Maverick. And that I sent him away. It was tough. But I carried on, playing my role as the perfect trophy wife on maternity leave.

The next Saturday, I found a rare chance to slip away. Nova had invited me to brunch. She'd texted me, urging me to get out of the mansion. I put on a simple floral dress, strapped the baby into the car seat, and sent Mark a quick text about meeting some girlfriends for a ladies' lunch. He barely acknowledged it, just typed back, giving me permission. He was probably off with one of his mistresses, anyway.

So, I drove to our usual spot, a cozy café near downtown. The city was baking, but the awnings provided shade on the sidewalks. People were walking around with iced coffees, couples had their dogs out. It was all so lively, a total change from my stuffy life at Mark's mansion. I missed this life.

Nova was already seated at a corner table, wearing sunglasses pushed into her dark-blonde hair. The instant I approached with the stroller, she jumped up to hug me.

"God, Lex," she whispered, glancing at the baby. "He's getting so big!"

I gave a tight smile, settling the stroller beside my chair. "Babies tend to grow," I joked weakly. Then I took a seat, ignoring the pang in my heart. He was Maverick's spitting image.

Nova studied me with sympathetic eyes. "How are you holding up?"

Fiddling with my napkin, I lifted a shoulder. "I'm... managing." My tone sounded hollow. "Mark's still controlling, still sees other women, but at least he's not on my case every second. The baby's healthy, that's all that matters." Except I couldn't quite meet her gaze.

She sipped her lemonade. "And Maverick? I know he visited. Are you okay?"

I remembered the intensity in Maverick's eyes. "He's gone now. I told him I was happy. Not to come back. I had to."

Nova frowned. "You had to?"

I was on the verge of tears. "Yes, because Mark, he'd use the mob to crush him if he discovered he knew the truth. I can't risk that. I can't lose..." My voice broke. "I can't lose Maverick... if the mob hunts him down... This arrangement is all I have to keep everyone alive."

Nova squeezed my hand across the table, silent empathy flowing between us. It was so great to have someone to talk to who understood my position.

The waiter approached, we each ordered, then waited in uneasy quiet until the server left.

"How's Chigger?" I asked about Nova's on again, off again fling, changing the subject.

She could talk for hours, telling me every detail of their adventures and their sex life. I was living vicariously through her as she babbled.

Finally, Nova cleared her throat. "You deserve real happiness, Lex. You shouldn't be living in fear."

I forced a wry laugh. "And how do I get that? I can't snap my fingers and fix the mess I created. Mark has the power to kill us all if I stray from my contract."

Nova frowned, glancing at the baby. "Still, maybe there's another way."

Our brunch arrived, eggs benedict for me, a fruit-laden waffle for her. We nibbled half-heartedly, the baby dozing in the stroller. When the plates were cleared, Nova dabbed her mouth with a napkin with a thoughtful look on her face.

"Don't hurry off. I want to show you my new place. You have never visited since I moved out of the city. Please come, even if it's just for an hour. I'll drive you home before Mark's back, promise."

I hesitated. Mark's schedule was unpredictable, but I craved any semblance of normalcy. "All right," I said softly. "But let me text him, say I'm doing some shopping."

Nova nodded approval. "Do it now. We can head out soon."

I typed a quick message to Mark, *Going shopping after brunch. Be home later.*

He responded with a curt, *Ok.*

Good enough.

Soon, Nova guided her SUV onto the highway, the baby strapped securely in the back seat, me in the passenger side. The city disappeared, replaced by endless suburbs. We chatted a bit or tried to. My mind was drifting to the day last year when we'd driven together for that ill-fated rally. My life had changed so drastically.

"It's wild," I murmured, gazing at the passing scenery. "A year ago, we were hitting book signings, squealing over hot cover models. Now I'm married to a man I don't love, and I have a baby who might never know his real father."

Nova gave me a sympathetic smile. "I know. Life's insane. But you're strong, Lex. We'll figure something out."

I gave a sad smile. "I wish I could be truly happy, you know? Like the heroines in those romance novels we used to devour. None of them had to face real mob threats. Only imaginary ones."

Nova gave a quiet chuckle. "True. Our real-life story is a bit more... real. But maybe we'll find a better ending if we keep fighting."

My smile faded. I knew Nova was just trying to cheer me up, but since Maverick showed up, and I learned he hadn't been happy with his wife, I'd been throwing a pity party for one.

We arrived in a quiet suburb outside Frisco, pulling into the driveway of a modest, single-story home with a neat lawn. Flower pots lined the porch, the paint fresh. It wasn't big or flashy, just cozy like her place before we got the condo. She helped me carry the diaper bag and ushered me inside.

The interior smelled faintly of fresh paint, boxes scattered around the living room. I blinked, taking in how half the place seemed packed up. "You just moved here, and you haven't unpacked?" I teased lightly, noticing labeled crates, kitchen, books, bedroom stuff.

Nova grimaced. "Yeah, about that..." She motioned for me to set the baby's car seat on the couch. "Let me get you something to drink. Have a seat."

Confusion gnawed at me. "Is something wrong?"

She just shook her head and gave a strained smile. "Relax. I'll explain in a sec." Then she disappeared into the small kitchen.

I gently unbuckled the baby, holding him close while scanning the boxes. A pang of worry fluttered in my stomach. Was she moving again so soon? Was it because of the mob threat?

Nova returned with a cold glass of iced tea, pressing it into my hand. "Here, sip. Put him down for a bit? The couch is wide. I have a blanket."

I raised an eyebrow but followed her suggestion, laying the baby on a folded blanket. He stirred, then fell back to drowsing, lulled by the house's cool air. Whatever she had to tell me, she thought I didn't need to be holding the baby. Was it that bad?

"You're stalling," I said, taking a sip of the tea. "What's going on?"

Nova settled onto a nearby chair, fiddling with her glass. "I have news," she began, voice trembling slightly.

She was taking her sweet time with it. I took a big gulp, waiting.

"I'm... going on the road with Chigger. All my stuff's going in storage. I'm leaving tomorrow."

I was so shocked, I almost spit out my tea. "You're what? Why?" She'd joked about seeing the country on the back of his Harley. But fuck. I didn't want her to leave, leave me all alone in Texas with Mark.

She exhaled, setting her untouched glass down with a clink. "Because I see how stuck you are with Mark. I know why you're there, fear, blackmail, all that. But as long as you think me, or Chigger, or Maverick might be in danger, you won't break free. You'll stay married to that prick. So, I'm removing myself from the equation."

"That's... that's ridiculous. I told you, I'm coping fine. Don't throw your life away on the road just because of me."

Nova's gaze hardened. "I'm not throwing anything away. I'm living my life. And I won't let you use me as an excuse to stay in a loveless marriage. If the mob threatens me or Chigger, we'll be long gone. They won't find us."

I felt tears welling up. "But I don't want you to vanish. You're my best friend, my only real friend in this city."

She reached for my hand, squeezing tight. "I'm sorry. But you deserve the chance to choose your future without worrying about me. If you want to be with Mark, that's your call, but I want to be sure it's actually your call and not fear for me or the others."

My head gave a shake, tears slipping. "Nova, that's... I don't want you to leave."

She forced a small smile. "I love you, Lex, but it's time. Now, look, I want you to understand something." Her voice grew firmer. "You do not have to stay with Mark. We can figure out a better plan. The baby belongs with you, you alone if you choose. But Maverick's the father..."

I opened my mouth to argue, but a woozy sensation twisted my vision. The room seemed to tilt, the edges blurring. My thoughts grew fuzzy. "N-Nova," I mumbled, blinking rapidly. "I feel... weird. Dizzy."

She shot up, alarmed. "Are you okay?"

I tried to speak again, but the words tangled on my tongue. My limbs grew heavy, eyes drooping. The baby's soft coo sounded distant, like I was underwater. What was happening?

Darkness rushed in. My body slumped, everything going black. I vaguely heard Nova saying my name, her voice echoing as though down a long tunnel. Then nothing.

CHAPTER 48

A throbbing ache pulsed in my temples when I drifted back to consciousness. I peeled my eyes open, squinting at a living room that definitely wasn't Nova's. My head pounded, mouth dry, disoriented.

Panic flared. Where's my baby?! I jerked upright, scanning the unfamiliar space. The furniture was old-fashioned, worn couches with a southwestern pattern, and a coffee table of distressed wood. Low lamplight revealed drawn curtains over a big window. I got a hint of engine oil and leather.

Nova's voice startled me. "Hey, you're awake." She was perched on a recliner, fiddling with her phone.

Relief and confusion lingered. "Nova?" My voice cracked. "What happened? Where's my baby?"

Her eyes flicked behind me. I turned, heart lurching, to see a broad figure stepping in from another room, cradling my infant. The child let out a gentle coo, and the man carefully handed him from one arm to the other. My breath caught.

Maverick.

He stood there, leather jacket shrugged off to reveal muscular arms, that same smolder in his gaze. My baby, our baby, snoozed in his grip, tiny head tucked under Maverick's chin. The sight nearly broke me.

I shot off the couch, vision swimming. "Give him to me," I said in a choked whisper, arms outstretched. Fear mingled with outrage.

How dare they take me from my home?

Maverick stepped closer, carefully transferring the baby into my waiting arms. "He's safe," he murmured, voice thick with emotion. "Took me hours to get him to settle, but I managed."

I clutched my son, half sobbing. "What the hell, Nova? Did you drug me or something?" I glared at her, fresh tears burning my eyes. "How could you do this?"

Nova lowered her gaze. "I'm sorry, Lex. You left me no choice. You were too locked in Mark's grip to see reason. Chigger and I, we just want you safe, truly safe. We planned this... got Maverick's help. It was the only way."

I stared in disbelief. "You... you kidnapped me?"

Maverick cleared his throat. "Think of it as a rescue." His eyes shone with a quiet intensity.

Anger flared, competing with relief. My baby wriggled in my arms, reminding me to keep my temper. "Mark, he'll freak out, call the mob. They'll kill us all. Don't you get it?"

Nova stood, pacing. "Let him try. Chigger's arranged for us to disappear if needed. The baby's father is here. You don't need Mark or his hush money. If we all vanish, the mob has no leverage. We have resources."

I shook my head, tears dripping. "You don't know how powerful Marciano is. Or Mark's father. They have their claws everywhere."

Maverick's jaw flexed. "So we run. As a nomad, I know how. And if they come after us, I'll bury them. I'm done letting you suffer in that bastard's mansion."

My breath came in ragged gasps. A swirl of longing and terror battered me. "I... God, I can't believe you two. This is insane."

Nova stepped closer, placing a tentative hand on my shoulder. "Lex, we did what we had to do. You and the baby deserve a life free from threats."

I glanced at the baby. He blinked awake, eyes so like Maverick's. My throat tightened. Could this truly be freedom? Or just another tragedy in the making?

Maverick exhaled slowly. "I'm sorry for scaring you. But I had to do something. The second Nova told me about her plan, I jumped at it." He ran a hand through his hair. "This is your chance, Lexi, to break free."

A whirlwind of conflicting emotions seized me. The child fussed, picking up on my turmoil. I rocked him gently. "He's hungry," I mumbled, sidestepping the bigger conversation.

Nova gestured to a small dining area. "There's formula and supplies. We planned for everything." She cast me a hopeful look. "Let's feed him, talk it through."

I bit my lip. "You expect me to just... be okay with this? You drugged me, took me from my home." I was so upset I could barely see. "Mark's going to lose his shit."

Maverick's expression flattened. "Let him. Let the mob come. I'll handle it." The fierce protectiveness in his eyes sparked a deep memory of the times I'd felt truly safe in his arms.

Still, my shoulders wouldn't relax. Maybe this was my only escape. My entire body yearned to collapse into Maverick's embrace, sobbing out the months of fear and loneliness. But a swirl of guilt clung to me. I lied to him for so long, insisted he had no role. Now I'm forced to rely on him.

Nova gently guided me toward a worn couch. "Sit, feed your baby. Then we'll figure out the next step. We have a plan, Lex. You're not alone."

My eyes burned as I sank onto the cushions, the baby in my arms. Could I trust them? Could we outrun the entire Syndicate, Marciano and Mark's father's resources? Questions hammered my brain, but a fragile hope glimmered in the distance. Maybe there was a way to keep my son safe without living in a fancy prison.

Kneeling beside me, Maverick's warmth evoked memories of our love. "We'll protect you." His voice choked with emotion. "Me, Chigger, Nova, we'll do whatever it takes."

I met his gaze, tears finally slipping free. "I'm terrified," I admitted. "But... I don't want to go back to that mansion. Ever."

A soft smile touched his lips, a promise blazing in his eyes. "Then you won't."

As the baby nuzzled against me, I let out a trembling breath, leaning into Maverick's shoulder for the first time in what felt like a lifetime. Outside, night descended, but inside, a light came on inside me. Hope flickered. My captivity was over, replaced by a new fight for freedom, and possibly a second chance at love.

CHAPTER 49

Maverick

I gunned the throttle, the wind slicing across my cheeks, tasting of dust and open road. The black SUV carrying Lexi and the baby trailed behind, guided by Chigger and Nova. We'd managed to get everyone safely into Oklahoma, just barely across the Texas state line, and holed up in a little rental cottage tucked away off some old highway. It wasn't much, but at least there was enough cover that Mark's men or the mob wouldn't find us easily.

One step at a time, I kept telling myself. First, get Lexi and the baby out of Texas. Next, head for Maine, where the Kings of Anarchy MC welcomed me once before. But the plan had changed a bit, thanks to Kingpin's meddling, or maybe to his benefit, hard to say.

With Lexi out cold, it gave me my first moments with the baby. I would never call him Mark. He was Adam, and he already owned my heart. Even though Nova offered to step in, I was determined to be the one to help him settle in.

Once Lexi woke, Nova broke the news to her gently as I cradled Adam. Of course, she was confused and then angry at us for taking her. Because she was also terrified that the mob would find us, kill us all. When Lexi rested her head on my shoulder, I knew there was hope for us. Still, that first night I gave her some space.

We rolled up to the next cabin just as the sun dipped below the horizon, painting the sky in purples and golds. Nova parked the SUV a ways down a gravel patch, and I pulled my Harley alongside. The air was muggy, cicadas droning in the trees. The baby cried from inside the car, and I saw Lexi step out, worry etched on her face.

"We're here," I told her, gently taking the diaper bag from her weak grip. She was exhausted, understandably, after being uprooted so unexpectedly. I hated the guilt gnawing at my gut. If I'd come sooner, maybe she wouldn't have spent a year in that sham of a marriage. If I'd never left her behind in the first place...

But regrets could wait. We had a job. Keep her safe from Mark, from Marciano, from all the mob connections. And that meant forging a new path north. This time, I wouldn't use phony names or hide behind the shadows. I was Maverick, still a Road Monster, but I'd called in favors from Kingpin. Hell, I basically sold my soul to the biker president for his help. It was complicated, like everything else in this twisted underground.

We crowded into the small living room with mismatched furniture and faded wallpaper. Chigger carried in supplies, bags of groceries, extra diapers, the random stuff Nova had prepped. Nova herself busied with checking windows, while I locked the front door, scanning for any sign of watchers.

Lexi stood at the center of the room, holding the baby tight. She looked so small, her eyes darting around the unfamiliar space. Her dark hair was tied back, revealing the worry lines on her forehead. I ached to hold her, to promise it'd all be okay, but I knew trust didn't come easy after I'd barged into her life again and practically kidnapped her.

"There's two bedrooms down the hall," Nova said, returning from her quick inspection. "One's got a crib. We did our best on short notice."

Lexi gave a strained nod, cradling the baby closer. "Thank you," she murmured. Her voice trembled, and I knew she was overwhelmed.

I reached out, wanting to rest a hand on her shoulder, but paused, unsure if she'd welcome my touch. Her eyes flickered to mine, and for a moment, I read a swirl of emotions, fear, longing, confusion. Then she looked away, heading down the hall to check on the crib.

Chigger cleared his throat. "So, we staying the night, or are we pushing on?"

I sighed, sinking onto the worn couch. "We'll stay the night. Kid needs rest. Tomorrow, we head north."

Nova nodded in agreement, then cast me a curious look. "Any word from Kingpin? Did he finalize that deal with Ralph Getty?"

I swept my hair back with my hand. "Yeah, called him earlier. He said he gave Ralph the intel on Marciano's double-cross about Lexi, so Getty's wanting to cut a new deal, one that sets Lexi free from her old arrangement with Marciano and Mark. But it requires some bullshit contract that ensures she's not the rightful heir to the Getty empire."

Chigger snorted. "Mob politics, man. So basically, if she's Alexander Getty's kid, that's a threat to Ralph's claim. So they want to disprove her heritage or something?"

I nodded. "Exactly. Kingpin said they'll have her sign a contract and do a DNA test, but they'll rig it so it shows she's not a Getty. They just need someone else to claim fatherhood. And apparently, Kingpin volunteered. He said it's not impossible, given how many men Dirty Diana was with back in the day while she was in Nashville."

Nova let out a disbelieving laugh. "So Lexi's father on paper will be Kingpin? That's twisted as hell. Then you'd be hooking up with the daughter of your mortal enemy."

My stomach knotted at the idea. "Let's not dwell on that," I muttered. "Kingpin is not as much my enemy as a necessary evil. Anyway, that's the plan, so Lexi can be free from any Getty inheritance nonsense and the mob's interest."

Chigger chuckled. "Damn. That's messed up, but if it works, it works."

I exhaled, glancing toward the hallway where Lexi had disappeared. "Nothing's certain. We'll see once the test is done. Then we go to Maine. Let the Kings of Anarchy provide cover."

Night fell, and we divvied up sleeping arrangements. Nova and Chigger claimed the smaller bedroom, leaving Lexi and the baby the slightly bigger one. That forced me to sprawl on the couch, a lumpy old thing that squeaked whenever I moved. Fine by me. I didn't want to push Lexi into sharing a room, not yet.

Early morning arrived with the smell of instant coffee that Chigger brewed in the tiny kitchen. I lumbered in, bleary-eyed, running my hand over my jaw scruff. Nova was packing a cooler of snacks while Lexi rocked the baby in the corner, wearing the same tired expression.

"We head out soon," I said, clearing my throat. "Got the route planned, straight up through Missouri, Illinois, then cut east. Should be a few days' ride."

Lexi nodded, adjusting the baby's bottle. "What about the DNA test Nova mentioned? How does that work if we're on the run?"

I leaned against the counter. "Kingpin said he'll have a contact meet us halfway, or we can mail a sample. Once it's processed, they'll handle forging the results, assuming you're a Getty. But if you're not, we might not need the forgery. Then you sign some contract, say you have no claim, and that's it."

She chewed her lip, eyes darting to her son. "And if I am Alexander Getty's daughter?"

My chest clenched. "Then they'll fake the test, using Kingpin's DNA to say he is your real father." The words tasted bitter. "He volunteered for that, said it's plausible enough."

A flicker of shock crossed her features. "Then I'd be Kingpin's daughter? Some random biker like mom always said. But I guess I wouldn't be an heir to the mob."

I forced a nod, ignoring the weird swirl of jealousy. I'd be in love with Kingpin's daughter? His fake daughter. That would make my ex, Eve, her fake stepmother. The universe had a twisted sense of humor.

We made the grueling ride north over the next several days, stopping only for quick motel stays and to let the baby rest. Chigger drove the SUV with Lexi and Nova while I rode ahead on my Harley, scouting. Each mile put more distance between us and Mark or Marciano's men. I checked my phone frequently, expecting some kind of pursuit. Nothing materialized.

Finally, after crossing state lines and winding through pine forests, we reached the Kings of Anarchy MC in Maine. Their president, Solo, greeted us with a curt nod. They'd prepared a small apartment above their clubhouse for Lexi and the baby, ensuring privacy. The place smelled faintly of sawdust and motor oil, but it was livable.

Lexi looked relieved yet wary as she settled the baby's car seat in a corner. "Thank you," she told Solo softly.

He just shrugged. "Any friend of Maverick's is a friend of ours. You'll be safe here."

We sent off Lexi's DNA sample, just a cheek swab. It took Kingpin a couple of weeks to process it through his contact. Those were tense days. We roamed the clubhouse, living in borrowed rooms, uncertain if Mark or Marciano had a clue where we were. But none of their men showed up. Maybe we shook them off for good.

Lexi was distant, though I caught her watching me with conflicted eyes whenever I played peekaboo with the baby. She never forbade me from holding him, but she never invited me either. It felt as if a storm were about to break. We needed a proper conversation, but she kept busy, holed up in the little apartment with the baby. I busied myself constantly on guard, watching for trouble that was bound to find us, eventually. Therefore, we hovered in a strange limbo.

Finally, Kingpin called. I took the call outside the clubhouse, pacing near a row of Harleys under the pine trees. The summer air in Maine was warm enough, not oppressive like the months that were coming, and the distant crash of ocean waves always provided a soothing backdrop.

"Maverick," came a gruff voice. Kingpin used the right name. "We got the results."

I was on edge, waiting. "And?"

He hesitated, then let out a low chuckle. "She's not a Getty. No forging required."

I froze. "Wait, so... the test says she's not Alexander's kid?"

A rustle on the line. "It did say she's related to... a powerful man."

"Who?"

"Handsome fellow, but a mean son of a bitch. Big dick."

"What the hell are you talking about, Kingpin?"

"Test says Lexi is really related to me. Dipshit." Kingpin sounded weirdly resigned. "I guess Dirty Diana was blackmailing me for a reason. She always threatened to reveal something big, but I never figured... Anyway, her DNA matches me. She's my daughter. Like I said, no forging required."

Shock pulsed through me. Lexi is Kingpin's daughter? That was a revelation I never saw coming. "You sure you didn't rig that test?" I asked, half-joking, half-panicked.

He gave a dry laugh. "I wanted to. But the doc said it was a perfect match. So that's the truth. I fathered a kid with Diana I never knew about."

I raked a hand through my hair. "Jesus. That means... She's your daughter. And I... we, uh..." My mind scrambled. I was in love with Kingpin's daughter? Had a kid with her. His grandson?

He growled. "I'm not thrilled about you being with her, Pig. Even if I never knew her. But it solves the Getty problem. She's not an heir, so Ralph and Marciano have no claim. She's free."

My head swirled. "So now what?"

He grunted. "If you truly want her, do right by her. Otherwise, stay the hell away. I never liked you anyway. But I guess, I'm a grandad." He ended the call abruptly.

I stood there, phone in hand, the pine-scented breeze ruffling my hair. Lexi is Kingpin's daughter. That explained Diana's threats. A wave of relief mingled with dread. At least she was safe from the Getty empire, but now we had the awkward reality that she was the daughter of my longtime enemy. So be it. I wouldn't let that keep me from her if she wanted me.

The clubhouse was quieter than usual, most of the Kings out on a charity ride. The small apartment above was quiet, too. I rapped lightly on the door. A second later, Lexi opened, baby cradled to her chest. She looked tired, but there was a glint in her eyes, some combination of worry and curiosity at my arrival.

"Hey," I said, stepping inside.

She shut the door behind me, fiddling with the baby's blanket. "Hey. Did you hear something?"

I nodded, keeping my voice low. "Yeah, Kingpin got the results. You're not a Getty. You're... his daughter."

"They forged the results, then."

"No, oddly enough, your mom had been telling you the truth all these years. Even if she was blackmailing Getty, you weren't his kid. You were a random biker's kid. Kingpin's. That's why when Ralph and Sky came after her and you, she wanted to spill her secrets on Kingpin. You weren't Getty's, you were his."

Her expression froze, color draining from her cheeks. "So, it's actually true?" she whispered. "I'm Kingpin's kid?" The baby fussed, as if sensing her distress. She tried to soothe him with gentle pats. "That's insane. I, I never imagined."

I stepped closer. "He said your mom used to… hang around his club, Royal Road, around the same time she was with Alexander Getty. Kingpin slept with her back then, too. It aligns with everything. Look, the bottom line is you're safe from Ralph. No more mob claims. No more Mark. You're free."

She exhaled, tears brimming. "Free. Right. But I still can't go back to my old life. I… I'm married to Mark, and even if he can't hold that arrangement over me with the mob, he might still fight me for custody."

Pain lanced my chest at the idea of losing her again. But I tried to keep calm. "You can divorce him, Lex. If he tries anything, you have me behind you. I'll fight that bastard if necessary. Besides, little Adam is my child. We'll prove it. He won't take him."

She swallowed, placing the baby in a portable crib near the wall. Then she faced me, her eyes flicking with panic. "Maverick, you have to realize how crazy this all is. I barely escaped with my life. Now I find out my father is… a man you claimed was your sworn enemy. And I'm here in Maine, with you, after you basically kidnapped me. My mind is a mess."

I reached for her hand, and this time she let me take it. "I know. But I'm sorry, I had to do something. I couldn't let you stay with that snake. You're safe now. That's what matters."

Her gaze locked onto mine. "I… I don't blame you for rescuing me, but it's a lot to process. And we have a baby, yours, not Mark's. What do we do?" Her voice cracked, tears pooling.

My heart knocked as I gently cupped her cheek. "We make a fresh start. I'll take you and the baby in. We'll stay in Maine if you want, or somewhere else safe. I want to be a family, Lexi. Marry me."

Her eyes went wide, tears spilling. "Marry you?" She let out a shaky laugh. "I'm already married, remember?"

I grimaced. "We'll get it annulled or divorced. Once Mark realizes the mob has no interest in you, he can't blackmail you. We have Kingpin's arrangement that you're not a Getty. He no longer has a stranglehold, right?"

She hesitated, looking down at our joined hands. "I guess so, but Mark might not give up easily. He's a vindictive bastard."

I shrugged, determination burning in my chest. "Then I'll make him. One way or another. I'm not leaving you or the baby. I want you both."

She trembled, tears falling silently. "I... I love you, Maverick. I never stopped. But you hurt me. You left me, and I ended up in that mansion. It nearly killed my spirit."

My throat closed. "I know. I'm sorry. I was so messed up, thinking you wanted Mark, or that you were safe. I was wrong. I'll spend the rest of my life making it up to you if you'll let me."

She blinked, voice choking on a sob. "I don't know if I can just... trust you completely again. Not yet. But we have a son. I can't deny that. And I'm so relieved I don't have to hide it anymore."

We stood there, gazes locked in a fragile moment. Then she sniffled, shaking her head. "I can't say yes to marriage until I sort out this divorce. Or see what Mark does. But... I won't run from you anymore."

Relief swept through me. I dared to lean in, pressing my lips to hers, tasting the salt from her tears. She gasped, but her arms slipped around my neck, and she kissed me back, a wave of longing surging between us. My heart pounded, breath hitching with the pent-up passion of a year's separation.

When we broke apart, I rested my forehead against hers. "We'll figure out the details. For now, can we at least try to rebuild what we had?"

She clung to my jacket, eyes glimmering. "Yes. Let's try."

A soft cry from the baby broke the moment. She pulled away, going to soothe him. I watched with a bittersweet ache. He's mine. Our child. My chest swelled with both pride and sorrow, thinking of all the milestones I missed. But maybe I'd be there for the rest.

Later that night, after dinner and an uneasy hush settled over the small apartment, I slipped out to the hallway. I found Lexi pacing with the baby, trying to get him to sleep. I touched her shoulder gently, offering to take him so she could rest. She allowed me to cradle him, my heart soaring at the weight of my son in my arms. The first of many moments, I vowed silently.

We'd face Mark's wrath soon enough. He'd probably unleash every legal trick, maybe send men to find her. But we had the Kings' protection, and the truth was on our side. Lexi wasn't a Getty, so Marciano had no claim. Mark had no leverage but threats. Let him come. I'd stand at Lexi's side now, not cowering in the shadows. She might be Kingpin's daughter, ironically making me the black sheep dating the boss's kid, but that was a worry for another time.

Right now, her soft breathing behind me, the baby's small hand grasping my finger... that was enough. I pressed a gentle kiss to his downy head, tears pricking my eyes. I'd never abandon them again, no matter who tried to tear us apart.

CHAPTER 50

Lexi

Time had a strange way of both racing forward and standing utterly still in those first two months in Maine. Some days I woke up and felt like everything in my life had changed overnight, separated, living in a cabin near the ocean with a biker, raising my infant son. Other days, it felt like I'd been in this limbo forever, caught between the hush money from the mob, the echoes of my old marriage to Mark, and the new life quietly forming with Maverick.

Those early weeks blurred into a routine that was half domestic bliss, half nervous watchfulness. We'd found a modest ranch-style house on the outskirts of a small coastal town, a place the Kings of Anarchy MC had arranged. It was bigger than the tiny apartment above the clubhouse, with a fenced backyard and enough space for my baby's crib in a cozy, light-filled nursery. I painted the walls in soft lavender, Nova helping me with the stencils of little stars and moons.

During the day, I nursed the baby, still named publicly as Mark Jr. in some official papers, but privately we called him "Adam" in honor of Maverick's and his middle name, changed diapers, read my dog-eared law textbooks, and tried not to obsess over Mark's inevitable legal meltdown. And each night, after dinner, Maverick would help me clean up, his warm presence both comforting and nerve-wracking.

I tried to keep him at arm's length physically, my body still felt foreign to me after pregnancy, and the emotional scars from everything that happened left me skittish. But Maverick was patient. He never pushed me for intimacy, never made me feel bad about my post-baby body. He just lingered, near enough that I knew he was there for me, yet distant enough to let me set the pace.

My phone calls with the divorce attorney progressed slowly. Mark's legal team, big shots from his father's firm, filed every delaying tactic possible. But eventually, the hush money and the fact that I'd left quietly worked in my favor. Mark had no interest in continuing a public fight if it meant risking the mob's attention. So the days dragged on, punctuated by tense phone calls with lawyers, until at last a settlement formed. I wouldn't get much financially. I didn't want it anyway. I had that hush money from Marciano sitting in a secret account, ironically enough. Illegal or not, Mark had no claim to it and was happy to wash his hands of it.

Nova joked that we should use it to open our own law practice somewhere in Maine. We daydreamed about a small storefront in the coastal town, painted white with a sign reading **Lexi & Nova, Attorneys at Law** or something like that, more likely our last names. Maybe my last name would be Hart by then. But it was just a fantasy, the firm and the marriage. For the moment, I was still adjusting to motherhood, living with Maverick, and trying to get out of a marriage that was, at best, a sham.

Despite the turmoil, Maverick found sweet ways to draw me out of my shell. Every Thursday, he took me on a "date" somewhere in the area. Once, we rode his Harley down the coast to a lighthouse, the wind in my hair and the ocean crashing below. Another time, we went to a quaint farmer's market. We wandered aisles of fresh produce while Adam snoozed in a sling pressed to my chest. Maverick would slip an arm around me protectively, his patched leather cut branding him an outlaw among the wholesome families. Yet he fit in so easily at my side, flashing a small grin whenever an older couple cooed over the baby.

He was gentle with me in every sense. If I shied away from physical closeness, he'd back off, but the longing in his eyes never vanished. I saw it in how he lingered over breakfast, in how his fingers grazed mine when handing me the sugar, in how he fixed the squeaky step outside our front door so I wouldn't trip carrying the baby. He was giving me space, but he was also quietly proving that this time, he wouldn't abandon me.

Still, I struggled with my postpartum body. My belly remained softer, my hips wider, my moods unpredictable with breastfeeding and hormones. I wore baggy clothes, not wanting Maverick to see how I'd changed. Late at night, I'd cradle Adam in my arms and remember how Maverick once traced every curve of my body. Now I felt unrecognizable, ashamed. If he noticed my insecurities, he never commented, just offered hushed reassurances that I was beautiful. But I usually laughed it off or changed the subject.

My heart still pounded with guilt. I'd been dishonest with him for so long, letting him think I'd chosen Mark, while I was forced into marriage. Even though I knew he understood now, a piece of me felt unworthy of his affection. So I kept him at a distance, physically and emotionally. He noticed, but never demanded. With controlling men surrounding me, Maverick's patience was a comfort.

Maverick was still a Road Monster. He wore the cut with pride, but also an undercurrent of weariness. Kingpin didn't call the shots here in the northeast, some other Ace of the Road Monsters had that territory. Meanwhile, the Kings of Anarchy MC, particularly their president, Solo, welcomed Maverick as an ally. The synergy between them grew stronger by the day. But as Maverick's ties to the club solidified, he found himself missing the solitude of being on the road alone. Except he didn't want to leave me or the baby.

Chigger had taken off on a run shortly after we arrived. Nova decided to stay with me, living in a small side room until she decided her next steps. I suspected she half-expected Chigger to come back, but she wasn't holding her breath. She had other plans, like maybe opening that law practice with me someday. We talked about it on slow afternoons, me nursing the baby while she perused local real estate listings on her phone.

"We could do it," she'd say, pointing to a listing for an old storefront in the harbor town. "Restore it, hang our shingle, become the dynamic duo."

I smiled at the idea, but a hollow pang reminded me. I can't start practicing until the dust settles. The last thing I needed was Mark's father's firm or the mob sniffing around. I told Nova maybe in a few months.

Two months crawled by. Adam sprouted from newborn to a plump infant, giggling whenever Maverick made funny faces. Nova found a part-time gig waitressing, paying her share of expenses. The hush money covered rent and groceries, so we weren't exactly starving. My divorce with Mark was finalized with surprisingly little fanfare. One final signature on a stack of documents ended that twisted chapter. A wave of relief crashed over me, I was free. But also, a sliver of fear. Mark was pissed to be losing his heir and claim to his father's fortune. Signing the divorce papers, his hand had been forced. What if he retaliates?

When I told Maverick that the divorce was done, I expected him to erupt in joy. Instead, he gave me a solemn nod and gently took my hands. "Good," he said, voice thick with unspoken emotion. "Now we can truly move forward."

Life shifted after that. Freed from Mark's legal grip, I breathed easier. Maverick and I grew closer in ways that went beyond physical desire. We discovered each other's hobbies, mixed martial arts was his passion and he liked tinkering with engines. I liked reading romance novels and cooking anything that took a million ingredients. Late evenings, I'd curl on the couch, devouring a steamy historical or dark biker romance, Adam asleep in the crib, while Maverick laid a warm blanket over my legs. Sometimes, he'd brush aside my hair, gently kiss my temple, whispering how peaceful I looked reading.

One night, I felt bold. I wore a slightly more fitted top, revealing a hint of my postpartum body. Maverick's eyes lit up, a slow grin curving his lips. As I read a passage from my current novel, he asked me about it.

"You're smiling," he said, resting his forearm on the back of the couch. "Must be a good part?"

I blushed, hugging the book to my chest. "It's... a spicy scene, actually," I admitted, heart pounding.

He raised an eyebrow, leaning in. "Tell me," he said, voice low. "Give me the gist."

My cheeks flamed. "It's a dark romance. The hero's morally gray, tying the heroine to the bed, worshiping her, then, it's, well, it's intense."

A spark danced in Maverick's gaze, a tinge of mischief. "I can do that if you want," he teased, brushing his fingers lightly across my waist. "I'll tie you up, re-enact it line by line."

A shiver ran through me, both intrigue and lingering fear. "N-no," I stammered, remembering the vulnerability. "I'm not ready for that kind of... scene. Just reading it was enough. But I... I might be ready for something else." My heart pounded as I shut the book, gaze lifting to meet his.

He exhaled softly. "Are you sure?"

I nodded, breath catching. Time to let him in. I set the book aside, leaning forward. My lips brushed his, tentative at first, but then the hunger we'd kept at bay surged. He cradled my face, kissing me with a reverence that made my eyes burn with tears.

We stumbled to the bedroom, my bedroom now. I felt self-conscious about my softer belly, the stretch marks. But Maverick's hands caressed every part of me, murmuring how beautiful I was, how lucky he felt. My heart soared, the insecurities slowly melting as his lips mapped my skin. God. I wanted him.

His hand swept across the tattoo on my belly, his property patch. "I'm glad you kept it."

"Me too," I said, before I got completely swept off my feet.

The first touch of his weight over me made me gasp. The baby was asleep next door, Nova out for the evening, so we had quiet privacy. A swirl of memories flooded me, our one night in that resort, the heartbreak that followed, the child we created.

Maverick was about to strike, claim me again, but I rolled away.

He laid on his back. "What's wrong?"

I climbed over him, straddling his naked form. "I have so many regrets, but one in particular has really haunted me."

"What?" he asked, his face tight with concern.

My hands ran down his chiseled abs before I wrapped them around his thick erection. "I never got to taste you."

A big smile grew on the biker's face. "By all means, gobble away."

"Gobble?" I laughed, but I licked my lips. "I'll show you gobbling."

Maverick guided me down to his cock. I opened my mouth wide. His hands clutched my hair. "I'm sure you will, princess."

His salty skin tasted divine as I slid my tongue up and down his hard length. Soon, I was swallowing a mouthful of satiated desire, fresh from Maverick and right down my throat. I licked my lips. The biker was delicious, not the milky substance, but just being with him again.

But even though we took our time exploring, checking off all the foreplay, when he entered me, the lovemaking was tender, unhurried, fueled by more than raw desire. We were forging a bond, healing old wounds with each shared jolt.

Afterwards, wrapped in sheets, I felt my tears roll down my face. He noticed, brushing them away with a calloused thumb.

"You okay?" he whispered, worry lining his brow.

I mustered a trembling smile. "Yes," I choked out. "Better than okay. I just... I love you, Maverick. More than ever. And I'm sorry it took me so long to trust you again."

His eyes shone. "Don't be sorry," he said, leaning in to kiss me gently. "I love you, princess. I'd wait forever if I had to." A pause, then he sighed. "But... I do have to leave soon. Just for a bit."

My heart constricted. "Leave? Where?"

He stroked my hair. "The Road Monsters need me on a run. With us up here, I'm technically under a different Ace's territory. They want me to show face, maybe do a job or two. I'll only be gone a week or two, max. Chigger or someone else will be here to guard you and the baby. But before I go..." He drew a breath. "I want to marry you."

A wave of breathless shock rushed through me. "Marry me?" My chest fluttered.

He laughed softly. "Of course. I wanted to marry you a year ago, before everything crashed down. Now you're free. I want to make us an official family, me, you, and Adam."

Tears brimmed again, but this time from sheer joy. "Yes," I whispered. "I want to marry you, too."

He grinned, relief washing over his face. "Good, because I already asked Nova to watch the baby while we go pick out a ring tomorrow."

The next morning, Nova happily offered to babysit, eyeing us with a teasing smile. "Go on your little ring-shopping adventure," she said. "I'll keep an eye on Adam."

We hopped on Maverick's Harley, and my heart soared at the familiar rumble beneath me. I clung to his waist as we sped down the coastal road, gulls calling overhead. It felt like a scene from one of my books, except it was real. We found a quaint jewelry shop in the nearby harbor town. The bell chimed as we entered, a friendly elderly clerk greeting us.

We browsed the glass cases, my eyes lingering on modest rings. I didn't want anything flashy, or that reminded me of Mark's extravagance. Finally, I spotted a simple band with a small diamond cluster. Something elegant, not ostentatious. Maverick slipped it onto my finger, and it fit perfectly. Our gazes locked, and I saw so much love in his eyes that my breath caught.

"This is it," I whispered, smiling up at him.

He pressed a tender kiss to my lips. "We'll do the wedding in two weeks."

"Just a small ceremony."

"The Kings will come, maybe Nova as your maid of honor. That enough time to get a dress?"

I laughed softly. "I'll find something. I'm sure Nova will be ecstatic to help."

He paid for the ring in cash, not with the hush money I'd offered him, ironically enough. Maverick always seemed to have enough cash, and I wouldn't let myself worry where it came from.

We rode back through the winding roads, the wind tangling my hair. I glanced at the ring on my finger, heart brimming with cautious optimism. My life was far from perfect. There was still the looming threat of Mark's reaction, the final steps to ensure the mob wouldn't target me, and the bizarre truth of Kingpin being my father.

When we pulled up to our little rental house, the sun was just setting over the pines. Nova stood on the porch, baby in her arms, grinning ear to ear when she saw the ring. She squealed, scolding me for not letting her help pick it out, but hugging me tight anyway.

Maverick hopped off the bike, took the baby from Nova, and cradled him in the crook of his arm. I watched them, my heart bursting. Adam looked so peaceful in his father's embrace, and I felt that same sense of peace wash over me, too.

Yes, I'd have to face the final storms. My father was a powerful outlaw biker with some hold over the biker I loved, and Mark might lash out. But tonight, in that golden twilight, all I saw was a man and a baby who were mine, and a ring on my finger that symbolized the promise of a new chapter.

I stepped up to them, gently kissing Adam's forehead, then Maverick's lips. He smiled against my mouth, murmuring, "You're mine, princess. For real this time. No one can take that away."

I leaned my forehead against his, inhaling the scent of leather and the faint baby powder. "Yes," I whispered. "I'm yours, and you're mine."

And as the sun set, I felt a calm I'd never known before. Together, we'd rebuild our lives, a real family, no lies, no blackmail, just love strong enough to face whatever came next.

CHAPTER 51

The sea air brushed my cheeks as I stepped barefoot onto the warm sands of Maine's rugged coastline. Two weeks had vanished since Maverick placed that ring on my finger, promising a new life free of the mob's grip and my old ghosts. Now, I stood here on a secluded beach, dressed in a soft ivory gown that flowed around my ankles, the salty breeze teasing strands of my hair from an updo. The tide lapped at the shore in a rhythmic hush, as if nature itself was blessing this moment.

My heart thudded, excitement and nerves mingling. *I'm about to marry Maverick.* Just months ago, I'd been trapped in a loveless arrangement with Mark, never imagining I'd be free to choose who held my hand forever. But now, I was no longer Lexi Martin, mob bargaining chip. I was Lexi, soon-to-be Lexi Hart, *Maverick's wife*, his ol' lady, embracing the wild freedom he offered.

Friends drifted across the sand, setting up a small semicircle of chairs. The Kings of Anarchy MC crew had come to celebrate, Solo, their president, Chainsaw, the Vice President, and a handful of members and their women who'd grown fond of us. Nova was there, in a light-blue sundress, cradling our son, Adam, while Chigger hovered around them, fresh off the road from some Road Monster's run.

I exhaled, smoothing my palm over the soft white satin of my dress. Nova had helped me choose it. Simple, sleeveless, with a gentle lace overlay at the bodice. My postpartum body still felt foreign, but looking at my reflection in Chigger's bike's chrome. I felt... serene.

A cough made me turn around. Standing there was Kingpin, towering in a black button-down and jeans that somehow seemed formal for a biker. He had a thick beard, dark hair with streaks of grey, combed back, and two restless toddlers clinging to his legs. My heart leaped. *My father.* The man who once opposed Maverick, who'd probably never imagined having a grown daughter, show up out of nowhere.

He cleared his throat again, casting a glance at the toddlers. One was fussing, the other picking up shells. Beside him was *Eve*, his wife, a few years older than me, yet not by much. She wore a flowy floral dress, her long blonde hair tied in a loose braid.

"Lexi," Kingpin said gruffly, stepping forward. His gaze flicked over me, a hint of awkward pride in his eyes. "You make a beautiful bride."

I released a nervous breath. "Thanks... it's nice to finally meet you... in person." We grinned a little awkwardly, as I recalled the night I got a call from him, and he asked if he could come to the wedding.

He shifted the toddler off his leg, handing her to Eve. The little girl looked at me with wide eyes. *Angel. My half-sister,* my mind supplied, reeling. I had a brother, too. *Named Prince.*

Life is so bizarre.

Then Kingpin handed me a biker cut embroidered with *Princess*, Maverick's sweet name for me. *It was for me.* It held the biker president's new patch. *Bastard Sons MC.*

And I was a son of the bastard or rather a daughter.

Kingpin scratched his beard, explaining, "I'm not the mob," he muttered, as if anticipating my concerns. "But I got enough pull in the MC world to protect you just as well. If you ever need anything, you call me, understand?"

I swallowed hard, emotion swirling. "Thank you," I managed. "I... we're a family, I guess. Strange as that might be."

His lips twitched, almost a grin. "Yeah, guess so. Your mother... Dirty... well, Diana and I had a fling a long time ago. Didn't realize she'd had my kid. I'm sorry I wasn't there, that you had to grow up without," He broke off, gaze dropping.

I blinked. *He's apologizing for something he never knew he should be apologizing for.* I forced a small smile. "Don't blame yourself. My mother kept a lot of secrets. But I appreciate you being here now, walking me down the aisle." The words felt surreal, but he'd said Eve had insisted he do it, some symbolic gesture of fatherhood. I wondered if he only used her as an excuse to do the right thing.

At the mention of the wedding, Kingpin straightened, repeating the excuse again. "Eve said I should do the fatherly thing, even if I've never had a day of practice. She's got more sense than me about these things."

Eve stepped forward, balancing a squirming toddler on her hip. She offered me a warm smile as Kingpin drifted back to talk to a biker I'd never met. Some ginger haired guy standing watch like he was protecting them. "I'm proud of him for showing up, honestly. And yes, you're almost the same age I was when I first got tangled with him. I know people talk about our age difference, but…" She shrugged, eyes shining with fondness for Kingpin, "I couldn't resist a big, sexy biker with a heart of gold. Looks like we have the same taste."

Realizing she spoke of Maverick, I swallowed. He was her ex, after all.

"I only mean Adam…" She used his real name, and the intimacy of it made my stomach tie in knots. "He's one of the good ones," she clarified. "And he loves you so much."

I found myself laughing softly, relief flooding me. "I'm glad you two found real love." And I meant it. Their dynamic might be complicated, but from the way Kingpin hovered near her, gentle with their kids, it was clear they shared something genuine, far different from Mark's coldness.

Kingpin gestured to the beach altar, a simple arch draped in white gauzy fabric. A handful of chairs faced it, sea gulls swooping overhead. "Ready?"

All the wedding nerves suddenly hit me. "Yes, I, I think so." I glanced around, noticing Maverick wasn't anywhere in sight. "Where is he?"

Nova popped over, wiggling her eyebrows. "He's waiting down by the shore with Sully." Kings of Anarchy MC had supplied their chaplain. "You want me to take the baby?" Little Adam dozed in her arms already, lulled by the ocean breeze.

I nodded, pressing a soft kiss to Adam's brow. My nerves fluttered again, *my wedding day.*

Kingpin cleared his throat, offering his arm. "Shall we?"

I took it, still reeling that this biker, my father, was escorting me. Eve shot me a playful wink, guiding her toddlers to find seats near the front.

A burly biker named Folklore played soft guitar chords as we approached the makeshift aisle. The handful of guests, King's members, plus random friends from Maine, rose, smiling. Chigger, Nova with the baby stood in honor with us. My bare feet sank into the warm sand. Kingpin's grip on my arm was steady, surprisingly reassuring.

Ahead, Maverick stood by a simple wooden arch, the waves rolling behind him. The sun cast a golden hue over everything. He wore dark jeans, a crisp white shirt with the sleeves rolled up, his Road Monsters cut left aside for the ceremony. My breath caught at the softness in his gaze as we locked eyes.

We reached him, and Kingpin gently placed my hand in Maverick's, giving me a firm nod before stepping aside. For a moment, Maverick and I just stared, hearts in our throats. *This biker*, who once saved my life, who fathered my child, kidnapped me from Texas, who fought for me and waited for me. He squeezed my hand, his features reflecting the love I felt for him.

The officiant, guy in the MC, Sully, a biker himself, spoke in a low, gentle tone about love, family, and second chances. The waves crashed softly, a gull cried overhead. Tears stung my eyes as I gazed at Maverick's face, lined with relief, devotion, everything I'd craved in a partner.

"I pledge to stand by you," I choked out. "No more secrets, no more lies. You gave me freedom when I had none. You believed in me when I'd lost faith. I... I love you, Maverick."

He blinked back tears, a faint smile tugging his lips. "You changed my life, Lexi. I was running from everything, my past, my heartbreak, until you showed me what I truly wanted. A home. A family. You. I promise to protect you and our son forever, to treasure every moment, and never let you doubt my devotion."

We exchanged rings, he slipped a simple band on my finger, shining next to the engagement ring. I slid a matching gold band onto his, heart thudding with every breath. Sully smiled, pronouncing us husband and wife. Cheers erupted from the small gathering, Nova leading the applause with Adam in her arms. Chigger whooped, the Kings hoisted up beer cans in salute.

Maverick leaned in, engulfing me into a passionate kiss, sealing our vow under the blue sky. My mind flashed through the memories, the heartbreak, the fear, the stolen kisses in motels, the baby's birth without him. Now we'd finally found our way here. Joy swelled in my chest. *We're married. We're free.*

We lingered on the shore for a while before heading to the party the Kings set up just a ways down the beach. People chatted in small clusters, sipping beer or whiskey. Kingpin was barefoot, at the brink of the water with Eve, their toddlers, my newfound siblings, squealing at the incoming waves. It felt surreal, my father, the man I'd never known, now part of my wedding.

I drifted over, with Maverick's hand clasped in mine, dragging him with me. Kingpin nodded in approval at us. "That was a nice ceremony. Simple, but heartfelt."

My cheeks warmed. "Thank you for coming, for... for walking me down the aisle, dad."

Shifting his stance, he smiled proudly. "I know I offered to have you come down south, with us. You'd be under my protection, no messing around." He spoke to us both. "But if you prefer Maine, that's fine. I'll have your back if anything arises."

Eve smiled at us both, but she spoke only to me. "We'd love to get to know you better, but we also understand if you want distance. Just know we're here if you need us." Her voice held genuine warmth, her gaze flicking to the toddlers chasing each other. "Our door is always open."

My heart softened. "Thank you," I said softly, as I tried to speak for both Maverick and I. "It's... a lot to process, being your daughter, or that Adam is your grandson. But I appreciate the support. Right now, we love being away from Texas, away from old trouble."

Kingpin's gaze slid to Maverick, a hint of grudging respect in his eyes. "You keep her safe, Pig," he said, using an old insult with no real malice. "If I hear any different, I won't hesitate to ride up here and whoop your ass, again."

Maverick stiffened, but a faint smirk tugged his lips. "She's my wife now, old man. I won't let her down."

Kingpin huffed a laugh, then reached out, patting Maverick's shoulder. "Good. Because if you do, you'll answer to me. Family is everything."

His words reminded me of the mob, but I exhaled, relief coursing through me. Maybe, someday we could bridge these bizarre family connections.

Nova joined us with my mother's urn. I felt it was time to spread her ashes, give her a final resting place. The fact that there was someone here who had also loved her in any way, made me smile. Together, Kingpin and I released her ashes into the ocean.

When the others were out of earshot, Kingpin started speaking low. "Your mom, she always loved the ocean. That's how she got wrapped up in the biker world to begin with. I met her at Bike Week in Daytona. I'd just gotten out of the slammer, and I was hung up on an old flame, if I hadn't been, maybe I would've loved her more, but that's a story for another day. She rode with me back to Nashville. We didn't stay together long, but she came back a few times... She worked at my club... well... Maybe one time there will be time to tell you more."

"I'd love that," I said, my eyes reaching his that shined with unshed tears.

As dusk fell, Nova sidled up to me, cuddling a sleepy Adam in her arms. "Smutty.... Go, have a honeymoon," she teased, grin wide. "I'll watch him tonight. We're safe here, right? Plenty of MC folks around, no one's messing with us."

We hadn't really planned to, but Maverick spoke up. His hand slid to my waist. "We can head to that B&B farther up the coast," he murmured in my ear. "Just one night, a few hours of quiet away from Adam's cries and Nova and Chigger. Think you can handle that, Mrs. Hart?"

A tingle ran through me at the sound of that. "You sure Nova can manage Adam?"

Nova rolled her eyes. "Please, I babysit him all the time. Go be newlyweds for once. You deserve it."

I gazed at Adam, guilt tugging me about leaving him. But a part of me yearned for a single night of rest and closeness with Maverick. Nova was right, we deserved it. I pressed a kiss to the baby's forehead. "Okay. One night. If anything happens… "

Nova swatted my arm lightly. "I'll text you. Relax!" She winked. "Now go. Your husband awaits."

Chapter 52

Maverick's grin shone big when he heard me agree to have a honeymoon. He led me to his Harley, which we'd parked near the dunes. I hoisted my dress slightly, laughing at the absurdity, freshly married, riding off on a motorcycle in my gown. He tossed me his helmet. I slipped it on, knowing I probably looked ridiculous.

We roared off, leaving the wedding party behind on the beach. The ocean wind whipped over us, headlights carving a path through the night. My arms wrapped around Maverick's torso, cheek pressed to his leather clad back. A thrill pulsed in my veins.

This was our future, wild, free, and together.

We arrived at a quaint bed-and-breakfast perched on a rocky cliff overlooking the Atlantic. Fairy lights twinkled around the porch railings, a warm glow beckoning us inside. The owner greeted us with a polite nod, handing over a key to a snug room on the second floor. She barely blinked at my dress or Maverick's biker attire, as if used to all kinds of visitors.

The room was small but charming, with an iron-framed bed, lace curtains, and a window revealing moonlit waves crashing below. The gentle lull of the ocean echoed through the walls. Maverick set our small overnight bag in the corner, then turned to me, eyes alight with both tenderness and desire.

I exhaled, letting the excitement of the day slip away. "This is nice," I whispered, stepping closer.

He wrapped his arms around me, the smell of leather and sea salt flooding my senses. "Yeah. Real nice." He brushed a thumb over my cheek, his voice thick. "My princess. My ol' lady. My wife."

My breath hitched. "My husband," I murmured back, tilting my head for his kiss.

Our lips met, soft at first, then deepening as the weight of every obstacle we'd overcome melted into that moment. He carefully slipped the lace straps from my shoulders, guiding me toward the bed, each movement carrying reverence.

The night stretched on in blissful warmth, me losing myself in Maverick's kisses, his hands tracing every line of my still-recovering body. But he never once made me feel less than beautiful. A tear slipped down my cheek as he whispered how perfect I was, how grateful he felt. We moved together in a slow dance of rediscovered intimacy, each whisper, each caress a vow of devotion.

But the night turned. Maverick stopped our lovemaking all together. "Lexi, I have to tell you something."

My heart was in my throat as I worried for more trouble on the horizon. "What is it?"

"This isn't me. This sweetness. It's just an act," Maverick admitted, hanging his head.

"What do you mean?" I croaked, on the verge of tears.

"No. I love it, I love you, anything with you, but I don't want to scare you."

"Maverick, what are talking about? Scare me?"

"I have some kinks. And I've been holding back, trying not to scare you off," he said, his voice real low.

"Okay, what do you mean by kinks?" I pictured him in a leather mask with a whip and grimaced.

Maverick blew out a breath. "I can't really describe it, not in words. Princess, basically, I want to tie you to the bed. You'll have little control over what's happening. Some of it might seem... harsh. It might hurt a little, especially if I decide to spank you or to test your limits. But I promise, you'll love it."

Spank me? Tie me to the bed? Test my limits? Maverick had no clue about the smut that'd read. "That actually sounds pretty amazing," I said offering my wrists to him, though I was still nervous as hell. Reading was one thing, but in reality, fuck... I was really moist.

Maverick proceeded to secure me to the iron bars of the bed. My naked body was laid out for him to do whatever he pleased. Tugging on the tie, I had no control. Maverick's hot and hard naked body loomed over me. Fuck. This was naughty, hot, and I was on pins and needles, anticipating his next move.

"This first time, I'll be gentle," he promised.

And by the time he finally slid his dick into me, I got off almost instantly. Then Maverick had another command. He planned to go again, and all night. Taking me to the big whirlpool tub, he planned for me to keep up with his stamina.

"Are you up to it, Ms. Hart?"

Sinking into the water with him, I was more than happy to oblige. But when he slipped his arms around me and shoved a butt plug into my ass, I couldn't lie and say I didn't have second thoughts.

"That's going to stay in while I wash every inch of you," Maverick said in a hungry voice. "His soapy fingers slipped down my breasts and inside my pussy."

I gulped. "And what do you get out of this?" I asked, clearly the winner.

"I enjoy watching you squirm. Believe me, I'll get mine once you're ready."

I was living a romance all right, but I'd leaped right out of Jane Austen into Fifty Shades.

Eventually, we drifted off in a tangle of limbs, totally spent, moonlight spilling across the bedspread. I was sore in the most amazing ways as I felt like the biker took my virginity anew. The first time had been easy. Now, the biker was introducing me to his actual wants and needs. I felt like a fish out of water all over again, but for the moment, I was one sated fish.

A gentle breeze carried the distant roar of waves, lulling us to a dreamless sleep, content in the knowledge that this was the beginning of a real marriage, one built on choice, love, freedom and an amazing chemistry in the bedroom. I looked forward to learning all about Maverick's desires and wanted to satisfy all of them.

At dawn, I stirred to the soft glow of sunrise edging through the lace curtains. Maverick still slept, arms around my waist, face relaxed. For a fleeting moment, I watched him, marveling at how his rugged features looked almost boyish in sleep. *My husband.* He looked so much like our baby Adam. The thought rippled with joy.

A quiet knock sounded on the door. I gently extricated myself from Maverick's embrace, slipping on a robe. The owner had left a small breakfast tray outside, fresh croissants, jam, coffee. I carried it inside, the aroma making my stomach rumble.

Maverick roused, blinking away sleep. He broke into a slow, lazy grin seeing me. "Hey there, Mrs. Hart," he teased.

I giggled, passing him a coffee cup.

We ate in companionable silence, sipping coffee, sharing small smiles. The sunlight painted his scarred arms golden. He caught me staring, lips curling in amusement.

"What?" he asked, brushing a crumb from his lip.

I shrugged, cheeks warm.

"I can't believe you got so much work done in the last year." I spoke of the tattoos he'd gotten covered up. When I looked at him, I would no longer be reminded of his other women.

"I needed a fresh start."

"Just... can't believe we're finally here. Married, happy, no one chasing us."

He nodded, hand sliding to interlace our fingers. "We still gotta figure out the rest. I leave this week, and it's going to be hard. But this is ours, princess. No one can take it." He lifted my hand, pressing a kiss to my ring. "I promise."

I swallowed, heart tight with gratitude. "Thank you. For everything. For saving me, for being patient, for loving me when I felt unlovable."

He set his coffee aside, pulling me into his arms. "You were never unlovable," he murmured. "And you saved me, too, from a life of running with no purpose."

I rested my head on his shoulder, letting the moment wash over me. Outside, the ocean crashed, a steady reassurance. We had battles left. But we'd face them together, forging a path that included our son, our friends, maybe even a new law practice for me one day.

For now, we savored the gift of a day without fear, cradled in each other's arms, the vow of forever sealed in the hush of this seaside dawn.

The End For Now

To read more of Morgan Jane Mitchell's Road Monsters MC in Mayhem Makers check out her website
www. morganjanemitchell.com

Read more about Nova and Chigger in the next Road Monsters MC book, Chigger.

Nova: I never wanted to fall for biker, especially not one who drifts in and out of my life without warning. Yet Chigger, the mysterious Nomad with a sinful grin and a carefree swagger, keeps crashing back into my world. Our late-night sexcapades used to be all sparks and no strings, but my heart might want more than just a fling.

Chigger: I'm used to living on the run, answering only to the open highway and the brothers I sometimes ride with. Letting Nova in means facing a commitment I've never been ready for. Now, danger from the MC underground is looming, forcing me to confront the truths I've been running from. I thought I could hide in the Road Monsters MC, but the man who wants me dead has other ideas.

Nova's determined to walk away from me before she loses herself again. I can't watch her slip through my fingers so easily, not when my enemies set their sights on her. Will I risk everything to finally claim her? And more importantly will we survive?

www.morganjanemitchell.com

For ARC and signed paperbacks & more
Join
Morgan Jane's Facebook Group
Read More By Morgan Jane Mitchell
Books by Morgan Jane Mitchell
Join my Newsletter http://www.morganjanemitchell.com/join
Like Morgan Jane Mitchell on Facebook
Bookbub
Books2Read
Instagram
Twitter

About the Author

Award winning, USA Today Bestselling Author Morgan Jane Mitchell spent years blogging politics and health trends before she rediscovered her love of writing fiction. Trading politicians for bloodsuckers of another kind, she's now the author of bestselling post-apocalyptic fantasy novel, Sanguis City. Her action-packed series of vampires, witches, demons and zombies is paranormal romance, dystopia, urban fantasy and erotica in one bite. When Morgan Jane is not creating the city of blood or conjuring up other supernatural tales, she's dreaming up erotic and dark romances including her latest bestselling erotic suspense, Asphalt Gods' MC series and bestselling romances, Royal Bastards MC: Nashville, TN series.

Morgan Jane Mitchell

Royal Bastards MC: Nashville, TN Chapter

Reading Order

Hallow's Eve (Hallow)

Kissin' Irish (Irish)

Royal Road (Kingpin)

Royal Surprise (Kingpin)

Catchin Levi (Leviathan)

Pagan's X-Mas (Pagan)

Valentines' Eve **(Eve)**

Royal Pain (Riff)

Lovin Opry (Opry)

Royal Ransom (Kingpin)

TBA (Villain)

TBA (Thorn)

TBA (Horror)

TBA (Memphis)

TBA (Haven)

TBA (Rome)

TBA (Prince)

To read more about the Asphalt Gods MC start with Scar for
Scar, Asphalt Gods MC

Scar, Asphalt Gods MC

Emery wants to die. Good thing she just ran into a killer. *"They say what doesn't kill you makes you stronger, but that's bullshit. What doesn't kill you leaves a scar. More than the eyesore down my torso, I was a scar, the jagged, fucked up remains of a tragedy."*

Scar's Nomad status gives him a chance to fulfill his one wish, but his lonely mission is interrupted when a possible one-night stand goes horribly wrong.

"They say what doesn't kill you makes you stronger, but what if I can't live with myself anymore?"

Finding the blonde face down in a puddle of her own blood jeopardizes everything. Saving her and keeping her quiet could get Scar killed, but when Emery wakes up, her shocking proposal for him to kill her starts the ride of his life.

Reading Order
Asphalt Gods' MC
SCAR
Seven Sunsets
Hell on Heelz (standalone)
Sunrise
Cowboy, Take Me
Picking Bones
Lucky Stars
Bone Daddy
Mud
Trax
Snakebite
Hawk
Freedom
Slayer (standalone)

Asphalt Gods' MC series

Hell on Heelz, an Asphalt Gods' MC novel
Morgan Jane Mitchell An Asphalt Gods' MC Novel. Full length, Stand Alone.

"They say time heals all wounds, but my time's done run out. I'm no spring chicken, but it's more than that. I've been mad as hell for far too long. It's made me a different woman, a bitter woman. No, they don't call me Rage for nothing—I'm a twisting bitch tornado and that's before you make me mad. When I'm not fuming, I'm secretly festering in suffocating smog of self-loathing. A man did this to me, and now that I've finally met another man, one who calms my storm, one I might let break through the thick thorny vines I've wrapped around my heart—I fear there's nothing left of me."

Edie Pearl better known as RAGE never thought her decision to leave her cheating husband and join the Hell on Heelz would land her as the potential President of the female outlaw motorcycle club when the Banshee is killed. Rage has spent the last two years mad as hell, nursing her broken heart with booze and fast men. When she's pitted against her fellow heel, Dixie, in a race to track down the Banshee's killer, she meets the man of her dreams. Mud may be the only man to get her motor running, but he's also her sworn enemy. Will Rage do the unthinkable and choose a man over her club? Or is time really up for her?

Mud's been a mess since his twin brother left the Asphalt Gods' MC. He'd hate to have to kill his own kin. When Scar shows Mud mercy by sparing his brother, he thinks everything will finally be back to normal. He's proven wrong. A ride to California is interrupted with by the Heelz. After he leaves his brothers and catches up to his enemy, he finds a beautiful woman, one he cannot resist. Him showing her the same mercy puts him in even more jeopardy. His heart on the line with his life, which road will he choose?

Made in the USA
Monee, IL
25 February 2025